Floyd, VA 2:42

A novel by Barbara Pleasant

AUTHOR'S STATEMENT

The purpose of this book is to entertain my friends and neighbors, the good people of Floyd, VA. It is entirely a work of fiction, and all characters and events are a product of my imagination. Most locations are fictitious as well, including houses, but established landmarks and businesses in the town of Floyd are real.

Copyright © 2025 Barbara Pleasant
All rights reserved.

Chapter 1   The Event

September 1

Dear Mom,

I've waited here at home for two weeks, but there is not much food left and too much to worry about, too many memories, and it's making me weird. Very weird. I've decided to move to Grantham's house on Brambleberry Road, so you can check for me there. You know, the brick house on the hill? I used to babysit there when I was a teenager. I know how their house works from taking care of Rebecca when she was little. You had told me they were on vacation in Florida, so I knew there would not be bodies inside.

I'm not abandoning the ship, but the Grantham house is on a main road closer to town, not back in the woods like ours, so it doesn't feel so isolated. There are stacks of dry firewood and I know how to work the wood stove, so I should be okay when the weather gets cold. If this thing goes on that long.

And there's more. The Grantham's next-door neighbors had a flock of chickens that survived, which I discovered when I rode up there on my old bike to check out the house. They acted like they were starving, the rooster crowed and crowed, so I found their food in the shed and now they are much happier. It helps to have someone to talk to, even if it's just chickens. Near the coop there is a water pump, the kind with the long green handle you pump up and down ten times before the water comes. But I do have clean water, which is a very big deal.

I cannot guess why chickens and birds and bugs survived what happened, but people and cows didn't, ditto for dogs, cats, squirrels, and horses. There are animal carcasses rotting everywhere, in the fields and some in the streams. Everything smells gross, even the water.

I hope you were somewhere safe at work in the hospital, maybe down in radiology, so now it's just a matter of making it back to Floyd. None of the cars around here will start, so getting home from work can't be easy! Seriously, I pray for you All-The-Time, and I do believe, must believe, will always believe that you are alive and will make it back home. Soon.

I have thought about trying to get to Roanoke to find you. I know, it's a stupid idea. But I do think about it.

Jeremy did not make it. There was nothing I could do, I'm sure you understand by now. His life stopped when the world stopped, sorry but I can't talk about it now. Maybe another time. Same thing with Mabel and Scruff. I buried them in the flower garden, together.

There are no airplanes in the sky, not one. Or lights after dark. Or sounds other than wind, rain, and a few birds.

I miss you so much.
S

Dear Mom,
I miss you All-The-Time, but especially when I come

home to check the house. All the way over on the bike I imagine seeing you waiting for me. Or maybe when I open the door, I'll notice something that only you would have done, like straightening the pillows on the sofa. Then I get here, and the air is stale, the house is dark and nobody's home and I can't wait to leave.

Today it's not so bad because it's sunny and dry, so I have the doors open to let things air out while I get some clothes and a few other things. It's starting to get cold at night, so I'm borrowing your puffy coat because it's better than mine. I hope you don't mind. I tried it on, and it smells like you. There is a crumpled tissue in the pocket, today's treasure.

How old is Rebecca Grantham now, 17? It looks like Mrs. Grantham went back to teaching high school, because there was a stack of composition books inside the front door, still wrapped in plastic, and a box of pens. I've been using them to keep track of what I find when I check houses, because I can't always bring back everything I want, or remember everything I see when I go foraging for supplies. It's my new hobby. Generally, I don't go into houses, only sheds and garages. If there are cars in the driveway there are probably dead people inside and I'm not that hard up. Yet.

In my own notebook I write down the addresses where I want to go back for things and make little maps of where I've been. Remember Lucretia, my friend from 11th grade? Her neighborhood has been a gold mine of good stuff, and it's like all the garage doors were left open when it happened. I've found two nice camp stoves and a case of bottled propane. Getting it back here was easy because one of the houses had a bicycle in the garage with a twin-size baby carrier hooked to the back. I loaded my loot into the carrier and got it back in one trip. I think the baby carrier will be great for hauling things once I get over the sad part about the babies. The cushions are blue, so I think they were little boys. Did you know them?

About Jeremy.

As you know, we had permission from Mr. Greely to go diving at the old quarry before Jeremy went back to the University. His last blast, remember? I only have one little brother, so I took the week off from work, rented some scuba gear, and drove home from Richmond. We spent two days getting our equipment ready, doing checklists and waiting for it to stop raining. You made that incredible beef stew and we played Monopoly. The game got put back in its box, but the box is still on the table.

We made it to the quarry late in the morning, let ourselves in through the gate, and had an uneventful first dive. The water was cool but not freezing cold, but it was muddy from all the rain. We rested in the sun, ate the sandwiches we brought, and talked about everything and nothing. He was happy that day, Mom, I promise. His last day was a good one.

After maybe an hour we went back in, looking for coins and fish but finding mostly beer bottles, cans and some really strange snails. Jeremy signed that he was cold and going up, so I nodded okay and stayed down a while longer. I found a truly gigantic snail and wanted to show it to him, so I surfaced and held it up, and was ready to pull my mouthpiece to call to him when a big boom came. I saw him lying on the rocks at the edge of the water, so I thought he'd been shot and that I'd be next. I went back under, felt some strange waves coming from the quarry rocks, and watched a big one crash through the water. I swam toward the shallows to get a better look at Jeremy. He had not moved.

I stayed under until my oxygen ran out, and I felt dizzy when I got out of the water and dropped my gear. Jeremy had taken off his tank and mask, and then it looked like he just fell over. No blood, no bruises, and his eyes were open and fixed like the dead people on TV. I shook him, even pinched him, and there was no response. Nothing. His body was not as warm as it should have been. He wasn't breathing.

I ran to the car to call 911, but the phone was dead, and the car engine wouldn't turn over, not even a click. I got Jeremy's jacket from the back seat and took it to cover him up, hoping he was only hypothermic or something, and then I took off running to the nearest house. I think I passed out, because time gets kind of wobbly for me. When I came to, I was lying in the driveway of the campground store down the road from the quarry. In the front yard of the house there were three bodies, a man, a woman, and a dog.

All I could think of was getting home. I tried to start the truck parked by the store with the keys in the ignition, but it was as dead as my car. The door to the store was unlocked, but inside it was pretty dim with no lights. There were a few display cases of chips and drinks, and a big clock on the wall stopped at 2:42. Same as my watch. In the corner there were two bicycles, ten speeds with fat tires that were probably rentals for people staying at the campground. I checked the tires, put on a helmet that hung on the wall, and started toward home.

It was only a few miles, but it was slow going. I felt tired and achy, and everywhere there were dead animals. Dead cattle in the fields, dead mice and voles on the edges of the pavement, squirrels that seemed to have dropped from the trees. A few cars were stopped in the road at strange angles, but I tried not to look inside. It was crazy quiet, but when I stopped to catch my breath or walk the bike up a steep hill, I noticed that there were still some birds alive, and a few bugs, too. If there were crows alive there could be people, too. You could be at home, clueless, cooking dinner. Powered by hope, I pushed on.

That was more than a month ago, Mom, and hope is in very short supply. It's getting late and I need to get moving. Thanks for the coat, be back when I can. Like I said, I'm at the Grantham house on Brambleberry Road. See ya?

Love,
S

September 21
Dear Mom,
Happy Birthday! I didn't bring you anything but good wishes, but I've been thinking of you All-The-Time because it's your birthday week. In our family one day was never enough for a birthday, so we stretched it into a week. You always wanted a lemon cake. Thinking of it makes me cry, but I've been crying a lot lately. Sometimes I can't stop, just kind of weep all the time. It helps to focus on something practical, like hoarding olive

oil and liquid propane.

The flies outside are really bad from all the carcasses. They were getting in my eyes, my ears, even my mouth, and then I remembered that Mr. Stanley down the road kept bees. I found a beekeeper's hat with face netting in his garage that helps a lot. I wear it to get water and tend the chickens and of course to ride, but I hope I won't need it much longer. When the flesh is all eaten and the weather gets colder the flies will disappear, right?

Today I came to get Mabel and Scruff's leftover dog and cat food, to feed the chickens, and Jeremy's muck boots and rain poncho. I can wear them to come and go from the chicken coop and water pump on rainy days, and I know he would want me to have them.

The blanket shroud I put over his body has shrunk down. Last week I covered him with wildflowers I picked by the road, goldenrod and some pretty blue flowers. I cried a lot. Then I went by the camp store and cleaned them out of matches, canned food, and boxed chocolate milk.

Mom, you should see my legs and shoulders. I'm telling you, I am buff. I ride around looking for supplies when the roads are dry, haul tons of water from the pump every day for myself and the chickens, and wash everything by hand, dishes, hair, clothes. It takes a lot of time, but then I have a lot of time.

I've gotten used to seeing death everywhere, or trying not to see it, but I'm afraid to go into town because I might see dead people I used to know. I have no reason to think anyone is alive there, because I have not heard anything, not the first gunshot. I think if there were people alive, they would be shooting guns for one reason or another, don't you? To get attention, or to scare each other, or just to shoot? Did you know that all three of the Granthams kept pistols by their beds? Loaded, too. I don't sleep in their beds, only on the sofa in the den, so I've moved the three pistols to hiding places near the doors. In case I need to scare a bad guy.

Sometimes we would take a picnic up to The Saddle for your birthday, and I'm planning to keep the tradition if the weather holds. It's the closest place on the Parkway where I'll be able to see the town on one side and the valley on the other. The roads are starting to get covered with leaves and sticks that make riding tricky, but if I get an early start and take it slow, I should make it there and back in a few hours.

Wish me luck! I'm wearing Grandma's ruby pendant necklace as my talisman. I hope it will help.

Love,
S

October 10
Dear Mom,

I'm missing you and Jeremy a lot today. It's not a good place to be, because feeling abandoned is awful, worse than you can imagine. I know it's not something that was done to me, it just happened, and I should be happy to be alive. Sometimes I am, other times not so much.

Ready to hear about my adventure to The Saddle? I know, it's an easy trip, what could go wrong? Here's what. I wiped out in an oil slick left by a group of motorcycles laying on their sides, which caught me by surprise when I came over a hill, but I should have smelled it first. Oil and gas are slippery beyond belief and your brakes become useless, and I was going too fast and lost control of the bike and went down. On a dead, rotting body! It broke my fall, I have only scrapes and bruises, but it was bones and mush and beard hair and gunk that got all over me and I was so freaked, it was the grossest experience of my life. I screamed and screamed until I was dizzy.

I picked up the bike and walked most of the way to The Saddle, only using the bike to coast level sections since I had no brakes. I had to keep moving because the decomposing goo on my clothes reeked and drew flies, and I didn't have water to clean up with. Usually I don't want to see dead people from 2:42, but hikers and picnickers at The Saddle bring bottled water, which I needed more than anything. I hoped there were lots of them up there that day.

When I got to the top, there were no signs of life, only death. Five tourists, posing for a group photo, their bodies in a semicircle of heaps on the ground like giant mushrooms, one wearing a cotton dress in a flowered print. The lovers, entangled on a blanket forever, a half bottle of wine between them still waiting to be drunk.

I looked in the empty cars for water, towels, anything to help me clean the stinking death sludge from my face, arms, and hair. If I stopped moving for a minute, my own stench made me gag. The clothes had to go, so as I made my way through the parking lot, I peeled off my shirt, shoes, socks and pants, leaving it all behind. I found two sun-warmed bottles of water in a back seat and used them to wash off as best I could. In another empty car I found a pair of lime green flip flops, which was great because the pavement hurt my bare feet. I did not open the doors of cars with bodies inside.

Finally able to slow down and breathe, I noticed The Artist. He had been painting the long view of the mountain valley when it happened. His rain-warped canvas showed forest, rocks and sky, with the glimmer of a lake in the distance. His body was folded into an almost fetal position beside his fallen easel, his box of paints slick with mold, a jacket lying in the nearby grass. I felt something heavy in a pocket as I spread the jacket over his body. A set of keys. I took them with me to the parking lot, where I checked more unoccupied cars for water or clothes I could wear.

I was especially drawn to the RV parked toward the end of the lot, a small, older model that had seen some road time. The door was locked and the windows were closed, and I saw no dead flies in the screens, meaning there were probably no bodies inside. I started trying The Artist's keys and got lucky on the fourth one.

I still smelled hideous, so I tried not to touch things as I climbed inside. It was warm from the midday sun, and there were four big bottles of water, a little bar of soap by the tiny sink, and even a clean towel folded on the mattress. I grabbed it all and jumped outside for a better bath, starting with my gunked-up hair. It took a while, but I restored myself to near normalcy, dried off in the late afternoon sun, and found a freshly washed NC State sweatsuit in a drawer inside the RV. It smelled great, and the mean-looking red wolf on the front of the shirt made me feel strong.

As I looked for food, I concluded that The Artist had planned to spend one night and then drive back to North

Carolina. He did not plan to cook. For dinner he would have had saltine crackers with sardines in mustard sauce with two warm beers. For breakfast there was bottled cappuccino and Cheerios with boxed milk. In a cabinet I found a few cans of fruit cocktail, baked beans, and Vienna sausage. I would not go hungry.

But the most interesting item I found was in the glove compartment. Instead of a gun, there was a pair of binoculars in a leather case. I took them outside to see what I came to see.

Which was nothing.

You know what I wanted to see. Lights twinkling in the town, maybe moving headlights on a distant road on the south side of the ridge. Instead it got dark, and quiet, with the best light coming from the stars and a quarter moon. So many stars! Talk about feeling small. And lonely, so alone that I felt my heart beating faster and I knew I was starting to panic, so I got back into the RV, wrapped myself in a blanket, and tried to calm down.

Which is easier said than done. I took deep, even breaths, and drank some water. Cried a little. Said a prayer. Talked to God about this mess and what I should do. That's what we humans do, they say that's what makes us special. But does it work? Wish I knew, but it's not like I have much to lose or anyone else to talk to. Even snuggled into The Artist's small bed, it was a rough night.

In the morning the valleys on both sides of the ridge were thick with fog, so there was nothing to see but white. I got my act together. The Artist had a pair of old loafers that stayed on my feet when I walked. I found a single speed bike in the back of a truck, and emptied a small kid's backpack for carrying the binoculars and leftover food. I left the Artist's keys dangling in the door of the RV. What if someone else needed a dry place to sleep?

After having so much trouble making it up to The Saddle, it felt like I rode down in ten minutes. I picked up the bike and carried it around the awfulness where the motorcycles were, keeping my eyes on the ground to avoid mishaps or unnecessary misery.

I think I was home by noon. I could tell the chickens missed me.

Love,
Sarah

Chapter 2   The Visitor

November 15, maybe
Dear Mom,
You know how you always wanted me to wear my hair in a short bob like the one I had in kindergarten? You got your wish! The Parkway accident left a stench in my hair that wouldn't come out, there was some kind of tar, so I got Mrs. Grantham's sewing scissors and cut it off. The back probably looks like I butchered it, but the sides are level with my ear lobes, with a few feathered bangs. It looks okay I guess, but the main thing is that it no longer stinks.

The nights are getting longer now, and candles don't give off doodly-squat for light. Why didn't I know that? Oil lamps work so much better! Why didn't I know *that*? Now I have to go back to the sheds and garages I raided before, looking for lamp oil. Unscented. The fake perfumed stuff makes me sneeze.

There is other news. The first winter storm brought wet sleet and freezing fog that coated the deck with ice and was starting to form icicles when I saw something moving out on the road, something large and dark, too tall to be a turkey vulture. I got a pistol from the coffee table drawer and hid behind the living room curtains to watch. It was a human, had to be from the way it shuffled to the front door, but the head was hidden by a droopy hat and the rest of the body was covered with a black garbage bag. When it knocked, I opened the main door but left the storm door locked.

Right away I saw the right hand jiggling under the wet garbage bag, the same way mine was doing. "Is that a gun?" I asked, and the figure nodded. "Please leave it out there," I said, pointing to the porch swing. A bony man's hand reached out from under the bag to lay down the black pistol. I opened the storm door to let him inside.

He was like the thin man out of every horror movie, dark and gaunt, but he was dripping wet and his teeth were chattering, so I led him to the den where I had the wood stove going. My big mistake? I did what I had to do, got some dry clothes from Mr. Grantham's dresser and a couple of towels, and told him to change when he was ready, that I would be in the kitchen fixing some food.

He had taken off his hat, the garbage bag and the top layers of his wet clothes, and I could see that he was older, maybe in his fifties, a lean man in many ways plain, but with startling blue eyes over a sharp, pointed nose. "Thank you, ma'am," he mumbled.

I lit a lamp and took it to the kitchen, and reheated some of the grits and Spam I made earlier when the light was good. It's become my habit to prepare food once a day, and make enough to eat until the next day, when I'll make something else. Today's special was grits and Spam, which you never bought because you said it was a super-processed food, which it is. It also goes great with grits, which are easy to make on the propane stove. I brought my visitor a warm bowl of grits and Spam and a box of milk. He thanked me with a nod.

He had made himself comfortable in the recliner, and his cheeks were now bright red instead of deathly pale. He ate slowly, pausing between bites, keeping his eyes focused on the bowl. I told him my name, and that he was the first live person I had seen since it happened. Another nod. He took a long draw on the milk and slowly looked up at me.

"Until I smelled your wood fire, I thought I was gonna die, or that I had died," he croaked, then coughed. "Now I'm just so tired." He handed me the empty bowl, pushed back in the recliner and started snoring in about thirty seconds. I covered him with a fleece blanket.

Man, does he snore! It's not as warm in Rebecca's room as it is on the sofa in the den, but I slept there anyway, zipped into a mummy sleeping bag I found in the closet, with the door locked and all the guns by my bed in a dresser drawer. I could still hear my visitor snoring through the wall, even with an extra pillow over my head. Sometimes there would be long, quiet breaks between loud, gasping snores. I think he has sleep apnea. When I got up during the night to put wood on the stove, I heard a mumbled "Thank you, girlie."

In case I've made a fatal mistake and this is my last report from Planet Sarah, I just want to tell you what a great mom you are and how much I miss you.

I hope all of this is a bad dream. All. Of. It.

Love,

S

Dear Mom,

It is not a dream. None of it. When I woke the next

morning before dawn, my visitor was already up and about, stoking the stove and trying to use a candle for light.

"Good morning," I said, and he returned the greeting. I lit the big oil lantern I use in the den and brought two jugs of water from their storage space by the wall to pour into the pot I keep on the wood stove. My hot water system. When the water is stored at room temperature, it doesn't take long for it to heat up on top of the stove.

"Let me get that, girlie," he said, calling me girlie, I swear he did, and then he took over the pouring of the jugs. Is that my new name? I went to the kitchen and set a kettle of water to boil on the propane stove.

"Coffee, tea, or hot chocolate?" I asked. He said whatever I was having, as long as it wasn't tea. I kind of went all out, made big mugs of real coffee sweetened with Swiss Miss, and warmed up a couple of Pop-Tarts, brown sugar cinnamon. "This will hold us for a while, then I'll cook some real breakfast," I said, sitting on the sofa. "Coffee first."

"You said that right, Girlie." He lit into the coffee and Pop-Tart, stopping twice to tell me how good it was. Then he told me about himself.

His name is Howard (Buddy) Troutt. He is missing the last two fingers on his left hand from a work accident at the sawmill, and he may be prone to over-sharing. I knew the Troutt name, there were a million of them in Floyd, some with one T and some with two. Buddy was on his way to the family home place to bury his mother and sister and take up residence. He assumed they were all dead, but if there were any Troutts alive, they would find their way home, just like he was doing. He had about six miles to go. I told him he could stay until the weather cleared. Daylight revealed thick freezing fog.

"Is this your house?" he asked, a fair question. I decided to be honest.

"No, it belongs to friends. My house is pretty far out, on a gravel road, and this one is better, with a water pump out back and the wood stove. I learned how everything worked when I babysat here a few years ago. It belongs to the Granthams. Gerald and Helena Grantham. He sells insurance. Do you know them?"

He fingered the insignia on the chest of the sweatshirt I'd given him the night before. "Ha! I'm sitting in Gerald Grantham's recliner wearing his clothes. Now, how do you like that?" He was kind of cute when he smiled, with deep lines that cut into his cheeks at just the right angles.

"I knew Gerald in high school. He was a jerk, at least to the country kids. Made fun of us, called us stupid, but of course he always had it made. Went off to college in a shiny car, came home and stepped into his daddy's business, then gave my mama a hard time about her homeowner's insurance. She quit him, I'm happy to say. Went to Farm Bureau." He looked around the room at the furnishings, windows, and skylight. "I reckon all's fair that ends fair. He's not here, is he?"

I reassured him that the Granthams had gone to Florida, then went to the kitchen to cook some eggs.

After breakfast, I asked if we needed to wash his clothes, and I must have made a face because he smiled again. "Nah, burn them," he said. You got a burn pile?"

The fog had thinned some, so I pointed out the stone-encircled burn pile in the backyard, the chicken house, and the well pump beyond. I showed him the garden cart I use to bring jugs of water to the house, and the wheelbarrow for hauling firewood, leaning against the stack covered with a blue tarp.

"I'll be glad to help with that, it's the least I can do. You reckon Gerald had a pair of boots I can borrow?"

We went down the dark hallway to the master bedroom. To bring in light, I opened the heavy curtains and blinds layer by layer, which I had closed tight against the cold. The closet held several pairs of fancy shiny shoes, perhaps too many, some nice slippers and running shoes, but nothing good for mud or snow.

"I might have seen some boots in the garage," I blurted, instantly regretting mentioning the garage. "You look for clothes you can use. I'll go get them."

I hurried to the garage, lit a candle, and found the two pairs of men's boots near the door. My mountain of hoarded food and supplies, piled against the interior wall, was none of his business. Trust does not come easy for me.

We met up in the den.

"Ha! They fit!" Buddy said after lacing up the boots. True to his word, he brought in enough water to flush and clean both toilets and then refilled the jugs while I fed the chickens. Then he dragged his wet clothes to the burn pile, carefully checking each pocket. He put his treasures in a small pail by the back door as light rain began to fall.

I asked what he might want to eat. He said he'd lived on canned beans, turnip greens and campfire potatoes until the tin foil and ketchup ran out, so anything but potatoes would be good, as long as he was having whatever I was having. For our meal du jour, I made spaghetti with cream of celery soup, good tuna, and a can of peas. Buddy said it tasted like something his mamma used to make, which was really sweet.

When night came I got out a checkers game, at which I am passably good because of all the times I played with Jeremy. Buddy, I quickly learned, is *very* good. He pretends to take his time with each move, but he's making plans, two moves ahead. The game gave us time to talk, and he told me his story.

"Why am I still alive? I don't know, can't quite make sense of it. It was my day off, when I like to take on little chores, and I was tired of trying to fix the old leaky window down in the root cellar. It's an old house, came from my wife Candy's mother. It was built back when they put in root cellars instead of basements. The window kept leaking, so I went down there to close it up from the inside with insulation and a piece of plywood.

"I was down there hammering away when Candy came and said she needed to close the hatch door for a minute so she could mop. The hatch opens into a corner of the kitchen floor, you know. I said that would be fine, I had the light on and a flashlight, so I went back to nailing and had almost finished when everything went black. The light went out, flashlight too, and with the window nailed shut there was no daylight coming in. I felt my way up the ladder and went to push open the hatch door, but it wouldn't move, like it was stuck.

"Then it's like I went to sleep or something. It was all just dark. After a while I tried pushing on the door some more, hollered for Candy, and started noticing how quiet it was. No Candy, no dog, no nothing. I found my hammer on the floor and pulled off the plywood, then broke my way out through the old window. I got cut up some, but not too bad.

"When I went into the house I saw why the hatch door wouldn't open. Candy was laid out on top of it, stone cold dead. My Candy was a big woman, she had some heft to her, which is why the dang door wouldn't open. Now it don't much matter. I managed to get her buried. Took some tarps and a winch to get her out, but I did."

"I'm so sorry," I said.

"Yup."

I told him my story and cried through most of it, but it was good to tell it out loud, share the misery. Or at least I thought so at the time. He's planning to leave tomorrow if the weather clears. I'm kind of hoping for more rain.

Love,
S

Dear Mom,

The skies cleared but now the wind is blowing like a banshee, which has never been my favorite thing. Remember how the winter winds used to knock out the power and we'd be stuck with no TV or internet and we thought it was the worst thing? We were so spoiled. Sometimes I see my reflection on the big, black screen on the wall, and have to remind myself what it's for.

It was easy to get Buddy to agree to stay another day. He said he'd seen some hay in a nearby barn, and he wanted to get a couple of bales to snug in the chickens. Buddy likes having something to do.

He found me in the sunroom, where I often read and write on sunny days. Even when it's cold outside, the sunroom warms up in the afternoon. "Welcome to my office," I said through the open French doors.

He carefully sat down in a wicker chair with flowered cushions. I told him I'd been making a list of things to put in his backpack for his walk home, which he thought would take one day, but might take two. "Did you ever go backpacking, or long-distance hiking?" I asked.

"Oh, I never had time for such things. Started working when I was fifteen years old."

Mom, I was too embarrassed to tell him about our trips to the Smokies, or up to the Monongahela in West Virginia, where we wandered the forest and camped, just to do it. Jeremy and I had so much fun, we didn't know we were being taken on cheap vacations. That's how I know how to pack and carry a backpack, of which I had at least three in the garage. There was a nice green one, used maybe twice, that would hold what he needed.

He cleared his throat. "If you don't mind, can we talk about you for a minute? Girlie, I don't like leaving you here. Where I come from, it's not right to leave a woman alone like this, much less a pretty young lady like you. Now I mean no offense, you've done a good job here, taking care of yourself, taking care of the house, but Girlie, it don't have to be this way. You can come with me, take my sister's room or any room you want, live in the house for the winter. I can't stay here, but you can come with me and let me look after you. All on the up and up, of course, no hanky panky. If it don't work out I can bring you back."

I'm sure I looked surprised, because I was, though the thought had crossed my mind. But I'd been in a lot of old farmhouses, complete with mold and mice in the walls, and I had no interest in giving up my warm den for something like that. Plus there were the chickens, and I was used to being in charge, and Buddy snores like a locomotive. I was edgy from lack of sleep. I told him it was a tempting offer, but I would decline.

"Give me a piece of paper," he said. He wrote down the address on Franklin Pike and drew a crude map of how to get there. I knew exactly where it was, not far from Hilltop Church, which had one of the prettiest views in the county.

"Why do you need to stay here?" he asked, handing me the paper. I said I didn't know, that I guessed I was waiting, that I was still hopeful you made it and will come back, just like Buddy did. He was in a root cellar. What if you were down in radiology behind three sets of doors?

"Yup. You gotta have hope."

Buddy left this morning well fed and properly outfitted, his pack filled with a change of clothes and enough food to last a few days, along with bottles of water and Mountain Dew and his pistol. I walked with him to the top of the hill, and we shared a long hug before he went on his way. He thanked me again for saving his life, and I thanked him for saving mine.

I still have hope, and maybe feel less alone. I know where Buddy lives, how to get to his house. But loneliness is a relative thing, and I may be sadder than I was before. When a pain is relieved and the medicine wears off, you definitely don't feel better when it comes back. Please come home soon.

Love,
Sarah

Chapter 3   The Pharmacist

December 1?
Dear Mom,
You know how you always said not to try to open things with your teeth? Wish I had listened better because I think I cracked a tooth trying to get the cap off of a tube of hippie toothpaste. I know, it was dumb, and it only hurts a little so maybe it will be okay. I don't think I'll be getting an appointment with Dr. Black anytime soon.

This week it snowed! Not a lot, only two inches, but it made the world pretty and you could go out and look around without seeing death. It's not extremely cold, either, so it was a nice change of pace. Melted the next day.

I'm planning a trip to town to see if I can get into the drug store for some tooth stuff, in case the pain gets worse. Mission two: Buddy took his wallet and keys, but left behind a couple of empty pill bottles with his name on them. I think I should at least try to refill them if there's a way to do it. Mission three: If the drug store hasn't been looted I'll also know for sure there are no people, because it's the first place they would hit, don't you think? Looking for drugs? If necessary, I plan to lob bricks through the plate glass windows. My crimes are

multiplying.
Love,
S

Dear Mom,

How are you? I miss you so much, and trust I will see you soon. I have to keep believing that, it's what keeps me going.

Ready to hear about my big town adventure? I knew from the great view from the Grantham's house that it was high up, but I had not realized it was downhill almost all the way to town. I stopped a few times to pick up some fallen limbs, and had to walk the bike around a logging truck left wedged in a curve, but it was basically a coast. Every house I passed looked deserted. No dogs came out to chase me.

Like the crows and vultures, some turkeys may have survived because as I rode over the bridge outside of town, I think I heard gobbling in the bushes. Remember that year when the wild turkeys found the bird seed you put out and started coming to be fed? It was those kinds of sounds.

Town was silent. There were lots of cars in the road at odd angles, but no wood smoke or other signs of life. It felt spooky. I got off the bike to walk.

There were only a few corpses, none that I recognized, though I tried to avert my eyes. As I neared the drugstore, I noticed that a body-size lump had been covered with a blanket. By who? Had Buddy been here, trying to refill his prescriptions? Not very likely, he wouldn't know where to start. Knowing someone had been there since 2:42 made the hair on the back of my neck prickle. I wondered if I was being watched.

He saw me before I saw him, when I tried to look in through the mirrored windows of the drugstore. Then I went around to the back, opened the unlocked employees only door and propped it with a brick to let in the daylight. I tiptoed through the storeroom and into the dim store, calling "Hello, is anybody home?"

"Who are you, and what is your business here?" a loud male voice demanded from behind the pharmacist's podium. I screamed.

"Step into the light, please," the voice said when I quieted down. I complied, trying to place the slight familiarity in the voice. I reached into my pocket to get my list.

"No firearms allowed, it's on the sign!" the voice yelled.

"I'm not armed. I am Sarah Margolis, and I came for a few things I need," I said slowly. "Can you help me?"

"Sarah Margolis?" The voice almost cracked. "For real?" A second later I felt something hit my shoulder. I jumped as another rubber band hit my forehead.

"Hey, you could put my eye out," I said. The dark figure behind the podium moved.

"Sorry, but I need to make sure you're not an android. You know, programmed as Sarah Margolis. They would pick someone familiar, someone I would accept."

"They?" I asked. He said we would talk about that later, and asked me to turn to the right. The sun was now shining on my face.

"Tell me something about Wyndell Crouch that's not accessible to AI. Nothing statistical. Something from our shared human experience. Do you recognize the name?"

"Give me a minute," I said, and then I remembered Wyndell Crouch, and something he did. "In our high school production of The King and I, when I was a senior, in the chorus, Wyndell Crouch played the trumpet in the scene where the children are presented to Lady Anna."

"Continue," the voice said. I was enjoying the memory. "As the children were presented, one by one, he made each introduction sound different, made the children more unique, which was the point of the scene. I didn't know you could do that with a trumpet." I turned to face him, shading my eyes with my hand. "Do you still play? Are you Wyndell?"

"Sometimes. And I go by Wynn."

There was a hissing sound, and the room was flooded with light from a kerosene lantern. He looked different from what I remembered, tall and angular, with thick dark hair, and I'm not sure I could have picked him out of a lineup. Two years younger than me, he was kind of shrimpy in high school, but not anymore. It was a lot to take in.

"I'm glad to see you. How can I help you today?" He wore a white pharmacy coat over a long-sleeved tee shirt and some running pants. His posture was stiff, formal, but cute in a "let's pretend to play store" kind of way.

I tried to smile, wondering how much I should tell him. I did need his help, so I told him about my cracked tooth, and showed him the list of toiletries I wanted, some shampoo and skin care products that could handle an acne breakout on my chin, and I showed him Buddy's pill bottles. "Hmm," he said, rubbing his chin. "Take anything you want out there." He waved his arm to encompass the store. "I'll see what I can find back here. I'll need to know more about Buddy, but we can talk about that later. Get it in the record book." He turned away and seemed to be making a list on a green memo pad.

I wandered the aisles, picked up two types of Pantene, two types of oral anesthetic, some Advil, and brand name skin care products I normally can't afford. In the food section I found some boxed milk, corn chips and bean dip. I took my backpack to the pharmacy counter to show Wynn my stash.

"You've been busy," he said, looking into the pack and raising one eyebrow. He added two white paper bags, which he said were antibiotics, one in case my tooth blew up on me, another for Lyme or other random infections. Then he pulled a couple of bottles from the vitamin rack, both multivitamins for women. "You probably need more iron, and the vitamins will help with your face."

Well, he had seen my list, but the remark felt a bit rude, and I sensed that he knew it, like he wanted to slap himself. I thanked him for helping me and was on the verge of asking if he was a pharmacist when he fessed up. "If you have any questions for the pharmacist, you're out of luck because she's dead."

"But you do work here?" I asked. He said he was a pharmacy assistant, which is why he is still alive.

"There were bodies in the store?" I asked. He used his thumb to point to the rear parking lot. "In the ditch behind the dumpster. I moved them before they went stiff."

"Good thinking," I said.

29

He said we would talk about that later, pointed to the back door, and turned off the kerosene lamp. I picked up my backpack and walked toward the light.

He said we needed to go to Headquarters, where he kept his records and maps, so we walked a block or so to a small brick house, which we entered through a long, attached greenhouse that covered most of the back wall. Inside it was toasty warm, and there was a small table, and a pair of nice folding chairs with cushions, as if he was expecting company. There was also a wooden drying rack with running clothes and shoes left to air, and stacks of books and papers on a shelf by the wall.

"Please sit down," he said, pulling out one of the chairs. "I won't be a minute."

He came back with a thick spiral notebook marked with orange sticky notes, a pen, two bottles of lemon Perrier water, and little packages of gourmet cookies, Pepperidge Farm and Butter Shortbreads. The guy knew how to serve tea.

He took notes as I told my story, not crying as much this time, and I related what I could remember of what happened with Buddy. He brought me a box of tissues and listened attentively, writing as fast as he could in neat, slightly slanted handwriting, a mix of printing and cursive. Then he got out a large map of the county to find our addresses. He marked the route to my house with a pink highlighter and used a blue one to show the way to Buddy's. Already there were neon yellow marks following different roads on the map, spiraling out from town like a spider web. He saw me studying them.

"Those are places I've already been. I jog and use a kickboard scooter on the downhills."

"Looking for other people?" I asked. He shrugged and almost smiled.

"Something like that." He folded up the map and opened his bottle of water.

"How about you?" I asked. "How did you survive?" He gave a little laugh, then started talking. This is the short version.

"I don't know if you knew our manager, Caity, with a C, but she was a pain in the neck. Loved to micromanage every little thing, and I don't like that, it bugs me. I'd been there longer than her and I knew how to do my job. So when she told me to go into the walk-in cooler and move and reorganize the stock in there, I said sure. I put on the hat and coat and took my time, thought I'd be in big trouble when I came out, but instead there were dead bodies everywhere, including Caity. No blood, just dead. The mom with two little kids was too much, sent me into shock and I passed out. When I regained consciousness, I went home and found my mother, and went looking for others, and within a couple of days I knew I was alone."

When I said I was sorry about his mother, he said we could talk about it later.

The day was getting on, I had an uphill ride ahead of me, and the winter sun was starting to lose its warmth, so I said it was time for me to go. That's when things started getting weird. Wynn started talking faster, getting excited and waving his hands, telling me about the Incineration, which is the next Big Thing that will happen. The first one, 2:42, was only the beginning. They, we know not whom, will next want to clean up the mess the humans and other animals left behind, which they will do by sending super surges of electricity through the power grid, causing every human-made thing to catch fire. The Incineration.

"That's a grim future," I said, standing up.

"Yes, it is, but not entirely hopeless. I'll come to your house tomorrow and turn off your power at the breaker box. It's a basic defense, with the switches off the wiring in the house can't activate." He said he'd shut down most of the breaker panels in town already, that he would bring his own tools.

Why not? I said that would be fine. If he is dealing with Things As They Are by flipping switches, it seems harmless enough. One thing I know for sure is that Wynn wants to be helpful. He makes obtuse remarks at times, said Pantene would not fix the problem with my hair, but he gives off an air of protection I like, crazy or not. I thanked him again for the supplies.

On the way out of town I stopped on the bridge to pee, hoping to get a turkey sighting. But the woods were silent except for the water gurgling in the stream. It took less than an hour to push my way home. I think the chickens missed me. I gave them some of my corn chips.

I miss you. Watch out for the Incineration.

Love,
S

Dear Mom,

Company's coming! You were always so good at that, planning food and activities, even when it was Grandmother who was coming. She drove you crazy no matter what you did. I don't have your gift, but I decided to try.

As soon as it was light I cleaned up the den and

sunroom, took the trash to the burn pile, did my chicken chores, and warmed up water on the wood stove so I could grab a bath, which is really a sponge-and-dip shower standing in the cold bathtub. I had a bad case of helmet hair from yesterday's ride, and I was more than ready for clean clothes.

Next, I went to the garage to find refreshments in my hoard of supplies. Wynn struck me as the health food type, so I chose lime and tangerine seltzer waters, a bag of avocado crisps, a can of almonds, and a jar of green olives. All I was missing was cheese. I turned to look for some cheese crackers when I saw a helmeted head in the garage door window, with an insect-like shield covering the face. I screamed. Wynn was grinning when he pulled off the helmet. I can't believe he thought it was funny. I motioned for him to go to the back door.

He also wore shiny black knee pads, which he took off as he came inside. "Sorry to scare you, but Sarah, I think you scare too easy. It's a skateboarding helmet with a face shield, there's a lot of debris on the road, you know? The scooter is like a skateboard with brakes, it can wipe out pretty fast." I could tell he was excited, and that he didn't quite grasp what he had done wrong. He slipped off his backpack and carried it in one hand. "The breaker box is probably in the garage," he said.

I led him through the kitchen to the garage, lit an oil lamp, and held it while he found the breaker panel behind stacked mini cans of ginger ale and orange soda. He opened the cover and flipped all the breaker switches off, including the main one. When he finished, he looked around and whistled.

Okay, I admit there's a lot, but under the

circumstances my hoarding is a constructive hobby. I have three bicycles, one with a baby carrier, a high-end enclosed baby stroller that cost a thousand dollars new, and three small mountains of provisions, from toilet paper to tuna. "We will now stop worrying about Sarah starving," he said into an imaginary microphone. I told him to take anything he wanted. He took a second look and shook his head, said he was pretty well fixed.

In the sunroom, he took the love seat against the wall, I suppose so he could survey the yard, the neighboring houses, and my overall situation. He popped a seltzer and chugged it down, then turned his head to listen to Chester, the little rooster. "You have chickens?" he asked, "Like for eggs?" I said I was only getting a few eggs because chickens don't lay much in winter, but he was welcome to some. He said he wanted to meet the chickens and I said sure. Then he opened a fresh seltzer and started in on the Cheez-Its. I tried the avocado crisps.

Between bites, he said he wanted to flip the breaker panels in the houses next door, because fire moves fast and you can't be too safe.

"I haven't been in those houses because there are cars in the driveway, which means bodies inside. I can't do the bodies. I haven't needed anything bad enough," I said. He looked at me doubtfully, his brows pulled together in mock concern.

"Oh, but my dear, you cover them. You take a sheet or blanket with you, and shroud that which you do not want to see." He said that's how he did it when he went into houses in town. "Speaking of which," he said, pretending to look at a watch, "Let's go flip some switches."

Armed with a stack of sheets from the Grantham's linen closet, we went to the first house, where the windowsills were lined with dead flies, not a good sign. The front door was locked, but the side door into the kitchen wasn't. Wynn motioned for a sheet and stepped inside while I waited on the small deck. I heard his footsteps, softened by carpeting, and then he reappeared at the door.

"You're safe in the kitchen, and I'm working right there in the next room, the breaker box is by the washer. You can come see what's here. Just don't open any doors," he said. I tiptoed inside.

The small kitchen was so cluttered that it was hard to find a place to put the reusable grocery bag I brought with me, so I hung it on the back of a chair. Dishes and boxed goods were stacked everywhere, covering most of the table and countertops, and what did the people do with all those little appliances? The top of the refrigerator overflowed with paper grocery bags. Talk about fire hazards.

The pantry held mostly store brand soups and pasta sauces, but I found some dried fruit and a gold mine of canned corned beef hash, which is really great as long as you don't read the label because of all the salt.

Wynn deactivated two more houses, and I found some bottled propane in the pantry of the second one, which filled up my bag. I led him home through the backyards, showed him the well pump, and then the chickens. My flock of eight was instantly alert, with little Chester, half the size of the largest hen, scratching at the dirt. I unwrapped some peanut butter crackers and threw a few pieces to Chester, who pretended to take a couple of bites and then made his "come get food" sounds for the hens. I gave Wynn the rest of the crackers to feed to the flock while I checked for eggs. Three eggs are better than none.

We hung around watching the Chicken Channel through another packet of crackers. "You know they are dinosaurs, actually existed before the dinosaurs and survived when the asteroid hit. Insects, too. That's why it's interesting that they survived this," I said, sharing something nerdy I'd been thinking about for a while. "Unless the birds are needed by the plants, for seed dispersal, and this is all about the plants."

He was quiet for a moment and then said "Yes, the re-greening of the blue planet. I'll consider it, get it in the book. There is a section on theories. Incineration is not the only one. And it's not inconsistent with planetary revegetation."

We were almost to the house, and he got strange the way he does, hyper and fidgety. I think he could have separation anxiety? "Whatever's going on, it's good that you're off grid now. You have to be careful, especially with astronomically significant dates like tomorrow. One less thing to worry about."

I asked what was special about tomorrow. "It's December 21, Winter Solstice," he said. "For us, the darkest day of the year."

I must have looked shocked because he said please don't scream.

"Like it's almost Christmas?" I asked weakly. He said you can't stop time as he gathered up his helmet and knee pads. And it's true. You can stop lots of things, but you can't stop time. The days, and nights, just keep coming.

"You'll come for dinner, on Christmas?" I asked, "Please?"

He hesitated and looked down at his shoes. "Yes, it will give us something to look forward to."

I asked if he was an android, because he was thinking my thoughts. "No, but it's always good to be on guard." He looked up at the sky, as if judging the time of day. "I'll get going, check on the turkeys." He'd heard the turkeys on his way to my house, not by the bridge but higher up the hill. He made me promise not to shoot and cook one.

Mom, I don't know how I lost track of three weeks! I knew I was wobbly on the dates, which I tried to mark off on Mrs. Grantham's wall calendar, but I had no idea I was so far behind! It's not like I can check my phone. Seriously, I thought it was somewhere in the December single digits, not the 21st! That's four months, Mom. Four months since it happened, the longest, most terrible four months of my life.

I hope you are faring well. See you soon.
Love,
Sarah

Chapter 4   The Turkey Woman

Dear Mom,

How are you? I hope you are comfortable wherever you are, holding it together in body and mind. My tooth is okay but I have a hard time keeping warm. Even with the wood stove running and wearing two layers of clothes, I need a knitted blanket and hat to not feel cold. Do you think it could be nutritional? The vitamins Wynn gave me may be helping and they just need more time to work. Meantime I am eating more beans. Canned black beans with Cheez-its crunched up on top is pretty good!

There is not much news to report here in the middle of nowhere with this crazy Armageddon going on. The chickens are well and I see chirpy little winter birds in the bushes, but have I told you about the crows? Murders of crows? They must have done well eating animal carcasses, because they are everywhere. I think maybe twenty live in the pine trees down the hill, and it's creepy when the whole clan swoops down into the back yard. Sometimes they perch on the patio furniture and look at me through the windows, creepier still. I try to ignore them.

One odd thing: A mysterious honeybun wrapper. I know every inch of the path from the house to the chicken coop because I walk it at least twice a day. I've raked off the leaves and evened out the gravel, so it's pretty clean, you would approve. The morning after Wynn's visit I was out there and found a fresh, partially crumpled honeybun wrapper on the ground. It could have been there the night before, maybe Wynn dropped it? Or the crows might have brought it in, but it sure looked fresh, with dry crumbs still inside. For the record, I don't eat honeybuns, too many empty calories, so it's not mine.

It is also possible that I heard the turkeys again. Today brought good weather for hauling water, so I filled the garden cart with empty jugs and wheeled it to the well. Just as I got the pump primed and the water started running clean, I think I heard those gobbling sounds in the bushes again, but I can't be sure because of the sound of the water. I listened as I filled a dozen plastic jugs with water, but heard nothing more, even on my second trip. In case the turkeys are thirsty, I got an old pail and filled it with water before closing down the pump. The more the merrier, right?

Speaking of merrier, I am walking a fine line between being dramatically maudlin about Christmas and trying to make something positive out of the day. Faith is really hard when the world you know disappears, and then I think why am I still here? I am thankful, sort of, but it has nothing to do with sins or forgiveness or being a good Christian. Confusing times here on planet Earth.

The silly side of Christmas is also out. I looked in the red and green storage bins in the garage and was not amused by happy Santas and Rudolph the Red Nosed Reindeer, because all the deer are dead. There were some elf figurines I like, and some scented candles and a wreath with nuts and pine cones, but my holiday decorating will be minimal this year.

I may reconsider the big box of angels. I think maybe Mrs. Grantham lost her parents in the last few years, or maybe she was treated for cancer or something, because one entire storage bin is full of angels. There are glass and ceramic angels in boxes, little angel rag dolls, and a large collection of stained glass angels, too. I was concerned about bad juju from leftover angels, but I'm thinking of going back for a second look. Angels are always good, right?

Love,
S

December 26
Dear Mom,

Merry Christmas, with a big bear hug that lasts an hour! That's what I wanted more than anything, but maybe next year? I keep hoping. Now that the actual day has passed, I feel a little better.

Not that it was totally awful. The weather was good, mild and sunny, and I was energized to cook a nice dinner, which kept me busy and made the house smell wonderful. It's amazing what you can do with a propane stove. I cooked a canned ham with pineapple sauce, made mashed potatoes, and green beans with mushroom soup and fried onions. Everything was finished and arranged in a big baking pan on the back of the wood stove, keeping warm. There were cookies and butterscotch pudding for dessert.

As you know I hate to wait, and I was just getting worried when Wynn arrived. He stopped at the patio table to take off his helmet, knee pads and an enormous backpack. The first things he pulled out were a bottle of wine and a trumpet case.

"Merry Christmas," he said, handing me the wine. I

went into the house and got wine glasses and the bowl of nuts I had ready. I poured two glasses and raised mine for a toast.

"To our continued survival," I said, smiling.

"And the rebirth of hope," he added. It was an appropriate toast. We both took a sip, and he motioned for us to sit down. The sun, the wine and the company felt warm and good. He said the concert would start with the second glass, and asked my permission to pick through the nut mix for pecans.

"All you want, and that's a nice touch, too," I said, pointing to a bright red Santa hat hung on the chicken coop door. He was wearing a tacky holiday sweater over his running pants, so I assumed he put it there. He looked at me like I was not quite right, cocking one eyebrow the way he does, and said he had nothing to do with it.

Crows don't hang up Santa hats. Only people do that. I told him I thought it was the work of the turkey girl, or boy, or whoever, and the reasons why I thought it was a human, moving closer. Turkey noises, garbage, a moved bucket, some grain scattered in the chicken run I didn't recognize. He listened thoughtfully, then refilled our glasses.

He made a sly face and stiffened his posture. "I have details to report as well, details that may lend credibility to your theory that we have a fellow human among us," he said loudly, then leaned in close and spoke in softer tones. "In addition to the road you took to town, there is another route that loops to the west, it's longer but more scenic. That's the way I came up today. Down by the horse farm some limbs and other debris have been pulled out of the road, piled up on the side. And the gate is open. It's been a while since I was down there, but I remember seeing the dead horses in the field. I swear the gate was closed then, chained and locked. Now it's open."

I asked if he knew the people who lived there, and he nodded and said that unfortunately he did, but it was confidential pharmacy business. He made me cross my heart and hope to die, stick a needle in my eye promise not to tell, which I did.

"I think it was a hospice situation. The people at the horse farm, Gina and George, they've lived there forever, and George came to talk to the pharmacist a few times. He was retired, but maybe he was a doctor? I waited on him once when he came in for a pick-up."

We both startled when we heard and saw stirring in the bushes beyond the chicken house. "Just in time for the concert," he said, again using a loud voice. He stood, picked up his trumpet, and turned to me.

"Trumpeters get popular during the holidays. I know so many carols by heart. Do you still sing? You were in the chorus. You can sing along."

I said I hadn't felt much like singing lately, but I did know a few carols. "And clapping, too," he added, nodding toward the bushes. "That will help flush them out." He wet his lips. "We will start with some Schubert," he announced, and then played a prayerful version of Ave Maria that gave me goosebumps. I clapped loudly, and definitely saw more movement in the bushes. He kept Have Yourself a Merry Little Christmas short, then launched into Jingle Bells, motioning for me to clap and sing along, which I did.

But it was We Wish You a Merry Christmas that brought an older woman into the open, crying and holding a box of chocolates against her chest. She wore a blue Christmas sweat suit embroidered with snowmen and a Santa hat that matched the one on the chicken coop. A gold bell hung from her neck. As Wynn finished the song, I instinctively stood up. "We're so glad you came to join us for Christmas dinner," I said. "I'm Sarah, and this is Wynn."

If a person can nod and shake their head at the same time, that is what she did. It was a don't-get-too-close move, and Wynn picked up on it, too. He sat down gently and motioned toward the empty chair with a sheepish look on his face. "We have wine, food and company to share."

This time the shake of the head was a definite no. She took a step forward and placed the box of chocolates on the patio, then stepped back again.

"Don't go yet," I said, and went into the house to get the take-home food I had already packed for Wynn. "Please," I said, slowly walking toward her, holding out the plastic bag, and then placing it on the patio when she didn't reach out to take it. "It's dinner to go, but you know you are welcome to stay."

She bowed her head, I think it was a thanks, picked up the bag and turned to leave. "Take care, I'll come see you soon," Wynn called after her. She stopped for a moment, and then squared her shoulders and continued on her way home.

I asked Wynn if we should help her and he said, no, it was only a half mile of gentle downhill to her farm. He said he would go check on her and her breaker box in the next few days. I said I thought she might like that.

The whole thing put me in a somber mood. I was having trouble wrapping my head around trauma so deep that you can no longer speak, because that's one of the ways I feel it, too. Since 2:42 I've gone months talking only to chickens, and it's been okay. I did like talking with Buddy, and now Wynn, but I can still keep my silence for hours and not be bothered. Gina and I are on the same continuum, but she's much farther down on the isolation scale. It is not always comforting to find someone worse off than you.

I suggested to Wynn that Gina might be more comfortable if I went to the horse farm with him. He agreed it was a good idea, especially after we read the card she tucked into the box of chocolates. Wynn said they were a fancy brand from California, very expensive, and not quite expired. The handwriting was weak and shaky, but legible.

Dear Neighbor,

I want to wish you happy holidays, and offer my sincere apology if I have frightened you. Certain people and animals have been my whole life, all gone now. I was ready to be gone, too, and then discovered your chickens. They have revived me. Please forgive my intrusion. I hope to be better soon.

Sincerely,

Gina Barris

It is definitely the most memorable Christmas card I have ever received, so I had to share it. I hope you got a Christmas card, too. And maybe a trumpet concert.

Love,

S

Dear Mom,

Happy day after Christmas, when you often had to work and felt guilty about that and about us not getting enough presents. We said we didn't care, and we really didn't, but things were tense. You were tense. Did Dad help at all with the presents and extra holiday expenses? Not likely! You lied to cover for him, we knew. I know you tried to keep it a secret that you had his paycheck garnished to get child support, but we knew that, too. He told us, the jerk! And no, we didn't think he ignored us because you made him pay. He ignored us because he wanted to. It's what he chose to do.

On to the news, because I finally have some.

On Christmas Day, Wynn and I were both yawning after the wine and big meal. When I invited him to stay and spend the night on the sofa, he immediately agreed. He's decisive that way. "It's so warm and cozy here, and I like the angels," he said. I had stationed some angels from the storage bin around the den, on bookshelves or hung by the windows. I thought they would be good company for my first Christmas alone, but Wynn was even better. We played gin rummy, talked about people we knew, and carefully avoided delicate topics like you, Jeremy, or Wynn's mother. For now, all of you are in the "talk about it later" category.

Other news. Wynn said he went to Buddy's house, but didn't find Buddy. He appeared to have been there, two fresh graves had been dug in the backyard, but after much knocking and calling there was no response. Wynn left the prescriptions on the front porch.

The last time I zipped myself into the mummy bag in Rebecca's room, Buddy was in the house, and I found myself listening for his snores. I don't think Wynn snores.

In the morning I learned that he prefers tea over coffee, a protein bar over a Pop-Tart, and scrambled eggs rather than fried. He is also full of surprises. While I cooked eggs, he moved the wicker table in the sunroom, spread a sheet over the floor, and placed one of the kitchen stools in the middle. When I asked what was happening, he said "Welcome to Wynn's House of Style! After breakfast, I am going to repair your hair."

Resistance was futile, because he came prepared with a cape and hair scissors.

Mom, this may be the best haircut I've ever had! He took his time, humming a little but not talking much, working through the mess I'd made layer by layer until it took on an actual shape. There was no mirror, but I could feel it happening. And even though I've washed my hair forty times since The Stench incident, having more taken off made me feel cleaner.

And Wynn loved doing it! It was almost like he did a slow dance with my hair, he was totally in the zone. "You're so good at this," I said. "Did you go to cosmetology school?"

He snorted a laugh. "I wish. Mother thought it would be an unseemly career choice."

"Oh," I said, knowing better than to follow up with a question about his mother. "Well, it's never too late. I'll recommend you to all my friends."

So now I have fluffy, even hair that falls back into place when the wind blows, all by itself. He says it's a medium layered bob.

The weather was still good, so we decided to go to

Gina's.

It was clear from the size of the house and property that Gina is loaded. Or was loaded. If you were a millionaire before, are you a millionaire now? I felt like a serf entering the royal palace as we walked through the iron gates, me pushing the swanky stroller loaded with canned goods, toilet paper and other necessities. It seemed like a good way to say "Welcome back to life."

The big house had a Spanish look to it, with a nice blend of stucco and stonework, with solar panels over part of the tiled roof. Another solar array was installed next to a spacious barn. "Do those things work?" I asked.

"Unfortunately not," Wynn said. "The big ones like this are tied into the power grid, which as we know is not working, and the small off-grid systems rely on batteries, which also are not working." He said he had checked on an off-grid solar house he knew of, and the power was as dead as the people inside. "Not that I'm an electrical engineer, I would need YouTube for that," he said, cracking a smile.

Gina must have heard us coming, because she met us by the front door. She wore a soft royal blue sweatsuit made out of velveteen or some other plush fabric, and had pulled her graying hair into a ponytail with a silver scrunchie. I don't know how old she is, maybe sixty? She has a lot of wrinkles around her eyes, maybe sun damage from being out with horses all the time, or they could be weeping wrinkles from excessive crying.

If not for the huge purple burial vault set on a metal stand, the main room of Gina's house would have been stunning. It has soaring ceilings, beautiful timber frame woodwork, and glossy floors made of marble or something like it. It was a bit chilly, which is probably best for corpses. Wynn looked respectfully at the vault, at least eight feet long, and asked if it was George. When Gina nodded, we both whispered "I'm so sorry." It did not seem like a good time to ask for details, which would not be forthcoming because Gina does not speak.

She led us through a door into the kitchen area, where it was twenty degrees warmer. A gorgeous white ceramic stove radiated heat into the room, dense with struggling houseplants. We put down the provisions we brought on the tidy countertop, and Wynn picked up his tool kit and asked if she knew where her breaker boxes were. The question seemed to confuse her, so I broke in and explained Wynn's Incineration Theory and why he wanted to attend to her electrical panels. I may have seen a hint of a grin as she pointed to a door near the back wall that had a cute hand-painted sign that said Control Room. As Wynn disappeared into the utility room, Gina reached out and tugged at my sleeve, then motioned for me to go with her outside, to the big barn.

The chickens will never go hungry. She has hundreds of pounds of horse feed of different kinds in a sealed room, which explains some of the mystery grains I'd noticed in the chicken run. She pointed to one barrel and made *bok bok* chicken sounds, indicating that they liked that feed best.

Being around a nonverbal person is interesting. You get to keep talking, you need to keep talking, but you also have to watch them because they're talking back with their face, hands and posture. "You can keep feeding the chickens all you want," I said. "I ran out of chicken feed long ago, I've been giving them dry dog and cat food. The grain is probably better for them." She clasped her hands together and nodded rather emphatically. I think she doubts my abilities as a chicken keeper, which is certainly justified. I'm strictly an amateur.

We didn't stay long. Once the breaker box was taken care of, Wynn was eager to get back to town. Even with no customers, he felt a responsibility to keep the drug store safe yet accessible, and he needed to get Gina into his record book, and put her on his map.

She would not let us leave empty handed. I saw her eyes get wide when she saw the coffee I'd brought, and at least twice she rubbed her stomach and smiled to thank me for yesterday's meal. As we turned to go, she gave each of us a paper bag containing a small loaf of bread. Bread! I think I screamed, but only a little. I haven't had bread in four months! On the outside of each bag she had written "From my pizza oven."

So there it is, the biggest news of all, which is that we have a source of bread, Gina's outdoor wood-fired pizza oven. I invited her to come to my garage grocery store when she needed more ingredients.

I have lots of cleaning up to do and the water needs replenishing, but I wanted you to know that Christmas wasn't terrible, my hair is amazing, and the only spooks in the backyard are crows.

Life goes on, and it's better with bread!
Love,
Sarah

Chapter 5 The Big Snow

January 15
Dear Mom,
Hello from Windy Ridge, where winter seems to be here to stay, along with the crows. Are you keeping warm? I'm in the den by the wood stove all the time, reading during the day and sleeping there at night. I also have taken up knitting, because Mrs. Grantham had a big basket of yarn, a case of assorted knitting needles, and several beginner books. So far I'm not very good, stitches disappear and reappear like magic, but I'm trying. I can cast off, knit, and purl.

Did you get snow? If there was a Winter Storm warning issued, I didn't get it. No sirens or beeps on the TV or text messages from Ap Power.

The snow started late in the morning with a few flurries, and then the flakes got bigger and by mid-afternoon there was six inches on the ground and it was still coming down. The thermometer outside the back door said eight degrees, and ten feet outside the door it was a whiteout. I had worried about the chickens all day, and decided I needed to bring them inside. I planned to keep them in the sunroom, so I gathered up the chair cushions, and covered the loveseat and coffee table with tablecloths. I got a pet carrier from the garage, put on boots, coat, hat and gloves, and trudged outside to capture chickens.

Despite their jumping and squawking, I caught three hens easily and carried them to the house. I slipped once, then got more careful. Not a good time to break a leg! Out in the coop, Chester was proving to be a problem. He may not have recognized me wrapped up in winter clothes, so I talked to him, explained about the snow, apologized for the snow.

I caught the black hen named Mocha and was zipping her into the cat carrier when I felt him jump on my back. His spurs couldn't penetrate my coat, but I screamed anyway. He backed off, but still got in the way when I reached for a hen. I was ready to kill him, seriously. It was snowing even harder, my hands were numb, and I wondered if I should just give it up. Then I discovered I was not alone. A dark figure in a puffy coat was crouched down beside me, making chicken sounds. Gina.

"He won't let me catch him!" I called into the wind, but instead of an answer she threw herself against me, knocking me against the wall of the coop. It was not a gentle nudge, and it shocked me into silence. I sat there in the snow while she touched Chester's back and talked to him in her *kerr-kerr* chicken voice, and gently picked him up. She tucked him under her arm and walked away toward the house. With Chester gone, catching the last two hens was easy. We were all crazy cold.

I delivered the last chickens to the sunroom, where Gina sat on a stool, talking to them in chicken talk. Good enough. I went to the far end of the den and peeled off my wet boots and clothes, down to Rebecca's thermal underwear with teddy bears on it. I saw her looking at me, and she was smiling. I went to the back of the house to get more clothes for both of us.

I showed her the clothes I found for her in Mrs. Grantham's drawers, various undergarments, socks and slippers, and a thick Virginia Tech sweatsuit, maroon and orange. I expected silence, then heard her clear her throat.

"I suppose beggars can't be choosers," she croaked. She said something! And, her teeth were chattering. She had gotten too cold, and this was not good. Unless that's what jolted her to start talking again.

"Come change into dry clothes," I said. "Here by the fire. I'll be in the kitchen making us some hot chocolate."

I have a lot of hot chocolate mixes, and I made what I think is the very best, a half and half mix of Swiss Miss with marshmallows and Ghirardelli Dark. The snow was still coming down, probably pushing a foot, and I suddenly felt happy to be warm and dry on the sofa by the fire, with a creamy mouthful of chocolate.

"Mmm, this is good," she said, as if she was surprised. "Hits the spot."

I said she should plan to spend the night, that it was too cold to go back outside. "Don't worry," she said. "I promised Chester I wouldn't leave. Birds of a feather fly together."

So, she made a deal with the rooster? To be honest, I was relieved to have the chickens in the house, and kind of glad to have Gina here, too. What more can happen? Lose power? Car won't start? Roads impassable? The usual problems caused by a big snow no longer apply, because they are already here.

Hoping for a better day tomorrow.

Love,
Sarah

Dear Mom,

Good morning from Cold Mountain! The snow finally stopped, and the wind, too, and now it's seriously gorgeous outside, with the snow a foot deep. Chester started crowing before dawn, which is really loud inside the tiled sunroom. Gina thinks this is funny. While I made coffee, she sat with the chickens for a morning visit.

"They like me better than you," she said, joining me in the den. What is this, kindergarten? Actually, I think she has designs on my chickens, like she wants to take over the flock, or maybe she already has? "The early bird gets the worm," she added, pointing her index finger in the air.

I felt the coffee kicking in and smiled. "It's good to hear you talking," I said. "You must be feeling better?"

I thought it was an innocent question, but her response suggested otherwise. "But I'm not sick! Do I look sick?" Her voice was loud, defensive.

"Well, no…"

"It's these awful clothes," she said, pulling at the pants of the sweatsuit. "No fashion sense at all."

This was true, it was a baggy sweatsuit, but what did it matter? "If you can't beat 'em, join 'em," she said with a sigh. While I cooked breakfast, she changed into her own clothes, now dry from being near the fire. The switch into blue velour and a hot meal improved her mood. "You can't make an omelet without breaking some eggs," she said, giggling like it was a good joke.

She offered to clean up the kitchen, but lost interest after washing the silverware, and went to sit with the chickens.

When you have nothing to do, time passes way too slow. It's hard to read with a rooster crowing in the next room, and watching icicles drip is pretty dull, so I got out a deck of cards and started playing solitaire.

This got Gina's attention. She came into the den, closing the French doors behind her, and sat down on the sofa. She said she didn't want to play, only wanted to watch.

"Did anyone ever tell you that you have beautiful eyes?" she asked.

"Thank you," I said, though my eyes are not that special, a neutral blue-gray, and at this point I have cavewoman brows. At least she was trying to make conversation, not in chicken talk. It reminded me of her days as a turkey.

"The turkey call," I said. "How did you learn it?"

She snorted, cleared her throat. "I used to hunt. Loved to hunt. Ever tried it?" I shook my head. "Didn't think so. You're a little soft for it," she said.

I'm a little soft? Five months on my own, and I'm soft? Too soft for what, for killing animals? It's Gina who has a mean streak. She comes off as gentle and kind, but it's an act. She says things that cut, like "I don't guess you had many friends before all this happened." What? I had friends, why would I not have friends? Sometimes I wished I had more friends but what business was it of hers?

Or how about this one. I was brushing my hair and she asked me if I liked wearing my hair this way and I said I really did. "Maybe you haven't had a good look," she said. As in, "You look ugly."

Ready for the capper? She asked me about my job while we were playing Go Fish, the only card game she will play. I thought this was a safe subject. You know I liked my job even though some people (including you) were not sure I would find happiness selling tires at the Goodyear store. It was a good job! I liked the people I worked with, I often felt like I was helping customers make good decisions, and I made more money than most of my friends.

"Kind of a stuck little occupation, don't you think? Get the pun?" she asked. I did get the pun, and her implication that I was a loser.

By evening I was ready to choke her. The snow can't melt fast enough.

Love,
Sarah

Dear Mom,

I am out of snow jail, are you? After three days with eight chickens and my crazy neighbor, the snow went slushy and mud replaced the ice. Good thing, because we burned up all the dry wood I'd brought in, and used most of the drinking water, too. It felt good to get outside and work.

In the early afternoon, when everything started melting fast, Wynn appeared wearing snow boots rather than running shoes. He knocked lightly as he came through the back door, pulled off his boots by the wood stove, and answered my call to come into the kitchen. Then Chester crowed at him from the sunroom, and he jumped. We both burst out laughing.

"New roommates?" he asked, rinsing his hands in my warm dishwashing water. I looked around warily. "Gina's here, too. And she's talking. She's in the garage, looking for chicken treats in my food stash." I offered him coffee, hot chocolate or tea, and put the kettle on the propane stove.

"I'll take tea!" Gina called from the garage. "Earl Gray if you have it," she added, knowing I did. She riffled through the tea selection several times a day, rearranging the packets. It's weird.

He went into the den to talk with Gina while I made tea, which I served on a big tray with three little plates of Biscoff cookies, the best ones for dunking. Gina turned to me and eyed her approval. We sipped our tea and talked about the snow, and Gina gave the chickens a few cookies to quiet them down.

What brought Wynn out in the slush? He needed help with Buddy, who he found drunk and slumped against the back door of the drug store in the falling snow, howling like a dog. Until the snow, he had been staying at the liquor store, which had no heat.

"I brought him home to my house to warm him up and dry him out, but he can't stay with me," Wynn said nervously.

"Don't look at me," I said. "He can stay in a neighbor's house, but not here. He snores! You've heard him. I can't do it." It felt cruel in the moment, but Wynn looked at me with a softness in his eyes. He respects boundaries, perhaps because he has so many of his own.

Gina fluttered her hands. "I have a cottage for my trainer. Would that work? He can help me with water, earn his keep."

I said I thought it was a good idea, but Wynn wasn't so sure. "Okay, but he wants to drink. Driven to drink, as they say." He rubbed his chin, which was unusually dark with stubble.

"I can hear! I've had drinking men work for me before. They're all right if they have just enough, but not too much." She reached for a cookie. "They know which side their bread is buttered on." So, Gina was experienced hosting alcoholics, who she likely found easy to push around. Poor Buddy. I hoped she would treat him better than she'd been treating me. If not, we could find a place for him in the neighborhood. We'd come up with something.

I am open to ideas.

Love,

Sarah

Dear Mom,

Good morning, and how are you? I am doing better. When the weather warmed up, so did I, and now I feel more confident about making it through the last of winter. After that, who knows? Wynn says I should move to town, and he has picked out a couple of houses for me to choose from.

I am seriously considering it. I moved to the Grantham house because of the wood stove, water pump and chickens, and because I knew you could find me here. It was a good decision at the time, but maybe not anymore. Being in town closer to Wynn will be way less lonely, and it will be easier to work with him gathering long-term supplies. We have both realized that this situation might go on forever, as in *forever*, and we should get our act together and do a better job managing our resources.

Wynn brought up the subject of relocation when he brought Buddy to move in at Gina's. I arrived first, bringing toilet paper, coffee, and cinnamon Pop-Tarts, which Buddy likes a lot.

Gina met me at the door. Decked out in designer denim and high leather boots that cost more than my car, she led me down a brick pathway that went around the house to the trainer's cottage, a roomy one-bedroom cabin next to the barn with marble countertops and an awesome piece of stained glass in the kitchen, which looked out over rolling pastures. It was decked out like a high-priced Airbnb!

"This place is gorgeous!" I said, which clearly pleased her. I had my doubts about Buddy being comfortable in such hoity-toity digs, but whatever. He arrived bathed and dressed in clean clothes, but he still looked rough. His death duties and drinking binge had cost him a little weight and his eyes looked tired, but he smiled and said "Hey there, Girlie," like he was really glad to see me. I was awesomely glad to see him. I'm not much of a hugger, it has to be my idea, but I hugged Buddy and he hugged me back. I hoped we were doing the right thing moving him in with Gina.

So far, so good. A few days later when Wynn went to check on him and take Gina refills of his medicinal vodka, he stopped by my house to give me a report. "He looks fine, maybe even happy," Wynn said. "I think he really likes that cottage, says it's peaceful."

I had trouble imagining living with Gina as peaceful,

but sharing two houses is different from sharing two rooms.

"I hope you're giving some thought to moving to town," Wynn said. "The chocolate situation needs attention, and it's kind of far to come see you." "The chocolate situation" is our phrase for our supply challenge, because when the chocolate is gone, there will be no more. There are no ships carrying cocoa beans from Central America, or factories making chocolate bars, or trucks bringing them to stores. If we go on living and living, chocolate will become a fading memory, like cheese.

"I am," I said. "I think I'm ready for a change."

Wynn can be so cute. "Ta-ta-ta-daaa! Excellent news," he said, touching my cheek with his finger. "I will be king, and you will be my queen."

Who knew it could be so simple to rule the world? Of course, this makes you royalty, too.

I'll leave a note in the mailbox when I know where I'll be. Hope to see you soon!

Love,
Sarah

Chapter 6   The Garden House

April 15
Dear Mom,
Greetings from home, where spring has arrived showing hope of better things to come. That's what spring is about, right? Say fie-fie to death, because little daffodils are blooming everywhere, and dandelions and purple wildflowers are popping in the unmown lawns.

Warmer weather also has brought back the bugs, and I'm not talking about a few bees and butterflies. These are little black biting flies, and they are bad! Wynn thinks they overwintered under cattle carcasses. You can be out after dark or first thing in the morning, but other than that you better protect yourself or stay indoors or they will get you. Insect repellents don't do much good. We've tried everything Wynn had at the drugstore, but nothing works for long.

I lost the beekeeper's hood in the yucky incident on the Parkway, but Wynn and I have figured out how to make head coverings using netting from the basement of Schoolhouse Fabrics, a gold mine of bug netting! You put a baseball cap on your head, then a piece of tulle or nylon net, which you tie around your neck with elastic or a loose bandana. Then a long-sleeved shirt buttoned to the top. It looks spooky, but makes it possible to go outside during the day without getting eaten alive.

This is one of the reasons I'm glad I moved to town (news!), and let the chickens go live with Gina. The flies were after them, too, biting their butts and eyes, so I had no choice but to keep them indoors. The sunroom was trashed, and I was ready to move on.

Besides, I knew Gina wanted those chickens. Needed them, in her way. And Buddy could fix up a place in the barn that would work as a coop.

Let me tell you about the house in town Wynn found for me. It's only two blocks from his place, higher on the hill, and I'm calling it the Garden House. The furnishings are spare, as if the woman who lived here had moved very recently. There is little food in the cabinets and none in the fridge, and only a few clothes in the closet, mostly old dresses. The drawers are empty. The furniture is plain but ample, with beds, a sofa and recliner, and a table and chairs in the kitchen. The scattered books on the shelves look interesting, and the house is immaculately clean.

But here's the best part. The house comes with a raised bed garden, with hoops and covers to keep out bugs and birds, and on the adjoining property there's a small spring-fed pond. Seriously! It's a dug pond, oval, and two pipes come out of the ground on one side and drip water all the time. Wynn says it's spring water, good to drink when collected straight from the pipe, he's been drinking it for months. I can use pond water for flushing.

I know you're laughing about me wanting to grow a garden, the kid who smirked when asked to weed the flowerbed, but times change! Eating canned and instant food is better than going hungry, but it won't last forever and Wynn and I are ready for real food anyway. Some of the reading material in my new house includes old issues of Mother Earth News, so I'm learning about how we might make this gardening thing work.

Back to the chickens. Gina comes to feed them every day, so I'm sure she noticed that I've been gone a lot. She's such a sneak that she's probably been watching me move stuff. One day I waited around for her so we could talk. You know I have no gift for manipulating others, but I know how to read them. Gina needs to win at whatever game is being played. I planned ahead to be the loser, even rehearsed what I had to say.

I waited until she was in the sunroom, talking to the chickens while sitting on the stool I kept covered with a towel to keep it clean. As usual, she was overdressed for the occasion. Under her protective bug hat, she wore a gauzy layered blouse over fitted cream-colored slacks. Perfect for feeding chickens.

"Gina, you once said the chickens like you better than me, and I think you're right. I try, but just don't have your instinct for it. I'm moving to town for the summer, and rather than take them with me, do you think they could move in with you?"

My direct approach took her by surprise, but I could tell from her surly grin it was just what she wanted.

"I suppose we could make do, come up with something," she said. "Buddy is rather handy, and there is a roll of window screen in the barn." Clearly, she had already thought about chicken housing, biding her time until I caved.

"I can see how much you care for them, and they know it. I would not try to take them back, not unless you wanted me to."

"Well then," she said, turning her face away so I could not see her pleasure. "You've been such a good neighbor. It's the least I can do."

I thanked her, and said we could move them in the pet carriers anytime she was ready, to just let me know. She didn't bother. The next day I came back from taking a load of stuff to town, and the chickens were gone.

It took me hours and hours to clean the sunroom. Chicken poo is no joke! The house got me through the cold, and I might move back sometime. There is enough firewood to last another winter. I left it in good shape.

More later,
Sarah

Dear Mom,

I miss you so much and think of you every day, but honestly, not all the time. Is that how it is for you? Only double because of Jeremy? The hurt and loss are not going away, but the sharp, killing pains are fewer and not as bad.

I do have survivor's guilt, which comes in little pricks. The Garden House has a thermostat in the hallway, and it reminds me of the thermostat wars we had over whether 74 was too hot in summer and 68 was too cold in winter. What wimps we were! When I asked for more heat, you told me to put on more clothes. Sorry if I whined.

Wardrobe adjustment is now a way of life. The day starts out with two layers of clothes, plus bug wear, then goes to one, then doubles up again when it cools off at night. You are your own thermostat.

I'm all moved in, and I've been working with Wynn to gather and store perishable packaged foods like flour and cereal before insects can get them. We're using the basement of the Methodist church for storage, because it's cool and dry down there, and there's plenty of room for plastic bins. Best of all, there was nobody in the church at 2:42. No corpses. We come and go through an upstairs door, and are meticulous about excluding flies.

I am back to scavenging for pasta and propane, which is less scary because Wynn used green spray paint to mark the houses with no bodies inside when he shut down breaker boxes. Back in the fall when I was by myself, I liked to get in and out of houses fast and clean, taking only what I thought I might need. Now things are different. I'm in less of a hurry, and can take my time looking for canned meats, oils, and other precious foodstuffs.

On yesterday's mission, I entered an older two-story house through the mud room, which opened into an orderly kitchen. The table was clear but for salt, pepper, and paper napkins, and the dishes were put away except for one cup in the sink. Did the owner take a last sip before leaving? I placed the cup in the dish rack and started checking the cabinets.

I was scoring big with Stovetop stuffing and canned chicken, maybe humming a little of that old song, Fly Me to the Moon, which Wynn played on his trumpet at sunset last night. Then I heard something bump downstairs, in the basement, not once but three times. I stood still, listening, thinking I would hear scratching animal sounds. Instead I heard heavy footsteps on the stairs and a man's voice calling "Mary Ann? Is that you?"

I screamed, dropped the cans I was holding and backed toward the door. The footsteps stopped.

"I take it you're not Mary Ann," the voice said from the stairwell. "Are you armed?"

"Who's Mary Ann? And no, I'm not armed. Are you?"

"No." The footsteps resumed, and a middle-aged man of average build, dressed in khaki pants and a cotton plaid shirt, came into the kitchen. "Walt and Mary Ann, this is their house. Old friends of mine," he said. "A long time ago I worked on this house. Helped install the solar panels. My name is Rob Lowe."

"Seriously?" I said. "Sorry, I'm Sarah. Are you staying here?"

He hesitated. "More like squatting, until I find what I need, and resting up for a while. It's safe here, right? Where I've been nowhere is safe, but I've been in Floyd two days and haven't heard a gunshot. Only maybe a trumpet?"

I couldn't help but smile. "Yes, Wynn plays the trumpet. So far we've been spared from guns. Where did you come from?"

"I have a place here, up in the county, but I was in Roanoke. Or what used to be Roanoke. We'd been living there, me and my wife Natalie. She didn't make it. Then things started blowing up, and I hunkered down."

"I'm so sorry," I said, suddenly feeling like I should be sitting. "My mother was at work, at Memorial Hospital. Do you think…"

"No way to know," he said quickly. "Don't get your hopes up." He went to the pantry and got a couple of Dr.

Peppers, and handed one to me. "We're better off here."

He said it took him three weeks to travel fifty miles, in part because he has a bad knee that can only take so much walking in one day. He'd been beaten once and shot at twice making his way out of the city, where looting was the only remaining occupation. He said his fellow survivors were drunk, high, or just plain mean.

"It got worse after a few months, when they banded together into gangs. Vicious, brutal gangs with nothing to lose, no consequences. What they did to bodies, it was savage, and sometimes you could hear screams, so you knew they attacked live people, too. I've never been so scared."

He looked to see if I was listening. "I guess so," I said, keeping my eyes on the floor. I didn't want to hear any more, but what was I supposed to do? Change the subject, put it on fast forward?

"Did things improve when you got out of the city?" I asked.

"Oh, yeah," he said, taking a slug of his drink. "Once I made it over the mountain, everything got quiet, too quiet. I might have PTSD, I keep expecting the crack of guns." He'd seen only two other people on the highway coming into town, unarmed, who he called The Yuppies. "They're camping along the way, up at the FloydFest site, like this is some kind of vacation," he said, shaking his head. "While the whole world's gone dark."

I was not feeling well, light-headed and nauseous. I stood up and started putting the food back in the cabinet. "Sorry about stealing your food."

"Honest mistake."

"If you need anything, between me and Wynn we

have everything from bottled water to propane stoves. Those are at my place, lanterns, too. But first you need to check in with Wynn." I drew a map to Wynn's house on a napkin, my hand shaking more than it should. I needed to get out of there, let Wynn take over. "There are four of us, you make five. Wynn will explain it. I need to go."

Mom, I couldn't bear it, the news Rob brought from the city. Where are you??? Under siege somewhere, or murdered on your way home, or gone forever? It sent me into a strange state, slightly dizzy and detached from everything except the ground underfoot as I walked to Wynn's to tell him the news. He was in the greenhouse, reading and hiding from the flies. I decided against opening the door.

"Expect a visitor, we have a new neighbor," I said. "He's okay, his name's Rob. I have to go. See ya." I heard my voice shaking, felt myself falling apart, and was glad my face was partially hidden by the bug screen. I walked home as fast as I could.

I couldn't bear it.

I went into the house, drank some water, changed into a tee shirt and pajama pants, pulled the curtains closed in the bedroom, got into bed and hid under the covers. After a while I felt safe enough to cry.

That's where Wynn found me a couple of hours later, after he met Rob and got him in the Record Book and heard his story. I had finished crying, but was still curled up in a ball.

"Hey, Sarah," he said softly, sitting on the edge of the bed. "Are you all right?"

"No," I sniffed.

"You're not hurt?" I heard a subtle panic in his voice.

"No." Sniff, sniff, blow nose.

He got up, took off his shoes, and laid down beside me, on top of the covers. "You don't mind a friendly visitor, do you?"

"No, I'm glad you're here." I stretched out my legs, then my arms, emerging from my cocoon. I yawned, suddenly exhausted. "Too much bad news at once."

He agreed with a grunt, but took a minute to choose his words. "Sarah, I know you worry about your mother, you have to, but please know this. The only one I worry about is you."

I reached out from under the covers and took his hand. I wanted to tell him I felt the same way, that he's the best semi-boyfriend I ever had, but I was afraid I would start crying again. I rolled over and put my head on his shoulder.

"I love you, too," I whispered. He squeezed my hand, and didn't pull away.

"Let's just breathe," he said, which is what we did, for a long time. It sounds weird, but it felt very intimate to lie together, barely touching, relaxing that way.

"Thank you," I said, "But now I need to pee."

A few minutes later we heard Rob outside. "Yoo-hoo, came to get some water," he called, and Wynn went out in the soft evening light to show him the dripping cistern, complete with plastic faucet, that we'd made from an old cooler installed at the edge of the pond.

Watching them through the kitchen window, I felt exhausted yet calm, but there was something else. I was finally starting to feel secure. There is magic in the power of two compared to going it alone, but three brings more strength, talent, even resilience.

Sorry, but I'm trying to NOT think about you right now in light of Rob's dark report. By tomorrow the angel of hope will return.

Love,
Sarah

Chapter 7 Saint Buddy

Hi Mom,

Hope you are well and able to enjoy sunshine and rain, like you always did. You would sit out on the deck when it was sunny, and stand by the window when it rained. I'm starting to do the same things, only in slow motion.

Remember texting, and how your phone would play Shake it Off when it was me, and my phone would light up with a picture of Scruff when it was you? After I left home, remember the buzz and lights of an actual phone call? I still have my phone, in the drawer by the bed, because there's always What If?

Here at Small Town Apocalypse, we use a more primitive messaging system. Wynn installed dinner bells behind the drug store, at his house, and at my house, so if any of us is needed, we can ring for attention. Ding-dong, dinner's ready! Or, should a stranger come to the drug store, there is a sign there telling them to ring the bell. So much for phones.

We had rain overnight, which made the flies slow to hit the air in the morning. I had about finished bringing in water when I heard the drug store bell. I scampered down the hill, expecting to see Wynn, but it was Buddy!

He smiled and held up a cloth grocery bag, heavy with bread and eggs. "From Gina and the chickens," he said. "How you doing, Girlie?"

He looked good, nourished and rested, better than I'd ever seen him. He had a shopping list, but first I invited him to my house for lunch. I'd been carrying water and he had walked two miles, so we were both hungry. He sat at the kitchen table while I sliced bread. I asked how it was going.

"Oh, we're getting along. She's different, all right, but she leaves me in peace for the most part. It's kind of lonely, but now that I know the way here, it don't seem so far. I can come visit more often, if you don't mind."

"Anytime, all the time," I said. I finished making peanut butter, jelly and potato chip sandwiches, one of my specialties when we have fresh bread. I made a third one for Wynn and ducked outside to ring the bell, but not too loud. He was out with Rob looking for DC converters, whatever those are, and I knew he would show up sooner or later.

Buddy loved his sandwich, said his mother let him and his brother put potato chips on their bologna sandwiches when they were little, and he'd always liked them that way. The bread really was remarkably good, and I asked Buddy if he had learned how to run the wood-fired oven.

He laughed. "You bet I have. She gets frustrated awful easy starting it up, so we sort of do it together." There was a kindness in his voice that got my attention, or maybe it was just his impulse to help the ladies. "This batch was a hot one, with hickory wood, that's why it's so smoky," he said between bites.

In other news, he said he'd built a screen house for the chickens, who were doing fine, and he was digging up the old paddock, where there was lots of horse manure, for planting sweet corn. He helped move most of the houseplants from the kitchen to the patio. "Them things need more water than the commodes," he said. "Gina ain't much on hauling water from the spring, but she has all kinds of buckets and pans she puts out to catch rain for the plants. Pours it into a watering can and talks to the plants when she waters them."

I told him I could understand that, because I was growing lettuce and radishes under a cover in the garden, and I checked on them every day.

"With her it's different," he said. "Which is why I want to talk to Wynn. About a prescription."

As if by magic, I heard Wynn coming through the vestibule door, pulling off his bug covers, and quickly hurling himself into the living room.

"What gives?" he asked, walking toward the kitchen, and then he saw Buddy. He raised an imaginary trumpet and played *Ta-ta-ta-daaa,* then clapped Buddy on the shoulders. "Good to see you, my man!" He sat down and smiled big when I gave him his sandwich.

"Buddy came to get some supplies, but he was also saying that Gina's been acting funny, and he thinks she might need a prescription."

Buddy leaned back and pulled three empty pill bottles from his pocket and placed them on the table. They had been prescribed for Gina Barris.

"If she don't need me for something, she stays in her house and I stay in mine, but I refill the commode tanks every day, and these were in the bathroom wastebasket last week." He paused and looked at each of us. "Now, y'all know I ain't no peeping tom, but I see her through the windows at night with the kitchen all lit up with candles, walking around and talking to herself, looking worried. And the thing is, I seen this before. Candy's daddy had a work accident, a boiler blew off half his ear, but he did good enough until he was about sixty, and then he went down with dementia. That's one of the reasons we moved up over the ridge, to help her mama take care of him. He'd be all right in the daytime, but when evening came he'd get all nervous and start pacing and it about drove everybody crazy. Then we got some medicine, a couple of different pills, and it helped settle him down."

"Wow," I said. He waved his hand at me.

"I ain't done. There's this other thing. The casket is empty, ain't nobody in that vault, but sometimes Gina closes herself up in there and I think that's how she survived. She uses a little step ladder and climbs in there."

"Whoa," Wynn said. "Escape death by pretending to be dead."

Wynn listened attentively, as is his way, and finished his sandwich with a flourish. "Thank you, my dear, as always it was absolutely delicious." He turned to Buddy. "The computers are down, but I'll see what I can do at the drugstore. If we're really lucky, there might be filled prescriptions ready to pick up." He invited us to come shopping, and blew me a kiss on his way out the door.

"So, where's George?" I asked as I gathered up the dishes.

"Don't really know, probably up in his room," he said.

"And it don't much seem to matter."

Does Buddy have a great attitude or what? There are things you can do something about, and other things that don't much matter. He chooses his sources of worry, just like Wynn, who pushes painful topics aside into his "talk about it later" box. I wish my mind worked that way.

We gathered a few food items from my stash and walked down the hill to the drug store, which was ablaze with light from the kerosene lamp. Wynn was refilling the pill bottles and looking up the drugs in a big book. "Almost done," he called. "Get one of those folding carts by the door and take what you need."

I helped Buddy find soap and aspirin and fancy skin cream, and added some stale crackers to his bag for the chickens. He picked up two flavors of nutritional drinks, chocolate and vanilla, explaining that sometimes Gina refuses to eat.

"Not surprised," Wynn said, coming up behind us with a white paper bag. "One is an antidepressant, and the other two are for dementia. I think she may have Alzheimer's Disease."

"Yup," Buddy said.

"I had it in my mind that they were hospice, but I was wrong," Wynn said. "There was a patient card in the special orders box saying special arrangements had been made with the pharmacist. Too bad she can't answer questions because she's dead." He apologized for not being about to print out instructions and precautions because the printer was down. He really does make a good pharmacist.

I offered to walk home with Buddy, but he said no, for me to wait and come in a couple of days, after he had a chance to see if she got better with the medication. "She really likes you, Girlie. She'll be real nice about everything if she knows you're coming."

Too bad I can't send her a text. And it's scary and embarrassing that I mistook poor mental health for meanness. Or maybe she's sick and mean? I'll know more in a couple of days. Stay tuned.

Love,
S

Dear Mom,
Good day to you, and I hope you are comfortable and well. I've been thinking of you a lot lately, nothing new there, but remember music, and dancing? We loved both, though Jeremy opted out in favor of video games. Well, you don't realize how great music is until you don't have any. Here in Nowhere Land, there's no turning up the speakers and bopping around the living room, or hearing public radio in the background while you cook dinner. At least there is Wynn, and the summer birds, which have miraculously returned from the tropics. I know some of them from how excited you got when they migrated each spring. I've seen the bright blue indigo buntings, a few hummingbirds, and there are robins everywhere. It sounds like a tropical rain forest outside first thing in the morning. I hope they have a good appetite for flies.

There is a stone fire ring in the yard next to Wynn's house, and we sit by it at night, after the bugs go to bed, as long as it's not raining. If he's in the mood, Wynn will play a bit of trumpet, which always makes my day. On Rob's first official night with us, he played Ode to Joy, which he said was Beethoven. It was awesome!

Then we debriefed about Buddy's visit, with Rob mostly listening and sipping a beer. He raised his hand. "I have a question. Is this Hemlock Ridge farm, the horse farm?"

"Yes, do you know it?" Wynn cocked his eyebrow the way he does.

Rob nodded. "A long time ago, when I worked doing solar installations, we put in an array next to the barn. Is it still there?"

I told him about the trainer's cottage, and the ground-based array beside it, but I'd never been behind the barn. "Plus the main house has rooftop panels," I added.

He said none of that was there back then, only the new barn and some construction trailers. Wynn fed the fire and described the house, which we call The Manse, short for Mansion. "Maybe there's some stuff there we can use," he said, looking at Rob hopefully.

"Could be. I'll certainly have a look."

This is how a plan emerged for Rob to accompany me to The Manse two days later. While I visited with Gina, he would get Buddy's help looking for solar parts, which he collects like gold bars. When he finds the right ones, Plan A is to power up a house that has older solar panels, and see if it works. Or it might blow up.

I got brownie points for finding the right house, which had to be smallish, near town but not on the main road, with its own well and septic system, with no bodies and good appliances, and a ground-based solar array. "How about the round house?" I suggested as we sat around the fire. "You know, the dome thing over by the Rescue Squad?

Wynn's palm flew to his forehead. "Of course, I know the place! That could definitely work." Everyone in town knew about the dome house because it looked so different, round instead of rectangular. The next day, while Rob and Wynn looked at wiring and switch boxes, I checked out the kitchen and pantry. I don't think the house was being actively lived in, maybe being used as a vacation place, because everything was clean and neatly tucked away. There were a few small treasures in the cabinets, spaghetti sauce and pasta, but I left most things as they were. Our fondest hope is to have a daytime power supply sufficient to pump and heat water, and dream-of-dreams, run a washing machine.

If nothing blows up and the activation works, we plan to write a song about hot water.

Take care, I love you.

S

Dear Mom,

How are you today? I hope you are well and enjoying the last of spring and the full lushness of May. I try to think positive thoughts about you, keep believing you will appear, but time is passing and it's scary.

Ready for the Gina report? The woman I found tending her plants on the stone patio was different yet the same from the Gina I'd seen a few weeks before. She wore a loose cotton shirt over black jeans, and her hair was pulled into a messy ponytail, no scrunchie. She was arranging a row of small buckets on a stucco wall.

"Hi, Gina, it's Sarah. And this is my friend Rob. He's come to see about getting the lights turned back on."

"Oh, that would be nice," Gina said, clapping her hands together. "We could just flip the switch!"

Buddy joined us when he heard voices, and I introduced Rob and explained that he was looking for old solar parts, maybe in the barn? "I thought you could show him around, help him look," I said. "I'll visit with Gina."

I sat down in one of the patio chairs and pulled my shopping bag closer. "You have such beautiful plants. I can tell you take good care of them."

"Oh, yes," Gina said, brushing her hand over a fern. "They are my friends, but they are so big, I don't think I can take them with me." While I sat, she stepped from plant to plant, picking off leaves or arranging branches.

"Are you going somewhere?" I had noticed a suitcase near the front door when Rob and I let ourselves in and wondered if she had decided to move to town. I opened two chocolate nutritional drinks from my bag and handed one to her. She took a tentative sip.

"Yes, I am, but I'm not supposed to talk about it. My sister is coming to get me, I don't know when, but I'm getting ready." She finally sat down in a nearby chair.

"I didn't know you had a sister," I said.

"Oh, yes, Olivia, you must meet her when she comes." I said I would look forward to that. Then she told a long story about Olivia and a pony they had when they were children, an ill-tempered pony that bit and once knocked Gina to the ground. It was a fond yet terrifying memory, its recall interrupted by flies that had begun gathering around our heads. We went into the kitchen, and I unpacked the rest of the supplies. I saw the pill bottles on the counter, and asked if she had been taking them when

Buddy told her to.

She smiled. "Buddy forgets, but Bumbo always remembers." She patted the head of a stuffed elephant that occupied one of the stools at the counter. "When Bumbo says it's time, it's time! A stitch in time saves nine!"

She really is getting bonkers. I mostly just let her talk, and tried not to ask many questions, which seemed to confuse her. When I invited her to move to town, she became irritated and her steely old voice made a brief return. "I do not need watching," she declared. "No, ma'am, not me."

Later, both she and Buddy walked with us to the gates, and Buddy and I fell behind so we could talk. "Are the pills not working? She says her sister is coming to get her any day," I said.

"The sister who's been dead twenty years," he answered. "She's a little better, but she did slip back some when she ran out of pills. Let's give it more time."

I said if he could bring her to town, we would work something out, that it might be better for both of them.

"I'll let you know. It don't much matter to me, but for her, moving might be hard." We left it at that, and I said I would be back soon, and meanwhile to come visit. He said he would.

It was an easy downhill walk back to town, and Rob talked the whole time about the house and what he'd found in the storage areas. "They went all out, didn't cut corners, did things right when they built that place," he said. If all the solar panels were fully operational, as in The Time Before, the Manse was likely energy self-sufficient. "Ah, we can dream," Rob said. As it was, he had found two components to possibly use at the dome house.

I'll let you know how it goes. I have started collecting fire extinguishers. Better safe than sorry.

Love,
Sarah

Chapter 8   The Yuppies

Dear Mom,

Good afternoon! I hope you are well and comfortable, and I suspect you are busy making others well and comfortable, which is what nurses do. You really are a great nurse.

I know you were disappointed when I quit community college and went to work instead, but I thought it might be temporary. I was tired of going to school, you know? Then the pandemic came and people like you and me needed to work to keep things going, so we did. I was thinking of making a change, and then everything changed.

Now things are changing again. The Yuppies have arrived.

I was the first to hear the loud clanging of the bell at the back of the drug store. And I mean loud. I ran down as fast as I could, and found the unlucky couple, a tall man in a wheelchair with one foot in the air, and his bedraggled but beautiful strawberry blonde companion. He had streaks of gray in his coarse beard and a receding hairline, so I'm guessing mid-forties? She's maybe ten years younger, which makes her older than me.

"He has an infected foot, from a cut," she said, brushing away flies from his face. "And a fever." The man's forehead felt hot and wet, and he said he was cold. His foot looked terrible.

"I'm Sarah," I said. "Rob and Wynn will be here in a minute." I rang the bell again. "Let's move him into the shade."

"I'm Clarissa. This is Claude." She apologized for her clumsiness with the wheelchair, saying it was all new to her. She found the chair in a vacant house with a handicapped ramp and pushed him the last four miles into town.

"Can you help him? Please?" She collapsed onto the wood bench Wynn kept under the shade tree.

"Don't worry," I said. "Help is on the way."

Wynn and Rob arrived together, breathless from running across town. Rob recognized them from the FloydFest site, and saw they were in trouble.

"He cut it a few days ago, and it never got better, and now it's worse," Clarissa said.

"Oh, my." Rob peered closely at Claude's foot, then held his hand against his forehead. Suddenly, click, just like that, Rob turned into a doctor. He looked in Claude's eyes, then at his fingertips. "Are you allergic to any medicines?" he asked. Claude shook his head. Rob rephrased the question. "Are you allergic to any antibiotics?" This time Claude croaked "No." He also was not a diabetic.

Rob turned to Wynn. "Do you have doxycycline? Two, with Gatorade? I'll be in to get the rest of what we will need. The light will be best out here." Then he asked me to bring two gallons of good water, a clean wash basin, some paper towels, and liquid soap.

By the time I returned, Clarissa had moved to a folding chair closer to Claude, and was coaching him to drink more orange Gatorade. "You should drink some, too." Wynn told her, placing two white plastic stools in front of Claude. "Unless you want something else."

She sighed and took a long swallow. "I don't think I've eaten since yesterday," she said. He went into the store and got some protein drinks and the last of the cheese crackers, and placed them on the ground beside her.

Rob carried a bin filled with supplies and sat down on one of the stools in front of Claude. "Here, Sarah, you can come help me," he said, gesturing to the other stool. Me? I thought, but only for a second. Then I leaned in. Together we got Claude's swollen foot soaking in water, and I used a washcloth to gently wipe off the dirt and caked blood. Then we changed to fresh water and a clean washcloth, and I did it again. Now we could see a big cut in the most tender part of the heel, with a small bulge in the middle. "That baby's going to bleed," he said quietly, and asked Wynn to bring a box of disposable mattress protectors or puppy pads.

"Immediately, sir," he said, and dashed into the store.

Rob rinsed out the basin and filled it with a half-and-half mixture of water and hydrogen peroxide and set the heel to soak while we cut open packages of gauze, bandage foam, tweezers, giant cotton swabs and latex gloves, and broke the seals on bottles of Bactine, rubbing alcohol, and a tube of prescription lidocaine.

"Showtime," Rob said. We put a pad under the foot, Rob and I gloved up, and he started talking softly as he worked. "This will sting a little," he said, pouring alcohol over the wound. Claude winced when he patted the gash dry with gauze, then relaxed when Rob smoothed lidocaine over it. It was starting to bleed. Rob reached for the tweezers, had me pour alcohol over them, and started poking at the wound with his fingers and the tool. Blood dripped, then gushed onto the pad, along with other gunk of an unknown nature. I asked for a new pad, but Wynn had disappeared. Clarissa jumped up and got one from the stack. Rob asked me to dribble water to help him see while holding the foot as tight as I could. This was a yoga move. Claude let out a groan, and then there was a plink as Rob dropped a shard of glass into the metal wash basin. "Got it," he said.

He and I were both splattered with blood, mostly me. "Sorry, Sarah," he said. "That will teach you to tell people your mother is a nurse."

"And you," Clarissa said to Rob. "When we met you before, at the campground, you didn't say you were a doctor."

Rob started laughing. "No, that was my father, he was a military doctor. I didn't follow in his footsteps, but he tried." He sprayed the wound with Bactine, then pressed gently at it with a gauze pad. No more funky stuff came out, and the bleeding was letting up. "And raising two kids gets kind of messy, too."

It hit me like a brick that Rob had two children, or used to have. How does he bear it? Seriously!

I gathered up the bloody things and carried them off behind the bushes, to deal with later. Bloody gloves, bloody pads, bloody handprints on the water bottles. I wiped my face, arms and legs with wet paper towels, and returned to the scene of the crime. Wynn had rejoined the group, though he looked pale and avoided eye contact.

"I think my place will be best, lots of room," Rob said.

Wynn said he would push the wheelchair and help get Claude settled, then find him some clothes. I told Clarissa to come to my place when she was ready, I would have warm water and a shower waiting.

She started crying. "You guys, you've been so nice to us…" Sob, sob. The only one clean enough to take her hand and comfort her was Wynn, and he rose to the occasion.

That's the report on the Yuppies, who had a very lucky unlucky day. But every event has ripples of energy rings that radiate from it, spreading and connecting and merging, and now I'm thinking about going to nursing school. Do you think I could get financial aid? Will your doctor friends write me recommendations?

No promises, but I thought you'd be excited.

Love,

Sarah

Dear Mom,

Greetings from Nowhere Town! I hope you are well and among friends. Have you made friends in your current situation? Of course you have! You always had friends, lots of them, and I remember asking "What took you so long?" when you went out for Saturday lunch with Deb. Aunt Deb, your Bestie, who always slipped me twenty bucks on my birthday. You would stay gone for *two hours*, and then you would come home tired, but in a good mood. "Get over it," you'd tell me. "Don't take good friends for granted."

Good advice!

We are all friends here, and Wynn is my Special One, but I needed to make room for Clare, literally and figuratively. Not Clarissa, it's Clare unless she's at work. As the guys got Claude ready to roll up the hill, she gave him a quick pat on the shoulder and turned to follow me.

"Sarah, wait up!" she called. Until she limped toward me, I had not realized she was wearing oversized shoes that flopped on her feet. For four miles? She had to have blisters. "Can I come with you?" she asked.

"Sure," I said, "It's right up here."

As we shuffled along, I commented that she seemed to be in pretty rough shape.

"You don't know the half of it," she began, then stopped. "I'll spare you the details, but Claude detests me, and the feeling is mutual."

"Got it," I said. "I have an extra bedroom."

She reached out and grabbed my hand. "Sarah, you are an answer to my prayers." She was crying a little, but then she was beyond exhausted. And dirty. I showed her the outdoor shower, with a solar hot water bag overhead behind a plastic curtain with pink flamingos on it. There's a little bench and a plastic soaking tub for filthy feet, and a shelf stocked with nice shampoos and soaps. "You can come inside and use the bathtub, but I think this is better," I said. "Lots of warm water today."

"Oh, I love this!" she said, picking up a jug of stored water to test its temperature. "You are so smart and resourceful."

I went inside to get towels and a robe while she peeled off her clothes and started soaking her feet, which were a mess. "I don't mean to take all your water," she said.

"It's okay, I have a pond," I said. "Slip in the front door when you're done. Fewer bugs get in that way." Then I gave her the privacy I would want if I was in her place and got busy making something to eat.

I think she likes me. I know she really liked the turkey tetrazzini I made from instant noodles with canned meat, mushroom soup and peas. I made a big batch, and let it steam while I got cleaned up. We settled in at the table, and she started telling her story.

"We weren't even a couple yet, not officially. It was only our fifth date, the first one on a weekend." She looked at me and winked. "You know, when you find out whether or not they're married?" I about dropped my fork.

"Been there," I said.

"He said, let's go to The Cliffs, this fancy resort in the middle of nowhere, and we drove four hours from DC to get there. It seemed like a long way, far off the interstate, which put him in a bad mood." She paused to take a bite.

"Once we got checked in, he had us set up for a romantic couples massage in the spa, but first we were supposed to get all lovey-dovey in the sauna. That's where we were when it happened. Bathed in hot steam, wearing resort robes, but not lovey-dovey. We didn't know anything was wrong until the hot rocks weren't getting hot anymore and he called for a drink that didn't come."

I got up to refill our bowls. I told her I was scuba diving with my brother, Jeremy, but that he didn't make it.

"I'm so sorry!" she said, her eyes filling with tears.
"Me, too."

She was traveling light. Beyond her grimy clothes, she had a small backpack with a few personal belongings – wallet, phone, some jewelry, a hairbrush – which she spread out on the table. "Not much left of my old life," she said.

I said it was time to start a new one. "Let's get you something to wear." I took her to the hallway closet where I kept unopened toothbrushes and packages of underwear and socks from the Family Dollar, explaining that it can be accessed through the back door, but not to go near the front counter. "The bodies are covered, but I don't do bodies and there are bugs in the store from the stuff in the refrigerators, so it's best to get in and out fast," I said. "We don't go to the Dollar General or the grocery stores at all because they are too gross."

"I'll remember that," she said.

We are about the same size, though she is a little shorter and with more curves. Even with her hair wrapped in a towel, she is naturally pretty. She has big hazel eyes with dark lashes that go on forever, even little teeth, and a light sprinkling of freckles on her nose.

I showed her my closet and drawers full of basics and designer finds from the Angels thrift store, and invited her to help herself. "It's absolutely fine at Angels, no bodies or flies. I'll take you tomorrow and you can pick out your own things."

"This is so nice of you!" she said, grabbing a vintage Madonna tee shirt and some soft pull-on capris.

"Don't start crying," I teased.

I got ready to take the rest of the food up to Rob's for the guys, and asked if she wanted to go.

"Not really. Tell them about my foot blisters."

Which is what I did. "Clare and I went ahead and ate, and she's dead tired and has blisters on her feet, so she sends her regrets." Gentle round of applause all around.

They appeared to have been snacking on corn chips and beer, with Claude propped up in the recliner with his foot elevated. He was back among the living, cleaned up and more alert to his surroundings, and he said that I was "quite the cook" after emptying his bowl of hot food. There was barely enough for seconds, but I'm not used to feeding five hungry people.

Wynn was quick to finish, and was his usual effusive self with his thanks. I asked him if he wanted to walk home with me.

"Always, of course," he said.

Since moving to town, and even before, I've found that the best way to talk with Wynn is to take a walk. There's something about moving his legs that helps him untangle certain thoughts, which is probably why he likes running.

It was a nice evening, getting late, so the bugs were gone and we didn't need to hurry. "We were a great team today," I said.

He snorted. "Speak for yourself. I was a wuss. I started feeling faint, had to go inside and put my head between my knees." He was so embarrassed, ran his hand over his head and pulled at his earlobe, and kept talking.

"I've never been able to stand the sight of blood, even my own. I fainted when I cut my finger when I was little, and I don't like shots, either. At work, I stayed as far from the immunization booth as possible. Mother called it being squeamish, said it was my nature."

I squeezed his arm. "I love your nature," I said. "And I'm glad you're not perfect."

He looked at me tenderly and kissed my hand.

We stopped in the middle of the main street, watching the last light settle over the empty town, listening to the evening birds. He took a deep breath, held it, followed by a long exhale.

"The air is getting better," he said. "Less death."

I told him a little about Clare, that she was nice and I thought he would like her, and asked what he thought of Claude.

"Blank check for now," he said. "He had money. Likes to impress. Still wearing his dead Rolex. That's all I know. But I don't get the vibe that we'll be BFFs."

We walked quietly for a while, bumping each other back and forth on the sidewalk, until I had a question.

"You're squeamish about blood and shots, but not dead bodies?"

"That's different," he said. "And I can't do the kids. I have my limits." This was another reason we steered clear of the grocery stores and the schools. There were too many little bodies with little backpacks waiting to get on the buses at 2:42, and the roads were clogged with carpooling parents. It was the worst of the worst.

"We all have our limits," I said. Then I noticed the dim light of a lantern shining in the window of my house. "Look!" I said. "Somebody's home!" I had forgotten what that was like to have someone waiting for you, someone sharing your safety pod. I would not be alone! I didn't know whether to laugh or cry as I gave Wynn a goodnight squeeze and started toward the house. Then I remembered a last bit of business.

"Almost forgot! Will you cut Clare's hair?" I called after him. "She wants a short pixie."

He stopped in his tracks and waved his arms like a

bird. "A pixie? By hand?"

It had not occurred to me that cutting a pixie required electric clippers.

"Well, think about it."

He gave me a soldier salute, smiled, and marched home.

I hope you like my best friend as much as I do. Dare I hope for a second one?

Love,
Sarah

Chapter 9 Solar Sam

Hi Mom,

How are you doing today, and what have you been up to? I hope you are well and happy, and finding good ways to fill your time. Having more people around is different, even though we are not much alike. The one thing we have in common is that we want what we don't have, can't have, never will have. We want our families, our homes, pets, phones and televisions back. But poor, poor Claude! He is the only one missing a Lexus, which he mentions in casual conversation whenever he can.

Wynn and Rob are busy installing elaborate grounding wires at the dome house, whatever those are, so I agreed to stop in and check on Claude during the early days of his convalescence. Clare said not to worry, that he would behave himself for a while. "That's how players play, to hook you in," she said, smiling.

Indeed, the first day he was quite charming, apologizing for not rising to his feet when I came in, and telling me how good it was to see me. Lunch was instant couscous with garlic and olive oil, of which I have a case that someone ordered on Amazon. He acted like it was high cuisine.

"Add a crisp glass of white, and this would be lunch for a king."

I said the antibiotics he was taking were better than

wine just now, and he answered with a drawn-out "Yes, Mother." It was only borderline offensive. Then he launched into a travelogue of Morocco, home of couscous, which involved riding camels and eating lamb. In a low-animal world, both sounded kind of icky.

I noticed the recliner was in the shadows, turned toward the blank TV, and asked if he wanted it moved so he had better light for reading.

"There are lots of books here, and reading is best in the daytime," I said.

"I don't know about that," he said when I handed him a John Grisham mystery from the shelf. "The kind of education I had, both undergraduate and graduate, makes it hard to enjoy reading on the same level as other people."

What? Was he making a joke? "Well, be like that," I said, taking away his bowl and replacing it with copies of The Martian and Lonesome Dove. Jeremy loved both of those books.

I brought him some water to go with the books, but left without moving his chair.

"He's not evil, just a spoiled little boy," Clare said as we checked out a house together the next morning. She found some comfortable sneakers at the Angels store and was eager to join me in a foraging expedition to an unexplored (and body free!) house two blocks away. "Money and women like me fed his ego. Now those are gone, so be careful. Good Claude won't last forever."

She quickly caught on to what we were doing with supplies. First we looked for foodstuffs in need of better storage, like oils, flours, grains, and unopened boxes of cereal, which we took to the Methodist church. We were also looking for solar equipment, especially a thing called a sine wave converter, which could be as small as your hand or as big as a mailbox. Rob drew a picture of a metal box with raised ribs and plugs at either end. If a house had solar panels anywhere, we checked the garage and outbuildings along with the kitchen, but we had yet to hit gold. Rob said it was an older piece of equipment that couldn't be used in grid-tied systems, so we were looking for a needle in a haystack.

"Why don't you just use generators?" Clare asked as we looked through a garage with a nice gas generator parked against the wall. When she and Claude were on the road, they stayed in vacant houses until the gas generator or propane ran out, then moved on.

"We don't like them." I said. "The ones with electric start don't work, and the ones you can start with a pull cord make a lot of noise and eat up fuel we might need for other things. We like it quiet, don't want to attract attention. The propane ones aren't as noisy, but portable propane is even more precious. And it's not like the small generators can deliver what you want anyway. In the Time Before, they were great because they could save the meat in your freezer, or keep your refrigerator running, but we don't have refrigerators." I was on a roll. "Water pumps need a big surge of power to get going, so we might use a big one as a last resort, if we had to."

"How would you cook if you ran out of propane?" she asked.

I said it would be hard.

"And what if this goes on forever?"

I said it could.

She said it was time to start praying for a miracle. I

already do that, twenty times a day.
Come home soon,
Sarah

June 10
Dear Mom,
I wish you were here. I wish you were here in the morning, and I wish you were here at night. I think I am a powerful wisher, so it's just a matter of time until we are together again, right?

It's safe and reasonably comfortable here. The bug situation has improved, and guess what? My radishes and lettuce are ready to start picking, and Wynn has grown a great crop of baby cabbage. Soon there will be strawberries! Remember Mountain Dew Farm, on Washout Road? In the fall Wynn gathered carrots and potatoes left in the field, and last week I took the kid carrier out there to see if there were any left. That's when I saw a row of strawberries blooming to beat the band, white flowers everywhere, swarming with bees. I covered the plants with a long piece of bird netting weighed down along the edges, and there's more. While I was working I heard a rooster crow, so I think there's a wild flock of fowl there somewhere. We will see about catching a few, because with more people, we need more eggs.

Wynn's peas and potatoes are growing better than mine, and it's time to start tomatoes, so I decided to ride my favorite bike to the garden center just outside town to get some fertilizer. They were closed on 2:42, so the shop was empty and there were no cars in the parking lot, but it's still depressing. All the plants in the greenhouses dried into brown sticks.

I was zipping a bag of organic plant food into my backpack when I heard an odd sound, a buzz or drone that was not a bug. I zipped again. The sound was not the zipper. "Anybody home?" I called loudly. "Anybody here?" No response.

I walked through the first greenhouse, which was quiet and empty, then followed the humming sound as it got stronger. In the third greenhouse, the newest and smallest of the three, a whirring fan on the far end clicked off as I opened the door. It had definitely been on, the blades were still moving! I went through the structure's back door, and there it was: a solar panel connected to a box that might be, could be, a sine wave converter that ran the thermostatically controlled greenhouse fan. I went back into the greenhouse, closed both doors, and waited. In a few minutes the fan clicked on and boogied down, I mean that sucker was moving some air!

I rode back to town as fast as I could, and found Rob inside his screened porch, studying equipment manuals. "I found something, you gotta come see," I said, gasping for air. "In one of the greenhouses. There's a solar fan, and it's working."

Rob is not as steady on his bike as I am, and we would need a way to carry stuff back, so he put a few wrenches and screwdrivers in a grocery cart, and we pushed it the mile to the greenhouses. The third greenhouse was quiet when we walked in, but sure enough, as soon as the sun came out from behind a cloud, the fan came alive and blew like crazy.

"Holy moly," Rob said, a big smile on his face. "This

will be fun." He flicked off a switch, started pulling some cords, and in no time we had the panels, converter and connectors packed into the grocery cart, cushioned with bags of potting soil. Before leaving, we checked the other greenhouses and looked around in the storage buildings for more equipment, but found nothing we could use.

Rob talked about wattage and voltage and other numbers that I'm beginning to understand as we walked back, but it came down to this. He thought the apparatus would run a coffee maker or a crockpot, which would save us some propane, and of course a fan in the heat of the day. "It's small, but it's a start," he said.

An hour later, we had the panels secured on the sunniest part of Rob's deck, connected and ready to run an oscillating fan he found in the house. Claude hobbled outside on crutches to observe and cheer us on. Rob asked us to stay back when he pushed the button, but no sparks flew. Instead, the fan started up with a gentle whirr, and soon began to swivel from side to side.

Tears filled my eyes, I couldn't help it, and I saw it was the same for Rob, and soon we were hugging each other hard, patting each other's backs, sniffling and laughing. Even Claude got caught up in our joy.

"It appears you have created a miracle," he said, pointing with one of his crutches. "Very impressive!"

I rode off to share the news with Clare, who was working in the basement of the Methodist church, and then Wynn, who was planting beans in his garden. "Big news! We have a small solar power unit that's working, over at Rob's," I said. "You gotta come see."

He looked at me closely. "Have you been crying?"

"Happy crying, it's okay," I said, punching his elbow.

"Something finally turned out. You're going to love this thing."

Indeed he did, as did each of us, as we discovered the small appliances it could run as long as the sun was out. The coffee maker, crockpot and rice cooker would be game changers in terms of kitchen propane usage, and we were all juiced up over what we could do with the waffle maker. We named it Solar Sam.

Later that night, when Wynn, Clare, Rob and I sat around the fire pit, our mood was unusually merry. The gardens were coming along, Clare was making good progress sorting our collection of stored fats and oils by expiration dates, and we had low-wattage power on sunny days. Enough to cook dry beans, which would help ease the pressure on our protein supply. We had a lot of dry beans, but it took so long to cook them that we wondered if it was worth the propane.

And so, it was a breakthrough day, and I'm only sorry you missed it. Will tomorrow bring more good luck? In the morning Wynn and I are going to the Farm to check on the strawberries, look for unharvested carrots or parsnips we missed before, and leave moth-eaten boxes of cereal to lure the chickens out of the woods. In the afternoon I'm taking Clare with me to deliver supplies to the Manse. If you were here, you could come with us.

Have I told you how cute she looks with her pixie haircut?

More later and love forever,
Sarah

Dear Mom,
Greetings from Planet Floyd, which is rich and green

with the shades of early summer. It looks really different, though, because the grass is tall and shaggy, and there are weeds crowding the edges of the sidewalks. Seriously, there are plants popping up in every crack in the pavement, even in the highway, like they were waiting there for the people to go away. Every time it rains, they double in size.

After a winter of hanging out and not doing all that much, I am suddenly busy with gardening and food storing, and the days are zooming by. I don't have time to cook and Claude does, so I have handed over food prep responsibilities to him. He knows his way around the kitchen and likes trying out appliances on Solar Sam, so it should be a good fit.

I asked him what he might want to make, so I could find the ingredients if we had them. "Like Italian, Mexican, anything specific?" I asked.

He sighed and rubbed his forehead. "When you've traveled as much as I have, it's hard to be dedicated to any one cuisine."

"Oh," I said, thinking too bad, there would be no more twice-yearly trips to Europe for Claude.

Clare does not trust him near our main stash of food at the Methodist church. "He'll tear into the oils and canned meats, I know his taste." These are among our most precious foods, stored out of sight behind the long rack of robes in the choir room.

We dole them out to him in small amounts as we make up a bag of things we think might work, and leave him to his own devices, kind of like Chopped Meets Survivor. At Clare's suggestion, we also include a bottle of wine from the little wine store downtown, which limits his complaints and seems to improve the quality of the food.

"Wine is his drug," she said. "And the only reason we made any progress on the road. He'd see a big, nice house that didn't look occupied, and if there was wine, food and propane, we stayed until it ran out."

I did and didn't understand why Clare didn't leave him and strike out on her own. What would I have done? Being alone is not easy, and who would choose it? She is also a city girl, though she worked at a summer camp in the mountains for three years and learned a few things about the outdoors. While we were walking and talking on our way to the Manse, admiring how the cattle carcasses had shrunk in size, I got the answer.

"He told me he'd seen evidence of wolves, and to not go outside alone, especially at night. Sometimes we would see torn up carcasses that could have been the work of wolves, so I believed him. Stupid me." She picked up a fallen limb and threw it to the side of the road.

Gaslighting 101, Armageddon style, but again, what would I have done? I don't know, but from then on, it was like Claude wore a big red warning label as far as I was concerned. Stay back! Toxic waste! I gave her a rump bump and reassured her that there were no wolves.

She was totally taken by the Manse, which I knew she would be. The long driveway was clear of sticks and debris, and the stone porch was swept clean. We let ourselves in through the front door, with me calling "Hello! It's Sarah," but getting no response. I showed her through the great room, where I noticed the vault had been moved to the wall, opened, and filled with stuffed animals. I couldn't help it. I walked over and looked inside. It just looked like an empty purple bed.

"Look at this art," Clare said, pointing to a large, colorful piece of textile art on a wall, then moving in for a closer look. "This is amazing." Then she noticed an old painting in a gold frame near the vault, and a metal sculpture hung from the ceiling. "Wow, do you think these are real?"

"You're the expert," I said. Clare has a degree in art history. Can you believe I never noticed the place was decorated with expensive art? The room felt cool and echoed a little, like a real art gallery. Maybe that's what it's supposed to be?

"I need to look up these works on the internet," she said, rubbing her chin. She said either Gina or George had a good eye for art, with money to back it up.

"There's more," I said, opening the door to the kitchen, which felt enormous with most of the houseplants moved outside. I unpacked the fresh carrots, strawberries, lettuce and supplies we'd brought onto the counter while Clare marveled at the appliances. The kitchen was immaculately clean, as always, but I didn't know if it was the work of Buddy or Gina.

"Well look who's here, Girlie, and ain't you a sight for sore eyes," Buddy said, coming in the back door carrying a basket of eggs. I gave him a high five and asked how he'd been.

"Oh, good enough, good enough," he said. I introduced Clare, who stepped forward, shook his hand, and gave him her most dazzling smile. "But now with two pretty girls here, I reckon I'm doing better." We sat down at the kitchen table to talk. I brought him up to date on Solar Sam and the gardens, then asked "Where's Gina?"

He looked at me, squinting his eyes, before answering. "She's at school, that's what she calls it. Out in the barn. Last week she scared me to death, wandered off and I couldn't find her nowhere, turned this house upside down and called myself hoarse. Then on into the afternoon, here she comes dragging in saying she was hungry. I fixed her some dinner and she was good as pie about taking her pills and getting ready for bed, calm and all. So the next day I kind of hid out and followed her when I saw her take off walking. She made a beeline to the back of the barn, to an old stall behind the chickens.

"She has old children's books and toys back there, says it's the school and she's the teacher. She likes it, keeps her busy," he said, grinning. "She don't like me there, but it's easy enough to check on her on the sly."

I asked if he had found George while he was searching for Gina, halfway meaning it as a joke.

"Sure did, glad you asked. Found him up in the big bedroom, looked like he'd been taking a nap when it happened. I rolled him up and got him buried proper out back. I think it just feels better having him out of the house, don't you?"

"Yes," I said, taking a deep breath. "It does feel different." This is a true fact. When a dead body that's been rotting somewhere is removed and put to rights, a house feels better.

"She don't seem to care about it, but I think it's what he would have wanted," he said.

It looked like rain might be coming, so instead of

hanging around, Clare and I hurried home with eggs, bread, and lots of questions about Gina and George for which we might never know the answers.

"What if he kept a diary?" she mused. "Or what if Gina did, until she couldn't? There will be records around the house for big art purchases, maybe in a safe somewhere."

"Probably so," I said. "You could ask her. Buddy once told me that he kept to the main floor taking care of things. Gina never went upstairs, so he didn't either. Until he had to."

"He seems like a really good guy," she said.

"Heart of gold," I said.

Like yours.

Love,

Sarah

Chapter 10   The Survivalist

Dear Mom,

I've been thinking of you a lot lately, but that's nothing new! Every day I wonder where you are and how you are getting along. I know you're not alone, that's way too much NOT your nature. I hope you are keeping company with people you like, staying in a place that feels comfortable.

Clare and I are proving to be companionable roomies. She is neat but not too neat, quiet but not too quiet. Once in a while I hear her crying at night, but don't we all? She doesn't talk about herself much, and when she does it seems to make her sad. We all have a lot to process.

There are many good things about the Garden House, but it's not perfect. Of interest today is the wall-to-wall carpeting in my bedroom, which has become gross. Seriously, I need a vacuum cleaner so bad! Rob says Solar Sam is not up to the task. For the record, you can't really sweep a carpet with a broom (I try) and the roller thing I swiped from the diner hardly does anything. There are sticks and pebbles and seeds and dirt that will stick in your bare feet, so I cover the place next to the bed with a towel to clean my feet before I get into bed.

How about these thunderstorms we've been having? They would have sent Scruff hiding in the closet for sure! Clare and I outran the big one that came the other day, and it's a good thing we did. There was no damage here, but hail hit the strawberries at the Farm pretty bad. We've picked off the bad ones, and put up a more secure cover in case it happens again.

We've also outfitted our houses with rain barrels we've found around town. Talk about having less water to carry! We're using water from the barrel by the back door for washing, and I want a second barrel for the garden, in case we get a drought. My garden is downhill from where the rain barrel will be, so I'll be able to run a hose and let gravity do the watering for me.

Solar Sam is saving us tons of propane not used for cooking, and when it's not running kitchen appliances it powers a fan that will keep bugs from biting if you get close enough to it. Since Sam was found in a greenhouse, we have expanded our search for equipment to include small farms, where we might find a direct-feed solar pump used to move water from a stream to a cistern. We'd also like to find prepper compounds, of which we know of one, thanks to Buddy. He knows of a survivalist guy who built a bunker close to his mother's place, down a dirt road off of Franklin Pike.

"You wouldn't want to mess with Jesse Doggett when he was alive. He had lots of guns and he was half crazy, but I think he's gone just like everybody else," Buddy said when I asked if he knew of any real preppers. "He would have seen me when I was at the house digging graves, heard me making noise, and he would have come around. He always liked Mama." According to Buddy, Jesse has been prepping since 2000 and might have a solar junkyard along with an arsenal of weapons and possible booby traps. "If you go, be careful back there," he said.

It was too far for Rob, but not for me and Clare on bikes and Wynn on his scooter. We decided to try it as a team. Buddy gave us detailed directions, along with a note he wanted nailed to his front door. "In case family comes, I want them to know where I am." I told him I understood completely.

The road was rough for riding, strewn with forest debris and a few fallen trees, so the going was slow. We found the place easily enough, just past Buddy's homeplace, which Wynn knew from his prior visit. I secured Buddy's note to the front door with tacks and a piece of duct tape.

Just down the hill, opposite a rusted mailbox on a wood post, the metal gate across Jesse Doggett's driveway was chained and locked. An old truck with Farm Use plates was parked just inside, empty. From there the driveway became a narrow four-wheeler track, overgrown with thigh-high weeds. Tick heaven.

"I don't think Mr. Doggett has been checking his mail much lately," Clare said, and she was right. So far, no signs of life. As we approached the house, I was surprised at how normal it looked, a trim double wide on a well-cleared lot, with baskets of dead flowers hanging from a covered front deck. Okay, it's flanked on either side by big metal storage containers painted in camo colors, but at one time, the place was probably pretty.

As previously agreed among us, I stepped forward to announce our arrival. "Mr. Doggett? Jesse Doggett? Are you here? We're friends of your neighbor, Buddy Troutt." I called loudly. No answer, but I felt Wynn jump.

"I think I saw something. In the house," he whispered.

"Mr. Doggett? We come as friends, we are not armed." Nothing.

Clare stepped forward to stand beside me. "My name is Clare, and this is Sarah. We know Buddy, he sent us," she called.

"Maybe it was a mouse," Wynn said, though none of us had seen a live mouse since 2:42. "Wait here."

He pulled on leather gloves and twisted the knob on the front door. It opened with a click. He disappeared inside, leaving the door open a crack.

I was used to waiting while Wynn disabled breaker boxes, but Clare was pacing around, looking in the windows, asking "What's taking him so long?"

She was right, it shouldn't take that long to find and cover a body. "Wynn?" I called, poking my head through the door. The house did not smell good, at all. I saw him crouched down in the kitchen area. He stood up and crossed his lips with his index finger, indicating quiet, and summoned us to come with his hand. Once we were inside, he whispered "Close the door behind you."

"Meet Prince," he said, squatting to pet the gray striped cat that purred as it finished a little can of cat food. A small medal on a thin gold-studded collar gave his name.

"He's so cute!" Clare exclaimed, and reached down to pet the cat, who purred and arched his head toward her like that's just what he wanted.

"Poor Prince, you poor boy," I said, feeling for bones through his fur. He seemed to be in pretty good shape except for a few fleas. "Did you run out of food?"

Fortunately for Prince, this had taken a while because

Jesse Doggett, who Wynn found dead behind the closed bathroom door, had prepared for The End with Prince in mind. As we explored the house, we found evidence that many large bags of cat food had been torn open and consumed, along with several boxes of breakfast cereal and flavored crackers. There also is substantial contamination from Cat Box Extremis (watch your step!). But what did Prince do about water? We got our answer a moment later, as Clare opened the windows to let in fresh air. One window was already partly open, with a corner of the screen cut away with scissors. Prince hopped through the do-it-yourself cat door Jesse had made for him, and let himself out.

The kitchen had some canned meats and Crisco we can use, and one wall was stacked with red label Budweiser, which Rob will love. I made notes of what I would need to get later, when I came back with the baby cart. Wynn found the breaker box and looked for interesting electronics. A thick rope of insulated cords led outside through a ragged hole in the wall, which opened into one of the storage containers.

Clare took a ring of keys from a peg on the wall to see if she could unlock the padlocks on the containers. "Sarah!" she yelled when she got the door open on the first one. "Sarah, come see!"

It was two-thirds full of bins and cases of supplies. Bottled propane, bars of soap, a tall pillar of boxes marked dried beef jerky, and enough canned cat food to last Prince the rest of his life. For starters.

"Meow," he said, jumping into the container. I scratched his head. It was like he enjoyed showing off Jesse's stuff.

Clare went to work on the second container, and she thought she found the right key, but the lock was stuck or rusted and wouldn't open. I went back inside to get some WD-40 I'd seen in the laundry room, thank you Jesse Doggett for leaving it there. After a good spray and a few solid licks, the lock opened.

The door hinges were rusted shut, too, so we sprayed them and the three of us pushed and pulled and got it open. More amazement! One side of the container was Jesse's shop area, cluttered with tools, screws and extension cords, and the other was a graveyard of solar panels and pumps and batteries and converters, plus a small wind turbine, still in the box.

"*Ta-ta-ta-daa!*" Wynn played on his imaginary trumpet. "I don't know what we have here, but it's something! Hey Sarah, grab some pics on your phone."

"Got it," I said, clicking away through a peephole made with my hand. That's when I saw Prince slip through the wall into the house. Wynn saw it, too.

"I bet he was in here when it happened," I said. "Asleep under something, airtight from the heat." Wynn agreed it was a definite possibility.

We did not find a sine wave converter, and the wind turbine was too big to carry, so we met on the deck to make a plan for what we would take home. Wynn said he would carry Prince in a canvas zippered bag he found in Jesse's closet, while Clare and I filled our packs with the most useful foods from the kitchen along with canned cat food for Prince, beer for Rob and beef jerky for Claude. We closed the windows and doors, relocked the containers, and hid the keys in a flowerpot. We knew we would be coming back.

Prince is such a great cat! I got to sit with him in my lap while Wynn went to the drug store for a flea collar and other feline supplies, and he purred so pretty. I wish I could keep him, but we agreed that he will live with Wynn because he loves cats and there is no point in being lonely if you don't have to. He plans to keep him in the house for a few days, but I don't think Prince is that kind of cat. I think he's more of a community guy, and it's not like he'll get hit by a car if he goes out wandering around.

Must go take a detailed bath in case I picked up ticks or chiggers today in Jesse's tall grass. They are everywhere.

Love,
S

Dear Mom,

Greetings from back home, which looks totally different with the grass and weeds standing waist high along the roadsides. Is it like that where you are, kind of wild and hairy? Inspired by Buddy's work with an old walk-behind mower at the Manse, Wynn started up the small push mower in my shed and cut our yards, then trimmed the edges of the sidewalks that we use a lot until Rob stopped him.

"Let's not show strangers where we are," he said. "The less inhabited everything looks, the safer we will be." Wynn agreed and put away the mower. After not hearing a gas engine for a long time, it does seem really loud! We cut the rest of the tall grass along the sidewalks with a manual weed cutter.

Thanks to Jesse's stash we are less frantic to store up

food at the moment, but we do need to go back for the wind generator, which should fit in the baby carrier. It easily carries 75 pounds, but we also need to bring Rob, who weighs 180. He doesn't trust his bad knee for a six-mile round trip hike, and biking wouldn't be much better because he would need to walk up the hills.

The hills. They are pretty tame going up to the Manse, but there are some big ones to climb to get to Jesse's. Then you have to be careful on the downhill because of stuff in the road. Everyone does their part keeping lanes cleared to the Manse and the Farm, but once you get out in the Netherworld the roads are bumpy with sticks, limbs and windblown debris. Out yonder, it's safest to travel on foot.

At fire pit meeting number 34, we discussed our need for some kind of bike or human-powered rickshaw with which to transport Rob to Jesse's compound so he could go through the equipment in the shop. Claude was still opting out of our evening debriefings saying his foot was sensitive, but he mostly wanted to finish his daily bottle of wine in peace. It was just me, Wynn, Rob, Clare and Prince watching the flames.

"Well, I did push Claude four miles in a wheelchair, though I wouldn't recommend it," Clare said. "With 200 pounds of dead weight in the chair, it was hard to control on those downhills."

"Don't those things have brakes?" I asked.

"Only the expensive ones," Wynn said. "Most people get the fold-up cheapies, like the one Clare found."

Rob protested that it was too much trouble, but that's Rob.

"Now to find a wealthy disabled person who is no

longer in need of their high-end wheelchair," Clare mused, squinting her eyes. She was on the case. Here's a cool thing about Clare. She is razor-sharp smart, and when she gets fired up about a task it's like a cyclone hit. Whether she's sorting boxes of Rice-a-Roni by expiration date or figuring out the best way to break into the locked wine store for Claude's bottled bribes, she finds a way. To get into the wine store, she whacked off the doorknob with a sledgehammer.

We went together to the small apartment complex for disabled people, where we did not find the right wheelchair. Only lots of medical equipment and shriveled bodies, which we covered with sheets we brought from the hotel. It felt very sad and yet oddly peaceful. Still, we got out of there as fast as we could.

"We should start looking for houses with nice cars parked outside with handicapped tags. That's where we'll find it," she said.

I knew of two such houses, one in town and one not far down a major road, both with cold breaker boxes, but with bodies. Clare said we could do it, that she would go in first, carrying sheets.

The first house, a small red brick ranch, was locked up tight with deadbolts, the way old people do. The car in the driveway was an old Corolla, like old people drive. We went around to the back, looking for open windows, then checked the sliding patio door. It was unlocked! Clare hurried in with a sheet, quickly covering the body in the recliner. Yes, the woman was probably old, but who can tell anymore? It appeared she had opened the sliding door to get some air at 2:42. Since then, leaves and poplar seeds had blown inside, creating a nest by the tiny feet that poked out from under the edge of the sheet.

We checked the house, garage and car for a wheelchair, but the closest thing was a rolling walker, nice but not what we needed. In the kitchen, we saved a few chocolate bars from ruin, along with several cans of tuna.

"Thank you for the goodies," I said as we left, closing the sliding door behind us.

"Bless your soul," Clare added.

The second house was outside of town, maybe a twenty-minute walk, and it had a big SUV with permanent handicapped plates parked outside. The car was locked, but the garage door was open wide enough for me to crawl under it. Inside, I released the manual handle and opened it all the way.

Daylight revealed several contraptions that made Clare say "My, oh, my, oh, my" over and over. A huge mower with extra hand controls filled much of the space, but what got our attention was a three-wheeled wheelchair with giant tires and brake levers on the handles. The design is slung back, like a reclining bike, but it's designed to be pushed. There was mud on the tires. Was it an off-road wheelchair? We rolled it outside and took turns pushing each other in it on the asphalt driveway, which was way fun and made us laugh. It would be perfect, not just for transporting Rob, but for moving other items too heavy for the baby carrier. We nicknamed it the Thing.

Mom, remember how you would read us stories from the Floyd Press, and I would act so disinterested because it wasn't cool? Well, later I would get the paper to read certain stories myself, like the one about the soldier who lost his legs to a land mine in Afghanistan, and how Easter Seals helped buy him special equipment to make his life better. Mom, it was him! I went into the kitchen and there it was, the newspaper story framed and hung on the wall.

I filled a shopping bag with mayo, grits and a few other short-date things from the kitchen, but we basically left the house untouched. It had given us enough.

I hope life is giving you enough. Of everything.

Wish you were here.

Sarah

Chapter 11   Heating Up

Dear Mom,

How are you? Well, I hope, as am I. Only I'm wishing for old times, wanting to pull the shades in the middle of a hot summer day, turn up the AC, and binge on reruns. I won't insist on controlling the remote, we can even watch Hallmark movies if you want. We can make real iced tea, with mint from your garden.

So much for wishing.

Lately, watching Claude has become my entertainment. His foot seems healed, but he doesn't want it to show. When people are around he still limps and asks for help carrying things, but he walks normally when he's alone. I know this because I spy on him when I bring produce and cooking supplies. From my hiding place in the bushes, I see him bopping in and out of the house tending to Sam. The limp returns when I make noise to announce my arrival, which makes me laugh. He doesn't know I know.

Did I tell you we have cherries? A nearby yard has a whole tree covered with them, and a double layer of bird netting doesn't keep out all the birds. But there are still a lot of cherries, and they're really good straight off the tree. Clare and I pick them every day, and everyone is eating them by the handful. Still, there are extras.

"And what do you expect me to do with all these?" Claude asked when I brought a big bowl of washed cherries into the kitchen at Rob's, where it appears he will stay forever. "They're full of pits!" He had a good point. It's one thing to eat a cherry and spit out the seed, another to pit several hundred.

"I think there's a thing called a cherry pitter," I said, opening the drawers to look for kitchen gadgets. There was no such item where it would have been, with the garlic press and can openers, but then I didn't know what I was looking for. "There could be one in the house with the cherry tree," I said. "Only there are bodies. I don't do bodies."

He laughed. Seriously, he *laughed*. "My dear Sarah, you are living on the planet of the dead, they are unavoidable. And it's not like they can bite you."

"I'm glad you think it's funny," I said, stalking out the door.

It was not a good time to be a weakling. Wynn was at the Farm staking up tomato and pepper plants that were growing wild in a torn high tunnel, Clare was busy doing her laundry, Rob was taking the electric apparatus off of the all-terrain wheelchair, and Claude was useless. I took a bedsheet from the pile we got from the hotel and went to face my demons.

The cherry tree was three blocks away, in the yard of a small frame house trimmed in stone, with a mulched flower bed by the mailbox. It was blooming with beautiful pink peonies! The tall grass was trampled down where we had been picking cherries, but otherwise the yard was overgrown, with only a strip of concrete walkway free of vegetation.

Old habits die hard. I went to the front porch and pressed the doorbell. Silence. I knocked on the door. "Hello? Is anybody home?" More silence. When I turned the knob, the door clicked open.

I wish it had been locked. As it was, I was feeling

shaky, heading to Panic City, so I sat down in a porch chair to get my act together and breathe. I told myself there was nothing to be afraid of, repeated it out loud, took a few nice breaths, and thought about Jesse's house and all the others I'd been in with bodies. It's not like they haunt you. So far. I grabbed the sheet and stood up.

"My name is Sarah, and I've come to look for a cherry pitter," I said, pushing the door open. The living room appeared vacant, so I stepped inside. It was a comfortable, lived-in space, with small piles of books and magazines, and a few newspapers between the sofa and cushioned chair. A swinging door, slightly ajar, led into the kitchen. "Do you have a cherry pitter I can borrow?" I asked, stepping quietly through the house.

I glanced at her for a split second before screaming and throwing the sheet. Ms. Cherry, slouched across the kitchen table, was in no condition to answer. She was wearing jeans and a tee shirt, still had hair, but dried gook over bones for arms. It was awful. I turned away.

"I'm just going to look for a cherry pitter," I said, opening kitchen drawers. "Your tree is producing a big crop, and we're trying to make use of it." I knew I was talking to a dead person, but it felt like the right thing to do, and the more I talked, the calmer I felt. "Any hints where to look?" There was one promising gadget among the knives, a lever with space for one cherry, which I put in my shopping bag. I kept looking for something bigger in the cabinets, then in the small closet pantry. "I hope it's okay if I take these anchovies," I said, taking the two small cans from the shelf. Then the thought of a waffle iron popped into my head, clear as a bell, and I went back to one of the cabinets, found the waffle iron, and next to it a small black and white case. It opened to reveal a six-seater cherry pitter. It made the hair on the back of my neck prickle.

"Thank you so much," I said as I closed the cabinet doors. "We really appreciate it. And thanks for the anchovies, too." Poor Ms. Cherry. I got out of there fast, making sure the door clicked shut behind me.

I cried some as I walked to the church to get ingredients to make a cherry pie: Pie crust mix, which expires in a year, and extra sugar and cornstarch and some almond flavoring. And two miniatures of cherry liquor, because why not? As I was leaving, I sat down in the sanctuary for a while to cool off and decompress. A while turned into longer, and I stayed in the soft, safe space for maybe an hour, just being there. Then I heard someone calling my name. It was Claude, out in the middle of the street, a half block away.

"Over here," I yelled when I reached the sidewalk, holding up the shopping bag. "I think I found one."

"I was getting worried about you," he said, hurrying in my direction. "I wondered if we should organize a search party. Here, let me carry that." He reached for the shopping bag and glanced inside.

I showed him the cherry pitters, and noticed that he had changed from slouchy bedroom slippers into the running shoes we brought him from the thrift store. Had he decided to rejoin the world? Clare predicted he would when he wanted something, like access to the wine shop, or a visit to the Manse. He was walking just fine, but I decided not to mention it.

He set up the fan to blow on us while we pitted the cherries, which is messy and leaves your fingers stained red, but goes pretty fast. It was too hot for rolling out pie crust, so we made the crumbly kind instead, and I'm telling you the beta version pie we put into the mini oven was a real beauty. Then came the unknowns. Would we get a solid hour of sun so Solar Sam could keep the oven going? Would the thermostat fail and burn our baby? It was a small thing, but I had to trust Claude and his knowledge of how the oven worked, and besides, he had been pleasant company all afternoon. Before things could go south, I excused myself to attend to gardening chores, and said I'd be back later for dinner and pie.

What I really did was sit in the shade in the backyard with Clare, telling her about Claude and the pie and Ms. Cherry. But not the waffle iron thing. Too weird.

"We'll see how he does in a small group, hope for the best. Sometimes people who can't pull off close relationships do well with several looser ones," she said of Claude, with whom she now has a cordial but distant relationship. He knows she's been choosing his wines, which gives her a bit of power.

Clare was a corporate trainer in The Time Before, and she pays attention to these things, analyzes what she sees and feels. After dinner, she plans to give him a map so he can find his way to the thrift store and wine shop tomorrow. After he receives the gift of autonomy, we wait and see.

The pie was delicious, but now it's gone. As long as there is good sun for Sam, we plan to make another one tomorrow.

Should I save you a piece?
Love,
Sarah

Dear Mom,

Hello from back home, where it's hotter than I ever remember, and it's not even July. Is it hot where you are, too, and have you found a cool place to pass the time? There are three ceiling fans in the Garden House, but my latent telepathy skills can't get them to spin. It's depressing. Clare and I got some folding fans at the thrift store, and they help a little, especially if you mist yourself with water from a pump spray bottle first.

Have you been anywhere, or do you stay in the same place? I miss my car, your car, all cars, and trucks, too. Man, did they make life easy! Seriously, I could have driven from town to Jesse's place in ten minutes, loaded up, and been back within an hour if only I had a car. Not really, because the roads are a mess, but I can dream, right?

We are still dreaming of getting the dome house up and running, which could really happen if the right equipment is waiting in Jesse's storage container. Running water! Fans! A washing machine! We decided to brave the heat to try to make it happen.

Clare and I left at dawn, each pushing a plastic shopping cart selected and lubricated by Wynn. Along with snacks and drinks, he tucked some bungee cords into each cart.

Even stopping to pick up sticks and admire the sun coming up over the mountains, we made good time. Pushing an empty shopping cart is easy because the cart does the balancing for you, and you can almost ride them on clear downhill stretches. We were nearing Jesse's place an hour later, when we heard the guys coming up behind us, exactly according to plan. Wynn is an excellent planner.

"Woo-hoo!" Rob called from his chariot. "And tally ho!" Both of them were grinning, having way too much fun with the all-terrain wheelchair. Wynn was sweating and breathing hard, like he'd been running, but that's what he likes to do. I handed them each a hydration drink. "It's like being on a ride at the fair, makes me feel like a kid," Rob said. "I just can't thank you guys enough ..."

"No more thanks!" Clare said. "You promised!" We were tired of hearing how grateful Rob was for the Thing.

Jesse's place was just as we left it. The shopping carts didn't do well in the tall grass, but the Thing had no trouble at all, so we used it to carry boxes and cords and reference books and equipment down the overgrown driveway. Rob rooted around in Jesse's shop, placed the wind turbine kit and other things of interest by the door, and we loaded the carts until they were full. It was hard, hot work.

"Break time!" Wynn called. We gathered on Jesse's shady porch to drink and munch and cool off. Rob was excited, and not just about the wind turbine, which he said could give us power at night in winter.

"I don't know what some of that stuff is, but it sure looks promising," he said. "And having the books, I mean, that's just so good."

After a few minutes Wynn went into the house and got two plastic jugs of stale water. "Old runner's trick," he said. "For the return trip, pour some water over your head, just don't get it in your shoes. It will keep you cooler."

Having wet hair and a wet shirt probably did help some, but it was still a steamy slog home. The loaded carts required serious pushing uphill, and got kind of scary on the downhills. Bless Wynn's heart. He pushed Rob home, then came back to help us make the last mile.

We did it! And in a surprise move, Claude helped unload the carts into Rob's shop. Clare and I dragged home exhausted and took naps, and I think Wynn did the same. He didn't come to dinner at Rob's, which is not unusual, so as I walked home I stopped to check on him.

"I can't get up, Prince is on top of me," he called when I knocked at the screen door. I let myself in and sat down beside them on the love seat. Prince turned up the volume of his purr when I scratched his head.

"Are you doing okay after your Olympic feats today?" I asked.

"Pretty good. And you?" He picked up my hand and squeezed it. "Any blisters?"

"How did you know? Right hand, left foot, but they're not bad." I said I wasn't ready to do it again tomorrow, but that we should all be proud of ourselves. "With major credit to you."

"We made a great team," he said, "But I am used up." He took a deep breath and slowly exhaled.

I got up, kissed his head, and went home to lay under the silent ceiling fan in my hot bedroom. Who knows? Maybe someday soon it will spin.

Stay cool,
Sarah

Chapter 12 Memories of Michael

Dear Mom,

Can we talk about God? What are your thoughts these days, with Jeremy gone and you/me missing and nothing like it used to be? Have you given up on God? Is that even possible? God always comes up when we talk about what happened at 2:42. There are many theories.

We have ruled out a world war because nine months later, there has been no follow-up. The skies are still empty of aircraft. No engines, contrails, or blinking lights at night. No big explosions. If some crazy nation is trying to take over the world, they are moving awfully slow.

Claude thinks it was triggered by a superior alien intelligence that saw the need to save the oceans. As dinner ends and he finishes his wine, he is prone to going on about his views, which are better informed than mine and often quite interesting. "In our solar system, in any solar system, water is life. The oldest life forms are in the oceans. When a massive asteroid decimated the planet and killed off the dinosaurs, the oceans remained. But now look. The seas are full of plastics, the fish are being driven suicidal by sound pollution, and water temperatures are warming too fast, killing the crabs. What if another intelligence was monitoring the situation, and punched the reset key to allow a few thousand years for the oceans to recover? It fits with Wynn's Incineration Theory, especially if it unfolds in stages."

"It doesn't have to be an alien, it can just be God," Clare said, getting up to gather the dishes.

"I agree," Rob said. "Too many things happen that can't be explained, on so many levels."

He had me there, and I already understood the basics of Clare's faith. "I don't have the time or energy to waste worrying over the past or being afraid of the future more than I have to. Instead I choose faith, every day," she said. "Soon after I wake up, I choose to believe in a loving God."

Clare's supreme being is not made of mumbo jumbo or supernatural stories, just God plain and simple. Later she told me that I lived in faith, too, only I didn't know it. "That's why you like to sit in church, and why you are so respectful of the dead. You're already letting God in, which is all we have to do."

What do you think of that?

There is big news from the Manse. Rob and Buddy found a small heat pump wired to solar panels designed to heat the floors, and they hot-wired it to the well pump. So, the Manse now has running water, at least during the day. I admit to feeling jealous that Buddy no longer has to carry water while I do. He even has a hose to water his sweet corn patch!

The heat wave broke two days ago with lightning and thunder that woke me up in the middle of the night, flashing and crashing like July 4th fireworks. After that it rained for hours, filling my rain barrels and giving everything a good soaking. Since then it hasn't been as hot. Time to cancel the excessive heat warning and get back to work growing food at the Farm.

The heat ruined the last of the strawberries and snap peas, but there are blueberries ripening under a bird/shade cover, and a few early squash. Wynn has a lot of stuff growing! He found the farmer's stash of seeds in a dry cabinet in the barn, and a box of shriveled potatoes, which he planted. You should see his potato plot, it is incredible! He weeds and waters it by hand, it's his baby.

As for me, I am the sweet potato queen. One of the big, vining plants in Gina's collection was a sweet potato, and Buddy took a bunch of cuttings off of it and told me to plant them with the tips just showing. "Keep them wet for a while and they'll grow. With no deer to eat them, they ought to do real fine," he said. They are growing like gangbusters, becoming a knee-high sea of green.

I like to work in the mornings when it's cool, though Wynn is usually there before me. By noon he likes to head home to check on Prince. We often clean up together by the stream that runs along the property.

"Sarah, I want to ask a favor, if you don't mind," he said yesterday.

"Sure, what's up?"

He took a breath. "I need to go to my old house to get some things. I don't want to go alone. Last time I went, it didn't go well, not for me. Will you come? Just wait in the house for a few minutes? It won't take long."

"Not a problem," I said. "Like when?"

"Like now? It's on the way to town. We can make a quick stop."

I may have gulped audibly, thinking about his mother's body.

"It's okay, she's behind a closed door," he said.

"I'm so sorry," I said.

"Me, too."

He talked as we walked, me pushing my bike instead of riding it.

"We moved here when I was twelve. My parents got a divorce, my mother changed jobs, and we landed here. She thought it would be a good place for me."

"Was it?" I asked.

"Yes and no. Let's just say adolescence was not my finest hour."

"Me either," I said. The sad truth.

Wynn's house was in a small cul-de-sac just off the main road. The houses were nice enough, but weeds filled the ditches and grew tall among the cars parked in yards.

"This is it, Chateau Crouch," he said, turning into an asphalt driveway. "Please come in."

Chateau Crouch was once a red brick ranch house, now painted light gray with a covered landing added to the front. The inside was updated, too, with interior walls removed to open up the space.

I suppose because Wynn can be particular in his ways, I expected his mother to be a strong ruler type, probably older and judgy, as in doilies and tea sets. Wrong! The décor at Wynn's is plush yet modern, with pale beige walls that change to faint mint green in the white-tiled kitchen.

"What a nice house," I said. "Your mother had great taste."

"She did," he agreed, looking around. "She was into light, and color. She thought they gave off vibrational energy. Please sit down. I'll only be a minute."

I didn't sit down, nor did I touch anything, or (banish

the thought) go looking in the kitchen cabinets. Instead, I tiptoed around the main room, checking out figurines, books, and framed photos of Wynn and his mother.

She was beautiful in a striking way, with dark, wavy hair and strong, angular features that were echoed in her son. Three framed photos, grouped together, showed the two of them at different stages of life. Mother holding a toddler at the beach. Mother helping a little boy jump across a stream. Mother smiling beside her son, several inches taller than her, at his high school graduation.

I sensed Wynn standing behind me. "What was her name?" I asked.

"Paula." His voice was soft, and not rock solid. Neither was mine, but I said what I wanted to say anyway.

"Paula, thank you for raising such a fine son. Your precious boy has grown into a very good man." Knowing I was heard, I walked toward the front door. He grabbed the sleeve of my shirt.

"Wait," he said. "Why did you say that?"

"What?"

"You called me her precious boy." His eyes brimmed with tears. "She called me that."

"Because she loved you." I didn't know what else to say. Mom, you called Jeremy your precious boy, but maybe it's not a universal thing?

He blew his nose and got a paper grocery bag to carry the sheet music, clothes, and running shoes he got from his old room.

"It wasn't so bad," he commented as we walked the rest of the way to town. "Much better than last time. Thanks for coming."

"Anytime. I really like your house." And I do. There is calmness to the colors and furnishings, perhaps intended to help bring peace to a tortured teenager. If I ever have my own house, as in my forever house, I know the style I want.

We bring our family photos to hang on the wall. You, me and Jeremy. What do you think?

Love,
Sarah

Dear Mom,

Hello from back home, where it's been raining for two days as you probably know. Are you safe and dry? Do you have windows, so you can look out at the rain? Do you get out at all? You always loved watching the water run through the mountain streams after heavy rains. If we were in the car, crossing a bridge with nobody behind us, you liked to stop to watch the water, listening to it with the windows rolled down.

How are things with you in regard to sanitation? You know, flushing? I learned about our septic system at home and how it worked, and didn't work, after Jeremy accidentally flushed a Ninja Turtle figure when he was a kid. No flushing, no drains after that, and one thing led to another until the nice man with the huge pump truck came and dug a hole and fixed it. I watched the whole thing, which gave me a new appreciation for what happens when you flush.

For the record, we don't have septic tanks in town. Instead, the befouled water gets pumped through a treatment system, only the pumps no longer work. After noticing early warning signs of drainage difficulty at his house, Rob placed those of us in town under a Flush Advisory. Because the Garden House is high on the hill, Clare and I are not in imminent danger of losing this important convenience, but it remains a concern.

It's not like one is tempted to make unnecessary flushes when you have to carry three gallons of water and pour it into the tank, every time, for every flush. Clare tends to her commode and I tend to mine, but each of us flushes only twice a day, or sometimes three. I don't think we are overdoing it.

Meanwhile, in the episode now streaming on the Claude channel, we are watching him try to wheedle his way to the Manse, complete with running water and unlimited flushes.

"Don't you look nice today, that color suits you," he told me when I arrived for dinner wearing a clean denim shirt. Seriously? I laughed and told him flattery would get him everywhere.

Claude is a handsome man, tall and broad-shouldered with lovely blue eyes and thick salt and pepper hair, and Clare says he looks even better now that he's lost some weight. He knows it, too. A couple of times when I've worked with him in the kitchen, I caught him checking himself out in the mirror by the door. Who does that? It's like he was studying his angles for the camera.

I think he fully believes in his own magnificence, so hearing him say nice things about me or anyone comes off as a bit thin. "Clare is one of the finest women I have ever known," he said to Rob, but loud enough for me to hear.

"I'm not surprised," Clare said when I told her. "He knows who the decision makers are."

And indeed, it's true that Clare and I hold the coveted keys to the kingdom. We go visit Gina every week or so, and we've spent the night twice. We have concluded that she enjoys having company, though she is still suspicious of me.

"I think she will love Claude," Clare said. "He will love-bomb her with praise and attention, and because of how she is, it will probably work." Clare learned to swim with the sharks from her work as a corporate trainer. She knows Claude's type. "You let them win, but on your own terms. Give them power, but only when you know it will go your way."

Intervening factor: Rob wants Buddy's help hot-wiring the solar panels to the pump at the dome house, so somebody needs to relieve him at the Manse. Clare says she will do it, but that we should give Claude a try. He feels entitled to a lifestyle upgrade, and being Gina's companion is pretty light duty.

You should have seen him when I asked him to come with me to the Manse to deliver supplies. I actually heard him catch his breath.

"Of course, if I can be of help," he said. "Anything I can do." It made me wish I had heavier things for us to carry.

"I can't believe it's so close," he said as we entered the gates. "Or that it's so big!" It's true. Even with the tall grass grown up in the pastures, the house stands like a castle on the sloping hillside, solar panels glistening on the roof. I guess I've been there so many times that I'm no longer impressed.

I knocked at the front door and opened it at the same time. "Gina? Are you home? It's Sarah the chicken girl."

No answer. There were suitcases by the door again. "Come on in, she's probably outside," I said. Claude's mouth was slightly open as he took in the room, the art, the burial vault filled with dolls and stuffed animals.

"All this, and running water, too," I joked.

"It's pretty amazing."

We found Gina tending her plants on the patio. She wore capri length khaki pants and a flowing floral shirt, her hair secured with a dark brown scrunchie. A good day. "Hi Gina, it's Sarah, Sarah the chicken girl. And I brought my friend..."

The metal watering can she had been holding clattered to the ground. "Michael!" she squealed. She ran to Claude, wrapped her arms around his neck and held him close, tears streaming down her face. "Oh, Michael, you made it!" She felt his arms, squeezing them gently, as if to see if he was real.

"It's so good to see you, Gina. You look well," he said.

"Oh, yes, very well indeed, and so much better now that you are here. Talk of angels, and you hear the flutter of their wings." He looked at me questioningly, silently mouthing "Who's Michael?" and I shrugged.

"Right now you are," I said. "Welcome to Gina-land." I excused myself to go talk to Buddy, who I found tending his corn patch.

"Hey there, Girlie, ain't you a sight for sore eyes," he said.

I asked if he was doing all right and he said, "Good enough, good enough. Gina's been eating and sleeping good, but she still thinks her sister is coming to get her."

"I saw the suitcases," I said. "Do you know who Michael is? I brought Claude with me today, and she thinks he's Michael, whoever that is. She's all over him, totally juiced up."

"I don't know, maybe a younger brother, or a cousin?" He scratched his chin thoughtfully. "There's a boy in some of the family pictures in the yellow bedroom upstairs. She talks about her sister, but I've wondered about that boy." Having spent the night in the yellow bedroom, I knew the photos he was talking about.

"He's going along with it. Should we tell her she's wrong?"

"Oh, my no, never cross her about something that don't much matter. You're asking for trouble. If it don't hurt nothing, I just go along." He made a crooked grin. "You pick your battles. I never cared much for fussing and fighting."

I asked him if he'd be willing to spend more time in town, helping Rob with the dome house, if we looked after Gina. "She likes Clare best, and it looks like Claude-Michael is a hit, too."

"I reckon they're cut out of the same cloth," he said, lighting up a little. "We could try it."

Buddy had met Claude during his visits to town, and though they got along well enough, because Buddy gets along with everybody, they will never be blood brothers. Claude's citified ways make me feel like a bumpkin at times, and it is not a good feeling. Make that double or triple for Buddy, who's never traveled farther than Myrtle Beach and barely finished high school.

"To tell you the truth, she's been testy with me lately. Says she's not sick, doesn't want to take her pills, twice a day pill time turns into a puppet show with those stuffed animals of hers. I've been thinking of asking Clare to come. You know, give us a little break."

"She's prepared to do exactly that, coming later today. But I have a question. Does this house have a wine cellar?"

He laughed. "Only about a million bottles. Lots of mold down there, though, so I keep it closed off. There's a door leading down some stairs in the main room, then double doors at the bottom. She ain't interested, it was George who collected the wine. Never cared for it myself, and thanks to you and Wynn, there ain't been no need."

FYI, our supply deliveries include medicinal amounts of vodka, rum or whiskey poured into small bottles. Not too much, not too little.

"Between having running water and good wine, I think Claude-Michael may be staying on," I said. "You won't have to be here all the time. In town you can stay with Rob, or at the dome house. Me or Clare will keep watch on what's happening here. Rob says he really needs you."

Another smile. "That's an offer I can't refuse. I always liked hot-wiring things."

Clare was expected later in the day, and until then it was my job to hang around and see how Claude and Gina got along. But my first stop was the kitchen sink, where I timidly turned on the cold water. It ran! Like, not a dribble, but with pressure! I soaped up my hands and gave them a good scrub under the running water. My nails are cleaner than they have been in weeks.

Next on my checklist was to count the pills in Gina's bottles so we could keep track better on the list Buddy kept of when she took them. Then I unloaded the food we brought, all the while hearing footsteps overhead.

Claude and Gina were in the east bedroom, the one with the high, four-poster wood bed, oriental rug, and dark, thick curtains. I thought I heard her laughing. I crept upstairs to eavesdrop.

She opened the curtains and walked around the room talking about a place she lived when she was a child while Claude sat in an upholstered chair, listening. "When you came, in the summer, we got to go swim in the pond, or paddle around in the boat. I was afraid of the snapping turtle, but you weren't, no sir, not Michael," she said. "You would dive right in."

"Those were good times," he agreed, crossing his legs, one of which was jiggling. He was nervous. I decided to announce myself.

"Hi Gina, it's Sarah. Would everyone like some tea?" A look of relief washed over Claude's face, but Gina looked at me suspiciously.

"You can't have my chickens," she said.

"I would never take your chickens. And look, today I brought you Michael. Give me some credit," I said, smiling.

She looked at him closely. "But you drove here, in the car, the big black one with the wings on the front. You always come in that car."

"Yes, but Sarah showed me the way," he said quickly.

"Well, then."

"This is like living in a movie," he whispered to me as we walked down the stairs. "Are you sure it's okay to lie?"

"Totally. Talk slow, ask yes or no questions, don't argue and be kind. She's entitled to her thoughts, even if they don't make sense. And remember, this is her house."

I don't know how much that matters anymore, but it's still true.

While I made tea, Gina showed Claude her dolls and stuffed animals and told him a story about her mother and a soup incident at a restaurant. He's a fast learner. With Gina, it's best not to listen for details, which are quickly changed or forgotten. Instead you do what Claude was doing, nodding and agreeing, which made her feel validated.

Confession. Clare and I left some caregiver books from the church library at Rob's over the last few weeks, placed on bookshelves here and there, hoping Claude would read one. I think maybe he did.

"Here is something you don't know about Michael, who I often call Claude, or sometimes Claude-Michael," I said as we finished sipping herb tea. He looked at me with raised eyebrows. "Michael knows about wine cellars, and I think you have one. A wine cellar, in the basement?" She nodded. "He says he will check it out later, make sure it's ship shape," I said.

Again, the look of Claude's face with his mouth slightly agape is priceless.

"It was my father who drank too much, not yours," Gina said, suddenly sad.

I suggested it was a good time to take Claude Michael to meet the chickens.

"Let's do," he said, standing up. He was getting the hang of things. I stayed behind to clean up while they went to visit the flock.

They were still in the barn with the chickens when Clare arrived to relieve me. Our plan was to tag-team as long as needed, until Claude proved himself worthy. I gave her a quick report and told her about the wine cellar.

"Our evening entertainment," she said, grinning and rubbing her hands.

I invited Claude to come back to town with me, but he declined (surprise surprise) even though it meant being watched by Clare. That was three days ago, and things are going crazy good, I'm telling you. One of us checks in at the Manse every day. Gina seems happy, and Claude-Michael expresses no interest in leaving.

And here's the thing. Since Claude's relocation to the Manse, the drainage problems at Rob's house have eased. Had he been committing acts of excessive flushing? Or was it all the cooking and dishwashing water running down the kitchen drain? In any case, our freedom to flush has been restored. At least for now.

Love,
Sarah

Chapter 13   Hiding Out

Dear Mom,

Hello from harvest central! Are you getting any summer vegetables and fruits, maybe some peaches? You always drove down to Wade's Orchard when the peaches were ripe, and then we'd have peach everything – cobbler, smoothies, peaches with our cereal. The only peaches we have here come out of a can, but I'm always on the lookout for a bearing tree in someone's yard.

Maybe it's beginner's luck, but Wynn and I have grown bumper crops of vegetables in our gardens, and at the Farm down on Washout Road. It's great to have fresh food, but there is way more than we can eat, and canning (if I knew how) takes too much fuel and extra ingredients. Instead, we are using an electric dehydrator plugged into Solar Sam, turning out many jars of dried tomatoes, peppers, squash, even some crispy kale. Dried veggies are new to me, but Rob says in winter they will be great for making soup.

Our active operations have moved to the dome house, where Rob and Buddy managed to hot wire the well pump to the solar panels in the side yard. It's a wonky system that doesn't work very well unless the sun is super bright, so we get water mostly at midday, which we store in jugs. Solar Sam is on the back deck, so we wash and pare veggies in the house and then put them in the dehydrator. It feels like we are making progress.

Two steps forward, one step back.

A week ago, Wynn was at his house in the early afternoon when he heard crashing sounds, then voices coming from up the hill, in the middle of town. He did his best stealth moves to see what was happening. The three men made no attempt to hide as they stood in the middle of the main intersection under the stoplight, talking.

"They were studying the highway signs and talking about whether or not to bash in the windows of the stores like they'd been doing to the cars in the road," Wynn reported as we ate garden vegetable soup with Rob on the back deck of the dome house. Two of the men carried baseball bats, the other a long crowbar. He assumed they also carried guns. He shadowed them for a couple of hours, until he was sure they were well out of town, heading toward Hillsville.

"No telling what will happen when they get to Liberty Grove," Wynn said. "It's a different kind of community, in good ways and bad. If there are survivors there, they have banded together and they are dug in." He used his hand to make the sign of a pistol, then blew the tip of his index finger. "Shoot first, ask questions later."

"We got lucky they didn't turn north," Rob said. "Pure luck."

"Do you really think the murdering hordes are coming?" I asked, trying to lighten things up.

"With a semi-automatic, it only takes one," Rob said. Good point.

Rob moved to the dome house the day after the incident, and I'm thinking of doing the same thing. Just as a short-term deal, until the garden food supply gets under control. Clare is at the Manse more and more, helping with Gina, who is not doing well. Now, when I'm home alone at night I find myself listening to every little sound, probably hearing things that aren't there. I'm not getting much sleep. If only Scruff were here! Seriously, I need a dog, but the world seems fresh out of them.

Peachy kisses,
Sarah

Dear Mom,

How are you? I wish I knew, because I know you are somewhere, and not in Heaven. I feel it in my bones. Please keep holding on, and be ready when you get the chance to come home. I'll be waiting for you at the Grantham house. Or someone will.

It's been rough around here lately. Fear is taking a toll on all of us. Now that I've started spending nights on the futon in the dome house, I know that Rob doesn't sleep much, either. He gets up during the night, comes into the main room and looks out the windows for a while, then tiptoes back to bed.

I get a definite Good Dad vibe from Rob, and being around him turns down my anxiety a couple of notches. I think his daughter was about my age, so whatever is going on between us comes naturally to him. Not so much for me. Sometimes I wonder if he's being overly cautious on the safety front, but that's what good dads do, right?

The main road doesn't feel safe anymore, but it's the only way to get back and forth to the Farm, or so I thought.

"We need to stop using the highway, stop cleaning it up," Wynn said. He was fully on board with Rob's plan to let town go ghost after hearing distant gunshots a few nights earlier. Prince heard them, too, and hid under the bed.

Wynn got out his maps to find an alternate route, if not to the dome house, then from the Farm to the Manse or the Grantham house, which everyone calls my house, Sarah's house. Is that not cool? I'm a homeowner! He did find a route, longer and part gravel, which we rode together yesterday. It was slow going, but we managed to clear a lane wide enough for a bike or the Thing. Along the way, we stopped for lunch on the porch of an abandoned house.

"I'm thinking of a plan," he said between spoons of rice and beans saved from last night's dinner. "Just because we started all spread out doesn't mean it's the best way. We should live closer."

"And not in town."

"Definitely not in town. Closer to the Manse."

I knew he was thinking about what was best for everyone, including Prince, who was now more important to him than the drugstore. Prince was terrified of gunshots and loud noises, and I felt for him, too. Jesse must have scared him with big bang weapons a few too many times.

"You and Prince should move into my old house," I said. "It's quiet, he would like it there."

He smiled. "We'll talk about it."

"You could have it to yourselves, at least for now. I need to step it up helping Clare with Gina, anyway. And

I do have my space at the Manse, in the yellow bedroom."

"It's been a long time since I've been to your house," he said. I could tell he was interested. We agreed to stop by on the way home.

I was glad I had cleaned up after the chickens in the sunroom, because the house smelled like lemon Lysol when I opened the door. There were still stained-glass angels in the den windows, and a few pieces of firewood by the wood stove, all swept and tidy. I left him to look around the house while I went to the garage to get some olive oil and a few other things from my stash.

"What do you think?" I asked, loading my backpack. "Can't beat the rent, fifty cents a month."

He whistled softly. "Sounds a little steep for my budget."

"Okay then, twenty-five."

"Where do I sign?"

In this way I became not only a property owner but a landlord. It's like I'm in a Monopoly game for real. Will I be assessed for repairs? Need to buy more insurance? Life can get complicated so fast!

Jokes aside, I will sleep better knowing Wynn and Prince are safe, which is not the case in town. As for me, I am needed at the Manse, but more on that later.

Love,
Sarah

Dear Mom,

Good afternoon from the Brambleberry Health Care Center, where a bunch of amateurs are trying to be doctors and nurses for a very sick patient. We really need your expertise right now, so please have yourself teleported here as soon as possible. The field in front of the Grantham house is big enough to land a helicopter.

I'm starting to sound kooky, like Gina, but not really, because Gina no longer has much to say. Last week she stayed in bed for almost two days, and when she finally woke up and started moving around, she wasn't the same. More confused, less talkative, and not as steady on her feet. Clare brought me up to date when she came to town to get a walker and portable wheelchair from the handicapped apartments.

"I can't believe how fast she's losing capacity," she said, using the term from the books. "Every day there's something else she can't do, because she's weak or because she can't remember how."

It's true. The next day I brought a stash of sickroom supplies assembled by Wynn that included wet wipes, straws, mouth swabs, rubber gloves, bed pads, and lemon drop candies. I sat with Gina while Clare took a nap, Claude-Michael made bread in the pizza oven, and Buddy covered ears of sweet corn with paper lunch bags to keep the crows from eating them.

"This is a lovely room," I said, looking around at Gina's personal space for the first time. "I love the soft colors, they feel cozy and warm." Because the large bedroom and bath is near the kitchen, separated by the laundry room, I think it was planned as a servant's quarters or mother-in-law suite. Deep brown woodwork is echoed in lighter shades of mocha and cream, with teal draperies bringing in texture and color. Of the five bedrooms in the Manse, it's the one Gina chose as her own.

Her eyelids fluttered open. "Who are you?" she whispered.

"I'm Sarah, the chicken girl. And no, I will never take your chickens."

She swallowed and asked for water. I broke into the package of flexible straws and helped her drink from the cup next to the bed.

"Where's Michael?" she asked. I reassured her that he was still here, in the kitchen.

"He better not run off again," she said, patting her hand on the blanket. Then she yawned and turned away from me to stare at the ceiling fan. After a while she started mumbling, which means she wants something, so I helped her to the bathroom. This took a very long time, because things move slowly these days in Gina-land.

We are developing a routine. In the mornings Buddy comes for a short visit, gives her a report on the chickens, collects the dirty laundry and brings in water. Claude-Michael doesn't do biological stuff, but twice a day he pulls up a chair, talks softly to Gina about the weather, and often thanks her for the fine wine he enjoyed the evening before. Sometimes she laughs in response. It's true, I've heard it. Then he opens a book, tells her a little about it, and starts reading a passage marked with a folded page.

Maybe it's the low rumble of a male voice, or the cadence of hearing good writing read aloud, but a calmness descends on Gina's room when Claude-Michael reads from books in George's library. He will often start with a classic, Shakespeare or Charlotte Bronte or even the Bible, then move onto something more interesting like Agatha Christie. I love to listen.

In the evenings, before it gets dark, I help Clare get Gina cleaned up and ready for bed, which is not always easy. Gina doesn't like being told what to do. Everything has to be her idea. Clare is really good with her, patient and gentle, and she doesn't let Gina's complaints and lack of cooperation bother her. While Clare takes her to the bathroom and helps her change clothes, I remake the bed.

"She feels warm to me. Does she feel warm to you?" Clare asked two nights ago as we finished our routine. I put my hand on Gina's forehead, then on my own.

"Maybe, a little bit."

In the morning Gina felt downright hot, and none of the digital thermometers in the house worked, so I went to town to get a mercury thermometer. I knew there was an old glass thermometer in the bathroom cabinet at the Garden House, and hoped there might be a newer one at the drugstore. No such luck. I left a note on Wynn's door that Gina was running a fever, and asked that he and Rob come to help us decide what to do.

In the afternoon Wynn and Rob arrived together with Wynn pushing Rob in the Thing. They brought a stethoscope, thermometers, some expired test kits for flu, antibiotics, and a hospice kit, which includes liquid valium and a small amount of morphine. Rob looked and listened and tried his best. Gina was listless and hot with 102 fever, and her breathing sounded rough and ragged.

"Definitely something going on, maybe a lung infection," he said.

We tried to get her to swallow an antibiotic capsule, but she couldn't do it, even with Claude-Michael coaching her. She was having a hard enough time with little sips of juice. We had no way to dose her with antibiotics, no fluids or drip lines, heart monitors, no way to read blood oxygen.

We sat together at the kitchen table, trying to come up with a plan.

"Seems like getting her some oxygen might help her breathe better," Buddy said. "Only I guess that's all electric."

"Or batteries," Wynn added.

Rob looked through the items in the hospice box. "A little liquid morphine might help her breathe," he said.

"Doesn't seem like there's much to lose there," Claude-Michael commented.

Clare said it was better than doing nothing, so that's the current treatment plan. We are open to ideas if you have any to share.

I'm just saying, if I ever end up in the fix that Gina's in, terribly sick and no longer able to take care of myself or talk or do anything, I want someone like Clare to take care of me. She is so soothing, so *angelic* in the way she talks to Gina, touches her, helps her change clothes.

She reminds me of you.

Please come soon.

Love,

Sarah

Chapter 14 Endings

Dear Mom,

Hello from Caregiver-Land, where I am on primary duty off and on during the day. Clare holds down nights. Are you caring for patients where you are? Anticipating their needs, keeping them comfortable? Being a nurse is what you've always done, but I am only now starting to get how it works. I wish I had your knowledge and experience. Caregiving is not easy, and in fact it can be really hard. For everyone.

I remember how sometimes when you'd had a bad day at work, like when you lost a patient, you'd come home and change clothes and go for a walk. You said it helped you reset and recalibrate, and you were right. As much as I enjoy listening to Claude-Michael read, I've learned to make the most of my break time by going out for a walk.

Buddy must have noticed me walking up and down the long driveway, because one morning after Claude-Michael settled into the reading chair, he waited for me in the kitchen.

"Hey, Girlie, I want to show you something," he said, stepping toward the door. "It's not far, down past those trees. The stream runs back there, with a sitting bench and all. I think you'll like it."

Walking to the stream gave us time to talk about Gina,

and about what might happen next.

"Her body is trying hard to fight the infection. Today she might be just a little better," I said. "Her fever was down for a while last night, and she drank some water."

"That's good news." He stopped, took off his baseball cap and wiped his brow with the back of his hand. "Girlie, do you think it could have anything to do with them chickens? The infection? She spent a lot of time with them in the barn, holding them, talking to them, back when it was hot. It wasn't sanitary, I could tell from the droppings she was tracking into the house. That's why I let them chickens loose."

I had noticed the chickens free-ranging around the house, but why not? There were loads of bugs for them to eat, and no predators to bother them. "You and Clare were around the chickens, too. She held and petted them, just like Gina did. You seem all right," I said.

"True enough, but it's been on my mind. But I guess it don't much matter."

I said we would need to call in the forensics team, like on TV, get some lab samples. Then try to get her to the ER.

"Yup."

The place by the stream is a treasure! The water cuts over stones and moss, and a few big rocks have been moved to create two small waterfalls with a waist-deep pool between them. It's like a perfect little park. You can sit on the bench and listen to the stream with your eyes closed, then open them and watch the sun play on the rushing water.

"She showed it to me when I first moved in," he said. "Then she forgot about it. I bet I've been down here a hundred times. When it was hot I came to cool off."

"I would have been in the water every day," I said. Tick-tock, time was passing, and I needed to get back to my patient. "You've been doing okay?" I asked.

"Pretty good, pretty good. How about you, Girlie? I hear everyone's hightailing it out of town."

I brought him up to date on Wynn's moving plans, told him all Rob and I wanted was to feel safe, and that right now I felt safest at the Manse, with him in the cottage.

"So you're figuring I'm staying on, even if she passes," he said. Buddy does not beat around the bush.

"Yes. The cottage is yours, for as long as you want it. You still like it there?"

"Nicest place I ever lived."

"Even with Claude-Michael around?"

"Yup. He ain't so bad. The way things are, we'd be hard up without him."

"I know I would," I said, getting to my feet. We walked back by way of the barn, where I looked at the old horse stall where the chickens lived for several months. They still roosted there at night, and laid their eggs in the nesting boxes. There was plenty of ventilation, but for a while the flies were so bad that the whole thing was covered with bug netting. The list of possible contaminants was getting longer, but like Buddy says, it don't much matter.

"I've done shoveled it out, put the manure to rest in a pile by the corn patch," he said.

"Smart move," I said. So much for evidence.

I washed my hands at the kitchen sink before returning to the sickroom. There was a note on the counter in Wynn's handwriting. "Bringing Rob and Solar Sam later today."

"Found it by the front door," Claude said, tiptoeing from Gina's chambers. "It seems we're having company."

He said she had been asleep for a half hour and seemed to be resting comfortably. "Snoring, but don't we all?" He riffled through the bowl of packaged snack foods I brought from my stash in the Grantham garage. A packet of Oreo Minis went into one of his pants pockets, a lukewarm diet soda went in another.

"Well, toodle-oo," he called, picking up his books, then stopped. "Agh, oh no, no," he muttered, reaching for the notepad where we write down Gina's medications. "She got agitated over something, after the first reading. She was jerking around, upset, so I gave her three drops of Valium. On a mouth sponge. She liked it, I could tell. I can't believe I almost forgot to note it." He put the pad and pen back in its place. "Let's not tell Clare of my carelessness," he said, winking. I heard him leave through the back door a short time later.

I did my usual thing, checked Gina's blankets, hands, feet and forehead, and fluffed her pillows to help keep her head and shoulders slightly raised, which helps her breathe. She was in a state beyond sleep, feverish and prone to twitching. I felt a weak response when I gently squeezed her hand, spoke her name and told her she had beautiful eyes.

I hope you get here soon because I have questions. How do you know when it's time? What do you do until then? Is the best you can do good enough?

Awaiting your prompt response,

Your unlicensed, and untrained nursing assistant daughter,

S

Dear Mom,

You always gave us curfews because you said that good things don't happen in the middle of the night, and you are right. Sometime in the wee hours, I was awakened by Clare sitting on the edge of my bed.

"She's gone," she said. I rolled over and opened my eyes.

"When?"

"A while ago." She took a deep breath. "She's not coming back."

"No," I said, scooting over to invite her to stay. "Want to talk?"

"Not really. I just needed to tell someone." I looked out the window and saw the odd light that comes just before dawn. I got up, gave Clare a long hug, made double-sure she didn't want to talk, and went downstairs to begin a very different kind of day.

I started by checking on Gina. Clare had covered her head and body with a blanket. I reached inside, touched her arm. She was no longer warm. No, she was not coming back.

I went to the kitchen to start coffee and wait for Buddy, who was always the first to appear. Everything felt different, I felt different, lighter and clearer somehow. Not profoundly sad. Not ready to cry. I found myself humming as I considered breakfast. Do you think there is something wrong with me, like I'm emotionally crippled or something?

Buddy said "Oh, no," when I told him, but he didn't seem devastated either. "She won't suffer no more." He went into her room to make sure she was "laid out proper." He returned a few minutes later.

After a cup of black coffee and a Little Debbie oatmeal creme pie, he talked about his plan for her grave. "I'll get started digging, but it will be tomorrow before I'm done, longer if we have to bury that vault." I could tell from his tone that he didn't want to include the vault, which is huge. "When I buried George, I wrapped him up nice and got him three feet down, just like I did with my people. I was going to put her next to him, not too close, but nearby."

"Sounds good to me. She never had nice things to say about him, did you ever notice that?" I asked.

"Yup."

Mom, burying someone at home is extremely slow, and reverent, and wonderfully weird. We all worked together, and I mean, all of us. After Buddy marked out the gravesite with a can of spray paint, he spread out tarps around the edges to hold the dirt. Claude searched the barn for extra digging tools and work gloves, and followed Buddy's lead digging out the hole. Rob stood by handing off tools and helping move big rocks. Wynn helped dig, and gathered ideas for the ceremony. A trumpet solo and Bible reading were on the program.

I kept the crew fed and watered, and consulted with Clare on flowers. I wanted flowers, lots of flowers. "I saw some dahlias blooming at a house up the hill, mostly red and yellow ones. Want to go get some?" I asked. Do birds fly? She was sooo ready to get out. We found Gina's pruning shears and some plant pails among the houseplants, and used the Thing to go up two big hills, then a hard left to the dahlia house.

"This is just so perfect," Clare said, trimming stems of yellow dahlias and placing them in a pail. "In her younger days, Gina would have been all over these." She was right.

"She also would have liked the sneaky feeling of taking them from someone else's yard," I said.

She laughed. "Like stealing chickens."

Back at the Manse, we found flower arranging supplies in a low cabinet, and worked together on the patio fashioning a spray of dahlias and shrub greenery to place on the grave. It was a good project that gave us time to talk.

"Gina was miserable so I'm glad it's over, and I know we did our best," she said. "Even Claude."

It's true. During one of the last days, in addition to reading to Gina, he went to town and helped move Rob and Solar Sam to the Manse. Just showed up, without being asked, pushed a packed grocery cart two miles and returned for a second load the next day. And now he was sweating shoulder to shoulder with Buddy, digging, laughing and drinking warm beer. It was hard not to notice. Does adversity bring out the best in some people? Or is it like Gina would say: A leopard never changes its spots?

Must go cook for the hungry crowd. It's a splurge day, canned roast beef and gravy with new potatoes and a vegetable mélange.

The funeral is tomorrow.

Love,

S

Dear Mom,

How goes your day? Did you have a singular, distinctive day, unlike any other, a day that may have made you a better person?

I did.

As you know, I have little experience with funerals. There was the funeral for the guy in high school who died from bone cancer, where everybody cried non-stop, and Grandmother's funeral, which seemed dark and sad and had too much organ music. Jeremy's funeral was a strewing of wildflowers and desperate prayers (We need a re-do there). None were stellar events, so when Wynn asked me to be host for Gina's funeral, I said no way.

"It's okay, it's okay, there's a program. You just have to keep things moving." He handed me his outline on a piece of paper.

Wynn can talk me into anything, including hosting a funeral for Gina, who none of us knew very well. By the time our paths crossed, she had withstood unbearable trauma while fighting a debilitating disease. We knew her former self from photos and stories and from living in her house, but our shared histories went back months rather than years.

The most somber and emotional part of Gina's funeral was the moving of the body from the house to the grave. The men carried the body wrapped up tight on an old door, and then lifted it into the hole. Buddy arranged a clean white sheet over her along with the items to be buried with her: a doll, a stuffed toy horse, a book, and a trio of hair scrunchies.

I cleared my throat and began, reading from my notes.

"Welcome to the celebration of life, and death, of Gina Barris. We did not know Gina well, only that she loved animals and certain people, and left the world with the innocence of a child.

"When we first met Gina, she was so traumatized that she could not speak. Wynn played a beautiful piece on his trumpet, a Schubert melody we know as Ave Maria, and she loved it. Now you get to hear it, too."

The trumpet solo sounded even more beautiful than it had at Christmas. Major goosebumps.

Clare's voice was shaky as she began reading the 23rd Psalm, but got stronger by the time she got to "Though I walk through the valley of the shadow of death, I will fear no evil, for thou art with me."

I loved hearing her read it, and then Buddy's short prayer, spoken from the heart. "I thank the Lord for being blessed with Gina in my life. I'll be grateful all my days for the home she gave me when I needed it, and the opportunity to be like Jesus wants us to be when she needed something of me. Amen"

Then he explained the doll in the grave. "Around here, people who kept the old ways liked to bury their dead with things they love, so I put Gina's favorite doll with her. It's a little worn, but that's Samantha, the doll who was her best friend."

Clare stepped forward. "Gina, I know how you loved your horses, the ones before and then after. This is the horse you called Legend, so soft and brown. Wherever you go, he will be with you. And we promise to take good care of your chickens. Rest well, my sweet."

It was my turn next. "One of the ways I knew you was from how you dressed," I said. "You took such care with your clothes, and looked so put together. When you felt strong and knew you looked good, I could see it in your outfit, with matching scrunchie. Here are three of your favorites, the sparkly silver, dark blue velvet, and burgundy satin one. Thank you for sharing your beauty."

Claude blew his nose in a cloth handkerchief and apologized. "So sorry, but this is all quite moving. But I do have something to say. The book there is Gina's copy of the Complete Poems of Emily Dickinson, which she especially enjoyed hearing toward the end." He straightened his back, making himself stand taller.

"She adored her cousin Michael, and as we all know, I became Michael, quite by accident. Being a suffering person's dream come true brings responsibility, sacred responsibility, and I've never had that before. Instead of taking, I had to give. Instead of being served, I had to serve. Being Michael for a few weeks made me a better man." He looked at the shroud and sighed. "Goodbye, sweet cousin."

Rob led us in the Lord's Prayer, which was over way too soon. As the grand finale, I was to start singing "Dream a Little Dream of Me," and I was terrified, as in stage fright. So instead of singing I started humming, and by the time I was ready to sing words, so were the others.

Sweet dreams till sunbeams find you,
Sweet dreams that leave all worries behind you.
But in your dreams, whatever they be,
Dream a little dream of me.

Wynn joined in on the trumpet once we got going, and it actually turned out pretty good. We clapped for ourselves at the end.

And then it was over. Refilling the grave went fast

because of the tarps, and it all looked quite proper with the spray of dahlias in place.

Now it really does feel like Gina's life is over, which is the point of a funeral, right?

I have no such feelings about you. I feel you alive somewhere, praying for me and loving me the same way you always have. It's like that energy channel is still open, I can still feel the buzz.

I hope to go back to the house soon, to get a few things. Maybe I'll see you there?

Love,
Sarah

Chapter 15   One Small Year

Dear Mom,

I've been thinking about the wall calendar in the kitchen of our old house. I might want to go get it. I marked the day of 2:42 on it, and the one-year anniversary is coming up. One year since we lost Jeremy, one year since I've heard your voice.

Right at first, I tried calling you, hoping to hear your greeting, but nothing happens when you call a dead cellphone on a dead landline, or vice versa. Since then I mostly call you on the Divinity Line. Have you been getting my messages? I miss you so much.

It's been busy and quiet since we buried Gina. As long as the weather was sunny, Wynn, Clare and I rode back and forth on the rutted gravel road to the Farm, hauling squash and peppers and tomatoes that we handed off to Rob and Claude to dry in the dehydrator. But then it started raining. It's still raining, which means limited running water and no Solar Sam. And it's hot again. The weather did this last year, when Jeremy and I were waiting out the rain to go diving, which spooks me and makes me worry that 2:42 could happen again. Are you thinking the same thing?

I'm settled into the Manse, feeling safe in the upstairs yellow bedroom, with Clare next door in the green room. Rob and Claude have the two bedrooms on the other side. We've started going through George's things in the big bedroom so we can make use of the space, maybe turn it into a game room, but we're leaving Gina's possessions alone for now. It just seems best to wait a while.

Clare is dealing with the loss by throwing her energy into new projects. "How do you catch a chicken?" she asked one day as we picked peppers and tomatoes at the Farm. I thought about it.

"The hens are pretty easy if they're in a confined space," I said. "Are you thinking about the chickens here? They're pretty wild, but there are a lot of them."

"We can use more chickens," she said. "For eggs and for meat. The homesteading book says three hens per person. And if we can get the young males, born this year, we can harvest them when they start crowing."'

"Sounds gruesome," I said. "But probably not to Buddy."

All summer, while working at the farm, we heard and watched two broody hens raise their little chickies, which make the most wonderful cheep-cheep sounds! But Clare was right. The dozen little chickies had grown into chicken-ettes we could put to better use, in the coop or in the pot.

Buddy was all in, and said he'd build them a separate pen because strange flocks don't like each other at first, but then they get over it. "To catch them, you need to get them used to going back inside at night," he advised, and gave us ears of overripe sweet corn to put inside the shed used as a chicken coop. We brought the pet carriers from the garage at the Grantham house for when we got lucky.

This turned out to be easy with the first captives. After

a few days of luring them with food, we started seeing a few eggs in the nesting boxes, so we knew some of the chickens were gathering in the coop at night. Clare started going to the Farm first thing in the morning to talk to them and give them treats.

"Aren't you the lucky ones," she might say, feeding them rice leftover from last night's dinner. "Do you want to come live with me? Of course you do!" The chickens became less skittish, gathering around her feet to beg for food, and one day she reached down and picked one up, just like that.

"Sarah, Sarah! I got one! Come help!" She held a shiny brown chicken against her chest.

I came running with a pet carrier, took the chicken from her, and slipped it in through the zippered door. "I want to try for another one," she said, breathless. And she did. In no time we had three hens ready for transport to the Manse. The next day we got three more, only Buddy said two of them were young roosters.

"You can tell from their neck feathers, and their combs. Pretty soon they'll start crowing." He seemed amused by Clare's dedication to chicken-nabbing, and warned her against getting attached to the boys. "It ain't just about the meat. A lot of them's mean. Not like old Chester." He wants to choose one young rooster to keep, and give the others another month to fatten up before their big day.

This sounds kind of gross, but I'm really looking forward to barbecued chicken, cooked on the grill, just like old times. With potato salad. Hope you can join us!

Love,
Sarah

Dear Mom,

Hello, and I miss you. How are you doing with the anniversary of the worst day of our lives coming up? Okay, I hope, or at least better than me. I don't feel like doing anything and my mind won't stay focused and wanders to places I wish it would not.

Deep sigh, life goes on.

The rain has put chicken-catching on hiatus, Clare is deep into a novel, and the guys are mucking around with the wind turbine in the barn. I went to hang out with Wynn.

He's made some improvements since moving into the Grantham house. Their family photos and curios are packed into a bin in the garage, and the dusty silk flower arrangements met their end in the burn pile. He swept and beat rugs and rearranged the dining room furniture to make it his music practice space. His maps and record books are arranged on the table.

"I like it," I said, admiring his good works.

"It's coming along. Good bones. The demo team will be here next week to cut through these walls, open up the kitchen," he said. He was wiping down the counters with a spray that smelled like oranges.

He made us some high antioxidant blueberry ginger tea, and we sat together on the love seat in the sunroom, watching the rain. Prince snuggled between us, purring. I felt myself relaxing. "This is good, I've been keyed up," I said.

"I know."

"It's that obvious?"

"Now that I know you, yes, it is." He reached over

and squeezed my hand.

"Wynn, it's been a year. A *year*. I'm having trouble with that. A year?"

"One twenty-seventh of your life, one twenty-fifth of mine. How do you like those numbers?" I said that was one way of looking at it.

"Do you think we're doing what we're supposed to do?" I asked.

"Like we have any choice?" he countered. Prince got up to jump at a bird that flew close to the window.

"I don't know. I want to go home, like to my mom's house, to get some things," I said.

"I'll go with you. I can check the breaker box. Just say when."

"Only maybe I don't want to go."

He allowed a second of silence. "Which circles back to your question. What do we do? Hold on? Let go? Be here? Be there?"

Prince returned and lay smack in the middle of my lap this time. He knows where he is needed.

"I want it both ways," I said.

I felt better the next day, not quite right but stronger, and the skies were clearing with a nice breeze. It was a good day for a ride, or walk, whichever it turned out to be. I took an empty backpack and pedaled toward home, alone. I hoped Wynn would understand.

I have never seen anything like these late summer wildflowers! Along the fences there are black-eyed Susans and purple spiky flowers and berries I've never seen before. There are weeds popping up in every pothole and crack in the pavement, and tall grasses crowd the edges of the road. In shady spots there are vines and creeping plants turning the sides of the roads green. There are birds everywhere, scarlet tanagers and red-winged blackbirds.

It is very weird, and not particularly terrible, to see the forest reclaiming everything. I had to watch curves for fallen trees.

It's a good thing I was going slow when I came to the bridge, because there was still standing water from the rain. Then something moved on the side of the road and I screamed. It was a turtle, a turtle in that exact same place where you stopped one time, got out of the car, and carried a turtle across the road.

"Are you the same one?" I asked him. Or her. "Is life better for you now? No cars to worry about?" The turtle very slowly walked away, pushing through the wet gravel, not engaged in the conversation. I forged on.

Sorry to say, the entry to our driveway looks like a road to nowhere. Seriously, it's like there's this tunnel into the woods that used to be our driveway. This is kind of good, because it gave me advance notice that I was once again entering an abandoned house. Only this time it was our house, our home. I checked the mailbox. My letter to you telling you where to find me is still there, safe and dry.

For a week I made lists of things I planned to get. Some photographs, the wall calendar, jewelry we both loved. Standing there by the mailbox, I asked myself "Seriously, Sarah, do you really want these things? Why do you want them, why do you need them?"

Or maybe that was you behind the questions?

Well, you know what? I ain't asking for much. A few mementos, that's all. I parked the bike, got a drink of water, and marched down the driveway. The shady part is still beautiful, but let's not talk about your flowerbeds.

I stuck to the task. I got only what I wanted/needed/had to have, which didn't fill half of my backpack. I made sure the door closed securely behind me, and hurried away. I didn't give myself time to see things I didn't want to see, or to cry. That's not what I wanted or needed, not anymore. When I got to the road, I felt like I was back in the free world.

I approached the bridge slowly, hoping to see the turtle again. It's a good thing, because Wynn waited for me there by the rushing water, wearing a bright red tee shirt over his running shorts.

"Halt! Who goes there, friend or foe?" he called, stretching out his arms, his brows drawn together to make a stern face.

"Are you the hungry troll that lives under the bridge?" I asked.

"That I am," he declared.

"You didn't eat the turtle, did you?"

"The turtle?" He dropped his pose and helped look around where I'd seen the turtle before, but it was gone.

"Did you make it to your house, find what you wanted?" he asked.

"I guess so. Nobody's there."

"Didn't think there would be."

We leaned against the bridge's concrete rails, watching the water rush toward us on its way down the mountain.

"I think it was DaVinci who said that when water is flowing toward you, you feel its oncoming energy as hope, as possibility. When it's flowing away, you sense its leaving as a departure, a loss," he said.

"I can see that." I moved to the middle of the bridge so I could look in both directions, the future flowing toward us, the past moving away. "I can definitely see that."

So that's where I am after a year. Standing in the middle of the bridge, seeing the relentlessness of the future and the fading of the past. It's time to move forward, take a ride on the river of life. Right?

Goodbye, Mom.

I love you so much.

Sarah

Floyd, VA 2:42

Part Two

Gabriel

Chapter 16   Homecoming

August 26

"If not for bad luck, we'd have no luck at all," Mama Beth would say when things went wrong, like when a newborn calf died, or the corn seed got washed out and we had to replant. I wonder what she would think about the world just coming to a stop the way it did. I tried calling her, sent her twenty texts. Futile efforts.

That was a year ago. One year and one day.

I knew they would be gone. That's not why I came here. I came to Floyd because it's the only place I could imagine where I could find peace. Even if it means living alone.

I can't believe I made it. I am not in Blacksburg anymore, where so many things are ruined, and no place is safe. Around here, weeds, fallen trees and wrecked vehicles make Floyd look pretty ramshackle, and I've seen a few smashed car windows and glass doors, but the town is intact. Maybe because it's so far from anywhere, hidden in the mountains. Why come here for the end of the world, unless you have a reason?

I think the town is deserted, but there are still plenty of summer birds around, chattery birds that like to talk and issue warnings to stay away from their nests, and I use them as my guides. Since my arrival I've spent a few sessions sitting quietly, watching and listening for signs of disturbance, waiting for the birds to react to another human, or another animal. So far, they are only reacting to me.

The biting flies were worse in Blacksburg, but there are plenty of them here, too. They are not as bad as last year, but you still want to have a head net ready in case you get discovered by a swarm. They are out for blood.

Wonder of wonders, the drug store in Floyd is semi-intact. In the 'Burg those were the last places you wanted to go, they got looted first, and the dollar stores and supermarkets were hardly worth the risk of being shot at or beaten. Granted, the drugstore in Floyd is half empty, with bare shelves in the pharmacy area, but it had insect repellant and the things I needed to doctor my eye. I hope.

About my eye. My injury occurred in Riner, near the high school. Someone didn't like the looks of me walking down the road and shot at me, or maybe over my head, I don't know. I jumped into the ditch and lost my footing and my head hit a rock. My right eye hit a rock. I got up fast and hurried on, and while I didn't get killed, it bled like crazy, and half of my face looks like hamburger meat. I cleaned it up with a kit from the drugstore, and now I'm wearing an eye patch, like a pirate. It's a good reason to lay low for a while.

August 27
Brief Report #1
When I arrived, I thought the town was empty of life, but now I'm sure there are other humans in the area. Or were. I have found two houses that show evidence of recent habitation: trash piles and rumpled beds, and rain barrels full of water. One house has a small vegetable

garden with ripe tomatoes, covered with bird netting. I ate three, put more in my pockets. Nothing like summer ripe tomatoes. Someone will be coming to get them soon.

I have not seen evidence of recent deaths. All the corpses are shrunken old ones, mostly covered with sheets or blankets. A few have been moved, but not many. The vehicles in the road have skeletons for drivers.

I'm staying at the other recently lived-in house because it has a good view of the main road through town. Whoever was living here moved on for a reason, which I guess was security. They needed more protection from strangers passing through, strangers like me.

Brief Report #2

I didn't think there would be anyone alive at the farm where I grew up, but you have to check into these things, lay them to rest. The weather was good, so I rode up there on a nice fat-tire bike I found, just to be sure.

There were no bodies in the house and the RV was gone, so I hope Mama Beth and Randall were off fishing somewhere when it happened, maybe down at Philpott Lake. I didn't stay at the house long. Being there was depressing with the grass overgrown and the lumps of dead black angus in the fields. And the world's best foster parents were not in the kitchen, waiting for me to get home for dinner. I got my hunting rifle from the gun cabinet, secured it for transport, and got out of there.

With no houses around, it felt safe on the Parkway. There was plenty of dry pavement without much debris, so I cruised for a while, feeling almost happy. I found myself whistling. I don't whistle unless I'm happy.

I stopped at the big outcropping of white rocks, which

everyone says have magical powers. I've been climbing those rocks since I was twelve, I know the cracks and crannies. I sensed no changes, no shifts. They still felt warm and oddly magnetic, as they always have. It felt good to check in with them.

August 29

It hasn't rained in several days and it's getting really hot, and though it cools down some at night, I could really use some AC, or at least a fan. I can't sleep inside because it's hot, can't sleep outside because of the bugs. It's a five on the misery scale.

In practical matters, the lack of water is creating a stressful situation. The creek that runs behind town is fine for bathing, but I don't think I should drink the water without boiling it first. There is not much bottled water around, and what there is has been sitting for a year, so it's probably loaded with microplastics. The water in the rain barrels at the tomato house is so scummy that I've been giving it to the plants.

It's about as bad as it was in Blacksburg. There we filtered collected rainwater through old tee shirts, boiled water from the stream, and hauled water from a pond for flushing. Water hauling was constant, often done at night. We thought about water all the time. Then flushing became an issue. You can still flush here in Floyd provided you have water you can pour into the toilet tank, but it's a long hike to the creek to get water.

From the sizes of the burn piles and trash heaps I'm seeing as I explore the neighborhoods, I think the town was occupied post-apocalypse for a while, weeks or even months. Lots of burned tin cans. Someone likes

Budweiser.

Medical Status:

The bright midday sun makes my eye burn and run, even with a patch on it, and it's too hot to be out doing much anyway. I found a shady place by the creek and took a folding chair down there to hang out. It's a good place to listen to the birds. Closest I can come to telehealth. At least it's free.

August 31

Big news, mega news, magnificent news. There are women, American women! Yes, acknowledged, I was around a good woman for a year in Blacksburg, a married woman who cooked for me and smiled at me in caring ways, but Mai only spoke Chinese, as in fast, rapid-fire Chinese. I understood what she meant, but not what she said.

The women here are my people, and it sounds so beautiful to hear gentle conversation in my own language! Their voices sounded like music, like birdsong, like home. One of them might be local, with a mountain twist to her words. I think her name is Sarah.

Watching from my perch on the deck, I saw them cross the back parking lots between the Exxon station (pause, look around), the propane place (pause, look around), and then scurry through the back door of the Methodist church, closing it behind them.

I quickly ran down the hill and plastered myself against the shady wall of the church, listening. The voices became more distinct as I crept closer to a partially opened window. Two women, talking about food and gardens and housework while they did something with their hands. They were planning to go pick apples. Their voices sounded so beautiful, I wanted to cry.

I stayed hidden until they left, then watched them leave by way of a narrow road I have yet to investigate. They lugged heavy backpacks. I don't think they carried guns.

September 1

Early this morning, before it got hot and the sun got too bright for my eye, I explored a road that led uphill, toward the high school. The edges of the road and sidewalk were less overgrown than most, as if the grass and weeds had been trimmed or mowed back in the summer. Shazam! At the top of the hill, I hit gold, a small house with a vegetable garden, rain barrels, and fresh spring water dripping into a small pond.

Too good to be true. Must be a trick. That's how it happens in video games, there are hidden traps everywhere, snares and bullets and poisons. No alarms went off when I opened the pink flamingo curtain around the outdoor shower, or when I picked up the bar of soap. It was dried and cracked, but it still smelled of coconut and spice. There were two hanging solar shower bags, ready to fill and use.

First things first. I gathered fresh spring water and filled the shower bags so they could start warming up. Finally, my body, my hair and my eye got the deep cleaning they needed.

September 2

My eye may be destined to survive. I got a decent night's sleep despite the heat, and this morning when I awoke, a giant sleep deposit had accumulated in my eye, complete with a chunk of grit. I must have rinsed it loose in yesterday's shower. I'm hoping it was the troublemaker, battering my retina every time I blinked. The eye is still sensitive, so I'm laying low on this too-bright, too-sunny day, treating it with my last bottle of fancy eye drops from the drugstore. Later on, I may explore some nearby houses for clothes and food. I could do with a good pair of cargo pants with a lot of pockets.

September 3

I gave up watching for the women late in the morning. It was getting steamy by then, not good working conditions for hauling food. I knew that's what they were doing. Last evening when the light was low, I explored the rooms in the back of the Methodist church and found two stashes of food. One was heavy canned goods, but in another room there were plastic storage bins filled with bags of flour and sugar that had been double wrapped in plastic. The food was prepared for long-term storage, safe from bugs. Eventually they would come to get it.

After a lunch of beans and franks with garden tomatoes, I set out to do some surveillance. I started with a stakeout of the downtown intersection, home to the only traffic light in town, though now there's no traffic and no light.

I thought, in error, that the courthouse would be an excellent observation point. Getting in wasn't a problem, the doors were unlocked, and I was met by a rush of cool air, captured inside by lots of old stone and wood. And a smell I couldn't place. I wandered into what was supposed to be a clerk's office, but the desks were huge, with leather chairs near the big windows that looked out on what used to be the courthouse lawn. Now it's thick with weeds and wildflowers.

Then it hit me, the memory of going with Mama Beth to see the judge at the courthouse. The hearing was not about me, it was about my foster sister, Alicia, a little blonde girl who lived with us for almost a year. I really, really liked Alicia, a year younger than me. The hearing wasn't in a courtroom like on TV. It was in the judge's office, which back then was this office. While the social worker, Mama Beth and I waited outside, Alicia went through a big wood door to talk to the judge. When she came out, she was crying.

Mama Beth sent us outside to wait on the front steps while she talked to the social worker.

"He didn't hurt you, did he?" I asked.

"No," she sniffed. "Just made me talk about stuff. Answer questions." She tried to smile. "No big deal."

A week later she was sent to live with an aunt in Missouri. I never saw her again, no calls, no letters. Welcome to foster care. It comes with baggage.

I decided that hanging out in the old judge's office was not good for my mental health. Before leaving, I looked in the drawers of the biggest desk and found the usual things, paper clips, rubber bands, extra pens and lip balm, and wonder of wonders, an unopened bottle of Visine. In the other desk I looked past the pistol in the second drawer to the real treasures, a trio of Dr. Pepper minis.

I left through a side door, listened for unusual bird sounds, and heard only a few robins and crows. I ran quickly to the two-story real estate office across the street, where I thought I'd find a county map. If the women and (presumably) other people who once occupied the town didn't come back soon, I would need to find them.

Chapter 17   Destiny

September 4

Newly dead bodies are hideous, smelly and slimy, but once they've been worked by insects and dried for a year, they're not so bad. They're more like piles of bones covered with patches of rawhide, but you still don't want to look too close. You don't want to see the hair, or the teeth, or the hands. It's best to cover them up, or to keep moving.

In checking houses for food and propane, I have discovered a correlation between houses marked with a chalked red X, and the presence of bodies inside. There is still plenty of food in the houses with bodies, even coffee and tuna. In comparison, houses marked with a green check mark have no bodies, but the kitchens have been cleaned out.

I must conclude that the food gatherers who came before me did not like encountering the dead. Nobody does. I suspect the gleaners were the women, moving food to the Methodist church. Furthermore, the markings on the houses indicate some level of communication between multiple people. How many survivors are there? Enough to occupy three houses? Where are they now?

I feel like I am living in a video game.

The maps I got at the real estate office helped me re-learn the names of roads in this part of the county that I'd almost forgotten, but they don't have the details I need to find a place that can accommodate a small community. Maybe it's a farm, or a group home, or a big family complex. I went back to the real estate office to look for more maps and pick up the guide to local farms I saw on one of the desks. The birds seemed quieter than usual, as if they were expecting something.

The air smells nasty inside the real estate office from the two bodies by the front windows, and the whole building is getting moldy, like everything else. Books, shoes, paper, they've all gone musty. I went upstairs to the private offices and looked out the windows at the quiet streets, then opened two windows that were not painted shut. Ah, fresh air. Ventilation improved even more when I opened a door to an old balcony. I settled in a leather chair to study maps and property brochures.

Voices carry, especially when you're not used to hearing them. I heard the bickering people coming over the hill behind the courthouse and crouched by the window to listen. A man, a woman, and an excited teenage girl, arguing. They stopped in the middle of the intersection. The woman, lean and wiry, wore a baseball cap and tight jeans. She held her hand over her eyes, looking around for signs of life.

"I thought there would be people here," she said, sounding disappointed.

"What does it matter? I'm home!" the girl exclaimed, raising her arms in delight. Her voice was squealy with youth, and she bounced on her toes, excited. She was oddly dressed in a baggy brown dress over purple leather elf boots. Her hair was a tangled mess, spilling over a small backpack.

The man was scary, and not just because of his big beard and belly. He carried a small semi-automatic rifle strapped against his back, and a pistol dangled from his belt. "Desi, honey, you're still a kid. We can't leave you here alone. No way," he said.

"You promised!" She stamped her foot. "I know my way around, this is my place. I can take care of myself."

He put his hand on the pistol. "Pipe down. You're gonna get us killed," he barked.

"I wish."

"Watch your mouth." He tensed up and pulled back, as if he was ready to hit her, and she froze.

"Don't you two get started," the woman said. "Not today. I can't stand it. I have a headache."

"Then give me the strap."

"No!" the girl yelled. "You can't do that to me, it's not fair!"

With the woman's help, the man tied the girls' hands together in front of her waist. She didn't fight them.

"We can't just abandon you," the woman said.

"You have to! You promised!"

"Shut up and stay here while we go shopping," the man said. "We can't visit Floyd without going to the Country Store." He laughed and put his arm around the woman's shoulders. "Get out the credit cards, honey, let's go have some fun."

I counted to twenty before going down the stairs and out onto the sidewalk. There she was, crying on a bench a half block away, wiping her face with the backs of her bound hands.

"Caw, caw," I called, mimicking a crow. She didn't look up, so I did it again, louder. No response. Was she deaf? I became a quartet of crows, caw-cawing like crazy, as if we were attacking a jay's nest. She saw me, let out a small shriek, and stumbled in my direction as fast as she could. I opened the door to the real estate office, then locked it behind us.

"I need help. Will you help me?" she said. Her face was wet with tears, her nose was running, her eyes were red, and she smelled terrible.

"Depends," I said, untying the strap. "Are those your parents?"

"My mother is dead. She was my only parent," she said, sniffing loudly. I handed her a box of tissues and she looked closely at my face. "What happened to your eye?"

"Accident," I said, leading her to an office in the back of the building, away from the front windows. She kept talking.

"We were traveling together is all. I wanted to come to Floyd, they were headed to Wytheville," she explained while I looked for the best place to hide if the man started shooting. "Then things started getting icky weird with Malcomb, how he talked to me, how he looked at me. I didn't like it, and neither did Marcy. She'll be glad to have me gone."

I opened the back door a crack to better listen for voices, and to get some fresh air. The girl smelled awful, like disgusting awful. "Will Malcomb shoot out the town when he sees you're gone?" I asked.

"I don't think so, but he might shoot some. If Marcy lets him." She blew her nose. "I really do smell bad, don't I? I can tell by your face."

I was relieved to know she was aware of the problem. "Why?" I asked softly.

She took a ragged breath. "To make him leave me alone, to make both of them stop acting like they owned me. The closer we got to Floyd, the more they were watching me all the time, making me stay close. It gave me the creeps. Then one day I got sick from something I ate, throwing up at both ends and all, and some of it got on my clothes. They said I smelled bad, and I did, but they started keeping more distance, not breathing down my neck. So, I decided to just stay dirty. I needed them to make it to Floyd, you know?"

She pulled the sack dress off over her head, wadded it into a ball, and threw it into a closet. Underneath she wore a stained Dollywood tee shirt and calf-length yoga pants. She still smelled bad, but not as bad.

"How old are you?" I asked.

"Sixteen last month," she said, sighing. "Sweet sixteen, gone sour." She blew her nose again and giggled. "How old are you?" I told her I was 23.

The birds outside suddenly went quiet. "Shhh, get behind the desk," I said, closing and locking the door. "It's out of range of the windows." We huddled together in the room's protected corner.

"Desi! Girl, get out here, now! You know we'll find you, so you may as well come on out!" the man yelled.

"Come on, Desi, it's hot, we need to get going," the woman called.

I felt her tense up beside me, ready to call back, but I shook my head and signaled for silence. "Be a gone girl," I whispered. "Disappear."

"Desi! This is not funny. You've crossed the line!" the man yelled.

"No, don't! It's a waste!" the woman pleaded.

A loud gunshot rattled the windows of the old buildings. We both jumped.

"Now get out here," Malcomb demanded. A second shot, followed by the muffled sounds of an argument.

The girl inched closer to me. "It's the pistol," she whispered. "Marcy won't want him to use the bullets. They're running low."

"What about the other gun, the semi?" I asked.

"I'm not sure it's even real," she said.

The voices were moving out of range. I tiptoed upstairs to look and listen through the open upstairs windows. They stood in the intersection, arguing.

"Enough, Malcomb, let's just go," the woman said.

"No, we can smell her out. How do you know she might not be worth a fortune?"

"A fortune of what?" she snorted. "A fortune of heartache if you ask me." She looked at the road signs and turned south on US 221. "It's this way. Let's find some beer, take a break, and then get moving. Let's go home."

"Empty handed." He put the pistol back in its holster and adjusted the tilt of the cowboy hat he'd picked up at the Country Store. Marcy told him to get over it.

I watched them until they were out of sight, then ran downstairs. Desi was standing in the open back door of the office, listening. "They're moving away," she said. "Right?"

"I think so. Should I shadow them, to make sure?"

She smiled. "In case you didn't notice, Malcomb and Marcy argue all the time. They can't not do it, they start early and have little fights all day long, so you always know where they are." We heard raised voices coming from the direction of the Food Lion. "When they drink, the fights get bigger, high drama. We should move to a safer space."

"Agreed," I said. "I know a place."

"One thing," she said, following me to the thrift store where she could get clean clothes. "What's your name? Or should I call you Johnny Depp? That eye patch makes you look like Johnny Depp, when he was the pirate."

I told her my name was Gabe.

"As in Gabriel, God's favored angel?"

"So I've been told."

"Explains a lot. About today. Your rescuing me and all."

Desi remembered the Angels thrift store from when her mother took her there as a kid, and she quickly found two pairs of shoes and an armload of clothes. I helped her carry them to the house with the pink flamingo shower to get cleaned up, rest, and recover. While she took her first warm shower in weeks, I sat sentry on a nearby hillside behind a bush, watching for movement. As close as I could tell, all was quiet on the Floyd front.

September 5
Labor Day

It's Labor Day, the banks and courthouse and post office are closed, today and forever, so let's celebrate the essential work done by everyone! Rest, have a barbecue, maybe go to the lake. Shed the burdens of life for a day.

When part of your job is looking after others, you don't get to do that, which is fine today, because I'm tired of being alone and Desi is good company. Still, one of the reasons I left Blacksburg was to get out from under excessive responsibilities.

At first it was exciting, teaming up with Mai and Chan

to break into the physics library at Tech to research clues to what might have happened. A geomagnetic wave caused by a humongous solar storm? A natural magnetic reversal triggered by the warming of the oceans? Was it natural, or did an outside force throw a switch?

And why are the dinosaurs still here, the birds and the insects, but not the higher animals? How did they survive? Chan says it probably happened once before, forty million years ago.

After months of study, we still didn't know the answer, but we did know how different and difficult life had become, and how much we had lost.

Both professors at Tech, Mai and Chan knew nothing about providing for themselves. As children, they had "aunties" who saw to their every need, and they had a housekeeper in the 'Burg. They didn't know how to cook, clean up, or wash clothes, and food safety was a nightmare. We shared a house for a year and I was on duty 24/7 showing them how to survive. It wore me out. When I couldn't do it anymore, I told them I needed to go home, and I left.

Now I have Desi, or Destiny, as she was named at birth. A new responsibility that scares me, but also pleases me in a fundamental way. It makes me feel alive to be a helper, and she's a good kid. She eats a lot, but she's probably making up for lost time. She also asks a lot of questions.

"Thanks, that was a great dinner," she said last night after finishing her second bowl of creamy noodles with tuna. "How come you're not dead?"

"Wish I knew. I was in a pressure chamber at Tech when it happened. Part of an experiment."

"You were like, being a guinea pig?" she laughed.

"Well, yeah. For extra money," I explained. "I was in graduate school in biology, working as a teaching assistant for Dr. Sharma. He had a friend in entomology who needed help with a mosquito project, and the gig paid well because you had to get inside a sealed glass observation chamber with bloodthirsty mosquitoes. My body gases would be measured and monitored when the mosquitoes started biting an exposed patch on my leg." Desi was glued, said to keep going.

"When I got in the box and Maria the lab technician wired me up with electrodes, it seemed hot and I was feeling a little weird, so I tried to relax and take slow, even breaths. I remember seeing Maria leave the room to go get the mosquitoes. It was scary quiet and stuffy in the booth with no ventilation. Something seemed wrong, but I decided to hang in there.

"A while later I awoke from what felt like a deep, slobbery nap. I clicked open the door, called for Maria, but got no answer. I pulled off the web of electrodes and crawled out of the booth.

"Maria was sprawled on the floor in the next room. No pulse, eyes fixed. Ditto for the three others in the lab, the maintenance guy in the hallway, and the students outside, so many bodies, it was like I'd gone psychotic and entered a nightmare world. I thought maybe they gassed me with something psychedelic at the lab? I did not feel well. I stumbled home, to my apartment, and locked the door."

"Farout," she said. "And then what?" I told her I'd stayed in Blacksburg for a year, and then felt like I needed to come home.

"I've only been here about a week, haven't figured things out yet. You're the first person I've talked to, but I saw and heard two others," I said, changing the subject. "Two women, moving some stored food, but I don't know where they went. I think this was their house."

"Mega cool, I love this house," she said. She got up, gathered our bowls and silverware, and placed them in the empty cooking pot along with a squirt of dishwashing detergent. "I can wash the dishes."

Wonder of wonders, unlike Chan and Mai, Desi knows how to do things. After her shower, she hung the wet towels on the clothesline to dry. She helped carry flush water for the commode. After dinner, she washed and rinsed the dishes outdoors with the last of the day's warm water. When I asked how she learned these skills, she shrugged and said her family camped a lot.

Desi is good at asking questions, not so good at answering them.

When it got dark, she went to sleep in the small bedroom and I settled in on the living room sofa so I could better hear noises in the night. I never heard voices or gunshots, but at one point I woke suddenly, thinking I heard a crash. An object, smashing into something else. I laid still, listening. There was no wind, and the cicadas in the trees were quiet. A distant hoot owl. The thump of a large moth against the window screen. I got up and looked out into the darkness, listening for movement. Nothing. Went outside and peed in the yard. Quiet. Maybe it was a dream, or I was back in the video game.

Chapter 18   Storm Warning

September 6

I was up before light to run down to the first house I stayed in to get my backpack and rifle. It was a successful, if disturbing, mission. Near the Subway, a small car has been bashed up like a tin can, and covers have been pulled off of several corpses. The front doors of the drugstore are totally shattered. This all happened within the last 24 hours, maybe when I was holed up downtown? Or is that what I heard last night? There also are metal shopping carts strewn about, so the marauders came from the direction of the grocery store.

It's weirding me out, because I don't think it's the work of Malcomb and Marcy. It's not their style. Desi agrees.

"Those people sought to destroy. Marcy won't allow that. She likes things nice."

"Now we know why the original Floyd survivors left. It's not safe," I said. I told her we needed to get out of town, pronto, and to pack her things into the backpack I'd found in the closet. "Aye aye, captain," she said, making a salute.

"We can grab breakfast on the road, but forget about Hardees. They hit it, too," I said.

"No sausage biscuits? I'm dying," she teased, clutching her throat.

My pack wasn't full, so I filled it with food, bottles of water, and the remaining first aid supplies for my eye. It is less painful but still sensitive. I am down to my last three disposable eye patches.

"Goodbye, beautiful house," Desi said, blowing a kiss to the flamingos as we crept away into the misty morning. She seems to have a special appreciation for comfortable housing and hot showers.

"Where are we going?" she asked, keeping her voice low. I said I didn't know.

We crossed a small neighborhood diagonally by jogging between houses, waiting a minute, and then crossing another yard. I was looking for one of two roads I'd seen on the maps that the women might have used to leave town. The first one we found was Brambleberry. Desi said we should try it because she used to know people who lived there, near a dairy farm. The road was blocked by a fallen oak tree, which I felt was a good omen. You had to want to go down that road bad enough to climb over the tree.

We then slogged up a curving hill, picking our steps among fallen branches. Tall grasses crowded the edges of the road and grew around the vehicles left parked in yards. After a year gone wild, pastures and lawns have become lush fields that ripple in the wind.

I find them quite beautiful, and so do the birds, singing their songs perched on power lines and fence posts. "Because of the tall grass, there are birds here that didn't used to be, meadowlarks and field sparrows," I said as we walked. "Amazing how fast they caught on."

Desi asked if I had always been a bird nerd, and I said yes. Just then a red-tailed hawk whistled overhead, and I whistled back.

"Impressive!" she said, pretending to clap her hands. I told her that some were easier than others.

We had gone nearly a mile, up and down a second big

hill, without seeing signs of life, or of road use by others. I was glad we didn't bring bikes, because the roads were a mess of limbs, windblown sheet metal and shingles with nails and screws attached, and oil and antifreeze leaking from disabled vehicles with corpse drivers. I was starting to worry that we were on the wrong road, but whatever. We were moving away from town, that was the main thing.

Next problem. The sky to the south was getting darker by the minute, and the clouds were moving in excited layers, wispy gray bottoms under dark billowing swirls higher up. We were about to get smacked by a monster of a thunderstorm.

"It's going to storm. We should find a house and hole up," I said.

"Want me to find one? I know the best ones, it's one of my specialties."

"Tell me about it," I said.

She fluffed her hair to consider her answer. "You don't want the big houses, they're no good, leaky and cold. Instead, you want a sturdy, simple house that's been lived in by regular people. Look for no cars in the driveway, like they've gone to work. The right house has food and propane, and it's clean inside. The best ones have a covered porch or deck with a gas grill."

Our search was slowed by a logging truck wedged across the road, but it didn't take us long to find a well-worn pathway around it. At last, a sign of human presence. There was another surprise on the other side of the truck, two grocery carts parked side by side, as if they had been put there.

"Somebody's been here," Desi said. A deep rumble of

thunder sent us trotting down the road, but she barely slowed as we passed three houses, none to her liking. "That one," she said, pointing up the hill to a small frame house with flowers blooming among the front yard weeds, dahlias and zinnias that had planted themselves. The front door was locked, but there was a key under the welcome mat.

"Good old Floyd," she said, letting us in. The air smelled acceptable and there were no dead bugs in the windows, but I checked the house for bodies anyway. It was clean except for the shrunken corpse of a small dog who had been curled up on the bed in the master bedroom. I wrapped it in the bedspread and took it outside.

"Kitchen's good," Desi said, after looking through the pantry. She leaned into a lower cabinet, pulling out big cooking pots. "We should put these out to catch rain," she said.

That's what I mean about Desi knowing how to do things.

I took the pots to the backyard, added a couple of buckets to the collection, and set a wheelbarrow to catch water from a broken downspout. The first drops were big ones that made quarter-size splatters on my head as I ran inside, and then there was a crack of lightning and a boom of thunder that shook the ground. I was never so glad to be inside a house.

The furniture in the den was arranged in the usual way, with a sofa against the long wall and a pair of recliners facing the TV. The coffee table was clear except for a few issues of Country Living and Birds & Blooms magazines and the latest Virginia Farm Bureau newsletter.

"Patrick and Leslie Nunley," I read aloud from the address label. "Thank you for your timely hospitality." An immediate rumble of thunder felt like an acknowledgement and made me think of Mama Beth. I thought she would like Mr. and Mrs. Nunley, who, from the looks of photos on the wall, had raised their children in this house.

Desi emerged from the kitchen carrying two bottles of Frappuccino and a box of breakfast bars, which she spread out on the table. "A good way to start the day, don't you think?" She plopped down on the sofa and opened her coffee. "Almond butter, peanut butter, or honey oat?"

We both chose almond butter, which went great with the rich, sweet coffee. It all felt quite cozy, being safe and dry and in good company while the rain poured outside. I hoped I wouldn't ruin it with my Big Question, but I asked it anyway.

"So, Desi. How come you're still alive?"

She laughed and reached for a second breakfast bar. "I don't know. Because Jesus loves me?"

"Well, there's that…"

"No, I'll tell you. Here's the deal. I've had a lot of time to think about it." She took a sip of coffee. "There's this place, down in Patrick County, we called it Wonderland. It's like a really, really marginal commune without much going on, but my mom had a thing for Leonardo, this old dude who like owned the place or something. Leo had a real house, not much but it was a house. Everyone else at Wonderland lived in old campers, and one old lady lived in a bus. But there were never more than a few people there except for Leo, because not hardly anybody wants to live that plain. Like, outhouse plain. When Mom and I didn't have anywhere else to go, we went there."

"Leo and your mom had a long-term relationship?" I asked gently.

She shrugged. "Yeah, I guess. Mom wasn't good with relationships, she had focusing issues, but Leo got her, had her back, and he was always kind. He helped get us through some rough times."

"Sounds like it," I said. She took another slug of coffee and continued her story.

"I didn't mind going down there when I was a kid, it was kind of like camping, but as I got older I liked it less and less, especially after my only friend there, Matt, moved away to live with his grandparents. Mom knew I was unhappy, and bored, as in b-o-r-e-d, and she always got tired of Leo after a while anyway, which is why we were getting ready to move back to Floyd. We had friends here, you know? On the day it happened, she told me to go find something to do while she talked with Leo about it.

"It was hot, so I took a book to the coolest place in Wonderland, a root cellar made from a buried VW bus. It was made by some paranoid person who later left the commune, and it was supposed to be a fallout shelter, for protection from radiation, but it morphed into a root cellar. We called it the Yellow Submarine because it was painted yellow inside. I liked it down there. To get in, you opened the hatch and went down a small ladder. There was a bench against one wall with canned goods stored under it and a red cushion on top, just wide enough for stretching out. It was made of red velvet, like it came from a church.

"That day, to keep from losing the cool air, I closed the hatch behind me, and took two flashlights for reading lights. I was moving along in my book, The Witch of Blackbird Pond, when everything went dark. As in very, very dark. The Yellow Submarine had vents, but they had been closed off to keep out the mice, so there was no light coming in. I decided to wait and give my eyes a chance to adjust to the dark, but I think I fell asleep or something. It took me a while to figure out where I was, find the pinpricks of light coming from the hatch door. I pushed it open and climbed out, and noticed how quiet it was."

I shook my head. "It was terrifying," I said.

"I know," she agreed. Outside, there was a flash of lightning, the crack of a splitting tree, and a boom of thunder. Desi barely paused, fueled by sugar and caffeine. "And it only got worse. I found Mom and Leo, leaning against each other on the couch in his house. I shook her, tried to wake her up, but her eyes looked funny and she felt cold. She wouldn't answer me. Leo was a lump.

"By this time I was hysterical, crying and screaming, and none of the four Wonderland dogs came out to follow me as I ran down the road to the nearest real house to call 911. I guess I thought everyone at Wonderland had been electrocuted or something, and the EMTs could bring them back. But the people in the brick house were dead, too, there was no dial tone on their kitchen phone, and their cell phones wouldn't turn on. Nothing would turn on. It was awful. I was so scared." She started crying a little.

"I know," I said, deciding it was time to lighten up. "But we survived. And you know what?"

"What?" she sniffed.

"We're going to keep surviving. We're going to be okay."

She forced a small smile. "If you say so."

I never thought my foster care experiences would be helpful to me later in life. I thought being an unwanted child would always be a tarnish on my imperfect evolution, a source of shame, but I was wrong. Those trials and tribulations prepared the way for me to look after Desi. My new foster sister.

September 7

The rain continued all day and night, and the dim light made it hard to look for emergency supplies like candles, lanterns, and a propane stove. There were none in the usual places in the kitchen or laundry room, where I noticed the door to the breaker box was open. Furthermore, the switches had been turned off, all showing red squares. How did that happen? The Nunleys sure didn't do it. The freezer reeks of rotten food.

I ran out to the garage during a break in the rain and found a couple of oil lamps on a high shelf, and next to them a box of matches and a butane fireplace lighter. Huge score! The lamps will provide light at night, until we do better.

I definitely get the feeling that the garage and house have been lightly pilfered for supplies. Not having candles or matches in the kitchen is simply not Nunley-like. There is still good canned and packaged food in the kitchen, but no peanut butter.

"Stale Fritos are better than no Fritos at all," Desi said when I gave her the lone bag of chips. She's right. They go great with canned beans.

I filtered some rainwater through one of our host's old tee shirts and it passed the taste test, so for now we have water for drinking and cooking. Thank you, Mr. Nunley. I only wish your shoes were bigger. You had small feet.

Desi hums. Just like I tend to whistle, she hums little tunes when she is focused on a task. After the rain tapered off, she found a rake and broom and swept a year's worth of leaves and pine straw from the back deck, humming the old Beatles tune, "Here Comes the Sun." After dinner, it was "Man of Constant Sorrow" while she washed the dishes.

"Do you sing?" I finally asked her. Her neck blushed red and she made a small smile.

"Not around other people," she said. "Social anxiety. But I can play the harmonica, and a little banjo."

"Do you have one, a harmonica? Because…"

"No, I lost it," she interrupted. "It was so stupid, I just left it in a house somewhere, like months ago."

I cleared my throat. "Because there's one here, in the top drawer under the TV. I saw it today."

"What? You're kidding me."

I went inside, got the gray case with the harmonica inside, and handed it to her.

She squealed and opened the case. "Jumping crocodiles, it's a Hohner Special 20! This is unbelievable, I've always wanted one of these," she said, holding it in both hands. "These things cost fifty bucks!"

"Happy birthday," I said.

"Oh, Gabe, this is so great. I've missed my old harp so much. Look, I don't think it's hardly been played," she said, showing me the like-new instrument. She blew a few preliminary notes. "Man, this baby is so smooth. Give me some time to limber up, then I'll play you something."

She took the harmonica out into the road in the golden evening light and walked around playing short pieces of tunes, bending a few blues riffs, and then stopping to think. When she started playing again, I recognized the first verse of Your Cheating Heart, but she was having trouble with the high bridge. I started whistling along, remembering the song. Then she switched to Danny Boy, such a wonderful tune. I could tell she knew it well. After a while, she joined me on the back deck.

"I love this thing, Gabe, I really do, but I'm nervous. I'm not ready to play."

"That's okay, but I heard you. It sounded good."

"Not good enough."

"Then let's do a duet. I whistle, you play. Here, I'll start." Hoping I had the right key, I started whistling Danny Boy. She quickly joined in, and we both gave it our best and it sounded beautiful. We made real music, and we both had tears in our eyes at the end.

But it wasn't the end. After a few minutes of silence, staring into the looming darkness, we heard Danny Boy echoing through the trees. It was being played on a trumpet. We looked at each other, eyes wide.

"The other people, they're here," she whispered.

"I know," I said. "And they know we're here, too."

Chapter 19   Cross Examination

September 8

We were both up early, getting ready to receive visitors. The weather turned cool after the rain, so we raided the drawers and closets for warmer clothes. Desi found a blue hoodie with Virginia Beach on the front. Mine said Shenandoah National Park. I liked that the Nunleys were into regional tourism.

"They probably know exactly where we are," Desi said, opening a drawer, unfolding a baggy cotton sweater, and then giving it a sniff. "Last night I was out parading around in the street with my harp, and you can't walk ten feet without whistling."

"Is it that bad?" I asked.

She said she liked my whistling, that it made her feel safe. "Like a good dog who barks, like that," she said. "And we totally killed that song," she added.

Wonder of wonders, our Danny Boy duet did sound awesome. I told her we should form an act, Gabe and Desi.

"Make that Desi and Gabe, and you have a deal," she said.

Heating water on a gas grill is a waste of propane, which we never would have done in Blacksburg, but this is now. Breakfast was hot instant oatmeal, one cup for me, two for Desi. We took our time enjoying the warm food.

"Are you scared?" I asked her.

"Not too much. How about you?"

"More like nervous. Excited. How does my eye look? I think it looks better."

She peered closely at my face. "Fresh eye patch is good. The scabby places are smaller." She hesitated before continuing. "And this is none of my business, it's your face, but you look great with a fresh shave. It was a good move. Gabe, you have a dimple! Right here." She pointed to her cheek.

"Thanks," I said. Shaving in the semi-dark was a pain, but her compliment made me feel less disfigured by my bad eye.

The sound of a trumpet playing Reveille got our attention. I went out on the front porch to await our visitors' arrival while Desi watched from inside.

The two men and woman who ambled over the hill did not seem to be on a mission to kill or take prisoners. They were talking and laughing, and the taller man gave the woman a quick rump bump. She smiled and ran her hand through her short blonde hair. Then they saw me.

"Ahoy, there," the tall man called, waving his hand over his head. "We come unarmed. Please put down your weapons."

"I am unarmed," I said, showing my hands.

The younger man, lean and sharp-featured, and who looked vaguely familiar, stepped forward. "Are you friend or foe, and where is the other one?"

"I am a friend, and she is in the house."

The three of them whispered among themselves. "And what is your business here?" the questioner continued. His thick, dark hair and angular build set him apart in my memory, but I couldn't place where.

"A homecoming. I was in Blacksburg when it happened, but I used to live here, I grew up here."

"Is that so? Then you can tell me the mascot of the high school."

"Buffaloes."

"And the team colors."

"Black and gold."

"Are you an android?" The question caught me by surprise, and I may have laughed a little bit.

"I don't think so."

"The eye patch. It's not a transmitter?" One dark eyebrow was stiffly arched.

"No. I had an accident."

More whispering. The taller man, a bit older, in his forties, folded his arms across his chest and took over. He had an amused smile on his face as he stiffened his shoulders. "Are you a heretic, then? Or a spy?"

"Probably," I said, playing along.

"And the child. Is she a witch?"

"I don't think so," Desi said, stepping out through the storm door. "I hope not, but it's too soon to tell. Witches get more power as they get older." In the oversized hoodie, with her hair pulled back in a tight ponytail, she did not look like a witch. She looked like a kid.

"Ah, so I've heard." The tall man was clearly charmed by lovely Desi, awash in the innocent bloom of youth. "As told in the oldest of stories."

"You guys lay off. I'm Clare, this is Wynn, and this is Claude," the woman said.

"You live up here?" Desi asked.

"Yes, and there are a few others. Six in all." She looked carefully at Desi, then at me, trying to figure us out. Desi saw it, too.

"He saved me from some bad people a few days ago, in town. Like, they were beyond terrible, and Gabe helped me get away. Now we're kind of a brother-sister act. We're okay," she said.

I nodded my head in agreement. "That's about the size of it," I said.

Clare seemed satisfied. "Did you guys come looking for us?" she asked.

I told them how I'd seen her and another woman at the Methodist church, and confessed to following them part of the way out of town. "Then, when we needed to move out fast, and with Desi to think of, yes, we came looking for you."

"We knew you existed because of the pink flamingos," Desi said, grinning. "Was that your house? We stayed there. It was great."

"Yes, it was a great house!" Clare said. "We called it the garden house because it came with a little garden. And it had water! You still had to carry it, but water is water. Sarah and I lived there half of the summer."

"Ahem," Wynn said. "Some of this goes in the Official Record, so I think it may be a good time to adjourn to the office." He turned to me and Desi. "It's a short walk, if you're willing."

"Strictly standard procedure," Claude said, winking.

As we walked together up the hill, Clare said that we were staying at the dahlia house, where they had gathered flowers for a funeral a few weeks before.

"Somebody died?" Desi asked.

"Yes. Gina died. She was sick before, and then got sicker, and we took good care of her, but then she died."

"Sorry for your loss," I said, and Desi added her "me, too."

We arrived at a large ranch house to which additions had been made, a garage, and a sunroom, where we were invited to sit for the first interview, as Wynn called it.

It was clear that we were expected company. A selection of small cans of fizzy drinks were set out in a broad bowl. Ginger ale, root beer, a couple of colas. Milano cookies on a plate.

"I forgot to ask if anyone is allergic to cats. I have a cat. He's hiding now, but he may come out," Wynn said, getting settled behind a small desk.

Desi squealed. "You have a cat, like a real cat?"

"Yes," he said. "Sit there on the love seat, and he will find you when he's ready. His name is Prince. He's a rescue, we found him a few weeks ago. He hears everything, and he doesn't like loud noises." Desi did as she was told, and I took a seat closer to Wynn. Claude and Clare each grabbed a soda and a cookie and kicked back in wicker chairs.

"Sarah will be here in a little while," Clare said. "She had first shower, didn't want to lose her place in line."

Wynn began by filling out basic bio sheets on each of us. Names, ages, places of birth. I gave my legal name and said I was born in Roanoke, my best guess. Destiny Elizabeth Snell was born in Pittsburg, where her mother was from.

Next, we were asked to explain how we came to be in Floyd, the details of our arrival. I told him I kept a journal, had a thing about keeping records, so I could get back with him on the actual dates, but gave him a fast overview of the last couple of weeks.

"Excellent, this is all just excellent," Wynn kept saying. He can write really fast.

"Is there a bathroom I can use?" Desi asked, directing her question to Clare.

"Sure, I'll show you." They disappeared down the dim hallway while the questioning continued.

Claude leaned forward and lowered his voice. "Good. While they're gone, can I ask you if the child has been treated acceptably? Are there traumas of which we should be aware?" he asked.

I appreciated the question. "Not that I know of. She had an unusual upbringing, hippie mom, plenty of love but not a lot of stability. On the road she made some narrow escapes, but she got away. She thought she would find safety in Floyd. That's about all I know."

We heard soft voices coming from the back of the house.

"They found Prince," Wynn said, leaning to either side to stretch his back. "Please help yourself to another soda. Sarah will be here shortly, perhaps bearing lunch?"

"Yes, I think so," Claude agreed. "Possibly not potatoes, if we're lucky."

"What's wrong with potatoes?" I asked. "I like potatoes." They both started laughing.

"We grew a ton of potatoes this summer at a farm we use. And another ton of sweet potatoes," Wynn said. "Lately we've been spending all our time digging, hauling and storing potatoes. And eating the culls."

"Stick around and we'll put you to work," Claude said. I said that was fine by me.

A woman I took to be Sarah pushed through the back door carrying two loaded cloth grocery bags, and Wynn jumped up to help her. They exchanged a few quiet words, and their low voices continued as they went into the kitchen. A moment later, Sarah walked into the sunroom. I instinctively stood up.

"Hi, I'm Sarah Margolis," she said, extending her hand.

"Gabe Shaw, also known as Johnny Depp."

"I can see that," she said, smiling. Her firm, confident handshake made me wonder if she was in sales before the world stopped. I think she's in her late twenties, a few years older than me, and extremely fit with shiny brown hair, still slightly damp, that smelled of fruity shampoo. She sat down in Wynn's chair. "Until Wynn gets back from Planet Cat to ask you more questions, you can ask me and Claude stuff you want to know. As long as it's not too personal." She reached for a cookie.

"Clare said there were six of you. Wynn lives here, and everyone else lives nearby?" I asked, trying not to sound nosy.

"Yes, exactly. This used to be my house, I mean I used it last winter, but then I moved and rented it to Wynn and Prince for a nickel," Sarah said, trying to sound serious.

"And the rest of us do live elsewhere, not far but it is a pretty good hike," Claude added.

"Is it, like a farm?"

"Not really," Sarah said. "It used to be a horse farm, but then the horses died. We grow food at another farm, Morning Dew. Ever heard of it? It was an organic vegetable farm." I shook my head.

"I've been gone a while, and my parents were more into raising black angus," I said.

"Wasn't everybody." She turned in her chair and pointed to the backyard. "For surviving an Armageddon, this house came with everything. A wood stove and lots of wood, and there's a hand water pump, one yard over. Even chickens. I knew the house, I babysat here when I was a teenager, so this is where I dug in for winter." she explained. "After Wynn moved in, he made some improvements, like the solar shower outside." She pointed to a brown shower curtain partially hidden behind some shrubs.

"You were alone last winter?"

"Yeah, for a few months. Me and the chickens. Then I met Buddy, and Wynn. Rob, Clare and Claude came later." The last low clouds of the morning cleared, with the sun shining for the first time in three days.

"Ah, well," Claude interrupted, standing and pretending to look at a watch. "I must excuse myself, as it seems to be turning into a solar day."

"At last! Tell Rob and Buddy I'll be down later to catch up on things in the house," Sarah said. "You taking Clare with you?"

"In my fondest dreams," he said, and called her name in a soft voice as he tiptoed down the hallway. A minute later, I saw them walk away together down a footpath that led through the mowed backyard.

"You have solar working?" I asked Sarah.

"Only a little. Do you know anything about it? We need help. We have the well hotwired to a panel that was intended to run radiant floors. It's direct feed, so we have running water, but only when the sun shines," she said.

"Rob and Buddy work on one idea after another trying to get more panels up and running."

"We did the same in Blacksburg. Never made the big breakthrough," I said.

She sighed. "We can always hope." She changed the subject. "Do you have any dietary restrictions?"

"None for me, but you'll have to ask Desi," I said.

"Like Desiree?"

"No. Destiny."

"Whoa. That's big." I told her I thought so, too.

Wynn and Desi returned to the sunroom, a gray striped cat sprawled in Wynn's arms. Desi sat on the love seat and Wynn placed the cat beside her. Prince eyed me suspiciously, and I held out my hand for him to sniff. He started purring loudly, so I think I passed his inspection.

Sarah and Desi introduced themselves, with thumb waves rather than shaking hands.

"Look, I found some Chuck Taylors, and Wynn says I can have them. I can't believe I'm wearing Rebecca Grantham's shoes." Desi stretched out her legs to show off the lavender Converse high tops with white laces.

"Did you know Rebecca?" Sarah asked. "I babysat with her, a long time ago."

Desi smirked. "You could say so. She was not a nice person. A mean girl, at least to me." She reached down and ran her hand over the pristine canvas shoes. "Long story short, I was in school here, in fifth grade, and she invited me to her birthday party, which was at the country club pool. At school she acted like she wanted me to come, but once I got to the party she and her friends treated me like a dog, swam away when I got close. It's like the only reason I was there was to be made fun of."

"That's terrible," Sarah said. "The parents didn't intervene?"

"At first. But Rebecca lied and told them it was a tag game."

Sarah sighed. "I'm so sorry that happened to you. Enjoy the shoes or anything else you want. But you know what they say, the apple doesn't fall far from the tree. One of our fellow survivors, Buddy, says that Rebecca's father was a real jerk."

The four of us had lunch on the patio, which included tuna salad sandwiches made with real bread (wonder of wonders) and real mayonnaise (double wonder of wonders) from an unopened, unexpired jar.

"We have an outdoor wood-fired pizza oven we use to make bread," Sarah explained. "The yeast supply is running low, so Claude is ramping up with sourdough. I'd say it's a good batch."

Desi said it was the best bread she had ever eaten in her life. "I totally want to learn how to make this," she said between bites.

Wynn finished his sandwich and folded his napkin. "Good to know for certain you're not androids. They can't eat tuna," he said.

"It kills them dead," Sarah added. "Sly choice of menu, huh?"

Desi and I looked at each other and started laughing, and we couldn't stop. It was the best joke I'd heard in over a year. Man oh man, have I missed laughing.

"Now for the plan," Wynn said. "We will set you up with food, water, and other necessities and comforts, and will meet with the others later in the day. Tomorrow one of us will return with the group's decision on how they want to proceed."

"We think they will invite you to visit, but we can't really say until everyone votes," Sarah said.

"Are you like a democracy?" Desi asked.

"No, a community. A community of committed survivors," Wynn said. "It's more like a weird club. You'll see."

We were taken to the garage, which no joke is like a bizarre grocery store. Various types of food items are arranged in stacks, some covered with tarps to protect them from light. There are also several bicycles and scooters parked against one wall, and two grocery carts. Wynn pushed one of them in my direction.

"My first few months alone I was in hoarding mode," Sarah said. "There was not much to do but check out houses." She removed a tarp from a box containing packets of instant noodles and rice. "None of this was prepped for long-term storage, so watch for bugs. Take all you want, of anything. We do have a limit on oil, one bottle per customer."

"This is a very impressive stash," I said, eyeing a box of ramen noodles.

"Do you have any Goldfish crackers?" Desi asked. "Or Lucky Charms?"

"All things are possible," Wynn said, abandoning the bikes to fetch a plastic snap-top bin from a shoulder high shelf. "We had an ant invasion. I threw a bunch of sugary stuff in here," he said, opening the lid. The contents looked like a sample shelf of kids' cereals, some in cups, some in boxes, some as bars. The corporations sure know how to shovel sugar at breakfast.

"Jumping bananas!" Desi said. "You have Cinnamon Toast Crunch! And Cocoa Pebbles!"

"Wait a minute, the Cocoa Pebbles are mine," Sarah said, grabbing the box.

Wynn hung back in the corner, grinning. "And you, Gabe, what will you have?"

I looked in the bin. "Has to be Honey Nut Cheerios," I said, picking up a big box. "Come to Papa."

We left with a grocery cart full of water jugs, canned meat and boxed carbs, a bottle of corn oil, and a single burner Coleman stove with two bottles of propane. Best of all: a half loaf of bread, half jar of mayo, and a bag of fresh potatoes, tomatoes, peppers and squash. We were set.

The road was covered with debris in the final stretch to our house, so Desi and I had to clear a lane for the loaded cart. After we made it to the house with our loot, Desi got the broom and went back out to finish the cleanup. She was motivated big-time, because Wynn said she could have a scooter and bike once the road was safe, provided she wore a helmet. He says that the road from his place to the main nest of survivors is well-maintained asphalt, but everyone is still expected to wear a helmet when on wheels. "We are not equipped to respond to traumatic brain injuries," he warned.

Wynn seems to be in control of a lot of things, like records, maps, and matters at the farm where they've been growing food. I got a quick glimpse at a complicated map in which several locations were labeled as depots, accompanied by letter codes. Is he coordinating a large fail-safe effort for survival supplies, or is he crazy? He seems to have Sarah's respect, so I don't think he's nuts.

I don't know what to make of Claude, who seems kind of goofy, but I pick up a quiet, noble vibe from Clare.

On one level I am relieved to have other humans in Desi's orbit, ready to provide care and support, but it feels threatening, too, like a leaving could be coming. Because of prior life programming, this is a familiar loop for my mind to follow, a persistent worry, a certainty of doom. You start caring about someone, you become important to each other, and then they leave.

It's also possible that Desi is indeed a witch, because sometimes she can read my mind. "Gabe, whatever happens, we should stick together," she said while she peeled and diced potatoes. "It's the best now for us." I asked her what that was, the best now. "You know, you have future, like tomorrow and beyond and all that, and you have now. I am totally into this now." She started giggling and reached for an onion to chop. "Can you tell my mom was on the moonbeam spectrum?"

"Stroke of luck," I said. She said it was looking that way.

Chapter 20   The Manse

September 9

Traveling from Blacksburg to Floyd, I often heard wild roosters in the woods and once ran into a group of hens in the road near a stream. The lucky free-ranging flocks with access to water at 2:42 made it through. They are survivors, true Hokies, like the big rooster that's the Virginia Tech mascot. They appear to be doing well. Last year they fattened up on animal carcasses, and this year the fields are full of insects, seeds and grains. I tried to catch a feral chicken once, intending to dress and eat it, but that bird outran me two to one. Now I interact with the wild chickens to amuse myself. When I hear a rooster crowing in the tall grass or woods, I often crow back.

Escorting us to the big house they call the Manse, Sarah thought my return rooster crow was hilarious. "Chester is going to love you," she said. "We only keep two roosters, and the older one thinks he rules the world."

Beyond the open iron gates, the grass had been mowed along a paved driveway leading to a sprawling two-story Spanish style house. It would have looked classy except for the racks and lines of laundry drying on the sunny front porch.

"We've been catching up on chores," Sarah said. "A sunny day means plenty of running water."

We entered through a heavy wood door that opened

into a cavernous room with lots of artwork on the walls, mostly paintings and complicated fiber pieces. There was a large dining table with upholstered chairs on one side, pushed close to the windows, its surface strewn with books and papers. "Study hall, for group discussions," she said, waving her hand.

"You mean like school?" Desi asked.

"Sort of. It's just about learning different things," she explained. "Participation is optional. It's for fun." She looked at the materials on the table. "Question of the week. Is beauty necessary in art?"

"Good question," I said, glancing at some of the art on the walls, including an old portrait of an exquisite young woman. The room felt like an art museum.

The big kitchen was a mix of white and blue tiles, with a long row of windows against the wall. Two men, both older, sat at a small table drinking water from canning jars.

"You must be Gabe and Desi," the shorter, stocky man said, getting to his feet. "I'm Rob and this is Buddy."

Buddy got up, too, and we all shook hands, even Desi. Sarah stepped back and told us all to smile while she took pictures with a pretend camera. A mechanical kitchen timer dinged on the counter.

"Duty calls. Come meet Solar Sam," Rob said, opening the back door and motioning for us to follow. Wonder of wonders, Solar Sam is a small direct-feed solar generator designed to run a greenhouse fan, only they are using it to run small appliances. Rob was drying apples in a dehydrator and cooking a crockpot of marinara sauce, switching the power supply to each appliance every hour. "We love this guy. Saves a ton of propane, and when we're not using it for cooking, it will run a fan," he said.

"Chan and I would have killed for one of these in Blacksburg," I said.

"I know what you mean," he said, looking at me in my good eye. "I stayed in Roanoke through the winter."

"By yourself?"

"Yeah."

"Fun times." The bright sun was making my eye start to water, which stings and makes the other eye tear up, too. He noticed it.

"Go on in, I'll look at that eye later if you want. Is it getting better?" I told him I thought so and asked him if he was a doctor. He laughed.

"No, but I raised two kids and I've lived a long time, so I'm the closest thing we got. Wynn worked at the drugstore so he's the pharmacist, and Sarah's the nurse because her mother was a nurse," he said. "If you need health care, we have it going on." He unplugged the crockpot and plugged in the dehydrator, which magically began to hum. Even on a micro-scale, electricity is such a miracle.

Next on the tour, Buddy took us to meet the chickens. A few hens were using the nesting boxes, and four young roosters croaked feeble crows from a wire enclosure. I knew that plans were being made for them. It was the same way Beth and Randall handled young roosters born to their flock.

"Planning a chicken dinner?" I asked.

"Yup."

"I can help dress them. Done it before," I said.

"Yup. Soon. We've been waiting for the weather to

cool down."

"Wait, wait. You're going to eat them?" Desi asked.

"Yup." It seems to be Buddy's favorite word.

"You can't keep all the roosters, they start fighting and some are mean. The meat is best when they're young," I said.

"Oh."

Buddy laughed. "We'll keep one, but the others are going in a pot," he said. Lean, tanned, and maybe sixty, Buddy seems to keep the Manse running. He showed us the pull start mowers he uses to cut enough grass to keep the ticks at bay, and the old horse paddock where he grew sweet corn. "It ain't a bad life, living here and looking after Sarah and the rest," he said.

"I think it's a dream life," Desi said, picking up a blue egg from one of the nesting boxes. "My mom would have loved this place."

Buddy smiled, took off his ball cap, rubbed his head, then put it back on. "And you ain't even seen where I live. Come on, let me show you."

Everyone else has bedrooms in the house, on the second floor, but Buddy lives in the former horse trainer's cottage. It's like the nicest Airbnb in southwest Virginia, with a stained-glass piece in the kitchen window, a leather sofa, and wood and stone details everywhere. Buddy says it's the nicest place he's ever lived. It's perfectly kept, smelling a little like oranges.

Clare appeared in the open door, calling "Yoo hoo! Looking for the guys. Have you seen them?"

"No. They ain't back yet?" A worried look showed on Buddy's face.

"No. They should have been back two hours ago. Me

and Sarah are going to look for them. At the potato house," she said.

"Now, wait a minute. I don't like you and Girlie running out when there might be trouble." He rubbed his chin.

"That's what Rob says," Sarah said, coming up behind Clare. "They're not here, either? Dang!" She stamped her foot.

I knew a little about what was happening, though I didn't have the full picture. On our way to the Manse, Sarah said that Wynn and Claude went to harvest potatoes at the Farm, and then take them to a house along the road, the potato house. When potato storage space at the Manse ran short, they started using an abandoned house with a handicapped ramp for easy loading. "The living room floor there is covered with a potato mountain," Sarah said, spreading her arms wide. "Like giant mice have been storing up potatoes."

The mice were missing in action.

"I can go with you," I said. "If Desi can stay here, with Clare." Desi made a small nod of agreement.

"Not a problem. Can you ride? One-eyed, I mean?" Sarah is not one to put on airs. She says what's on her mind.

"Sure," I said, only slightly embarrassed. "I just need a helmet with a face shield." This is how I ended up riding a primo gravel bike, best I've ever ridden, which retails for over $1500, wearing a metallic blue helmet that made me look like a bug. Sarah said it was only a few miles, but she's strong and fast and wastes no time. In the first leg, on pavement, I had to push up the hills to keep up with her.

She stopped near a place where mud had washed across the road and turned off into an opening in the tall grass. The entrance to an old dirt road was likely marked at one time, but now it's so overgrown with weeds that you would never know it was there if you weren't looking for it.

"We walk the next part. It's too rough to ride," Sarah said. The single-lane road through the woods was not well maintained in The Time Before, and has degraded into a mess of rocks, roots, tree limbs and mud. We stuck to the shoulders of the road to avoid slick spots, and then wonder of wonders, the trees opened up overhead and we were on good gravel, looking out over open fields of tall grass, waving in the breeze. "Our secret road that connects to the farm on the other side of town. The potato house is right up there. Let's park the bikes and take a look."

She led the way to a handsome brick house with a killer view, and a handicapped ramp in the front, almost hidden by tall weeds and grasses. From our hiding place behind a large oak, we could see the two bikes in front, one pulling a kiddie cart loaded with potatoes. But the house seemed quiet, with no sign of the men or other activity.

"Should we call out to them?" Sarah whispered.

"No. Be quiet a minute." I listened to the birds, a jay in the side yard, some doves in the grass. They were not feeling disturbed by whatever was happening in the house.

I whistled the first few measures of "Don't Worry, Be Happy," then stopped. Silence. I whistled it again, a little louder. Nothing. This was not good.

"I think I saw something move," Sarah said. "Do it again."

That's when Claude peered around the back corner of the house, wearing a camouflage hunting cap, trying not to be seen. I was relieved he was alive, but where was Wynn?

"Claude," Sarah called, waving her arm. "Are you all right?"

"Stay away from the ramp! There's a hornet's nest!" he called. "Come in the back!"

With Sarah behind me, I trampled a path through the waist-high weeds to where Claude waited on the back deck. "Wynn got stung, but he's doing better. It was touchy there for a while, but I think he'll survive."

We found Wynn on the sofa in the den with one leg elevated on a stack of cushions, smiling and seeming happy to see us. His eyes looked heavy, as if he had been sleeping. "I'm kind of out of it," he said, yawning. His lips seemed puffy, too.

"Three wasp stings and three Benadryl will do that," Claude said. He said Wynn was carrying potatoes up the ramp when he got stung on his leg, which didn't seem like a big deal at first, but then he felt hot and dizzy, and started getting a rash on his neck. He laid down and gave Claude instructions. Look for some Benadryl. Put a baking soda paste on the stings. Elevate the leg.

"He took three Benadryl I found in the medicine cabinet, less than six months out of date. So far, so good." Claude said.

"I might be starting to feel normal, maybe," Wynn said. Sarah sat on the edge of the sofa, feeling his head. "No fever," she said.

I stepped closer to look at the stings. One still had an intact stinger, caked with baking soda. "Okay if I take that out?" Wynn nodded. I went to the kitchen to get a sharp knife, then returned and scraped out the stinger. "It's in the Scout manual," I said. "Illustrated."

"What else are we supposed to do?" Sarah asked.

"Mostly wait for the EMTs, stay still, keep up the Benadryl," I said. "There can be a delayed reaction."

I was not making this up. Learning what to do for allergic reactions was part of the first aid merit badge I earned in seventh grade. Plus, for a while I had a foster brother named Ernie who was allergic to everything. I went to the special training session with Mama Beth and Ernie where we learned what to do if he got stung and the epi pen didn't work.

As Claude and Sarah discussed their next move, I was at a disadvantage because I did not know what they were talking about when they said they needed to go get the Thing. They needed the Thing to get Wynn home with minimal exertion.

"I'll go," Claude said, heading toward the back door. "Better to have it and not need it than to need it and not have it." Wynn laughed with his eyes closed and said Claude was starting to sound like Rob.

I brought Sarah a more comfortable chair and said I'd look around for some water. "Don't go into the bedrooms. They're closed off for a reason," she warned.

In what was once the formal living room, the floor was covered with potatoes, piled on bed sheets to protect the carpet. Thoughtful of them. There was a short stack of mail on the table by the front door, mostly junk. We were guests of the Neal family, rest their souls. Margaret and Joe. I wondered who needed the ramp, Margaret, Joe, or someone else?

It's a little weird, but I like knowing the people's names when I go through their houses. I like to know who to thank for the food, the shelter, the firewood. The pantry off the kitchen had several six packs of canned drinks and bottled water on the floor. The shelves included a selection of pastas in pest-proof plastic containers, a lot of stuff in cans, and an unopened bottle of canola oil. Under the sink was a half-full can of wasp spray.

"Plenty to eat and drink," I said, placing several canned drinks and bottles of water on the coffee table next to Wynn, who appeared to be napping. "Not much water, but I'll look out back for more." Sarah told me to be careful.

It was dark in the closed garage, occupied by a maroon Subaru that blocked access to the door's emergency lever. I climbed up on the car to reach it, popped the latch, and then opened the overhead door. I wished I hadn't. An older man, presumably Joe, was slumped in the seat of a riding mower, still wearing a white slouch hat and blue plaid cotton shirt. At least his face was turned away. I grabbed the cover from the charcoal grill and covered him up.

Good old Margaret and Joe. They kept their emergency supplies in a sensible place, on a shelf just inside the garage door. Candles, matches, an oil lantern, plus useless battery-powered flashlights. There were six plastic jugs of water on the floor. Except for the hornet's nest, it was a good house. I carried two of the water jugs into the kitchen.

"I found more water," I said, poking lightly at Wynn's leg to check on swelling. The mid part of his shin was blowing up like a balloon. "But we could use an ice pack."

"Fresh out," Sarah said. She went to the kitchen and dampened a dishtowel, then draped it over Wynn's leg. "Best we can do," she sighed.

"I've been wondering about something," I said, taking a break in the creaking recliner. "This house. Why is everything still here, when you're in and out all the time with potatoes? Did you even know about the guy in the garage?"

"There's a guy in the garage?" she asked.

"Yeah. Old dude getting ready to mow his grass."

"Not a bad way to go," she remarked. She had a point.

Wynn stirred and rubbed his eyes, halfway awake. "This is a third-tier house. It's in the plan, on the map. It might stand through The Incineration because of no trees, not much to burn. We might need it, and it's close to the farm."

"The Incineration?" I asked. He said Sarah would explain, and closed his eyes again.

"It's one of the theories on what might come next," she said. "That's why Wynn flips the switches in breaker boxes. The electrical grid could be reactivated, resulting in widespread explosions and fires. The Incineration. We have plans for various evacuations, safe houses with food and water in different places. This place is on the list, just not high up. Meanwhile, it's a convenient place to store potatoes."

"Assuming you can get to them," I said. "I'll go cut a path to the back door." It was a good excuse to go outside, take in the scenic vista, and make myself useful.

The gas-powered weed trimmer had fuel in the tank and it should have started, though it didn't because they never do. Instead, I whacked at the weeds by swinging a manual weed cutter, making a passageway around the house from the driveway to the back deck. The tool hit cracked flowerpots and some wood stakes, and I uncovered the edge of a large, circular hole that had recently been dug, probably just before it happened. The shovel was still there, sticking up among the weeds, which were rich with ticks. I picked two crawlers off my forearm as I was stashing the tools. Then I brushed off my pants and shirt and looked around the garage for treasures.

There were storage bins on metal shelving, folding lawn chairs and an extension ladder on the wall by the car, and a workbench on the other side, complete with a lifetime supply of nuts, bolts, screws and nails.

Under the worktable, a large, opened box caught my eye. The colorful label showed goldfish and koi swimming in a pond, and said it was a solar waterfall kit. The hole in the backyard! Margaret and Joe were putting in a pond with a solar-powered waterfall. Their project in progress came to a sudden end.

Wonder of wonders, the box still had the shipping invoice ($449) and the instruction manual. Double wonder of wonders, the submersible solar pump was direct current, no batteries, designed to push water on sunny days. I carried the box to the back deck.

"Hey Sarah, come see this," I said through the open patio door. "Solar Sam may have a little brother."

She looked at the box. "A fountain, seriously?"

"Yeah, with a solar pump." I explained how it worked. "You put the pump under water, like in a deep container, and it will pump the water out through a hose, probably pretty far if it doesn't have to push uphill. Like, it could deliver water from the pump behind Wynn's house way closer to the back door. Or it could pump water from a spring."

"Definitely the find of the week," she said, patting the top of the box. "Rob is going to love this."

A short while later, as I was finishing moving the last of the potatoes into the house, a hot and tired Claude appeared pushing what looked like a three-wheeled wheelchair. It had big tires, like bicycle tires, and the seat was slung back, like a reclining bike. It must be the Thing.

"Wow," I said, admiring the dark red frame. "Where did you find this?"

"Clare and Sarah found it, to help Rob get around. He has bad knees. As the story goes, it belonged to a disabled veteran who liked to get outside," Claude said. The path I cut was just wide enough to push the Thing close to the back door. We went inside to cool off and get something to drink. Claude collapsed in the recliner. His legs were caked with mud.

"We should take him the long way, on pavement," he said. "The mud is too slick." Sarah agreed. In this way, we trekked four long miles to Wynn's house, with Claude and I clearing the roadway ahead of Sarah pushing Wynn in the Thing, holding the solar fountain box in his lap. It was a slow, hot trip, but we made it. Claude went to share the news with the others.

I helped Sarah get Wynn comfortable on the sofa with

his leg elevated, and dabbed his stings with calamine lotion from the medicine cabinet. I thought about going after Desi, who might be feeling abandoned or might not be missing me at all. But I also felt persistent crawling sensations here and there on my neck, back and legs, which made me feel like a giant tick bomb.

"I need to go get cleaned up. I think I got into some ticks," I told Sarah.

"Yuck." She went to the hallway closet and came back with a couple of stiff, sun-dried towels. "Use Wynn's shower out back. There should be plenty of soap and hot water," she said. It was an offer I couldn't refuse.

Wynn keeps a fabulous shower. Behind the brown plastic curtain, two bulging black water bags are clipped to an overhead rod, and a small shelf holds an impressive selection of soaps, shampoos, even silicone body scrubbers. It's like Wynn cleaned out a CVS or something.

I peeled off my clothes and filthy eye patch, and lathered my head with peppermint shampoo. Scrub a dub, dub, man, it felt good! I soaped and scrubbed my whole body and was ready to rinse and repeat when I heard a small voice outside the shower curtain.

"Hey Gabe," Desi said.

"Hey Desi." I opened the spicket to slowly rinse more soap from my hair. "I got into some ticks. Should I use mint conditioner or tea tree oil?"

"Definitely tea tree oil," she said. "Can I like, get you anything?"

I said I had towels, but needed dry clothes and a pair of sunglasses, which Sarah could provide.

"Are you graduating to sunglasses?" she asked. I said

one could hope. As I finished up, I carefully washed my face and rinsed out my eye, which stung at only a two on the misery scale. I examined my face close up in Wynn's small shaving mirror. The road rash on my cheek and forehead were almost healed, but the eye socket was still purple, even brown, and the lid was puffy. I looked left and right, and saw that the pupil moved.

    I may not end up as a one-eyed guy after all.

Chapter 21 Missing Persons

September 16

"You never know when you'll need to know how to do something," Randall liked to say, whether he was showing me how to replace shingles that had blown off the roof or teaching me to pull a fence line tight. Like most farmers, he knew how to do a million things, and I loved following behind him, picking up little skills. Good thing I did. The more you know how to do, the more you can contribute, which makes life better for you and everyone else. This is one of my first observations about becoming a member of this funky post-apocalypse community.

As I learn about how things operate around here, I'm truly impressed by the Hokies, the name of the group of which Desi and I are now a part. It's like a weird, spread-out complex that includes Wynn's house, the Manse, and now our place, the Dahlia House. We share resources in terms of food, work and water, but what amazes me is the absence of friction. Part of this is natural, and part is due to Clare, who was a corporate trainer in The Time Before.

"It saves so much time and trouble when you stick with things you do well, or that interest you," she told me as I washed clothes in the outdoor sink Buddy and Rob installed on the patio at the Manse. Our laundromat. "You want to look forward to being able to do good work, you know?" Clare is crazy cute but she doesn't know it, with a tight pixie haircut and honey hazel eyes lined with dark lashes. According to Desi, Clare is 34, and she's thinking about marrying Claude and having a baby.

"She's thinking about it, that's all I'm saying. Don't make a big deal out of it," Desi said. "Apparently Claude used to be a jerk and then he changed. Now she's waiting him out, making sure good Claude is here to stay."

I said that made sense to me.

Rob and Prince are the official listeners. Prince because his hearing is five times better than that of any human, and Rob because he doesn't sleep very much and is up at all hours of the night. After a long string of quiet days, the listeners issued the first report of gunshot. It was early, barely light, when Rob heard a single shot as he sipped his sunup coffee. As Wynn was getting up, Prince ran under the bed to the darkest corner and refused to come out.

I was clueless when I arrived at the Manse to help Rob sort through electronic components.

"Did you hear a shot?" Sarah asked, handing me a mug of warm tea. I shook my head. "Me neither. Rob and Prince did, though."

"It was right at daybreak?" Buddy asked Rob.

"Yes. Early. First light. I was outside. Very quiet, no wind."

"And it was only one shot?"

"Absolutely. There was an echo to it, so I listened close, for a while."

"People don't fight at daybreak, that's when they hunt," Buddy said. He had a point, except that there were no deer or rabbits or even squirrels to hunt. Turkeys, maybe?

People hunt at sundown, too, which is when the next shots came, two of them, a minute apart. Desi and I were on the back deck, chilling after dinner, and we heard them clear as day. The first shot made the birds and the bugs in the trees go silent. They were just starting up again when we heard the second shot.

"Somebody's whooping it up," she said, assuming the shots came from town. I was not so sure, and thought they might be much closer, but I didn't want to scare her. I waited for a third shot that never came. I heard no shots while I waited to fall asleep, or when I went out to pee at dawn, but I kept thinking about what I'd heard. Rob was right, there was an echo to it, and that's when I knew. It wasn't a rifle or a pistol. It was a shotgun, with a fuller, more reverberating sound. Was somebody really hunting birds?

"Guns don't fire themselves," I told Desi after our breakfast of scrambled eggs, bread and syrup. "Someone is out there, maybe a hunter. Let's be careful. Wear bright colors."

"Okay, but I'm not picking up scary vibes. No freak out alert on the goddess channel," she said, swallowing her last bite of bread. "Did I tell you that me and Clare are going on a sugar run today?"

"That will be cool," I said. A sugar run means going into houses to look for sugar, canned meat, propane, and other precious supplies, and it's one of Desi's favorite things to do. Sarah and Clare are scavenging experts, so she's learning from the best. She changed into a neon pink tee shirt that matched her bike helmet and pedaled off to the Manse.

I clocked in to work at Gabe's Bike Repair, which is located next to a neighbor's house. It's a primo little shop for sharpening blades, replacing lost screws, cutting pieces of wood, or fixing bicycles. Thanks to Sarah, we also have a supply of replacement tires, tubes, seats and helmets, because she looks for bike supplies in houses where she finds good wheels.

"Once into treads, always into treads, makes me a groovy person," she jokes, because her old job was selling tires. She liked her job, and I think the things she learned about tires and friction and curves helped make her the great rider she is today. She can push up hills and jump or dodge obstacles with the best of them. If there is a future Olympic competition for biking post-Armageddon country roads, Sarah will take the gold.

I had one flat to fix and a disc brake to clean and adjust, but it's not like it was a high-pressure workday. I started with the brake, always fun to spin, and whistled "I've Been Working on the Railroad" as I cleaned the disc with WD40, such a refreshing smell. Working on the Railroad is one of my favorite comfort songs, because from a whistler's point of view, it has everything. Long notes, short notes, a change in tempo, the step-up lift for Dinah Won't You Blow Your Horn. In retrospect, I was whistling kind of loud.

I put on a helmet to take the bike for a test run when I thought I saw something move in the rearview mirror mounted on the handlebar. I stopped, moved the handlebar, and looked again. There was a tall man with a long gray beard standing in the road, looking at me and my shop. I parked the bike and slowly turned around, grabbing a tire iron from the worktable and holding it behind my leg.

"That was some good whistling, and I do thank you for it," the man called.

"You're welcome," I said instinctively.

"Music being hard to come by and all." He struggled to adjust his load, which included a shotgun over one shoulder and a bulging Walmart shopping bag over the other, with a small backpack in between. Then he laid it all on the ground, stood tall and stretched out his arms. "I won't shoot you if you won't crack my head with that tire iron," he said.

"Deal." I put down the tool, wiped my hands on a damp rag, and traded the helmet for my favorite sunglasses, a pair of black and gold Versaches that Desi found on a sugar run. They made me feel bolder, more confident. "Who are you, and what brings you here?" I asked, exploiting my home team advantage.

He cleared his throat. "Fair enough. My name is Jasper Higgins, only everybody calls me Hoot, and I'm looking for my cousin, Buddy Troutt. We ain't got the same name but we're blood kin through our mothers," he said. "Do you know Buddy? He left a note at the old homeplace, said to look for him on down yonder at Hemlock Ridge Farm." He waved his arm toward the top of the hill.

I walked out to the road to get a closer look. Like Buddy, he was tall and naturally lean, but his thick, bushy beard hid the lower half of his face.

"What did you say your name was?" I wanted to hear his voice again.

"Hoot," he said, coughing a little. "Hoot Higgins. Looking for my cousin, Buddy Troutt." He took off his ball cap and wiped his head with his hand. It was a familiar move, a familiar hairline.

"One T or two?" I asked.

He made a crooked grin. "You from around here? It's two. T-R-O-U-T-T."

"Your cousin. He had a wife. What was her name?" I thought it was a neutral question, but a look of pain crossed his face.

"Oh, sweet Candy, she must not have made it," he said. "I suspected as much." He cleared his throat and spat on the ground.

That was it, he was legit. I'd heard Buddy talk about Candy several times, his sweet Candy.

"I'm Gabe," I said, extending my hand. "I know Buddy, great guy, he's doing well."

I thought he was going to cry. His shoulders trembled and there were definitely tears in his eyes, but not enough to drip. "Praise the Lord," he said, taking a ragged breath. That's when I noticed what appeared to be an orange duck's bill poking from the shopping bag. "Been hunting?" I asked.

"Yeah, had to. I stopped for the night by this little pond with a tiny house next to it, and after a while these ducks start marching in from the woods, jumping in the water. Not wild ducks, meat ducks," he said, reaching down to pick up one of the dead birds by the neck. "See? They're all white. Like they used to be pets, or people kept them for eggs. There's a big old flock, and they're nice, heavy birds. I got three here, didn't want to show up on Buddy's doorstep empty handed."

"Good thinking. He'll like this a lot."

"They ain't been dressed. I didn't have a hatchet, and

227

my knife has punked out and gone dull anyway."

The sight of the dead ducks made me homesick in a happy-sad way. I remembered duck hunting with Randall on a cold winter day and the whole drama surrounding it. Mama Beth got up early to make us sausage biscuits while it was still dark. She said not to bring her a Canada goose because she didn't want to mess with it, and we had to clean any ducks we killed. Which we did. Huge learning experience.

"I always heard it was best to pluck when the feathers are dry anyway," I said. "But we'll need more water. There's a pump well not far from here, on the way to Buddy's. Give me a minute to gather some tools."

He said he wasn't hungry, but changed his mind when I said we had stale bread with Mrs. Butterworth's syrup. He sat on the back deck, enjoying his first bread in over a year, while I gathered the supplies we would need to pluck and dress three fat, delicious ducks.

I took him to the well pump by Wynn's house from the far side, and we worked on a picnic table in the neighbor's yard. First we plucked feathers, which took a while, and talked.

"I was up in West Virginia, like way up in coal country, had a job welding in a mine. It's good money, you know. Had my hood on, working away, and noticed it was awful dark. Then I killed the torch. You ain't seen dark until you seen that kind of dark." He crawled over bodies and equipment and made his way out by luck, and by smelling for fresh air. "I don't breathe so good anyway, got the emphysema, so it could have made my nose a little sharper. When I finally saw daylight and made my way out, it was raining outside. Nothing ever smelled so good. Except for maybe apple pie."

He said he camped out in a mountain resort for the winter, then started back toward Floyd in the spring. "You don't want to know some of the things I've seen," he said, shaking his head, "But I kept feeling like I needed to make it to Floyd, you know, get back home. I figured that even if everybody was gone, I'd find plenty of supplies at Jesse's place in the holler. Jesse was always thinking the end of the world was coming, only his storage containers are locked up tight and the house has been trashed. It looks and smells like there was cats living there. Might have even been bobcats."

I think Hoot likes having an audience, and I know how good it feels to talk after too much time alone. I asked him where he got the nickname. He slapped his leg and laughed.

"When I was a baby they said I looked like a little owl, so they called me Hoot. It stuck. Been Hoot all my life."

When the plucking was done, we chopped off the ducks' heads and feet with a sharp hatchet, slit open their bellies and pulled out the innards. The birds needed more plucking, with tweezers, but they were pretty clean when we washed them in a pail of cool water from the well. Mama Beth would approve.

"Whooee, I hope Buddy likes duck. These are gonna dress out to five pounds each," he said. He was clearly enjoying the work, but it had left his clothes a gory, feathery mess, and I didn't look much better. Wynn had never appeared, so I assumed he wasn't home, which turned out to be true. After calling his name and hearing a timid meow from Prince, I tiptoed to the back bedroom, got two polyester dress shirts Wynn would never wear from the closet, and took them with me to the scene of the crime along with a trash bag for the feathers and entrails.

Hoot said he thought we looked pretty sharp, but I don't think his standards are all that high at this point. I carried the bag of ducks and led Hoot down the hill to the Manse, which sparkled in the late morning sun. "Well, I declare, Buddy knows how to pick a house," he said, grinning.

"Actually, he lives in the back, has his own place," I said. "Right now everyone's busy doing other things, they'll be back later. Buddy and Rob should be here, though." I led him around the house to the stone patio, which serves as an outdoor kitchen. Rob had something cooking in a crockpot plugged into Solar Sam. I heard dishes clinking in the kitchen.

"Hey Rob," I said, poking my head in through the back door. "Is Buddy in there?"

"No, he was. Came up for a shower, but that was a while ago," Rob said. I smiled and motioned for him to come outside.

"I have a double surprise," I said. "Fresh ducks and a visitor."

I introduced Rob to Hoot and showed him the ducks. "That was the shooting we heard," Rob said, relieved. He poked at the top duck with his finger. "These will be fun." He put them in a deep bucket of salty water in the shade and started making plans for cooking them.

I whistled as we walked to Buddy's place, so he would hear us coming. The front door was partly open. "Hey Buddy," I called. "You have a visitor." I heard the squeak and thump of the recliner's footrest.

"I got a what?" Footsteps. I moved back and Hoot took my place.

"Cousin Buddy, it's Hoot," he said in a soft voice. "I made it home."

The door swung open. Buddy said nothing, but he was blinking hard when he started hugging and slapping Hoot, and then they both were crying, and laughing, and pushing each other, and wiping their faces with their sleeves and then hugging again. I'll be honest, I was sniffing a little, too, and it felt really good, to feel an emotion so pure and deep, though the tears left salty deposits on my sunglasses.

I spent the next couple of hours with Rob. He brought me some clean clothes and I grabbed a quick outdoor shower, an unexpected treat. Then I helped fire up the charcoal grill, which he said would be perfect for ducks because we could collect the drippings in a pan and it wouldn't matter if we made a mess. "Duck fat is like the next best thing to butter," he said. "We're gonna need more bread."

From time to time we heard voices and laughter coming from Buddy's place, but the Troutt men kept to themselves for a long while. I don't know how they did it, because the aroma of duck legs smoking on a hickory fire is so intoxicating! It's a primal pleasure, as if humans are hard-wired to dig barbecued meat.

Sarah, Clare and Desi were the first to get home from their day's mission, asking "What smells so good?" as they followed their noses. Their backpacks were loaded with sugar, shortening, coffee, and wonder of wonders, pie crust mix and instant topping in boxes. With the sun still shining brightly and Solar Sam available for use, they had time to bake an apple cobbler in the mini oven, a plan they'd been talking about all day. With the additional news of Hoot's arrival, it was turning into a party.

"I can't believe he showed up like that, walking down the road," Sarah said as she snapped green beans Claude and Wynn picked at the farm. We were outside at the picnic table under the shade of a big oak tree, me, Desi, Sarah, and Wynn, who was lying on the bench next to Sarah, pretending to be asleep. "That's how it happened with Buddy. He just found me." She smiled a fragile smile. Something was bothering her, she was snapping beans really fast. "Isn't that great?"

"You don't think they're androids, do you?" I asked.

"Don't think so," Desi said. "But until we meet Hoot, we can't know for sure."

Wynn sat up and started helping with the beans, pulling out the phantom strings from the small pieces. Wynn is into details. "Don't worry, Rob plans to share his beer. Androids don't drink beer."

"I can't believe Buddy has a living, breathing blood relative," Desi said. "Not like me, I'm end of the line."

"Me, too," Wynn said.

"Not me," Sarah said, sighing. "I mean, I know my brother's gone because I saw him, but Mom just went missing. I try to believe what is likely true, that she's gone, and I was doing good until today. If Hoot can show up, why not my mother?"

"My beautiful lady, hope is permitted, even recommended," Wynn said, leaning over to touch his head to hers.

I couldn't help myself. I stretched out my palm and

cleared my throat. "*Hope is the thing with feathers that perches in the soul and sings the tune without the words and never stops at all,*" I said slowly. "Emily Dickinson."

Sarah gave me a questioning look. "You hear hope, in birdsong?"

"I hear all kinds of things in birdsong," I said.

The Hoot Higgins I escorted to Buddy's doorstep was hardly recognizable when he appeared for dinner. His beard and mustache were gone, so you could see the tight Troutt jawline and strong teeth below bright blue eyes. He wore dark jeans and a light blue oxford shirt, and smelled of Gillette, citrus and menthol. He went around and shook everyone's hand.

"Thank you for helping me out today," he said when he got to me. "It's all working out even better than I thought."

Part of this assessment was due to the presence of Desi, who takes new people by surprise with her loveliness. She seems aware of this. He couldn't stop looking at her.

"You can call me Ms. Desi," she said as they were introduced, quickly withdrawing her hand. "I'm Gabe's sister, at least in our present circumstances."

"True enough," I said, raising my sunglasses to wink at her, which I can now do. "We both got lucky."

"And she's my little sister, too," Clare said, coming up behind Desi to kiss her on the cheek.

"And mine, too," Sarah called out from the food prep area.

Hoot got the message that Desi was protected by an electric fence of fake family. Not that he did or said anything wrong. It's just that Desi is our girl.

233

Claude and Rob produced a fitting celebratory feast of roast duck legs with green beans, sweet potatoes, and a tart sauce made from dried cherries. Plus, there was apple cobbler with whipped topping for dessert.

"Now I know I've died and gone to heaven," Hoot said, belching a little too loudly. "That's the best meal I've had in years, I'm telling you, in years." Then he coughed, but at least he didn't spit.

"Well, what do you think?" I asked Desi when we were back at home that evening. We were out on the deck, practicing a Beatles medley we'd been working on, her on the harmonica and me whistling. "All You Need Is Love" was starting to sound especially good.

"About what?" She wiped off her harmonica.

"I don't know. About Hoot. About your new sisters." I was trying not to sound jealous.

She giggled a little. "That was so sweet, wasn't it? Made my heart do a crocodile flip." She changed the subject. "Did you know Clare had a real sister, two years younger than her? Sarah had a younger brother, like your age."

"Nobody gets off easy in this video game. Rob had a wife and two grown kids," I said, pretending to push a joystick.

She played a quick riff on her harmonica, the opening to What a Wonderful World, then stopped. "But don't you see? It all makes us more meaningful, you and me. Because we're young, we can be reflections of their lost sisters, brothers, children. It makes us more useful. Me, anyway. You're already useful. You know how to do all kinds of stuff."

I whistled my response, the bridge in Wonderful

World, thinking the words in my head.
The colors of the rainbow
So pretty in the sky
Are also on the faces
Of people going by
I see friends shaking hands
Saying, "How do you do?"
They're really saying
I love you
    We finished the song together.

Chapter 22   Gone Fishing

September 23

The topic of the week is home. Desi and I are dug in at the Dahlia House, but summer is fading fast, with every day shorter and cooler than the one before. The propane tank is almost empty. Finding a house with a wood stove and firewood is not a problem, but then you need water. We've been checking out houses close to Wynn's, so we can share his pump, but most of them have heating issues and would need to be cleared of bodies and bugs. Desi says we should keep looking, maybe find a place close to a stream.

Moving into the Manse is an option, but not a good one, because the big house has a heating problem, too. There is a huge European stove in the kitchen that burns coal or wood, but only the bedrooms above the kitchen would be warm.

"We might need to camp out in tents and sleeping bags in the gallery," Rob says. "Or turn the kitchen into a bunkhouse. And that's if we can get the wind generator to run on windy nights." There were a lot of questions, and no sure answers.

Hoot got me thinking about home, too, what he expected when he came here, and what he got. When I came to Floyd a month ago, I definitely felt like I was coming home. Never mind that I was a foster kid, I really did finally find a home here with Randall and Mama Beth. Was I mountain born and bred? Who knows? Mama Beth said she would help me look it up after I turned 18, but then I got busy at Tech and didn't think about it much. Now that chance is gone. I'll never know.

"When I got back to the house, I seen Buddy's note and the new graves out back, so I knew he was alive," Hoot said as he finished tuning up and re-stringing a gas weed trimmer. "I thought I was gonna have a heart attack." The trimmer started on the third pull. When it comes to small engines, Hoot has a magic touch.

On the other hand, his social instincts are not so good.

Hoot, Buddy, Rob, Sarah and I were on the patio at the Manse, cutting up bruised pears gathered from a tree down the road. Solar Sam was running a fan to keep the yellow jackets away from us and the fruit. Rob and Sarah were making jokes about taxes, which we no longer have.

"I missed my quarterly deposit again, but since I didn't earn anything, I don't think I'll owe a penalty," Rob said.

"Probably not, with all these sales taxes we've been paying," Sarah added, grinning.

"It's the gas taxes that are killing me, twenty cents a gallon," Hoot said, shaking his head. "It's enough to drive a working man broke. And what for? To support a bunch of illegals come to take our jobs." He didn't mean it as a joke.

Buddy frowned and waved his hands in the air. "Let's not get riled up. Got no reason. You know it don't much matter."

"I'm hearing you," Rob said, looking at Hoot. "Not saying I agree, but I'm listening." He continued in a gentle voice. "It's kind of our policy not to discuss politics, causes tempers to flare, people get upset. It's okay to talk about why you think the world stopped the way it did, like if you think it was the Martians or the Russians or the Chinese, but not the political parties and presidents and people who are gone. Focus on the future."

Hoot's eyes brightened. "Everybody knows they've been bringing in Chinese spies, some dropping in parachutes," he said.

Sarah stifled a laugh. "Seriously?"

"Of course. Common knowledge. There was video of night drops, on YouTube. That way they didn't have to cross the border."

"Interesting," Rob said. "First I've heard of it."

Hoot folded his hands across his chest. "Let's just say I know things you don't know." His voice took on a defiant tone.

"Which is why we don't discuss politics," Rob said, getting to his feet. Sarah followed his lead, picking up the bowl of pears.

"Where you going? Not ready to hear some truth for a change?"

"Nope, not ready," Sarah said.

Hoot's face started turning red. "Last time I looked this was America and a man could speak his mind," he said, placing his hands on the edge of the table. "I know things you don't know because you never looked."

Sarah silently shook her head, which seemed to irritate him even more.

"You're not interested because you got what you wanted, right? You city folks, with all your smarts and money. Coming in with your windmills and solar and vegan what-not while coal and beef goes begging and good men can't get work. You don't know squat about these mountains, but you took them over anyway, jacked up the price of everything, then said we was too country. Run us out like rats." He stalked off toward Buddy's cottage.

His tirade left us in stunned silence.

"Sorry about that," Buddy said. "He's a little out of sorts I reckon."

There were many murmurs that it was all right, understandable, blah, blah, but the truth is that we were in shock. We took the mountains from the people to whom they rightly belonged? That was a new one on me, unless we're talking about running off the real Native Americans who lived here for thousands of years.

Buddy tried to explain. "Hoot was an only child, my mother's sister's boy. His daddy ran off when he was little, and his mama raised him like he hung the moon. Couldn't do no wrong. He got kinda wild, quit high school and took up welding. Worked at the Volvo plant for a while. We'd see him two or three times a year for holidays and reunions, always driving a shiny Chevy Silverado. Then he took a fall, broke a shoulder, and he got on that pain stuff, the pills, I remember Mama and Aunt Jill talking about it. He got himself straight, but he couldn't get the good jobs no more. That's why he was up in West Virginia."

"Tough life. And then making it all the way here. It's pretty incredible," Rob said. Sarah walked around the table and put her hands on Buddy's shoulders.

"I'll try to be more patient," she whispered, and he patted her hand.

"Thank you, Girlie."

It's the time of the year when the birds are changing. The blue indigo buntings have already left for Mexico, and the warblers are no longer singing over their nests at dawn. Instead they flit through the woods silently, staying low. There seems to be a lot of them.

There are also herons, or it could be one heron, who often flies over the Dahlia House, always heading southwest. I have seen him wading along the edge of a nearby creek, but where is he going? A larger stream, or maybe an open wetland or a pond?

I got out the maps from the real estate office. The topo map showed a creek flowing under a dirt road that joined another creek, and then the two blue lines flowed together onto a flat area. The map did not show a pond, but there was a dotted line for a driveway, and the little orange square that denoted a house or barn. As the crow flies, it was close to the Manse, farther down the valley.

While Desi enjoyed a petting session with Prince, I showed Wynn the map and asked what he thought. I said I wanted to go bushwhacking back there, to look for a pond.

"All things are possible," he said, getting out his own substantial collection of maps. He pulled out the master map, where the dotted driveway and beyond had not been marked in yellow highlighter, meaning they were unexplored territory. "There must not be a mailbox," he said. "And at this point that driveway would be tricky to find if you don't know it's there." He held his index finger in the air. "When to go? Tomorrow?"

Desi said she was going, too. I had no objections, because she has gotten really good swinging a double-edged manual weed cutter.

If I'd been looking by myself, I might never have found the overgrown driveway. That's because I tend to look straight ahead, but Wynn looks up and follows the power lines. "Ta-ta-ta-da! There she blows," he said, waving his machete in the air like a sword. Sure enough, a connector box on a pole had a smaller line that led into the woods. We hacked our way in through waist high grass, weeds, cockleburs and blackberries.

It was less overgrown in the shady woods. We crossed a drainage pipe that carried a small stream under the gravel road, then encountered a wide swinging gate, closed but not locked. A small "Private" sign dangled from a lopsided chain. Another sign said 549, as did the big plastic bin placed outside the gate for packages. Someone wanted to be found and not found at the same time, which is about right for Floyd.

"Smile, you're on Candid Camera!" Wynn said as we pushed the gate open through the high weeds. "They're watching us, waiting to see what we'll do." He pointed to a camera high in a tree, and another closer in, mounted on a post with a No Trespassing sign.

"I'll play them something," Desi said, pulling her harmonica from her back pocket as we walked along. She'd been working on Country Road, Take Me Home, and was halfway through when she suddenly stopped and called out "Jumping bullfrogs!"

Coming over the last rise, the view opened to a sparkling lake. Not just a pond, an actual lake, at least three acres, wooded on two sides, with a nice house built into the slope. Make that two houses. In addition to a modern log cabin, there was what looked like a small guest house, up on the hill where it would have a great view of the lake.

We hacked our way to the main house. "Hello!" We took turns calling, mostly out of habit. No answer, because the man in the rocking chair on the front porch was dead, like a year ago dead. There was a dead dog next to him, a big one. A man and his dog, rocking by the lake on a late summer day. Not a bad way to go.

I covered them with a bedspread while Wynn disabled the breaker boxes and Desi explored the house.

"The kitchen is gross," she said, joining me on the front porch. "Roaches and bugs I've never seen before. And mold, lots of mold."

"It's because it's so close to the water, never dries out," I said. We went around the side of the house to the garage door, and we about gagged when I opened it. It reeked of rotten fish or whatever else was in the big chest freezer. I let it air out for a few minutes, then held my breath and dashed inside to grab some fishing poles hung on the wall and a small tackle box.

"I love to fish," Desi said as we spread out the gear on the front porch. "Especially with crickets. I can catch us some crickets." She picked up a small black spinning rod outfitted with a bobber and hook. I said we should also try worms.

"Going fishing?" Wynn asked, pretending to cast out a line. He had finished disabling the power supply to both houses.

"Definitely. Are you feeling lucky?" Desi teased.

"More like hungry, for a fish fry. Does the biologist think the fish will be fit to eat?" he asked.

"Don't see why not. No septic inflow or animal visitors for a year, and it's fed by a spring-fed stream," I said. "But the fish could be small, from overpopulation. We'll see what we catch, if we catch anything at all."

"With that in mind," he announced, raising his machete, "I'll blaze a path to the shore." He whacked his way through to the water's edge, which was paved with flat stones. Along the way he uncovered a dilapidated wood chair, a fire ring, and a small aluminum boat, turned upside down.

"Don't touch it," Desi warned, coming up behind him. "Could have wasps."

"Good thinking," he said, checking his pocket for his expired epi pen. He bent over to rinse his hands in the water. A big frog plopped into the water just down the bank, then another.

"That's a good sign, seeing frogs," I said. "They're sensitive to contaminated water."

I helped Desi get set up to fish, though she basically knew what she was doing. I showed her how to hook a live cricket, and her first cast was a good one, upwind from us and out in deeper water. In no time the bobber started to jiggle. "Wait," I whispered. "The little fish are nibbling. See if they take it under." The bobber disappeared.

"I got one, I got one," she squealed, holding the rod high as she slowly reeled in the line. She landed a hand-size bluegill, flopping in the cut grass. "We're gonna need a bucket," she said excitedly.

She was right. Where there is one bluegill, there are a hundred more, and they're nice fish to eat as long as you take your time and respect the tiny bones. Panfish. I went back to the garage to get a pail and some folding chairs. Time to settle into fish.

Fish are spooky creatures so you have to be quiet, speak in whispers, not exactly Wynn's style, but he tried. "It's less than a mile to the Manse, right?" he asked. I said that was a good guess.

"I was thinking I'd go let Buddy know the fish are biting. That okay with you guys?"

"Absolutely," Desi said softly. "Tell Hoot we said to come." Her bobber went down again, and this time the fish gave a better fight, darting back and forth, and it was heavier, bending her rod.

"Hold tight, hold tight, keep her shallow, play her on in." I found myself coaching her, using exactly the same words Randall had used with me.

"Oh baby," I said, holding up the black and silver fish by its gills. "You have caught a crappie, and in September." I couldn't help it, I was excited, and so was Desi. "Crappie only bite when everything is right, the water, the moon, the everything." Wynn pretended to take commemorative photos, and then he was off in a flash, jogging to the Manse with the news that the fish were biting.

The fish stopped biting when the sun got high at midday, as they always do. "The sun hurts their eyes," I said, "And mine, too." My eye is way better, like at only a two on the misery scale, but squinting into blasting sun is a problem.

"Then let's check out the tree house," Desi said. She is not afraid of many things except snakes, especially copperheads, and the small guesthouse on the hillside looked like a great place for them. "Right behind you," I said, picking up a long stick and following her up the path.

The wood stairs leading up the hillside are steep and splintered, but the one-bedroom not-quite-tiny house nestled among the poplars is a prize. There's a small kitchen, sleeping nook, and a living area that once had full electronics, a TV and an internet router.

"It's called the Lakeside Treehouse," I said, picking up a brochure from the table by the front door. "Don't forget to sign the guest book." The brochure said the proprietors were Janice and Kevin Goodfellow. "If you need anything, just ask!!!" Then there were two cell phone numbers. They would not be answering.

We brought two folding chairs onto the front deck along with the food and drinks from the kitchen cabinets. There were two bottles of fizzy water, some lemonade Capri Suns, and a bowl filled with packets of trail mix, animal crackers, and granola bars, stale but edible with no visible bugs. It was a lot of sugar, but lunch is lunch, and you couldn't beat the view of the tall trees reflected in the sparkling lake.

"I used to love these things." Desi stuck a plastic straw into one of the drinks. "The fruit punch is the best."

I handed her my lemonade. "How did you learn to fish?" I asked.

She grinned. "There was a pond at Wonderland. Not a nice one like this, it was kind of a mudhole. The neighbor's cows weren't supposed to get in there, but they did, so the edge was deep black muck that would suck your shoes off. There were fish in the pond, bream and catfish. They weren't hard to catch but you couldn't eat them, you'd get sick at both ends, I'm not kidding. We buried the dead ones in the garden, Leo liked to put them under his tomatoes." She sighed. "Wonderland could be really boring. Fishing was something to do." She tore open a packet of trail mix.

"You're not bored here?" I asked.

She almost choked on a mouthful of peanuts. "Are you kidding? The Hokies are great! I have you, and everyone else is interesting, nobody's mean, and it's kind of fun, with different things to do. Compared to some places I've lived, this place is awesome."

She had a point. We watched as a kingfisher soared across the lake, barely touching the surface. After a minute another bird followed, hitting the water for a split second. "Even Hoot?" I asked. "He's a little unusual."

"Yup," she said, mimicking Buddy. "I heard what happened, Sarah told me." I asked if Sarah was mad.

"Are you kidding? She's kind of embarrassed about it, not mad. She says she sold tires through the pandemic, which meant listening to people, her customers, what they had on their minds. She says she heard it all. She just doesn't want to hear it anymore. But she's not mad."

"Good to know," I said, and it's true. I hoped Sarah was up to the challenge of accepting Hoot, because I desperately want Sarah to be perfect, and to not take sides. I can't explain it, but Hoot is my man.

"She has a thing with Buddy, she wants whatever's best for him," Desi added, twisting her ponytail. She started gathering up our lunch trash, stuffing the wrappers into the pockets of her cargo pants. Like me, she has taken to wearing loose cargo pants treated with bug spray, stuffed into the tops of her high-tops. Cuts way down on ticks, but with lots of pockets.

"I want to look around for a better boat," I said, getting to my feet. "The boat by the lake looks leaky. I thought I saw a plastic kayak out back."

"I want to look in the house some more. Did you go into the bedrooms?" I shook my head. She made a shy smile. "Would you mind doing body patrol?"

"Not a problem."

When it comes to accepting corpses, we are not all created equally. Some of us, notably me, Claude and Clare, can barge into unexplored houses and quickly cover human or pet remains with sheets and blankets with minimal psychic trauma. The others can do it if they must, but it often comes at a price, paid in sad days and sleepless nights. Here's my theory. The people who saw loved ones die, who touched their bodies, tried to talk them back to life, they are the ones who saw too much, who can't bear to be reminded of their lost wives, mothers, brothers, children. Lost family, but I barely had a family to begin with. I always step up when asked to do body patrol.

I found Mrs. Goodfellow in the laundry room, slumped against the open dryer door, wearing black yoga pants and an oversized flower-print shirt. "Rest in peace," I whispered as I covered her with a sheet. The rest of the house was empty, and more orderly than the kitchen. But there were a lot of bugs.

"Stay out of the laundry room," I told Desi, handing her some disposable latex gloves I found in the hall closet. "Watch what you touch. There are a lot of creepy crawlies."

"Check," she said. I got the feeling she was looking for something, and that I had been dismissed.

Chapter 23   The Messy House

September 30

Our housing situation is getting dire. Nights are now nippy, and the propane heater we use to warm up the house in the mornings is running on empty.

What's more important? Finding the perfect house, or fixing up one that's close to Wynn's manual water pump and the Manse? Several times Sarah has mentioned what she calls the Messy House, which is on a side road around the corner from Wynn's. "Wood stove, close to water, it just needs some TLC," she said. "And there's the issue of bodies."

One morning, after Desi left to do chicken maintenance with Clare, I went to take a look. I found the house easily enough, a brick rancher with blue trim. The front door was locked, but the side door to the kitchen was open.

I saw why Sarah named it the Messy House. Every surface in the little kitchen was cluttered with open boxes, dishes, small appliances, coffee mugs, and old mail. A cascade of plastic grocery bags filled the bottom of the pantry closet, which still contained edible canned goods despite Sarah's pilfering. Finding two cans of pineapple chunks felt like a welcoming sign.

In the main room, I opened the blinds and the sliding patio door to let in light and air. The wood floor was newish, and an interior wall had been modified to open the space for a large wood stove installed in the middle of the room on a stone hearth. There were ashes inside, indicating that it had been used. The living room was littered with shoes, papers, drinking glasses, and tissue boxes. A large black heating pad was tucked into the recliner. The side pocket held an impressive selection of remotes.

A mail piece from Direct TV said I was in the home of Marvin and Pat Petry, and the family photos on the wall suggested they had a grown daughter, but perhaps no grandchildren. Pat liked figurines of ducks and geese, and Marvin had two rifles and a shotgun nicely stowed in a locked cabinet. Next to it, there was a musical instrument in a brown hard-shell case. I opened it to find a banjo, in pristine condition. The brand said Deering, and there was intricate mother of pearl inlay on the neck. I set it aside behind the sofa for Desi.

The main bedroom was a little better, but the tops of both dressers and the bedside tables were jumbled with pill bottles, eyeglass cases, drinking glasses, books, tissues, and empty cans of Diet Coke. Had these people never heard of trash cans? Bedroom number two had a single bed, a waist-high work table, and several open shelves overflowing with craft supplies.

Both bodies were in bedroom number three, a small room that was being used as an office. One skeleton, presumably Marvin, sat at the desktop computer. Another skeleton, presumably Pat, had melted into a pile of bones and fabric a few feet away. What were they talking about at 2:42 that August afternoon? What to have for dinner? I backed out and closed the door.

I checked the ceilings for water damage, looked in the toilets, and went outside to the back deck, which was covered with leaves, sticks and pine needles. There was a gas grill with a black cover, and a glass-topped table with three metal chairs. The view to distant hillsides was spotty but would probably open up some in the winter.

Would Desi like it? I wanted to show it to her, but it needed to be cleaned up first, starting with the bodies. I needed help, and the go-to man for that kind of thing is Claude.

It was still early, so I thought I'd find him at the lake, fly fishing from the kayak. It was his new favorite thing to do. While everyone else fished from the bank using crickets or worms, Claude paddled to the far end of the lake with Mr. Goodfellow's fly rod across his legs, and cast his line into the shadows, over and over. He was quite good at it, the arc of the line was beautiful to watch, but I can't say he caught more fish than us peasants.

The red kayak was across the lake, deep in the shadows. I whistled the tune to the old John Prine song, Whistle and Fish, to get his attention. He waved and paddled my way.

"Catching anything?" I asked.

"Actually, no. I was just coming in. Nobody wants what I have to offer, and the water gets colder every day." He pulled the kayak to dry ground and sat down in a folding chair to put on his pants and shoes. "But I still like coming here. We all do."

I agreed it was a special place. "Speaking of places, I may have found a winter house for Desi and me, but it's kind of a disaster inside and there are two bodies. I was hoping you would help me with them," I said. "Before I show it to her."

"Sure thing. Where is it?"

I explained the history and location of the Messy House, close enough to Wynn's to share the water pump.

"Well, it so happens that I am free right now," he said, getting to his feet. "Let's go have a look."

We were almost to the road when we ran into Hoot and Buddy on their way to go fishing.

"I got skunked, so I'm going to help Gabe with something, get a house ready to show Desi," Claude said. Buddy asked where it was.

"Up behind Wynn's house, still close to my shop. It has a wood stove, but it's a mess," I said.

"Uh, huh," he said, scratching his chin. "Good luck with that."

As Claude and I walked the half mile to the Messy House, he explained how he likes to handle bones, a job he takes on with a certain degree of reverence. At the Lake House, he moved Mr. and Mrs. Goodfellow to lie side by side among lichen covered rocks, their dog at their feet.

"I thought it was best to keep them separate, but close, the way they may have lived in real life," he said.

For Marvin and Pat Petry, that meant that each collection of bones was placed on a blanket with gloved hands, rolled into a giant lumpy cigar, and carried to the far side of a large forsythia hedge at the edge of the yard. Marvin on the left side in a beige blanket, Pat on the right in mauve pink. I suggested adding some personal mementos before covering them with mulch, and Claude agreed it was a good idea.

"And now for a prayer," he said, taking me off guard. He then launched into The Lord's Prayer, which we finished together. Amen.

I was feeling better about the house with the Petrys set to rights. Garbage and bugs came next. The windowsills were lined with dead flies, and moths ruled in the closets and cabinets. We opened up the doors and windows and got to work gathering garbage and sweeping up bugs.

I was out in the backyard, looking for a place to burn trash, when I heard clattering on the road. It was Buddy and Hoot, pushing a garden cart loaded with string trimmers, brooms, and yard tools.

"Ha! We found you! This here is Troutt's Country Homes and Landscapes. We're good, and we're cheap," Buddy announced.

"You can't beat our deals," Hoot added, pulling out a weed trimmer.

The guys were on a mission. They might have been drinking, but whatever. Within an hour the yard was reclaimed from weeds and briars, the deck was raked and swept, and garbage smoldered in a burn barrel. Buddy started a small fire in the wood stove to test the draft, saying it was a good idea to smoke out the bats. Only there are no more bats, I don't think. He says the wood stove works fine.

It was ready to show to Desi.

Back at the Dahlia House, I grabbed a quick, barely warm sponge shower and changed into clean clothes. I was in the kitchen eating leftover macaroni in marinara sauce when she burst through the door.

"Why am I the last to know you found us a house? Buddy but not me?" I could tell by the way she stuck out her lower lip that she was only pretending to be mad.

"Sarah found the house, she's been telling me to look at it, but there were issues. There are issues. Claude helped me with the bodies and some of the mess. Hoot and Buddy reclaimed the yard from the wilderness. The house still needs a lot of work, but it's way less gross, like down from a nine on the grossness scale to a four." I felt that was a good assessment. "Do you want to see it? It's close to Wynn's house."

"Jumping wildcats, you mean close to Prince?" She delicately reached for one of the last pieces of macaroni. I handed her the bowl to finish.

"We'll get water from his pump, but it's downhill to the new house, an easy carry. Or we might be able to do something with that little solar pond pump, I don't know. The house isn't perfect, but it should be warm."

"That's what Buddy said. He and Hoot think it's a good house. Can we go see it now?"

"Yup," I said, mimicking Buddy. "It's all ready for Little Girlie to see." She burst out laughing.

"That's exactly what he said!"

I had peeled back the tops on a couple of Citrus Magic air fresheners before I left, and between the open windows, the scent of oranges, and the removal of bodies and trash, the place felt recharged. I launched into a proper real estate showing.

"The kitchen is compact yet practical, and of course there is efficient wood heat in the main living area. You can have the large bedroom with the en suite bath, but we will probably both be bringing our beds in here when it gets cold. Look around, see what you think. We still have a lot of cleaning up to do."

"Clare and Sarah said they would help," she said, wandering down the hallway, gently touching the walls with her fingertips. This was starting to feel like a done deal.

I went to the bedroom that would be mine and looked in the closet. It was stuffed with clothes and shoes and assorted bins that appeared to be craft supplies. I opened a bin with an opaque lid, thinking it held spools of thread. Instead there were rolls of money, fives and tens rolled into inch-thick stogies taped in paper wrappers.

Desi ambled in from the back bedroom to show me the rings on her fingers. Diamonds, sapphires, maybe a ruby. "I think the lady of the house liked getting jewelry for her birthday," she said, taking off one of the rings and dropping it in her pocket.

"And there's something else, a banjo," I said. She followed me to the living room, and I heard her catch her breath when she saw the Deering.

"See how it sounds. You said you could play a little?"

"Very little," she said. She started picking out the notes to You Are My Sunshine, getting about half of them right, and then stopped.

"How about you? Do you like this house, or are you choosing it for me?"

"A little of both. Winter's coming, we'll be warm, and it's close to the rest of the Hokies. Check, check, check. And there are two cans of pineapple in the kitchen, a banjo, and wads and wads of money."

"Money?"

I told her about the rolls of cash, and that it was probably the tip of the iceberg. No telling what we might find among what the Petrys left behind.

She said she was in.

Speaking for Desi & Gabe, not incorporated, we now have more money than we have ever had in our lives. As we cleaned, we found cash in coffee cans in the kitchen cabinets, in envelopes in the underwear drawers, in shoe boxes on closet shelves.

"She wanted her nest egg here in her nest," Clare said as she tossed another roll of cash into the money collection bin we set in the middle of the living room. We now had thousands of dollars of cash, with which we could buy nothing.

Not that we're in desperate need. While I worked in the garage making room for bikes and carts, Clare, Sarah and Desi purged the kitchen of garbage and moth-infested grits, rice, and Jiffy cornbread mix, which the chickens will love. Wynn used the garden cart to deliver a 20-gallon plastic water tank, filled it with water, and then came back with ten more gallons to use for cleaning. The whole house got mopped twice.

As we are prone to do, Desi hummed and I whistled while we worked. From time to time I heard Clare singing along with our tunes if she knew the words, then laughing. Sometimes there would be a lower alto voice, Sarah's, singing harmony.

As a whistler I am always melody-forward, so I found this fascinating. I also desperately want to hear more music. More of Desi's harmonica, more of Wynn's trumpet, more of everything. I've been thinking that I should learn to play an instrument myself, something simple like a string bass. Should one become available.

For now, it's starting to rain, a steady drizzle that's bringing down the first poplar leaves, so we are using the time to settle in and get familiar with things. We need to figure out how we want to cook in the new kitchen, how we should store water, what décor stays and what goes.

As they used to say in the home renovation shows Mama Beth liked to watch, we are putting our stamp on it.

Each time we move a piece of furniture, we find more cash. What was Pat afraid of? Bank failures? Societal collapse? We have all that and more, and we're doing okay. Safety is important, we all work at it, but it can't be measured in money, and it's not something you can do alone.

Chapter 24   The Feast

October 15

The nights are getting long and dark, and there are no lights, no Netflix, and nowhere to go. Reading by lamp light is a struggle, and a few games of checkers or Yahtzee are enough for me.

And so we make a small fire in the wood stove and tell stories, not just about ourselves, but also old stories we know and can tell by heart. I'm pretty good with the old Tailypo spook story, where the creature comes calling at the hunter's cabin, demanding the return of its tail. "Tailypo, tailypo, gimme back my tailypo," it wails at the door. Things do not end well for the hunter.

Desi is really good at fairy tales. Goldilocks and the Three Bears. The Three Little Pigs. She can get quite dramatic when the wolf huffs and puffs at the pigs' houses built of straw, sticks, and bricks. It's like it's her story, outlining her search for a safe and secure home. For now, that need is being met.

One chilly morning Sarah came knocking at the front door. "Telegram for Desi and Gabe!" she called, letting herself in.

Desi jumped from the sofa, threw off the blanket she was wrapped in, and greeted her with a big grin.

"We got a telegram?" I asked, joining them from the kitchen. "I never got a telegram before. Nobody died, did they?"

She grimaced. "Not exactly, but we can talk about that later. It's actually a dinner invitation for this afternoon at the Manse. I can't tell you what we're having, it's a surprise, but the guys are going all out," she said.

Of course, we said we were in. She accepted my offer of a cup of tea.

"I'm so glad you're settled in here. Seriously, it's a good place, has a good vibe," she said, dropping into an upholstered chair.

"We really like it, even without cable," Desi said.

Sarah sighed and waved one hand through the air. "Not the important thing, it's the people. I didn't choose them any more than I chose my real family, but for as long I live, I'm staying with the Hokies." She sipped her mint tea, waved me a thank you with her fingers. "Seriously, I never thought of myself as someone who needs people, and then life smacked me a good one. Last winter, alone, it was awful. For me, I mean. Magnificently, monumentally terrible. I won't do it again. Life got better when Buddy came along, and then I found Wynn, and then everyone here, including you guys." Her eyes were wet with tears. "This is what makes me really happy."

"Even Hoot?" Desi asked, smiling and wrinkling her nose.

"Even Hoot." She ran her hand through her hair, damp from being out in the morning fog. "And you know, he may be wrong about some things, but he's right about others. Not that they matter anymore."

"They still matter to him," Desi said.

She had a point.

"And do you know what? He still believes in America,

always will. As long as we are still here, so is America, and it's okay to care about that," Sarah said.

"Our new America is more like the one that was here before the Europeans came. We've become hunter gatherers again," I said.

She laughed. "Only this time instead of nuts and berries we're after peanut butter, propane, and solar hardware." She stopped and clapped her hands once. "Oh, oh, speaking of solar hardware, we are changing our search strategy. Instead of looking for old stuff to reuse, Rob thinks we might do better if we looked for newer equipment, solar power stations with built-in inverters. He says some of them will have a switch for bypassing the battery."

I knew what she was talking about. Until it got too dangerous to be out in Blacksburg, Chan and I looked for portable power stations that might work for running small appliances. The problem was that the solar stations homeowners bought were all about battery charging, with no inverter for direct output. Those setups cost more, as in more than a thousand dollars. We never found one, and eventually had to stop the search for safety reasons.

"Where will you look?" I asked.

"Expensive RVs, some of my favorite places."

"Why do you like RVs?" Desi asked.

"Not sure," Sarah said. "But back when I was alone and foraging for food, it always felt good to go inside a sun-warmed RV, sit in the big seats, and have a snack. Helped me stop worrying. Most of the time they were empty, and clean. No bodies, no bugs. All I was looking for was food and comfort. That was then. Now, Rob says to look under beds and in storage compartments of nice RVs. We're looking for a thing the size of a suitcase with plugs on the sides."

Desi said she wanted to help.

"Sorry, kid, you're not invited. It's an overnight trip, seven miles one way to the RV park, and we're thinking me, Wynn, and Gabe." She turned to me. "Want to be on the dream team?"

"Sure," I said. "No problem." I could tell Desi wasn't happy about being excluded, but she has good instincts and knows better than to challenge Sarah and Wynn.

In answer to the question of what we should bring to the meal, Sarah said a song, or actually two. "You bring a song of your choice and play it, sing it, whatever, and then be ready to sing along with America the Beautiful. It's the finale. I can't explain it, but I got appointed musical director. I'm looking for a banjo. Hoot says he can play it if we can get him one."

"Really?" Desi asked. "He told you that?" Sarah nodded.

I knew she was frustrated trying to teach herself to play, but it still surprised me when she got the banjo from the hall closet and opened the case to show it to Sarah. "It came with the house. I'll let Hoot borrow it. I'm busy with the harmonica anyway." she said.

"Wowza, that's generous," Sarah said.

Desi shrugged. "It just feels right. No big deal. We'll bring it later."

The banjo was a light load as we walked down to the Manse, where the woods were showing more reds and oranges every day. Desi insisted on taking her turn carrying it.

"Confession, Bro. Are you ready?" I said sure. "It was my mom who played the banjo, not me," she said. "She wanted me to learn, but I said no way, mostly because I didn't want to be like her. Not in that way. She sang, too."

We stopped to pick up a limb that had fallen across the road. "It's okay if the banjo's not for you," I said. "Just don't stop humming, singing, and playing your harmonica. You could be gifted. We can see about getting you into the governor's school for genius teens."

"Fat chance," she said, handing over the banjo. "But my reading has gotten better, practice I guess, and Yahtzee really and truly is helping with my math. I like the Hokie high school. I'm learning a lot." Then she insisted on a final practice of our song.

We knew to arrive in midafternoon, because all serious cooking takes place when the light is good and Solar Sam and the water pump are running. Wonder of wonders, we smelled hickory barbecue as we entered the gates of the Manse.

"Jumping roosters, we're having barbecued chicken!" Desi said excitedly. "Does that smell good or what!"

I had to laugh. "It doesn't bother you, she who helps look after the chickens?"

"Not one bit," she said. "That's what they're for. And the big black and white one was mean." She disappeared into the house to get Clare's help with a costuming detail for our performance. Carrying the banjo, I walked around to the back where Buddy was working the grill.

"Ain't you a sight for sore eyes," he said, grinning and wiping his forehead with the back of his hand. "Good to see you down here in the holler."

261

"It looks like quite a do," I said, admiring the two tables set with dishes, napkins, tableware, beer, wine and bouquets of wildflowers. A third table was prepped as the food buffet, with several bowls covered with dish towels to keep out flies. "What's the occasion?"

"Might be we don't need one," Buddy said. "Might be we just wanted to eat us some chicken. I'm calling dibs on a thigh. Always been my favorite piece." We discussed who had the best chicken thighs in the time before, KFC or Popeyes. I took a stand for KFC original, though we agreed that the way Popeyes cut their wings was better.

"Where's Hoot? We found a banjo at the house. Sarah said he could play."

"That he can, or he used to. We'll see. He's down yonder, resting up. Got to coughing after he breathed in some smoke." He fed the fire a few hickory sticks, then looked at me with furrowed brows. "That ain't the half of it, Gabe. He coughs a lot, at night, and I seen blood on his bed pillow."

"He told me he had emphysema," I said. "I don't know much about it, just that it's a lung disease."

"Yup. He's had it a while. Says he used to take medicine for it. I talked to Wynn about it this morning, he said he'd see what he could do." He poked at the chicken pieces, then rearranged them on the grill. "Rob says he could be depressed, too, on account of feeling like he don't fit in."

That hit a nerve. I know how it feels when you're new, and different, and you're supposed to fit in but you don't. Foster kid 101, but those experiences were so long ago, and I've come so far since then, that I don't think of them much anymore. Hoot, his mother's special boy, never got those lessons.

In case he was napping, I whistled Working on the Railroad as I knocked on the door, and then let myself in. He was sitting up in the recliner, halfway to his feet when I told him to sit back down. "Whatever you say," he said, waving hello. He looked tired.

"Look here, Hoot, I brought you something we found at the house." I opened the case and picked up the banjo and put it in his lap. Then I handed him the pouch of finger picks. I looked up to see his mouth hanging open. He reached out and squeezed my shoulder.

"This ain't no dream is it," he said, running his hands over the instrument's strings and metal body. "I always wanted to play one of these. It's a Deering, American made." He started tuning it by ear, then put on three metal picks. After a few false starts, his fingers found their places and he played a slow version of a bluegrass song that was familiar to my ears. Salty Dog? *Let me be your salty dog, or I won't be your man at all. Honey let me be your salty dog.* Yes, that was it!

We heard clapping from the doorway when the song ended. It was Wynn, carrying a white paper bag. "Wonderful music, my man, you are full of hidden talents!" he said.

Hoot visibly blushed, which was touching. He said he was a little out of practice.

"Aren't we all?" Wynn said. "I have your prescriptions, some steroids and a mood moderator, plus a bottle of good cough medicine. Start with two steroids now, the others in the morning. We can try different cough medicines. Does that seem like a good mix to you?"

"Indeed it does," he said. "Might help me get some rest."

"Good, then. Clare says dinner in an hour." Wynn headed for the door. I left a few minutes later after getting Hoot some water to swallow his first round of pills. He was picking out notes he wanted to hear from the banjo as I closed the door.

Sarah rang the dinner bell to call everyone to the table. Desi had changed into a long, flowing blue dress with a high, ruffled collar, and she was already stealing the show. Rob clapped his hands, asked that we bow our heads, and led us in the God is Great, God is Good blessing. *By His hands we all are fed, thank You for our daily bread. Amen.*

Things got quiet after we filled our plates and sat down, because you can't talk when you're savoring your first barbecued chicken in over a year, with potato salad and beans and cabbage slaw and baked apples. It was a most excellent feast!

When second helpings had been taken, Clare got up and welcomed us all to the dinner. She wore a yellow cape over a black leotard, which was really quite fetching. "A special welcome to Desi, Gabe, and Hoot, because you're the newest arrivals," she said, raising her can of ginger ale into the air. "Today we are celebrating you being here with us, and the changing of the seasons. Claude will begin by reciting "Fall Leaves Fall," a poem written by Emily Bronte in 1846.

Claude took his place front and center, opened a small poetry book and cleared his throat. As if on cue, a breeze set off a rain of falling leaves. He read the poem in a strong, deep voice, as if to defy the leaves to stay on the trees.

"*Fall, leaves, fall; die, flowers, away;*
Lengthen night and shorten day;
Every leaf speaks bliss to me
Fluttering from the autumn tree.
I shall smile when wreaths of snow
Blossom where the rose should grow;
I shall sing when night's decay
Ushers in a drearier day."

We clapped quietly. It felt right. Sarah got up to announce the music. The first act was Wynn playing Autumn Leaves on his trumpet, which was perfect and beautiful and made the hair stand up on the back of my neck. The silence at the end, before the applause began, also was breathtaking.

Desi and I were next. She looked at me nervously and I told her it was okay. "We're going to play a song many of you know, you're welcome to sing along," I announced. We launched into our special rendition of End of the World, which started with me whistling a verse, and Desi answering on the harmonica. We hit the second verse together, then I whistled the bridge. Desi took over the last verse, without the usual key change, using a big breath to draw out the last note. She was awesome.

There was much clapping and shouting, and Sarah called for an encore. So we did the song again, and this time I heard voices singing the words. *Why does the sun go on shining, why does the sea rush to shore? Don't they know it's the end of the world since you don't love me anymore…"*

Not bragging, just saying we were great. Clare said

she wanted to be our agent.

Sarah retook the stage. "The last song is a sing along, and you better sing because otherwise you'll be listening to me. And here's the thing. I can sing with other people, but I can't sing alone. We will Sing America the Beautiful, which will start on this note." She blew into a silver pitch pipe, and raised her hands into the air, with the rest of us following her lead. *Ohhhh beautiful for spacious skies, for amber waves of grain…*" We were on a musical roll, and though everyone didn't know the words to the last verse, Claude's rich baritone carried us through.

"Thank you, thank you, that was such wonderful singing," Sarah said, bouncing on her toes. I think it might have been her first time leading a chorus.

The weather signaled the end of the party. The sky went cloudy and the wind puffed from the east, which often means cold rain. We worked together carrying the last food into the kitchen, washing dishes on the patio and cleaning up our mess outside. I was picking up some dropped silverware when I saw Hoot walking toward the house with the banjo tucked under his arm.

The main room in the Manse is often the scene of small performances and events. Claude has a wonderful reading voice, and right now he's reading The Hobbit for an hour every afternoon. While the kitchen clattered, Hoot got comfortable in Claude's reading chair and started playing the banjo. His hands remembered, his brain remembered, his soul remembered the instrument and its songs. The gospel classic, Life is Like a Mountain Railroad, echoed through the big room with its hard acoustics. I knew the song, and so did Desi. It drew her from the kitchen, her head cocked sideways to listen. Sarah was two steps behind her. Soon everyone was assembled for Hoot's impromptu concert, with Buddy and I standing in the open kitchen door.

"I don't know what done him more good, them pills or that banjo," he said, "But it sure is good to see."

"Funny how things work out," I said.

It was only later, when Desi and I were back at the house, debriefing about our big afternoon, that we appreciated what it meant for Hoot to set up in the gallery and start playing. It was the moment he joined the Hokies, accepted their invitation.

"A step anyway," Desi said. "He's trying. We all are, and that's good. But do you know what?"

"What?"

"We absolutely killed that song."

She had a point.

Chapter 25   The Mission

October 21

Fall is reaching its peak, and every day is an explosion of reds, oranges and greens against a deep blue sky. The tall grasses in the fields echo the wind in giant waves. Autumn was always beautiful in Floyd, but when you're not distracted by phones and jobs and school and all that stuff, it's spectacular.

There's a stand of pines near the house that's become a favorite roosting place for some crows. They know the house, and sometimes perch on the back deck to look in the windows. At first Desi felt spooked, but I told her they were just curious, needed something new on their tabloid feed.

"They live in family groups. Those are brothers, sisters and cousins who will report back to the parents," I explained. "We're no threat to them, and they know it. People don't eat crow."

"Why not?"

"Supposed to taste bad," I said. "But maybe not if they're eating seeds and insects instead of carrion."

She said she'd wait on the turkey. Once the weather turns really cold, turkey hunting is on the agenda. Based on what I saw when we hit the road for Mission RV, we may be hunting for Muscovy ducks and ringneck pheasant, too.

We met at Wynn's early in the morning, where Desi

received her instructions on caring for Prince, her consolation prize for not being included in the mission. Wynn, Sarah and I each carried a backpack with extra shirts, socks and shoes, binoculars, bungee cords, and plenty of food and water. We didn't think we would encounter other people, but we were prepared. A small maroon Hokie banner and white flag waved from Sarah's long walking stick, and I found space in my pack for a gift bag, assembled by Rob. It included a small jar of peanut butter, a chocolate bar, and fruit flavored lip balm still in the package. All precious, all good.

"Like a peace offering. You hit a dicey moment, you say see, I brought you a present."

He had a point.

The route was familiar to all of us, because we grew up here, learned to drive on these winding roads. There was a lot of tree debris for the first few miles, with several tough hills. Only a few vehicles were on the road at 2:42, and they're still there, pointing this way and that, a big white Citizens truck partly in a ditch. All are being driven by skeletons. It's easier to look away now that the windshields are clouded with dirt.

Then we turned onto Franklin Pike, where the road is flanked on both sides by what were once hayfields and pastures, now gone wild. Pheasants aren't supposed to be here, they're not native, but I definitely saw two, feeding on dropped grass seeds along the edge of the road. They must have escaped captivity and adapted, like the wild chickens. With the wildflowers and grasses providing shelter and showering the ground with seeds, they have managed to survive.

We also passed some turtles sunning themselves on a

log in a small pond, which delayed our progress. Sarah has a thing for turtles.

"Freeze," she said as soon as she saw them. "Look."

One at a time, in quick succession, a line of painted turtles plopped into the water. "Is that cool, or what?" she said, smiling.

The sign that announced we had reached the Floyd Family Campground was almost lost in the weeds, but a red welcome flag still fluttered in the breeze. We passed a cluster of rental cabins, with only one car parked in the lot.

"We may be looking at tonight's accommodations," Sarah said. "Bet those cabins are on Airbnb."

The wide gravel road to the campground had not been mowed but was still easy to follow. Maybe too easy. Sarah, who was leading the way, signaled us to stop.

"Do you think some of the limbs on the side of the road have been moved?" she asked in a quiet voice. "And look. There's a trail through the grass, see? I just noticed it."

She stepped aside so we could see the opening in the weeds, a very slightly trampled trail. "Could it be turkeys?" she asked.

I walked a short distance ahead, then turned around. "Don't think so. No poop, no feathers, no signs of foraging."

"All right, then," Wynn said. "Let's go see who's home."

We saw no sign of movement as we walked to a small building that was once the campground store. The chalkboard on the front porch that had been used for the day's weather forecast now bore two messages.

LOOTERS WILL BE SHOT in all caps, white chalk, but over that in orange chalk was 911 underlined three times, followed by the number 18.

It was a mixed message, perhaps from site number 18? Not wanting to look like looters, we moved to a picnic table to take a lunch break and look at the campground map I got from a rack outside the store. It was a gorgeous day, and we had good snacks and drinks, but we were preoccupied studying the map and checking out various RVs and tent setups with our binoculars. Number 18 was down the hill, in the main cluster of RVs.

"What if someone was terrified, at first, and then something happened, and they needed help?" Sarah mused.

"Then we should be helpers," Wynn said. "Offer assistance."

"We're good at that," Sarah said. "Let's go with Plan A."

Plan A consisted of Sarah leading with her flags flying, calling Hello! Hello! while I whistled Yankee Doodle with Wynn at my side.

We stopped outside number 18, where things did not look good. An older fifth wheel camper took a bad lick from a tree limb, which made a deep gash in the high windshield and roof. Was someone inside when it happened? I volunteered to look. The walkway to the RV was thick with fallen leaves, like nobody had been there for a while.

I knocked at the door. "Hello, my name is Gabe, and this is Sarah and Wynn. Are you in need of assistance? Did you call 911?"

No answer. The door was unlocked, and inside the

place looked lived in, but not nasty. No bodies, which is easy to see in a space that small. Lots of broken glass, though.

"Looks okay to me," I said.

It did not fit our profile for the type of RV that might have what we wanted, so we quickly checked under the bed and moved on. We were looking for adventuring types who fancied themselves rugged and invincible, armed with a piece of equipment that costs two thousand dollars. There were at least a dozen likely candidates among the RVs in the main campground, with more scattered on the hillsides. We had a lot of work to do.

With the larger RVs and buses, Wynn and Sarah looked in the low storage compartments and other utility areas, while I checked roofs for solar panels with attached wiring. We found no treasures after searching four high end RVs, but we got better at looking. We stopped to compare notes.

"I think our guy wouldn't use one of these cushy full hookup sites," Wynn said. "He's more of a free spirit, wants to be away from the crowd. We should look at those sites up on the hill." He had a point.

I said I thought someone had been there since 2:42. "In one of the RV's, the black and gold one, there was a body covered with a blanket."

Sarah nodded. "And have you noticed that there's no water anywhere, like none? Seriously, there's no bottled water, and the storage tanks in the RVs are empty. The propane tanks are empty or low. It's like somebody was here long enough to use up the water and the propane," she said.

"One winter would do it. And then what?" Wynn

said, making a deep frown. We were tired from walking all day, so it was hard to feel optimistic about human endurance.

"I think if they wanted to shoot at us, we would have heard from them by now," I said. We made no attempt to hide as we trudged up the hill to continue our search.

We worked our way through the first campsite and started on the next one when the noises started. I froze when I heard what sounded like cowbells coming from the direction of the cabins. And a foghorn. Someone was signaling us with game day noisemakers. Which is better than guns.

"We are being summoned," Wynn said, raising his eyebrows with interest. We stumbled down the hill as the cowbells continued. As we neared the cabins, I whistled Yankee Doodle as Sarah called "Hello! Hello!"

A middle-aged woman sat on the top step of the second cabin, ringing a pair of maroon cowbells. She wore baggy jeans and a flannel shirt, her hair hidden under a triangular kerchief. She made no attempt to get up, or to smile. We stopped in the middle of the yard.

"Hello, I'm Sarah, and this is Wynn, and Gabe," Sarah said, trying to sound friendly. The woman looked at each of us through slitted eyes.

"Let's get one thing straight," she said. Her voice was hard and steely. "I don't care who you are or where you came from, but you're not leaving here without me."

"Oh, no problem," Wynn said after a short pause. "As long as you're not an android."

"A what?"

"An android. An artificial being created by aliens to sabotage our survival."

"Do they really have those?"

"All things are possible," Wynn said. "Do you like tuna fish?"

"It's all gone," she said.

"As in, you ate it?"

"Yes. What is this about?"

"Androids don't eat tuna," Sarah said, laughing a little. "But you can't be too careful."

Finally, the hint of a grin, but just barely. I stepped forward to deliver the gift bag.

"We brought a present. Seems like you could use one," I said. She peered inside the plastic bag, saw the chocolate and lip balm.

"Oh, my, you shouldn't have," she said, not meaning it as a joke.

"Back to the topic of the day. We don't plan to leave until morning, but you're welcome to come with us," Wynn said. "It's a long hike, might take five hours. You'll need good shoes. And we'll need to know your name, for the record book."

She nodded. "My name is Evelyn Dubois, and I've been ready to go for a year. Or maybe longer? How long ago did everything stop? I lost track sometime last winter."

"That happened to me, too," Sarah said. She reached out to touch Evelyn's hand, but Evelyn quickly pulled it back.

That evening around the fire ring, after finishing off three cans of chicken noodle soup along with a loaf of Claude's sourdough bread, Evelyn explained her circumstances. She and her newish husband were in Floyd as tourists at 2:42, traveling in an RV she bought after selling her condo in Florida. "Danny talked me into it. I had my doubts but it made him happy, and now it's water under the bridge," she said. Danny was the dead guy covered with the blanket.

When the time felt right, Wynn asked why she thought she was still alive. "I've always been electric, never could wear a watch. They'd last a day, maybe three, then be dead as a doornail. Maybe that's why I didn't get it. I got something, but I didn't die like everybody else."

"Where were you when it happened?" he asked softly.

"Down by the creek. I had a nice little dog, named Daisy, and she liked to go walking down to the water on a hot day. I'd take a blanket and a book and grab a nap in the shade. At first that's what I thought happened that day, that I'd fallen asleep. And I had, but when I woke up it was almost dark and Daisy was dead. Cold dead. So was everybody else, Danny, all the dogs, all the people."

She had been alone since then. She tried and failed twice to find her way to town. The first time she took a wrong turn and got lost on a gravel road, and the second time she turned back after hearing gunshots.

"I missed you this morning because I went to get water. There's a good stream on down that way," she said, motioning to the south. "On the way back, I saw where it looked like a herd of elephants had flattened down the grass, so I knew somebody was here. Never felt so happy and scared at the same time."

"We've all had similar experiences," Sarah said. "But now the worst is over. Believe me."

"It has to be," Evelyn said, shaking her head. "I was

not built for this, not at all."

I sensed an opportunity to change the subject. "We came here in search of electronics equipment, and I wonder if you can give us tips on where to look. There might be fold-out solar panels involved," I said. "We're especially looking for the gizmo boxes that go with solar or wind units. Do you know of anyone who was staying here who might have been nerding out on solar stuff, or maybe have a survivalist streak?"

She smiled. "I think you are talking about Zachary, the blue bus at the top of the hill. He'd been here a while, got packages all the time. I know because they leave them on the porch at the store for all to see. When I went to pick up a package, there were always one or two for him. He was always fiddling with solar panels. He liked Daisy, wanted to pet her when we passed by on our walks. Nice young man."

"Interesting," I said. "We'll give it a look at first light."

It was a still, cloudy morning, with leaves falling in gentle waves. Sarah waited behind for Evelyn so she wouldn't feel abandoned, and Wynn and I headed up the hill, eating the boiled egg sandwiches, dried apples and cold coffee Rob packed for us.

Zachary's converted school bus, named Julie according to the sign on the door, is a wonder of wonders. There is a cushioned bench along one side, a small kitchen and computer workspace on the other, and a double bed at the end, with side tables and lamps and a plush comforter with accent pillows. Every corner is attractively decorated in light blues, greens, and creamy white, all in perfect order and camera ready, down to the empty red mug next to the sink. In the front of the bus, the rider's seat was a clutter of tools, components, and a Samsung tablet on a stand. This is where he worked on things, maybe shot some still photos.

"Wowza," Wynn said, climbing the stairs into the bus and looking around. "This is nice!"

"I think he was a vagabond influencer," I said. "I don't think he lived in the bus, just used it as a set. You know, your happy traveler in a refurbed bus, reporting from the Blue Ridge Parkway. It looks like the video crew could arrive any minute."

He agreed with my assessment. Zachary wasn't inside the bus, so we thought he might be in the cabin tent outside, now low-slung and lumpy. Two of the support poles were bent, but we managed to get the structure semi-upright by lifting together from opposite ends, one, two three. Then we gagged and ran. Whatever was in the tent stunk to high heavens, acrid and sour and moldy and bad. Anaerobic decomposition that would choke a dog.

Wynn looked pale and sat down at a picnic table, trying not to lose his breakfast. I held my breath and zipped open the doors and windows of the tent to help it air out. Glancing inside, I saw a cot, a chair, and what appeared to be two corpses.

Things were not looking good for Zachary. In the time before, what if he was a YouTube star, with a zillion followers on Instagram? The techie equipment in the front seat of the bus was mostly computer peripherals and photography items, not what we needed. The contents of the tent were ruined, and the storage bins under the side of the bus were locked. At Wynn's suggestion, we decided to wait for Sarah, who is an expert at breaking into things.

She soon appeared with Evelyn, talking and pushing baby carriages, which are actually quite useful for transporting things. Sarah pushed a three-wheeled carriage, which is nice to have when the road is funky. Evelyn pushed a rectangular pet stroller. Her hair was covered in a splashy turquoise and yellow turban, surprising but not unattractive.

"We've been waiting for you, my darling. Perhaps to unlock the goods!" Wynn called out, getting to his feet. "Come and see this beautiful bus, but go nowhere near that tent." He shook his finger for emphasis.

Following a quick tour, we sat together in the bus and brought them up to date. Evelyn thought the second body might be that of "the China Man" who arrived in a rented RV at a nearby site a few days before everything stopped. "He didn't speak English, just nodded and smiled. I know it's not proper, but me and Danny just called him the China Man. He was friends with Zachary," she explained.

"Well, then, we'll need to check it out," Wynn said. "But first there's the matter of the storage bins here in the bus."

Sarah stood up and pretended to crack her knuckles. "Watch a pro at work," she teased. First she checked the two glove boxes, then the floor mats and under the front seats, then the refrigerator, looking for keys. She found the ignition key by itself on a key ring, but no locker keys until she looked inside a tiny cabinet above the stove.

"Zach had things he didn't want stolen," she said, dangling a small key ring with a pink rabbit's foot on it. It was ghetto cool, must have made good video.

Then things got weird, as in this-can't-be-real type weird. On the metal shelves under the carriage of the bus, there were three closed plastic bins full of solar interface hardware. These included small capacity sine wave inverters and surge controllers, a new hybrid inverter, and two shoeboxes full of connectors. Sarah screamed.

In the next bay there were folded solar panels and small appliances, a coffee maker, crockpot, two bins of clothes, and an assortment of electric fans. Was one of his interests running small appliances from a direct solar feed and making videos about it? Was that a niche thing in The Time Before? If so, I never got the memo. Could have been easy money.

Sarah and Evelyn went back inside the bus and checked every drawer, shelf and cabinet for items of interest. They gathered several nice toiletries, a few tins of smoked oysters, and small pillows and towels to use as padding for the electronics in the carriages.

The four of us went to the China Man's RV together. The boxy Cruise America RV was unlocked, unoccupied, and clean. A laptop was open on the table, and the spaces behind the front seats contained cloth shopping bags filled with Asian foods like rice noodles, soy sauce, sesame oil, and a tub of gochujang paste.

"Zachary's friend was Korean, not Chinese," I said, setting the bags aside. "Big difference, at least to him." My Blacksburg buddy Chan, who was upper class Chinese, thought the Koreans were stuck-up cultural thieves, but that was his opinion. I was happy to get the food, because living with Chan and Mai taught me to appreciate Asian flavors.

Sarah scooted behind me to inspect the open suitcase on the bed. She riffled through the neatly folded clothes before finding a wallet and set of keys in a storage compartment beside the bed.

"His name was Kwan, from Greensboro," she said, returning the items to their storage space.

"Thanks for the food, Kwan," I said, bowing slightly. "I am honored by this gift." Sarah said "Amen" as she went outside to check the storage compartments.

Call me a nerd. Call me an optimist. Call me a sneak. All true, which is why I closed Kwan's laptop and slipped it into one of the food bags along with its charger and his wallet. What if we found a way to bypass the battery and run it? What if polarity reversed in such a way that batteries would recharge again? WHAT IF? Before everything stopped, there were some awesome Korean video games that might work from Kwan's hard drive. Rather than think too small, I grabbed Zachary's tablet from the bus, too.

We can always hope.

Chapter 26   Keeping Secrets

November 1

One of the things you learn going through people's houses is that everyone keeps secrets. Secret money, secret bottles, secret letters and photographs. I know how it feels to live among things hidden or unsaid, because being an unwanted child is a major secret. You never tell it, and you never outgrow it, even when you become wanted or are no longer a child. Someone will spot your fatal defect if they know your parents abandoned you. There had to be a reason for that to happen, so you keep it a secret.

Desi is a keeper of secrets, too. Others were not to know how crazy her mother got at times. Living out of the car was their private business. She keeps most things to herself out of habit, if not need. If I want to know about something going on at the Manse after she's been there all day, I have to ask.

Evelyn is not a big talker, so she may have similar tendencies. On the way back from Mission RV, we stopped to rest at New Haven Baptist Church, familiar territory since we use it to store food and supplies. Among the houses and buildings used as storage depots, the hilltop church with its tall steeple is our most distant outpost. Wynn chose it because the big parking lot, open fields and nearby wetlands make it less likely to burn up in The Incineration compared to say, my house or his, which are surrounded by trees.

We were all tired, but Evelyn seemed nervous as we talked about what we would do when we got home. It was getting late, so Sarah suggested parking the carriages in Wynn's garage and unpacking the next day.

"Works for me," I said. "I don't know about you, but I'm beat."

"What do you say, Evelyn. Ready for some rest?" Sarah asked.

Instead of answering, Evelyn looked up toward the sky, blinking back tears while crossing her heart with her right hand. "I don't know what to do," she whimpered, starting to cry for real. "Promise you won't leave me," she begged between sniffs.

"That's not going to happen," Wynn said, with Sarah nodding in agreement. Evelyn had given the afternoon trek her best shot, helping clear debris for the carriages and keeping up despite a limp due to foot blisters.

"I am afraid I am unclean," she blurted between sobs. "You wondered about my hair? I have nits. Head lice. I have cooties!" She took a deep, ragged breath. "I'm so embarrassed."

"Oh, Evelyn, take heart. We have a shampoo for that, safely stored and ready to go," Wynn said.

"You do?"

"Indeed. You'll be right as rain in no time."

Sarah explained that Wynn used to work at the drugstore, and had moved as many useful items as he could into safe storage.

Evelyn's sobs subsided, but she continued to sniff and wipe her face with the front of her shirt. "I tried to fix it, cut my hair, washed it in the stream and then put baby oil on it," she said. "I haven't felt any crawling things, so it could be working," she said hopefully.

"Good job. Seriously, Evelyn, it will be okay," Sarah said.

It was time to declare my knowledge of head lice. During my early teenage years, when Randall and Mama Beth were still taking new foster children, several times I served as assistant nit remover. Anyone could catch head lice in school, but our kids came from dirty homes with under-functioning parents. They were the ones who carried the head lice to school.

Not after Mama Beth got hold of them. After a long, soapy bubble bath with medicinal shampoo, she would sit the child at the kitchen table, dip her fingertips in a bowl of herbal conditioner, and slowly snip and comb through their hair. My job was to keep the kid entertained by giving them Teddy Grahams, making faces, telling them stories, or whistling. The kids loved it. They loved getting cleaned up, loved being the center of attention, loved smelling like lavender.

"I've been around this before, it just happens. You can come to my house, where I live with my sister. We'll get you fixed up," I said.

I may have heard Wynn breathe a sigh of relief. Newcomers to the Manse require an invitation from the group, and Wynn is much too particular to entertain a guest with head lice. He said he'd deliver a box of Nix asap.

Desi was waiting for me at home, with water warming on the wood stove. She was stunned into silence by the appearance of Evelyn behind me as we stumbled through the kitchen door.

"We have company," I announced. Evelyn made a small curtsy.

"Your brother and his friends rescued me. He offered me shelter, with your approval of course, despite a delicate problem," she said.

Desi stiffened her back to make herself look taller, and touched her hand to her collarbone. For a second, I was so proud of my little alpha female, showing off her nice feathers. "A delicate problem?" she asked.

"Yes. Head lice." Evelyn met her eye to eye.

"Oh," Desi said, trying to dramatize being disappointed. "Is that all you got?" She looked at Evelyn's turban, slightly askew from the day's exertions. "You don't have like, dreadlocks under there do you? Because if you do, they have to go."

"Not at all," Evelyn said, and explained how she washed and conditioned her hair, cut it by pulling it into a ponytail at the top of her head and lopping it off, and then rubbed her head with baby oil. Desi listened carefully.

"It's a start," she said.

Wynn is so good at arriving on cue that I wonder if he waits outside the door for the perfect moment. He rapped at the front door.

"Special delivery for Evelyn Dubois," he announced. He brought the promised box of Nix, two gallons of room temperature water, and a women's personal care kit designed to go through airport security that included a toothbrush, toothpaste, skin cream, and random other stuff. Two steps behind him, Sarah brought an inflatable mattress, pillow, and blanket, and a small stack of clothes she thought might fit.

Evelyn started crying again. "You've been so kind, I don't deserve this," she sputtered. I saw Desi blinking back a few tears, too. Sometimes accepting help is harder than giving it.

The next morning I awoke to feminine voices. "You can't comb nits in the dark, we have to wait for good light," Desi said. I liked hearing confirmation of their agenda, because I had plans of my own. To speed breakfast along, I made scrambled egg and mashed potato sandwiches. When there's no meat or mayo or butter, you can use mashed potatoes mixed with homemade ketchup instead. Evelyn said her sandwich was delicious, and she ate every bite.

Wonder of wonders, we were just finishing up when Clare knocked softly at the kitchen door. "Good morning!" she called. "Is everyone decent?"

"We're always decent," Desi said, rinsing the dishes in a dribble of water. She introduced Evelyn, who looked different with her hair down, older and less exotic. I guessed she was in her mid-fifties, or maybe older but well kept. She wore a baggy blue sweatshirt over black yoga pants, and despite her first shampoo the night before, her hair hung in greasy, uneven chunks

"I came to give Desi a hand, and also to tell Gabe that Rob is plugging in the wind generator. The wind is up, and he wants to try it again."

"I'm in," I said. "Maybe the third try will be the charm."

Evelyn objected that she didn't want to be so much trouble, but Clare gave one of her dazzling smiles and said not to worry, helping with hair was one of her jobs when she worked as a summer camp counselor when she was a teenager.

"You were a counselor?" Desi asked. "I always wanted to do that."

"Watch what you ask for. Now you're camping all the time," Clare teased.

I put on my jacket, replenished the water warming on the wood stove, and trotted up to Wynn's house. I let myself in through the side garage door, relieved to see that the buggies were still fully packed, as we'd left them the night before. I pulled out Kwan's food bags and quickly rearranged the contents, placing the laptop, tablet and Kwan's wallet in one of the bags, hidden behind a tall package of rice noodles and various sauces. I set the bag outside the door. The other bag would go to the Manse.

I began sorting through the solar interface treasures, setting aside the large-capacity components, no longer trying to keep quiet. In short order Wynn and Prince joined me, the cat meowing hello and Wynn handing me a warm cup of tea. "Raspberry hibiscus with lemon grass, supposed to support radiance," he said.

He looked at the converters and controllers I had placed next to the food bag. "All of this to go?" he asked.

I sighed. "Maybe not all of it, depending on what you think. I'm wondering about keeping some of the low-amp stuff here, taking some to my place, to see what it can do. Maybe set up another Sam, I don't know. The more powerful modules will go to the Manse." I told him that Clare had come to help with Evelyn's hair, and I was heading to the Manse to help Rob fire up the wind generator.

"All things are possible," he said.

I filled the dog buggy to capacity with electronics, and stopped at my workshop to stash my secret Korean treasures.

"This is unbelievable!" Rob said as I unpacked controllers, inverters and other mystery components and arranged them on the kitchen table. He noticed me glazing over when he started reading amp and voltage ratings, because he snapped his fingers to get my attention. "Gabe, this may not be your thing, but somebody has to learn it. Claude, too. Your future, or at least the quality of it, could depend on how well you can fit pieces like this together."

"Did I hear my name?" Claude asked, yawning in the kitchen doorway. He helped himself to the carafe of warm peppermint tea and joined us at the table. The dwindling supply of coffee was reserved for weekends.

"What have we here?" he asked, surveying the loot. He reached for a large inverter with several connector wires attached with masking tape. "This one's been out for a test run."

"See if you can find a controller that matches, same manufacturer." Rob said, getting up from his chair. He got a spiral notebook and pen from one of the kitchen drawers and handed it to me. "For your inventory," he added before disappearing into the gallery.

"He's been a bit testy," Claude said quietly, picking up a small controller. "You know he doesn't sleep."

"So I've heard," I said. "Must be hard."

Claude sighed. "I think he's lonely. For his wife. They were together almost thirty years. It must be like missing a hand. Speaking of which, has Desi told you about our covert operation?" he asked, half smiling and pulling his earlobe.

"Not that I recall. What's the deal?"

He cleared his throat. "I want to ask Clare to marry me, but I need a ring. Desi is collecting them on sugar runs, when Clare isn't watching."

"Like a diamond ring?" Now that he mentioned it, I had noticed Desi wearing a sparkly ring one day, but it looked like a little ruby.

"Not necessarily. Just so it's beautiful and she likes it."

We developed a sorting system by listing items by manufacturer and carrying or charging capacity. Claude didn't question me when I added a column for country of origin, which turned out to be quite global, as in Denmark, China, Korea, Japan, the US, and Unknown because we can't read Cyrillic. Could be Russia, Bulgaria, Slovenia, hard to say since we can't look it up on the net.

He handed me a rather heavy inverter. "Here's something, Gabe. See the battery bypass switch? This baby swings both ways." It was an impressive haul, and then I pulled out the Super G food bag containing sesame oil, rice wine vinegar, canned curry sauces, dried salted fish and rice noodles.

"My man, you have outdone yourself," he said, clapping me on the shoulder. He got up and called up the stairs. "Hey Rob, come see this!"

We heard fast, quick footsteps overhead. "Sorry if I was short earlier. This is not my time of year," he said when he entered the kitchen. He picked up the hybrid inverter and looked at its connections. "But maybe winter won't be so bad after all. Solar panels in every home!"

As Rob oohed and aahed over the cool foodstuffs, I

sensed my moment. "Speaking of internet," I said. "Rob, have you tried to run a laptop from Solar Sam? I'm wondering if it might be possible to get some games up or something should we have available power. There are some smaller modules that wouldn't fit in the buggy I might fiddle with."

Rob said he didn't know, but we could try. "Sarah put a couple of laptops in the wine cellar last summer when it got hot. We'll need a steady output, solar for sure, but there's not much to lose." He hesitated. "You know, it really could work. The adapter would work as an extra controller. Look through the panels in the barn and see if there's something you can use." Music to my ears.

Buddy came in through the back door along with a rush of windblown leaves, smiling when he saw there was company. "Hey Gabe, nice surprise," he said, then turned to Claude. "Hoot's having a hard time with the dry air, wants to know if you'll fix him some of that slippery tea."

"Be happy to, one order of slippery elm with anise tea, coming up." Claude walked around the kitchen counter to start on the project. "Tastes terrible, but the herb books say it will help with a cough."

"He needs oxygen, but we're fresh out," Rob said, turning to me. "Any ideas?"

I looked around the big kitchen, crowded with houseplants that spent the summer on the patio. "Is there a wood stove down there, for heat?" I asked.

"Definitely. A nice one," Rob said.

"Then you move some of these plants down there. They won't actually increase oxygen, but they will humidify and purify the air, and maybe improve his mood. Plants can do that."

Rob smiled. "Ask the biologist a question, get a biology answer," he said. "You guys ready to pull the trigger on Mr. Spin?" He got up and walked to the door, picking up a heavy pair of gloves. Claude got his jacket and the fire extinguisher, while I donned a lighter pair of leather gloves and took my place by the converter.

"Ready?" Rob called, and we both gave the thumbs up sign. He turned on the turbine switch and nothing blew up. He motioned to me and I turned on the converter. The needle on the display started to bounce, but no sparks flew.

"It's in the normal range," I called, "Way better than last time." Rob scampered over to see for himself.

"Very nice. On to phase two," he said. Claude followed Rob into the house, fire extinguisher ready, and a moment later a miracle occurred, a ten on the wonder of wonders scale. A table lamp outfitted with an LED bulb shone through the window, light as day. I checked the output display on the converter, and there was no change. I gave the thumbs-up, and a second lamp turned on.

I couldn't help it. I jumped in the air and cheered, then ran into the house to congratulate Rob and Claude. We did it, turned wind into light, and nothing caught fire. This was becoming a very big day. In addition to producing light, Rob thought Mr. Spin could run a couple of electric blankets on blustery nights. "It won't match the output of Sam on a summer day, but every little bit helps," he said, a big grin on his face. It was rare to see him so happy.

I helped Buddy carry some houseplants to his place

and get them installed near the windows. Then I stayed to visit while Hoot sipped his tea, which really did help him stop coughing as long as he didn't talk too much. I carried on a one-sided conversation, reporting on the previous day's adventure and doing my best to describe Evelyn, whose arrival was hotter news than Mr. Spin.

"I hardly know her, but she seems very nice. Kind of ladylike in her ways, maybe. She's been through a lot, I think it's been rough, surviving alone," I said.

"Sarah says she might be kinda pretty when she's cleaned up," Buddy said, winking at Hoot. It made me laugh.

"Don't talk about women like they're horses. They hate that," I said.

I wished I hadn't made the joke, because Hoot started laughing and then coughing, and it wasn't pretty. I went back to talking, telling him about seeing the pheasants and saying how it was about time to start tracking a Thanksgiving turkey. He said he'd be right behind me.

Before I left, Buddy showed me around the solar graveyard in the horse barn, which was an assortment of small panels collected by the Hokies on their sugar runs. Everything was dusty, but there was a set of folding panels, still in the case, rated at 110 watts, enough to power a reading lamp and most certainly a laptop. I said I'd take it, as well as two smaller rectangular units because why not? I loaded them into a shopping cart.

When I stopped by the kitchen to say goodbye to Rob, he was busy filling a shopping bag with food items he thought we might need. Along with eggs and a box of cilantro-lime rice, there was instant cappuccino, ginger candies, and a tin of smoked salmon in olive oil. I knew he kept a stash of items of which there was too little to share, but smoked salmon?

"Welcome wagon," he said, dropping the bag into my cart. "And be careful out there," he added, patting the case that held the solar panels.

I appreciated his confidence in me. On the way home, I stopped at Wynn's well to pump water. It was a bright day, so I set up the solar fountain pump. You pump water into a tub manually, and then the solar pump pushes it through a hose that carries it down to a cistern by our house. There's a second line to Wynn's house. When the sun is shining and the pump is working, it takes no time to fill our cisterns, which are large coolers with spigots. We have fresh water right in our backyards that we didn't have to carry.

I like to think of us as space age peasants.

Chapter 27   Family Jewels

November 15

Desi and I didn't need an active mother in our lives, but when Evelyn moved in with us, we got one. It was mostly little things, like the way she would stare at a jacket on the floor that needed to be picked up, and then move her gaze to the offender and sigh. This technique was highly effective on me. I would jump up and pick up rather than risk trouble. Not so much with Desi, who might shrug and go back to reading her book. She would attend to her mess when she was ready. She always did.

On the other hand, Evelyn was getting stronger day by day, less frightened and more animated. The more I got to know her, the better I understood how terrifying the past year was for her. When she says, "I was not built for this," I think she means she cannot be alone. She needs a mate, or perhaps a flock. When we found her, she was on the verge of giving up.

I got her full bio when I took her to Wynn's for her initial interview. As was his custom, he had snacks and drinks on the table in the sunroom, and Sarah and I were present for moral support and to ensure moderation. Wynn can be intense at times, and Evelyn was still in rough shape. Both feet had blisters from the long walk, so she wore fuzzy pink bedroom slippers.

Wynn had already written up her version of 2:42, and now he added her personal information. Evelyn Renee Dubois, age 57, lived much of her life in Georgia, remarried and moved to Florida, and more recently was living the RV life. She has no drug or food allergies, but said she might need reading glasses because she had been having periodic headaches. She could play a little piano. "I used to like to draw, and paint," she said when asked about hobbies. "But that was a long time ago."

Evelyn has an interesting marital history. Danny was her fourth husband, an unusual occurrence in Floyd where one to two husbands are the norm. Everyone gets a pass on number one because mistakes happen, and marriage number two could end in death, or divorce due to mistreatment or incompatibility. Then what? Do you keep looking for Mr. Right, or are you somehow Mrs. Wrong?

"I kept picking badly," she said in a soft voice. "When I left my first husband, he was cheating on me and I'd had a miscarriage, and we were both a mess. He was a sweet boy, and I still think of him sometimes, miss him in a way."

"My second husband was physically and emotionally abusive, but we had a child together, Sky. I finally divorced him because I was afraid that he might hurt or kill us. After that, Sky was my life." She started weeping quietly. "I wish I knew where he was, if he made it. He was in Atlanta, Midtown." Sarah handed her a box of tissues. "I don't even know if he tried to call me," she said, pulling her dead phone from her bra.

"Oh, that's pretty," Wynn said, admiring the floral art on her phone cover. "Keep it safe. Just in case." He does have his soft side.

Sarah spoke up. "And then you married again?" she asked gently.

"Unfortunately, yes." She sat up straighter in her chair. "Maybe I saw myself as damaged goods, not worthy of a good man. My other two marriages aren't worth discussing, except for what I learned. I can't be married to an unfaithful partner, I know that, but I can't be alone either." She blew her nose.

"You might like living with a group. There's a similar feeling of protection," Sarah said. Evelyn said she was ready to give it a try.

Even so, she declined invitations to visit the Manse. We told her about Claude, Buddy, Hoot and Rob, but she said she wasn't ready to meet them. "When my feet are better, and we're a hundred percent sure about my problem," she told Sarah, touching her hair, which looked fine, even shiny. "Give me a few days."

Meanwhile, gift bags from Rob arrived, containing surprising little treats from the kitchen and pantry. When she delivered some eggs, Clare also brought a bag of Werther's caramel candies and three little cans of V8.

"Your Rob is a very thoughtful fellow," Evelyn said to Desi, handing her the bag of candies.

Desi slowly unwrapped a piece. "He was married forever, lost his wife and two grown kids. He doesn't sleep," she said, licking her fingers. "He is a beautiful, gentle soul, a truly good man. Caring, smart, funny, better than your best imaginary favorite uncle."

"He sounds wonderful," Evelyn said.

"He is. Which means, which means if you hurt him, we'll have to kill you."

"I see," Evelyn said evenly. "I'll keep that in mind."

The next day Claude delivered three pouches of Spam singles and a package of chocolate wafers along with a loaf of bread, still warm from the oven.

"Hello, lady Evelyn, so happy to meet you," he said,

extending his hand. For the record, Claude is handsome and charming, the kind of man who attracts women without trying. Plus, he was born into old money, which reportedly affected his character, not in a good way.

"He used to be a jerk, but not anymore. Did you know they used to call him Rolex? It was his nickname, for showing off his non-working watch. Now it's like he's a reformed narcissist," Desi said when she told me about the rings. "Sarah says helping take care of Gina, the woman who died, changed him for the better. So I've been helping him find a ring so he can propose to Clare."

"Does Sarah think they should get married?" I asked.

"I don't know. Clare is kind of religious, and for her marriage is for life, till death do us part. If Claude committed to her that way, I think Sarah would be happy for her," she said. "Clare and Sarah get each other. They're pretty tight."

She knew Claude was coming to look at her stash, which she arranged in a black velvet ring tray according to type. She showed it to Evelyn and me after breakfast as soon as the light was good. On the left there were a dozen sparkling white diamond solitaires, other rings with blue jewels in various shades, and a few accented with tiny green emeralds. On the right were vintage rings with rubies, sapphires and other gems in elaborate engraved settings.

"What have we here?" Evelyn said, instantly alert.

"For Clare. Claude wants to propose, but not without a ring. It's his way. So I've been collecting them on sugar runs. These are all in her size, I checked."

"May I?" Evelyn reached for one of the diamonds.

"Of course," Desi said.

Wonder of wonders, Evelyn knows her way around jewelry. "This is a three-stone ring, supposed to symbolize the past, the present and the future. Harry gave Meghan one of these," she said, returning it to the tray. She plucked out the only ring with a black stone and squinted at it. "Do you have a magnifying glass?"

The best I could do was a little plastic magnifier from an eyeglass repair kit, which she used to examine the ring. "Look at the cuts," she said, passing both to Desi. "It could be a black diamond, very rare in that large size, but we need jeweler's loupe to get a better look. If that's what it is, it's quite a find. Valuable, too. And dark gemstones, the authentic ones, are thought to have special powers."

"How about the others? Which costs the most?" Desi asked, slipping the black diamond on her middle finger.

"Hard to say. The stones in the older rings are the real thing, not cultured, and any big stone, over a carat, is worth more. That's about a quarter inch." She picked out four rings and placed them on the table. "I think these cost several thousand dollars each."

I whistled a little wowee and picked up a ring with a dark red gem surrounded by small diamonds. "Perhaps a Burmese ruby," she said. She thought the emeralds in a vintage ring might be from Colombia, the black diamond from Brazil. She told Desi that she had a good eye.

"I still don't get it. I mean, if Claude wants to give Clare a ring, that sounds fun, but is it really necessary? Like, maybe a tattoo would be better?" Desi asked, exchanging the black diamond for a white solitaire.

Evelyn laughed, a gentle trilling sound. I wondered if she had been alone so long that she had forgotten how to laugh and was just finding her happy voice. I think that may have happened to me.

After delivering his food gifts, Claude was ready to shop for jewelry. "I don't think Clare is a big rock kind of person," he said as he looked over the rings. "I like the ones with a bit more art to them." He pulled a jeweler's loupe from his pocket.

"Me, too," Desi said. "You should put the ones you don't like on one side, and your favorites on the other."

"Good idea." He quickly rejected the diamond solitaires with high, spiky settings, muttering something about too many sharp points, and he seemed drawn to the rubies and emeralds. He picked out four rings and took them to the window for a closer look.

"Evelyn says the red one might be a Burmese ruby," Desi said.

"Myanmar. I've been there," he said. Then he got a strange look on his face, sad and wistful. "These could be the last of all that for a while. Diamonds from Africa, rubies from Myanmar. Assuming the whole world stopped, these jewels are what we have, what will always be. Those places, those people, do they even exist anymore? Myanmar is mostly jungle, it would grow over in a year."

"No way to know," Evelyn said, speaking up from her place on the sofa. "But I'm not betting on it."

This got Claude's attention, because he loves speculating about what happened at 2:42. "You would think there would be planes in the sky, if civilization survived," he said.

"The fact that we're here confirms some level of survival, bare bones though it may be," Evelyn said.

"Whether by grace or luck, look at where you are, and what you've accomplished. It's really quite impressive."

Desi looked at her and wiggled her shoulders. "The little green men will be here soon. They just want to fatten us up some first," she said.

"If they want to eat meat, why did they kill off all the animals?" I asked, following her lead. "Except for birds. Does everything taste like chicken to them?"

"Actually, I heard they like to snack on the batteries in electric cars. Some say that was the cause of it all," Claude said, laughing.

Evelyn started laughing, too. "The car we pulled behind the RV was a Chevy Volt. Don't tell anyone."

It was great to hear her sounding normal, because Evelyn is definitely different, like she came from another time or place. This is reflected in her handwriting, which I saw when she helped make up an inventory list of the electronic components I kept. She wrote quickly, printing letters so neat and square that they could have been made by a machine.

"Working as an executive secretary will do that," she said when I complimented her penmanship. "Everyone must be able to read your notes." Our equipment spreadsheet is more elaborate than the one Claude and I put together at the Manse, because Evelyn added columns on battery type, Wifi, and Bluetooth where appropriate. Her interest in our future connectivity seems quite keen, but she has a motive. At least once a day she mentions wanting to get in touch with her son, Sky.

Chapter 28   Hands Together

November 20

It's been a long time since we heard guns fired in town or up on the ridge, a couple of months. We don't want to make loud noises either, don't want to call attention to our presence in case someone is listening. But the woods are thick with turkeys, and Buddy says if I bring him a couple of young ones, he'll dress them and cook them for Thanksgiving dinner.

The Hokies are hungry for meat. We still have eggs, but the extra roosters have been eaten. The pond where Hoot found domestic ducks has been vacated, the fish stopped biting in the lake, and canned meat is in short supply.

Claude volunteered to be my hunting partner. "I once had a good eye with skeet, and turkeys are so much bigger," he joked.

"I haven't fired a shotgun in years," I said. "We'll be on the same level."

"Don't worry, shotguns are easier than rifles," Hoot said. He thought we should practice using his shotgun and the one that hung on the wall in Buddy's cabin. "You know, to get the feel of it." Mostly he wanted to be around shooting. I knew how much he wanted to hunt with us, I saw the mix of joy and sadness in his eyes as he offered advice. But some days he had trouble walking to the Manse. He was in no condition to go tromping through the woods at dawn.

I said we were too close to town for shooting, that up on the Parkway would be better.

Buddy wanted to be involved, too. "Don't take out the big daddy gobbler, the meat would be tough and the flock needs him. Get the young ones, the jakes, they're big and ugly but way better eating," he advised.

We still needed another lesson on handling the shotguns, but we were feeling almost ready to hunt turkey. The weather was not. Cold rain kept temperatures in the 40's, nippy but not unbearable unless you're wet. But with no solar anything, staying inside was getting unbearable, at least until Evelyn left.

Maybe it was the vibes she picked up from Desi and me, but on the first morning after the weather cleared, she asked to be taken to the Manse. "I'm ready now. Do you think there will be anyone at home?"

"There is always someone at home," Desi said, trying not to sound too eager. "Rob, Buddy and Hoot never go anywhere. I'll take you down there. Just give me a minute to change clothes." I went along to pick up some cables for a solar station I've been working on.

Evelyn seemed nervous at first, but her mood lightened as we entered the gates and she saw the big, beautiful house. Clare was on the front porch, hanging laundry on the line. She stopped when she saw us and ran to greet us.

"Finally you are here, what a wonderful surprise! Come, come, let me show you around," she said, motioning to Evelyn. Desi slipped away to go visit with Hoot, and I went to the barn to look for solar panels and cables. I was loading two promising models and an extension cord into a yellow Dollar General grocery cart when Clare and Evelyn came through the barn door.

"I'm giving her the tour, which of course includes the chickens," Clare said, leading the way to the corner of the barn that was partitioned off for her flock, now fifteen strong.

"I've never been around chickens," Evelyn said. "Do they bite?"

Clare laughed. "No, they're only interested in food." To prove her point, she picked up a pitchfork of seedy hay and tossed it to the rowdy group, who began scratching and pecking as if they were ravenous. Maybe they were. In winter there were few bugs for them to forage, which is why Buddy cut and dried several gigantic heaps of hay in late summer, when the weeds and grasses were loaded with seeds.

Clare picked up two brown eggs from a nesting box and handed them to Evelyn. "Oh," she said, holding them in an open palm. "I've only had white ones, in a carton. They won't hatch, will they?" She seemed genuinely afraid.

"Not unless a hen is taking care of them," Clare said.

See what I mean about Evelyn being a little odd? Maybe I should have felt guilty for leaving her with Clare, but I was ready for a break. I took my grocery cart of solar panels and headed homeward, whistling America the Beautiful and practicing my bird calls on the uphill walk. I immediately felt better.

I stopped at Wynn's to pump water and look at locations for solar panels on his patio. I knew he wasn't home, being off with Sarah and Claude to rescue a tank of propane for the Manse kitchen. Prince watched me through the window. I told him I was hooking up power so he could have a heating pad, and his mouth made a big meow.

The system for Wynn's house was similar to the one I'd set up at our house to run a crockpot, but with different components. I'd been enjoying working on it in part because Wynn never asks for anything for himself, which is why his house is the last one to get plug-in solar power.

I jogged home to pick up the controller, inverter and surge protector. I was almost finished setting up the solar station when I heard voices coming over the hill, then saw Wynn and Claude pushing the garden cart, where Sarah held on with one hand, struggling to sit upright.

"Let's stop," she said weakly. "Please?"

"No, baby doll, we have to get you some help," Wynn said, touching her forehead.

Claude met me as I came closer. "She's hurt, has a piece of barbed wire in her hand. We need to get her to Rob," he said. His face was red from keeping up with Wynn pushing Sarah in the cart. He put his hands on his thighs and took deep breaths.

"Is it bleeding?" I asked.

"Not so much, but it will. The wire is still in there."

My stomach lurched into a hard knot. One of my most serious childhood injuries involved a spur of barbed wire in my leg, and I remembered how hideous it was, and how much it hurt.

"She tripped on a downed fence hidden in the grass, and her hand landed on a wire," he said. "We had to cut her out, thank God we had the tools."

I could not turn away, not from Sarah. She was sitting

on the edge of the garden cart, telling Wynn she wanted to go inside.

"Can I see?" I asked, stepping closer. She uncovered her right hand and turned it over to reveal a piece of old barbed wire, eight inches long, with a rusty barb embedded in her palm like a fishhook. The skin around it was white and purple, not much bleeding, but there probably would be when it was removed.

"When was your last tetanus shot?" I asked.

She squeezed her eyes shut. "2020? It was just before the pandemic, I had to get one for work, and then a few months later the Covid shots came out."

"Good, you should be good," I said. I turned to Wynn, who touched Sarah's face but avoided looking at her wound. "Where are the first aid supplies?" I asked.

"Most of it's here, in the garage. That's why we stopped."

Sarah got up and started walking slowly to the house. "This is as far as I'm going," she said. Her face was scary pale. That sucker was starting to throb. Wynn and I helped her to the sofa. Claude had disappeared, hopefully to get Rob.

"Do you have some Lidocaine?" I asked Wynn. He nodded. I followed him to the garage and helped assemble a bin with gloves, gauze, scissors, alcohol, hydrogen peroxide, bandages, and antibiotic ointment from his stash. I doused Sarah's wound with Bactine, which made her wince at first, but then made all those injured cells settle down.

"We need a light," I said, to which Wynn replied "So what else is new?" He was teasing the fire in the wood stove back to life.

"I think the solar station I was setting up is ready," I said, and went outside to thread an extension cord inside through an open window. I connected the components, turned the panel to the sun, and watched the red bars bounce into the normal range.

"In the sewing room," Sarah said when I came back inside. "There's an adjustable lamp with a magnifying lens, folded up in the corner. It's black." I returned with the lamp and plugged it in. Wonder of wonders, there was bright light at the touch of a button. It was only a 10X lens, not like what we had in the biology lab, but it would do.

"Wow," she said from the sofa. "Every time we get new solar, I am simply amazed."

Wynn handed her a mug of tea and three Tylenol, which she dutifully swallowed. When he returned to the kitchen, she leaned toward me and whispered, "There are some old towels on the floor in the hall closet. Wynn is squeamish. You're the nurse."

I said I would try.

Rob arrived in record time because he was being pushed in the Thing by Desi, who is all muscle these days, fast and strong.

"Oh, my," Rob said, examining Sarah's wound under the light. Then he moved the lens to examine the next knot of wire, how it was twisted and cut. He motioned for me to look. "Maybe some old four-point that went in at an angle?"

I said that was a good guess.

"Now all we need are some wire snips," he said. "We can take off that top piece, see if the rest will spin out."

I ran to get the set of electrical tools stored in a blue

box in my shop. When I got back, Desi was in the kitchen, boiling water on the propane stove for sterilizing my tools.

"It's what Rob told me to do. What else?"

"Think of a way to get Wynn out of the house," I said, swishing a pair of wire snips through the hot water. "Sarah says blood is not his thing."

"Mine either." A few minutes later, when our tools and bandages were ready, I saw her grab Wynn's sleeve and pull him toward the door. "No wimps or children allowed," she said. "It's the rules."

"Since when are you a child?" he asked, pretending to resist her pull.

"Since now."

As soon as the door closed behind them, Sarah whispered "Showtime" and extended her arm over the towels spread over her lap. I sat beside her so I could hold her forearm firmly with both hands. My job was to keep the hand still while Rob cut out the barb. He poured hydrogen peroxide over the wound, which erupted in bubbles. Then he squirted on more Bactine, explaining that it contained a local anesthetic. I averted my eyes and concentrated on holding Sarah's arm. She was shaking.

"Too tight?" I asked.

"It's okay," she said and then jumped and yelped.

"Easy, easy," Rob said, dropping a piece of the wire into a bowl. He picked up a pair of cuticle scissors and made a couple of small cuts that made her wince. She needed a distraction. She was breathing through her mouth, in and out, so I started talking about yoga, which Desi was learning from a book.

"She says the breath is key to extending your life

force, which is what the practice of yoga is about. She could use a proper teacher, I think. The book seems a little dry. Have you ever taken a yoga class, Sarah?" She shook her head. I prattled on as Rob clipped off another barb through the slits he had made in her skin. Blood dripped from her hand, forming red blotches on the towels.

"Hold steady," Rob said, and I gripped her arm hard. She screamed a little when he twisted out the embedded wire, and she was crying when he held it up for her to see. "We got it, the other two points are intact." He leaned in to take another look at the gash in her hand through the lighted lens. "I think you're going to live." When I released her arm, I could see my handprints in her flesh.

After the bleeding slowed, Rob cleaned the wound and dabbed it dry with gauze. Then he applied a set of butterfly bandages that tightened like zip ties. He wrapped the hand in gauze and taped it in place. "You have to keep it dry, that's the main thing. It's going to hurt, but let us know if feels hot, or bleeds through," he said, taking off his latex gloves.

"Yes, doctor," she said, halfway smiling. I gathered up the bloody towels and bandages and took them outside to the burn pile. Desi and Wynn were up by the water pump, talking. I whistled and motioned for them to come back to the house.

All things considered, Sarah seemed okay, but tired. Wynn made her some ramen noodles, which revived her enough to ask Desi to help her change clothes. "I don't think I can do buttons or zippers," she said, looking at her bandaged right hand. They disappeared into the front bedroom, with Sarah holding her hand high to keep from bumping into anything.

"I don't know how to thank you for your help," Wynn began, but Rob interrupted with a wave of his hand.

"You're not the only one who loves Sarah," he said.

I wanted to say that I loved Sarah, too, but I didn't. I couldn't trust my voice to say the words out loud. Instead of sounding warm and nurturing, what if they sounded husky and raw, the way I felt? Instead, I told Wynn he was welcome to keep the solar station, but to keep an eye on it and bring it in at night.

"It will run a light, a fan, or a slow cooker, that's about all," I said.

He said it seemed like a miracle to him.

Chapter 29 Wild Turkey

November 22

There was a lot riding on the success of our turkey hunt. Clare thought Hoot and Sarah needed meat and bone broth to restore their health, and Rob felt like the minerals would help his knees. Buddy and Hoot were excited about fresh game, mostly because it's the most authentic type of meat, always has been.

"Just bring 'em to me as they lay," Buddy said. "I'll pluck 'em and clean them up proper." He was a meat prep perfectionist, and described how he'd want to rest the meat for a couple of days before cooking it. "Four days is better, but we do the best we can," he said, grinning.

We were breaking all kinds of laws as we prepared for the hunt, but what good are hunting regulations when there's so little to protect? Like, it's illegal to bait animals with food so you can shoot them, it's illegal to take turkeys out of season, it's illegal to take hens, and it's illegal to hunt on the Blue Ridge Parkway.

"It don't much matter," Buddy said, handing me a small bag of cracked corn to scatter in the spots I had chosen as our killing fields. "With nothing after them, nary a fox, seems like there's plenty to go around."

"But taking down turkeys ain't easy. You got to get them out in the open, which ain't how they like it," Hoot said. "Let them come to you, and get ready to fire as soon as you hear them. Pull the trigger at thirty yards." Buddy nodded his head in agreement.

"They'll give you one shot. You just have to take it."

I'd already been up to the Parkway to scout likely spots once. Claude joined me on the second trip, to add his opinions and lay out tempting tidbits of corn and cracked acorns, which he'd been collecting for a week and smashing with a hammer.

"The book says it's their favorite food, after insects," he said. He'd been reading The Old Pro Turkey Hunter, which he found in the library at the Manse. "It's helping me think like a turkey. Until I started being around the chickens, I'd never thought about birds, wasn't much aware of them."

"They're dinosaurs," I said. "Birds go back much longer than humans."

It was a sunny afternoon, and we made it to the Parkway in less than an hour even though we stopped often to clear away sticks and debris that might trip us up in the dark. As we walked, I called to a few jays and cardinals who decided to stay through winter, and practiced my turkey call. I was pretty good at making the chirping distress calls of a young hen separated from the flock. They were coarse, barking sounds that echoed the honk of a goose at the end.

"We get settled in, ready to shoot, and you give out the call, just like that," Claude said, excited. "Then we stay silent and wait."

"As the birds come filing out of the woods, ready to be shot."

"More or less." I admired Claude's confidence.

He didn't like the first site I showed him, an open intersection where a gravel road crossed the Parkway. "I don't know, it feels risky. If the flock comes out to feed, the tom has to be watching in all directions. We'd do better with a curve in the road, facing east and near water."

"You learned all that from a book?" I asked.

"Yup. And Buddy."

We turned north and walked a short distance to what we both agreed was the perfect spot, a tight curve in the road that would get good morning light, with a stream running down one side and a gentle tumble of rocks on the other. But the best part was the silver Honda CRV that had come to rest against a roadside tree and was now mostly swallowed by tall grass and wild grapevine. We tramped behind it, taking in the broken windows and two corpses that had been thoroughly worked by bugs and birds. I looked away after noting jawbones and baseball hats.

"I don't think they will mind the noise," I said. "Rest their souls."

"Indeed." Claude opened the car's hatch and found a blanket, which he spread over the heaps of bones.

We experimented with sight lines from behind the car, walking off thirty yards three times, and we felt like we had a decent target range to work with. The car's position also made it possible to stand up straight while firing, leaning back against a tree, which made me feel like I had a better chance of making the shot. We scattered cracked corn and acorns where we wanted the turkeys to feed, and I made a few turkey girl "help help" barks just because I could. It was probably my

311

imagination, but I think I heard a gobbler respond from deep in the woods.

Claude spent the night on our sofa so we could get an early start. I was too keyed up to sleep much, and he was, too. He murmured "Hey" when I tiptoed outside to pee.

"Any idea what time it is?" I whispered when I came back in.

"Might be time to go," he said, stretching under the blanket. I lit the small oil lantern we would take with us, stoked the fire in the wood stove and got dressed in a black sweatshirt over camo cargo pants. Claude's outfit was more authentic, a National Guard uniform that said his name was Maberry.

"Were you in the service?" I asked.

"Not unless you count this."

We checked our guns, laced up our boots, and picked up the backpacks we'd packed the night before with food, water, and carrying bags for our booty. Rob is such a great guy. In addition to making our to-go breakfast, he sent a canister of vanilla caramel instant coffee, which was so good that we made second cups for the road. I left the rest of it next to Desi's favorite mug. She would not be up for hours.

We were buzzing. We used the lantern to light our footsteps until we got to the Parkway, then traveled on in amazing darkness. Only the stars and white parts of our shoes were not black. We shuffled down the center of the road, trying not to stumble, hoping we were ahead of the turkeys, who would awaken at first light.

We found the spot, the Honda showing a dull pre-dawn gleam, and silently placed more corn and acorns on the open patch of pavement. There was not enough light to see well, but I thought some of the grain we left the day before had been eaten. We walked around the far curve to pee and have breakfast, which consisted of water and stale Cinnamon Life cereal, which is actually quite tasty.

"Are you ready?" I asked in a quiet voice.

"I think so. But I'm worried about the moment when I squeeze the trigger, about missing."

"Don't breathe," I said between bites. "It's movement. A lot of people breathe out and hold before shooting, then breathe in. Keeps the gun still."

He chewed his cereal, took a slug of water, and whispered something about a statue. I wanted to say more, to describe the stillness of being one with the gun, but morning light was coming. It was time to take up our positions and get quiet.

Dawn arrived quickly, and with the milky light came waking sounds from the woods. I heard a pair of doves and a woodpecker, and then the chatter of crows as three descended on our feeding station. Claude and I shared sour glances, but I was not ready to give up hope. If there were turkeys in the woods who had fed on our grain the night before, they would hear the crows and be eager to return for their share.

I wanted to get the crows' attention without alarming them, so I whistled a bit of chickadee chatter, *chickadee-dee-dee*. It was enough to get the largest crow to look our way. Did it see two still and silent humans posed behind a wrecked car, or recognize us from Hokie-Ville? The big bird jumped back a step before cawing twice and flying away, with the other two close behind him.

313

We waited another twenty minutes or so, until I thought I heard movement in the woods. I made three of my turkey-hen calls, then lifted my shotgun and got into firing position. The moments ticked by, the way they do when you're waiting, and your ears are ringing and your feet and fingers start going numb. I jumped at the sudden loud gobbling from the biggest turkey I've ever seen. With his head tucked and tail feathers extended into a gigantic fan, the massive tom seemed to float on a pillow of feathers, turning this way and that as if on wheels. He looked our way and then turned away to check the food for the flock. A few birds were already trickling in from the edge of the woods. There were a couple of tall jakes and perhaps eight smaller females, all in perfect range.

"Three, two, one," I grunted, and we fired within a half second of one another, our shots erupting into a shower of feathers. I counted three birds down, and a fourth injured. Claude put down his gun and ran toward the birds, but I kept mine with me, hoping we would not be attacked by the tom.

"Sorry, son," Claude said, and he picked up the struggling bird by the head and wrung its neck. The flapping stopped.

"Don't tell me, it was in the book," I said.

"That it was. Shotguns don't always give a clean kill."

I told him we did a good job. Both of the hens had their heads halfway severed, and the second dead jake looked like he took the hit in his throat. We put the birds into cloth grocery bags with their heads sticking out the top, secured our guns, and started home just as the sun glowed pink over the ridge.

"It all happened so fast," he said, adjusting his load as we bushwhacked a shortcut downhill through the woods. "Like wham and it was done!"

"We got lucky, very lucky," I said, laughing.

"Take me to the blackjack tables, I'm hot," he said, pretending to throw dice. I asked him if he was a gambler.

"No, but I was a schemer, a player," he said, throwing his head a little. "Which may be why I like hunting, learning to stalk and kill your prey. Only this is not a sport, not an indulgence, not even a sin. It's a necessity."

We walked and thought for a few minutes. "Now Clare will have to say yes when I propose," he said, moving his bag of turkeys from one shoulder to the other. "It's the American way."

"You mean the Thanksgiving dream fulfilled?" I asked.

"Oh, no, none of that. I've been reading to Hoot from a book about Native American traditions pertaining to courtship and marriage. In the Cherokee ways, a man brings fresh meat to the household of his beloved. If she cooks the meat and she and her family eat it, she is accepting his proposal. If she refuses the meat, he's history. It's so much better than dinner at an expensive restaurant, don't you think?"

I started laughing when I pictured Claude on one knee, a dead turkey in front of him, asking Clare to be his wife.

"I don't see how she can refuse," I said. "But Desi says for Clare it's about commitment. That would make a good talking point."

He looked at me in a profoundly grateful way. "But

that's what I want, too," he said.

We stopped at Wynn's garage to get a grocery cart to carry the turkeys and guns the rest of the way to the Manse. Sarah heard us, and came through the door wearing a pink velour robe and fuzzy slippers. She held her bandaged hand close to her chest.

"Did you get one?" she asked, looking at the bags.

"Four. I think Buddy will be pleased," Claude said. "It all went according to plan."

I asked if she heard the shots. "No. And Prince didn't either. He freaks when he hears gunshot, and he's been fine." She peered into the shopping bags. "They're not exactly pretty, are they?"

"Astute observation. No, they are not pretty, which is why killing them feels less awful. But the tom turkey, the big male, let me tell you, he was something," Claude said, and started slowly strutting around the garage, turkey style.

"That's it, that's it," I said, laughing. "Win her over with your turkey dance." Sarah smiled, like she knew what we were talking about.

"Hey Gabe, I'm wondering if you will take a look at my hand. Desi will be here in a little while, to help me dress, but checking bandages is out of her league," she said. "I can go see Rob, but there's something going on with Evelyn at the Manse. Clare came by early with a pharmacy order, like for a migraine or something. Wynn's down there now."

"As I should be," Claude said, getting behind the loaded grocery cart. "You help Sarah. I'll deliver the birds."

Inside the house smelled of toast, comforting and

warm. I washed my hands in a bowl of soapy water in the kitchen sink. "I'm not experienced with this," I said.

"Me neither. My mother was the nurse, she took care of gory things." She sighed, then let out a ragged breath. "Having this claw hand makes me think of her, makes me wonder what she would do." She sat down in the sunroom, where there was good morning light.

"What would she do?" I asked, pulling on a pair of latex gloves from the bin of first aid supplies.

"She would tell me to be careful, ask for help, and remind me of how much I need my right hand."

"Has it been hurting?" I asked, slowly cutting the gauze.

"Yes, it throbs off and on. And it feels heavy. I expect it to be swollen."

"That was a nasty piece of wire," I said, gently pulling away the bandage. "No fever, aches, anything like that?" She shook her head, then leaned forward to look at the wound.

"Give me your other hand," I said. I tore open a package of sterile wipes and cleaned her left hand, finger by finger.

"Thanks," she said, and pressed lightly around the wound. It was puffy and raw, with the remnants of the dissolvable bandage flaking off. There was lumpy purple bruising, but no scary red streaks. She surprised me by holding the wound close to her nose so she could smell it.

"That's a biologist's trick, sniffing for trouble," I said.

She said it was a nurse's trick, too. "I think a nurse would want to clean it. Can you fix me up with a bowl of boiled water mixed with hydrogen peroxide? For soaking?"

I didn't think it would hurt. I prepared the soaking solution and she moved to a comfortable position on the love seat, next to a small table. Every few minutes as the wound soaked, I used sterilized tweezers to pick away loose bits, which is gruesome unless you view it as a medical imperative and beloved Sarah's right hand is at stake.

"There's drainage," I said when I saw a droplet of milky liquid oozing from one edge of the wound.

"Oh, good. I thought there might be," she said, taking a close look. "Would you mind making a fresh bowl of solution? Let's keep this going."

"Right away," I said, relieved that she was getting the result she wanted, that I had done the right thing. I sanitized her fingers a few times and dabbed seepage with gauze and Bactine, but she basically drained the wound herself, pushing and squeezing until it ran clean.

"That's enough for today," she finally said. "Now I just want to wrap it up. No sutures, no dressing."

"Got it."

Desi arrived when we were halfway done wrapping gauze. She put the finishing touches on Sarah's new bandage while I cleaned up our mess and got the first aid bin restored to order.

"Thanks for everything, Gabe," she said just before she and Desi disappeared into the front bedroom. "Though today you are Saint Gabriel, seriously."

I told her she would do the same for me.

I went home, brought in some water and firewood, and took off my boots. Desi had loaded the wood stove, so the house was warm. I was running on three hours of sleep and felt like it. I laid down on the sofa to take a nap. When I woke up to the sounds of Desi in the kitchen, midafternoon shadows played on the wall.

"The great hunter awakens," she said, stirring a pot of rice that steamed on the propane stove. "Hungry? We've been summoned to a meeting at headquarters, and I thought you might want to eat something first."

"Thanks, I'm starving," I said, and gently pulled her ponytail before sitting down at the kitchen table. "What kind of meeting?"

"An Evelyn meeting. She wants to fire up a laptop, try to check her messages, see if there's something from her son."

"Fat chance of that. The servers are down, you know."

"If you say so. She thinks Starlink is worth trying." She stirred a packet of flavoring into the rice. "Listen to this. Within hours after she got to the Manse, she asked Claude if he had tried running a computer with Solar Sam. He laughed and said there was no point with no batteries or internet, but she was welcome to try. They got a laptop from the wine cellar, plugged it in, and tried to get it to run. Total failure, even after they pulled the battery. It was a Mac and she said they needed a satellite-enabled PC, which about made his mouth drop open. How does she know stuff like that? And for what?"

"I know. She doesn't fit the computer nerd profile," I said. I did not tell her about the secret laptop stored in my shop, which was likely very much satellite enabled. Assuming there was still such a thing as Starlink. I decided to keep it to myself. Loose lips sink ships.

"Clare says we should meet to discuss it, at Wynn's

house." She filled two bowls with rice, vegetables, with thin snips of salty beef jerky on top. We finished the whole pot.

Chapter 30   Connections

Nov 24

Wynn's furniture was arranged so we could sit in a semi-circle around the wood stove. Our host sat in a kitchen chair, a spiral notebook in his lap, and he handed another notebook and pen to me. "Clare's in charge because she's good at running meetings. You and I should both take notes."

Clare sat in the recliner, smiling at the assembled group of six. "It looks like we're all here. Hoot, Buddy and Rob opted out of the trek, but they are with us in spirit to discuss our concerns about Evelyn, and what she needs," she began. "In case you haven't heard, she has asked for a satellite-enabled PC with a Starlink dish. We are here to discuss if that is safe and desirable for her, and for us. I'd like for each of us to briefly share our own experiences and opinions on this. We can go around the circle. Okay with everyone?" We all nodded. She motioned for Claude to go first.

"I was there when she tried a laptop at the Manse, and the remarkable thing was how she approached the keyboard, like a pianist. If it had come on, she was ready to play. When I told her I wasn't surprised because Macs could be so tricky, she said she knew that, and what we needed was a satellite-enabled PC, like from someone who was running Starlink."

Desi popped up from the pile of cushions where she

sat with Prince. "With Starlink you still have to have an account and pay the bill. That's why we never got it at Wonderland. I think it's okay to try, because it's going to be a dead end." She wiggled her head from side to side and sat down.

Clare asked Wynn what he thought. He finished making a note, put down his pen and leaned forward in his chair. "Medically speaking, Rob and I can't figure out the headaches, which come and go, so maybe migraines aggravated by anxiety? Rob thinks that if it was a brain tumor, she would be having seizures. In a way, even a failed attempt could be the medicine she needs."

Sarah listened, her brows drawn in worry. "It's no secret that I've been challenged letting go of my mom. I can see how Evelyn can't stop believing, why she wants to try anything," she said. "She was alone longer than any of us. Maybe believing got to be her way of life."

Then all eyes turned to me. My mouth felt dry, but it was now or never. "We might have the right kind of laptop, from the Korean guy's RV up at the campground. It's in my shop, along with his wallet. And there's a tablet, too, which was Zachary's." I turned to Sarah. "Remember, the guy with the bus and all the solar gear?" She nodded, encouraging me to continue. "I have no idea if they work. To be honest I'm a little afraid of them. Like they might send out signals about where we are, and then the little green men will come it will be my fault. When I brought the stuff back, I was thinking more along the lines of games or movies that might be on the hard drives." There were nods all around, so I kept going. "In college I had a roommate whose battery went dead in his laptop, and he kept it running for a couple of months by never turning it off. But since we can't provide power 24/7, it may not work, or maybe it will."

"All things are possible," Wynn said.

Claude raised his hand. "The new computer is of interest. We should have a look at it tomorrow when we have good light for power. Without Evelyn's involvement. Perhaps in an unoccupied space like the dahlia house. You know, to create location confusion." Claude can be a sly dog. I said we would need a dish.

"What kind of dish?" Wynn asked, cocking his eyebrow. "I know of a few."

It was quickly agreed that Wynn, Claude and I would form a technology team to test drive the Korean guy's PC. "Is that okay with everyone?" Clare asked, and there were unanimous "ayes" around the circle.

I for one felt stunned by how nicely a plan had come together, a plan in which I was responsible for some things, but not everything. Opening up about the computer felt freeing, too. Keeping the secret had become an uncomfortable burden.

"What about me?" Desi asked, getting to her feet.

"Oh, but you're our good witch, our lucky charm," Claude said as he pushed the sofa back into place.

"And you have to keep being my right hand," Sarah said.

"Come down to the Manse and help keep things rolling," Clare said, nudging her with her elbow. "Buddy needs help with turkeys, and with Hoot. We can spy on Evelyn, and Rob."

Desi wrinkled her nose. "Like, there's something to spy on?" she asked.

"Too soon to say."

Desi said she'd join the turkey team.

It would be midday before we had bright light or dishes to work with the computer, so Desi and I walked down to the lake house the next morning. I wanted to check the kitchen for chafing dishes or a crock pot to run with our solar setup, and Desi loves going to the lake. It was a weird weather day, foggy and still, and the lower we got, elevation-wise, I realized that the fog was really smoke. As in woods-are-on-fire smoke. It clung to the water in the lake in a floating layer that showed no signs of lifting as the sun rose higher.

"It's smoke. I remember it from before," Desi said, frowning. There were wildfires in the local forests a few years ago, plus more in North Carolina and the Shenandoah, and the air stayed gray for months.

"It's not good. Pray for rain," I said. I tried to remember the last time there was lightning, and it was at least ten days ago, maybe longer. If a forest fire had been burning that long, it had to be a big one. Humans could start a fire, but who? And where? Time to call 911.

The inside of the lake house had lost some of its mustiness but still smelled of mildew and rot. We cased the kitchen and pantry for small appliances we could use. I found a slow cooker, a slightly moldy electric sandwich maker, and an unopened can of Folgers coffee, black gold. Before she started coughing, Desi found two tins of sardines and a jug of canola oil. We had as much as we could carry.

"I call French fries," she said as we compared our booty on the front porch. "Fried potatoes, just one batch." I went back to the kitchen to check for salt and dishwashing soap and came back with half-full containers of both. We had stirred up a lot of dust, and between the dust, the mold and the smoke, I started coughing, too.

We walked down to the lake to clear our lungs. "What scares you more? A forest fire or invasion by aliens?" I asked when I reclaimed my breath. The smoke was moving, lightening up some, so I wondered if we had wandered into a temporary pocket of bad air.

"Totally forest fires, no question. In all the books and movies, girls like me are big prizes when the aliens come. Everybody wants us, it's the way things are. Courageous men like you, Claude, and Wynn risk their lives for us." She fluffed her hair and redid her ponytail. "Fires, they go their own way, feed on everything, don't care what they kill. We were down at Wonderland when the big fire happened, it came really close. My mom got very, very freaked out. She sang songs, said chants, made prayers to the goddess of water. Then one day Leo gave her the keys to his truck and said for us to leave. To go someplace safe. We checked into a cheap motel in Martinsville."

"There's a goddess of water?" I asked.

"Not really, it's more like the Goddess is in everything. Like God only different, more liquid."

I found myself staring at the surface of the lake, dark and mysterious. "She is moisture," I mused. "Where life always begins."

"Yes. The only force that can put out fire. Wait, wait, there's a rain chant, let me see if I remember it."

She stepped to the water's damp edge and spread her arms wide.

"Raindrops dance and wind entwine,

*From mystery realms, your powers align
Send forth your tears, so wide and vast
Quench the earth, from first to last."*

Then she repeated the chant, turning a quarter turn with each line, toward the north, west, south, and east. "That ought to do it," she said, picking up her bag. I asked her if she thought it would work. She shrugged. "Like Wynn says, all things are possible."

We parted ways on the road to the Manse, and I headed uphill to drop my loot and join the tech team at the dahlia house. The air was clearer, which made me wonder if wood smoke from the Manse had settled on the lake overnight, and I was worried about nothing.

At our old homeplace, the dahlia house, Claude and I moved the solar panels to a sunny spot in the front yard. We snapped the system together and plugged in a box fan to test it. All systems were go.

"We should disable the camera and mike," Claude said, picking up the laptop. "I think we can do it after starting it in safe mode, but I brought tape anyway." He pulled a roll of masking tape from his pocket and tore off small pieces to cover the camera and mike.

"I'm glad you know your way around computers. I only used one for work, games and Netflix," I said.

"Age and experience have benefits, plus a healthy dose of paranoia," he said, turning the laptop over to look at the sides and bottom. "Write this down. J947+. It's in marker, might be a password. This is probably a work computer, it's not unusual to keep them accessible."

Wynn arrived red-cheeked and excited, carrying two rectangular Starlink dishes, one with a tripod stand and another that had been mounted to a pole, and a bag of connecting cables.

"The Airstream people, I thought that's where I'd seen these things. Have you been inside one of those, a new one? This silver beauty is truly high end, summer quarters for some people building a house. Sarah found it, down a side road. Do you think this will work?" He handed me the cables and unfolded the stand for one of the dishes. "There was a computer, but it had water damage, like of the biological sort," he said, squeezing his nose. I pictured a skeleton holding a laptop.

"If this machine powers up and has an internal router, we might connect to something," Claude said, adjusting the cable to the dish. We decided to keep it plugged in for a while before trying to turn it on. Give it time to warm up.

"On another topic, did anyone notice smoke in the air this morning?" I asked. "It was thick down by the lake."

"I saw it, from the hilltop," Wynn said. "It was most unusual, not a fog, it was different. More like a mass."

I said it made it hard to breathe, and that Desi was sure it was wildfire smoke. Wynn said he would jog over to the overlook in the morning because where there's smoke, there's fire.

While we waited for the computer to warm up, Wynn went through its owner's wallet to look for password hints or other useful information. Kwan P. Kim from Greensboro was on faculty at a small university, and his photo ID showed a compact, middle-aged man with a receding hairline and dark, guarded eyes. His wallet contained three credit cards, two hundred in cash, photos of an elderly couple, and a small gold pig attached with a short chain.

"For luck," Claude said. "Let's hope it holds."

We agreed that he would run the computer while I took notes and Wynn rode shotgun. The ON light lit up when he pressed it, and the machine began to hum. Toggling a couple of F keys started it in safe mode. "Windows is working," he said, sounding surprised. Wonder of wonders, the computer managed a full startup, and Claude looked through the lists of apps and software.

For a few seconds the blue screen shone brightly with familiar icons, Chrome and Adobe and YouTube, and then it went blank, followed by a scattering of pulsing lights that seemed to follow a pattern, moving together and apart. Claude typed in "Hello," hit enter and waited, then typed it again. The lights slowed and suddenly disappeared as he typed it a third time. An oblong entry box appeared over a bright green screen.

"Try the access code," I said, and read off the series of letters and numbers. He keyed them in, read them back to me and pressed enter. A new box appeared on the screen, multiple choice, written in an Asian language that none of us knew.

"What tha?" Claude said, squinting at the letters.

"It must be Korean," I said. "Hangul. I can't read it. Is there a translator?"

While Claude looked for a translating app, the screen went blank again, did its swirling lights thing, and came back with *Hello* in a green box with a blinking cursor like you might see if you were hooked into chat support somewhere.

"Who are you?" Claude typed quickly. There was no immediate response.

Language adjustments are being implemented. Please wait.

Claude: "Our power supply and connectivity are limited."

KARLA requires contact with Dr. Kim. Please enable camera for authentication.

Claude: "Sorry to say, Kwan Kim is dead. Most humans are dead. Who is Karla?"

KARLA is a satellite-based monitoring and observation system. KARLA requires contact with Dr. Kim or another Aggregator.

Claude: "Sorry to disappoint. We are human survivors using Dr. Kim's computer. Do you have our coordinates?"

Request acknowledged. Please wait.

A few seconds later, Karla came back with our proper location, 40N/80W with decimals, and displayed the day's weather forecast.

Claude: "Are you a weather satellite?"

Negative. KARLA has telescopic functions, but has limited access to related information.

Claude: "Are there other surviving humans near our location?"

Request acknowledged. Please wait. Scanning 500 miles…

Affirmative. The Pirates. Location is 353.8 miles north/northeast at 40N/79W. Disclaimer: There could be others surviving humans with no connectivity. Many Aggregators failed beyond repair. We are sorry for the inconvenience.

"Ask her what happened," Wynn whispered. "This could be our only chance." Claude nodded.

"Can KARLA tell us what happened to cause the changes to Earth that killed the people and other animals?" he typed.

Request acknowledged. Please wait. Scanning...

Affirmative. A convergence of asteroids created a magnetic abnormality that was amplified by the accumulation of space debris. Many satellites were lost in the storm. KARLA needs repair. Most Earth-based Aggregators failed. We are sorry for the inconvenience.

As Wynn hurried to write everything down, Claude began typing a longer question about whether or not Earth will return to normal, but some high clouds were mucking with our solar feed, making the meter jump around. I didn't think it was good to run the computer on a wonky power supply.

"Tell it we have to go," I said when the screen dimmed slightly.

There was one last incoming message from KARLA.

Are any of you fertile females?

Claude quickly typed NO, and we powered down the machine and pulled the plug.

"That was big," I said, pushing back in my chair.

Claude closed the laptop and gathered up its cords. "Karla doesn't exactly have the gift of gab, but she knows some things," he said.

"I think it's for real because she was looking for Kim. Like, he was supposed to be an Aggregator, whatever that is," I said. "And he was here before 2:42. For what? Did they know it was coming? And why Floyd?"

We all agreed Kwan Kim might have been an Aggregator, an advance spy for Armageddon, which made Karla's last question more chilling. Fertile females? To mate with who? We are not a herd of cows. I don't think.

I like the way Claude summed up our contact with Karla when he reported it to the group. "Much depends on who owns the satellite, and what they want, and whether or not they still exist," he said thoughtfully. "It could simply be on auto pilot. We also should remember that rare things tend to gain value, and we are rare. In addition to being survivors, we are a solid sample of our species. Whoever, whatever it is, wants us to live."

The more I thought about this, the more I knew he was right, just like Desi. Let's say we get captured by invaders, human or alien. They want the women, so she and Sarah and Clare are safe from some things. Maybe they will also be interested in a young man who whistles and understands birds, and in the rest of the Hokies. My tribe. They feel like a real family to me, only maybe better. Because of the way things are, we've all had to let old worries go, put down some baggage, make ourselves useful. We pull together.

I will not let anyone or anything take away my new family. We will prevail.

Floyd VA 2:42

Part Three

Destiny

Chapter 31   Departures

November 27
By Destiny
I hate the fire.

I hate the smell, and I hate how your eyes and throat burn if you don't jump out of the way of the smoke just in time. I did not have fun stomping around the edges of the grass fire we burned along the creek that runs by the Manse. A backburn they call it. Now Gabe and I are home for a while because his eye has blown up again, and we were dead on our feet anyway.

He thinks he caught a cinder from the brush fire. I dribbled water into his eye and told him it mostly just looked irritated. Which it did. He said he'd take that. The good news is that it's not his good eye.

He's snoring in his bed now, but before he passed out, he got out this notebook and said we needed to make a checklist of everything going on. Which is a lot. I'm too keyed up to sleep.

We don't have equipment for measuring air quality, but we do have Hoot, whose lungs are so messed up that he's like a smoke detector. He was having trouble breathing at the turkey dinner at the Manse, though the windows were closed tight and the air didn't seem that bad to me.

Now the smoke is horrendous down in the valley, mostly because of our own fires. Hoot has been moved to higher ground at Wynn's house where he is being looked after by Sarah. Her hand is better, but the wound is still tender and her fingers tingle sometimes. Rob says she could risk nerve damage by not giving it more time to heal. She is trying hard to be a good patient, playing a lot of checkers with Hoot.

The rest of us are fighting fire with fire. And water. The day after we gorged on turkey thighs, legs, breasts, you name it, Wynn and Gabe jogged to the closest overlook to get a fix on the forest fire. It was not good news. There were at least three fires giving off smoke two ridges to the west, which meant something bad was coming our way.

A meeting was held to discuss our options. When we took a vote between staying put or moving to the Baptist church on the hillside with the praying hands, the Manse won.

First reason. Last summer, Buddy mowed near the house to control ticks and other bugs, and thanks to a mild autumn, the grass is still lush and green. Beyond that is a band of short stubble from where he cut hay for the chickens, then tall grass until you get to the stream. Buddy said we should burn it to make a fire barrier, and Rob agreed it was a good idea.

"The stream with a backburn may be an effective barrier," he said. "Fire can't burn where there's no fuel."

Second reason. Wynn, who has long thought an Incineration was coming, pointed out the benefit of the Manse's slate roof, which makes it more fire-resistant compared to the church. "Water can be poured from the upstairs windows to dampen the downspouts. We can fill all the bathtubs with water."

That's how I ended up stomping smoldering brush alongside Gabe and Buddy, while Clare, Rob and Evelyn stockpiled water. Claude and Wynn went off in search of dynamite.

That's reason number three. The dynamite was Buddy's idea. We were on our second section to be burned, taking a break down by the edge of the stream when Gabe said the stream was too straight to be natural, that it had to be man made.

"Yup," Buddy said, pulling down the kerchief that covered the bottom half of his face. His eyebrows were gray with ashes. "It maybe used to be a swamp. You know there's a spring out back. There's probably drainage tiles down there, been there fifty years."

Gabe asked how hard it would be to dig a hole in the bank to flood the area we'd just burned. "Put in a pipe or something so the water can run."

"Real hard without a Bobcat. It would be easier to blow a hole in it," Buddy said, showing a sly smile. "One big boom would do it." He said he knew what to do. As a young man, while working for a timber company down in Stuart, he helped blow up half a mountainside to put in a new logging road.

The plan caught fire. Everyone liked the idea of a mud moat. Wynn knew where there was some dynamite, because he'd found some a year ago in an open trailer at a construction site. He closed up the trailer and marked it on his map.

Claude volunteered to go with him to get it, about six miles round trip. They don't expect trouble, but Claude took Buddy's shotgun just in case.

I know they will make it back safely mostly because

it's Buddy's deal. My witch radar tells me that Buddy is a pure soul. His energy is always the right kind, so if Buddy is in it, it's good with me.

He calls Sarah Girlie, and he calls me Little Girlie. It gives me a happy feeling, I can't explain it. He's kind of old, and easy in his ways, like a dream grandpa. I met my own grandpa a couple of times when I was little, and saw him more often those last few years, when Mom called him for help. He didn't have much money but sent what he could. He took the bus from Philadelphia to come see us. I remember picking him up at the bus station in Roanoke, and then going out to Bojangles for chicken and biscuits.

Claude is also a force for good, and man alive, does he have a reason to work it. He is now married to Clare, the most wonderful woman in the world. It's true! At the turkey dinner, after we had all eaten seconds of turkey and sweet potatoes, Claude got up and said he had an announcement.

"Family, friends, whatever you are, I am honored and proud to announce that Clare and I have made vows to one another, and from now on will be husband and wife." Clare stood up and showed off her left hand, where she wore the ruby ring, my favorite. She picked up a broom that leaned against the wall, brought it to where Claude stood, and placed it on the floor.

"Shall we?" she asked, taking his hand. He kissed her, smiled, and together they jumped the broomstick. We all clapped, it was really great. Except maybe for Hoot's coughing, which got worse when we all sang the old Beatles song, I Will. *Love you forever, and forever, love you with all my heart. Love you whenever we're together, love you when we're apart ..."* It's a good wedding song.

Observation of the day. When you feel afraid of one thing, and then another scary thing comes along, instead of melting down you get stronger, more willing to fight. Like, when it's the end of the world and somebody you care about is sick and there's a wildfire on the ridge, you hunker down and carry on.

On big blast day, Gabe came in from his morning pee and said the wind had changed. "It's from the east, with fog. Sometimes that means rain," he said. "It could buy us some time." He said his eye was better, but he put on sunglasses as he left the house, so I know he lied. I made him promise to wait for me before they lit the big firecracker.

After I got dressed, I went to Wynn's house to see if Sarah needed anything. "I think I'm good, see?" She waved her hand in the air. In place of bandages, she wore a padded white leather golf glove with open fingers. Hoot smiled from the recliner, where Prince purred in his lap.

"You sure you don't want to come?" Sarah asked, and I offered to push him down there and back in the Thing.

"Y'all go on, it wouldn't be right to leave Prince alone. In case he gets scared."

"All right then," Sarah said, putting on her jacket. As we left, she kissed her good hand and transferred it to Hoot's head. Whatever might have been wrong between them once upon a time was long since over.

Down at the Manse it felt like a party. Evelyn had hot water ready for tea and Clare made eggy little apple pancakes to order. Outside, the guys were busy preparing for the blast. I slipped on the same sooty boots

I'd worn the day before and went to join them.

Using shovels and picks, they dug a hole for a piece of plastic pipe. "The dynamite goes in there," Buddy said. "It needs to be kind of buried."

"It's going to be huge!" Claude said, standing up straight and stretching his arms over his head. "Like Jason Bourne, even Star Wars."

"Yeah, the explosion of the Dark Star," Gabe said, laughing.

"It ain't gonna be nothing if we don't get moving," Buddy said. "Without electric ignition we need a dry wick, and this fog ain't helping."

"Yes, sir!" Wynn said, jumping down the bank. "Safety positions, everyone!" he shouted, clapping his hands to alert the people in the house. We all gathered behind the corner of the barn to watch, and Wynn blew a whistle when all heads were counted. Sarah nudged me from behind and handed me a small pair of binoculars. I watched while Buddy and Gabe lit the wick, and then ran behind the dead tractor we regard as yard art. The fog made it hard to see, but there were a few seconds of sizzles and sparks, and then a muffled boom as the charge went off.

It was not Star Wars.

When Buddy gave the sign, we came in for a closer look. Instead of sending rocks and dirt into the air, it's like the dynamite lifted a chunk of the stream bank and then put it back down. Gabe whacked at the loose dirt with a pick, and like magic a cascade of water started flowing over the top of the bank.

"There she blows," Buddy said, smiling. "Won't take long for the water to make that hole even bigger, flood us a nice little pond."

We were all feeling happy about our new moat, and about the damp weather, too, though it meant no solar power. It wasn't actually raining, just misting, and it felt good to hang out in the warm kitchen, talking and eating Clare's pancakes. You never want to hurry into a dark, cold, no-solar day, because it won't be much fun no matter what you do. But after a while Sarah said she was heading up the hill to check on Hoot and Prince. I said I'd go with her.

The fog got thicker as we walked higher, so you could hardly see the outlines of the houses set back from the road. "This could be one of those set-in winter fogs that stays for a couple of days," she said, then told a story of when she was my age, new to driving, and she almost rear-ended a school bus in the fog. "I didn't see it, seriously, I was just tooling along and there it was, and I braked hard and went a little ways off the road, but not quite into the ditch. Scared me to death, I was shaking so bad. Driving in fog was never my thing."

When we got to the house, she called out "Honey, we're home!" as she pushed open the back door. I said, "Hey, Hoot, you missed it!" Only there was no Hoot. Prince looked up from where he was curled up on a pillow by the woodstove and yawned.

"Hoot?" Sarah called, looking into the bedrooms. No Hoot. I went outside and called for him as far as the dahlia house, then ran down the hill to our house, too. No Hoot. Back at Wynn's, Sarah carried an oil lantern to check every closet and shower stall. "Look," she said, leading me to the garage. "Wasn't the Thing here before?" I was pretty sure it was. She said I should go tell the others, that she would stay and wait, just in case.

Like, maybe he went out for a stroll or something?

Was he cold? That's what I keep wondering. Or did it happen so fast that he didn't have time to feel the cold? We found the Thing at the gate to the lake house, so he would have stumbled the rest of the way to the water's edge. By that time, was he struggling to breathe so much that he just fell in, and was gone in seconds? That's what I'm thinking.

Hoot's body was still floating and Gabe swam out to get him, but it was too late. He was blue and going stiff. Claude quickly covered the body with a tarp. Gabe was shivering cold, and his teeth were chattering. I was starting to panic, not about Hoot but about Gabe. Everything in the house was gross, and he needed dry clothes. Then I looked up and saw the little loft house, where there were probably a few semi-clean sheets and blankets. I ran up those steps so fast my lungs hurt. Score!

Claude helped strip off Gabe's wet clothes, and then we wrapped him in a double toga of sorts made of sheets. A mattress pad became an insulating shawl that made him look kind of like a marshmallow. While Claude waited with the body, I got Gabe into the Thing and pushed him as fast as I could to the Manse. He said I could slow down, he was doing okay, but he didn't sound right, so I kept running through the fog.

We almost crashed into Buddy, who was waiting by the gate for news, wearing a camo rain slicker. "I'm so sorry," I said, reaching out to touch his hand. "At the lake, Hoot had a fishing accident. He drowned." That's how I had decided to tell it. "Gabe went in to get him and now he needs to warm up."

"So sorry, Buddy," Gabe said weakly. "I'll miss him."

"Yup." He leaned over to look closely at Gabe, whose lips were slightly purple. "Little Girlie, I want you to go put him in Hoot's chair by the wood stove, right now. There's hot water in the kettle and some Swiss Miss in the drawer. Make him drink something hot." I don't think I said anything because I was blinking back tears. But I did exactly what he told me to do, and once Gabe was in the warm recliner holding a hot mug of cocoa, still looking like a marshmallow but grinning a goofy grin, I went to the big house to tell the others. I was still kind of crying, a mixture of grief and relief.

Wynn left immediately to notify Sarah and go help the others, but my sad mood was shared among those who remained. Rob and Evelyn sat beside each other at the kitchen table, sniffling and patting hands. Clare made me change into a dry sweatsuit that was nice and baggy, and she took Gabe flannel PJs and a robe from Claude's closet. She said he needed hot food, and fixed him a precious can of Progresso Beef with Vegetables soup. As she carried the pot out the door I confess, I felt a little bit jealous.

She hesitated. "C'mon, you know he won't eat it all," she said.

In true Gabe style, he only ate half, and gave the rest to me.

Chapter 32 Fog

It was good to see the tall grasses on the side of the road bending over with the weight of accumulated water, but the moisture came from a thick mist, with only little bits of actual rain. It sure wasn't enough rain to put out a big wildfire, and it might have made the smoke worse. Hoot's lakeside burial was shrouded in a mystic fog, or at least it felt that way to me.

We had no way to haul Hoot's big, stiff body back to the family homeplace, so should he be buried lakeside or at the Manse? Everyone gathered in the kitchen of the big house to make a plan.

"He was never exactly happy here, said he felt like a visitor," Buddy said, and Rob and Clare nodded.

"Back when the weather was warm, he fished almost every day, we both did," Claude said.

Buddy took off his hat, ran his hand over his head, and put his hat back on. "Yup. Might be Hoot already decided the whole thing," he said.

The next day, a grave site was chosen where a big rhododendron bush had died, and the guys dug as deep as they could before they hit a boulder. "Looks like a nice bed to me," Buddy said, and the hole was enlarged enough to fit Hoot's body, wrapped in blankets and tied to a board to keep it flat.

I couldn't help it. When I heard those first few clods of dirt hitting the body, I pulled out my harmonica and started playing Knocking on Heaven's Door, which it turns out everyone knew because it's been recorded so many times. Clare, who had been gathering pine boughs to lay on the grave, actually knew the words and led the second verse. Sarah brought in a soft harmony on the repeat of *Knock, knock, knocking on Heaven's door*. Gabe whistled the third verse, which brought in an eerie yet angelic touch. Many voices turned the last set of *knock, knock, knocking* into a fabulous finale, and we all clapped at the end. Hoot would have loved it.

He also would have understood why we didn't hang around long, being wet, cold and dirty. His memorial service would be another time.

Before leaving, I dashed into the stinky kitchen of the house to grab the small fire extinguisher I'd seen there, while Clare and Sarah checked the garage for a second one. Instead they found a box of water toys that included several Styrofoam water blasters, which Clare said would shoot twenty feet. Definitely useful tools for Hokie firefighters.

We dragged our damp behinds home to rest, recover and prepare to evacuate.

I won the coin toss for first bath, which isn't really a bath but feels like one. You stand in the bathtub with a pot of warm water from the wood stove at your feet, and start with your hair and soap your whole body, then rinse in dribbles from the top down. By then there's barely enough water for a second rinse, and it isn't hot anymore, but that's okay. While Gabe took his turn, I made some canned chili beans over ramen noodles. Don't knock it 'til you've tried it.

"I can't believe this might be our last night here. I love

this house," I said as we finished eating.

"I know. I like it, too. I hope we can spend the winter here," he said.

I told him I was praying for it, which is true. Since I first smelled smoke, I've been chanting and praying like crazy. Thanks to Mom, I know a lot of prayers. In her most desperate moments, she always prayed.

I was whispering "Hail Mary, full of grace," as I carried jugs of water to the upstairs bathrooms in the Manse, and passed Clare on the landing.

"What did you say?" she asked, stopping me.

"Hail Mary?"

She told me to put down my jugs and took hold of both of my hands. "Let's pray together." She bowed her head and recited the holy words.

Hail Mary, full of grace, the Lord is with thee.

Blessed art thou among women, and blessed is the fruit of thy womb, Jesus"

"Holy Mary, Mother of God, pray for us sinners, now and at the hour of our death. Amen."

She squeezed my hands and asked if I was Catholic. I told her I just liked prayers. She said she did, too. All this time I've been thinking the prayer thing was hereditary, but maybe it's just a willingness to believe that someone is listening.

"Have you decided what to take?" Gabe asked, placing his shotgun and the laptop on the kitchen table. To get ready for the possible Incineration, we were to pack up things we wanted to keep safe from the fire. These will be piled into Treasure Mountain, which is a heap of solar and electronics equipment, food and personal possessions that's being constructed on the far edge of the stone patio at the Manse. It will be covered with several layers of wet tarps and blankets. If all of the houses go up in flames, we will still have our most valuable stuff. We hope.

"It's not like I arrived here carrying luggage," I told Gabe. "And most of my clothes are dirty." He said his were, too. But he still had his old wallet, his journals, and some clean tee shirts to add to his pile. My stash was mostly jewelry, a few books, and my most comfortable shoes.

We both noticed the lantern light bouncing outside in the darkness, and then Sarah knocked at the door. "Is this the packing party?" she asked, letting herself in. Along with the lantern, she carried a well-filled shopping bag.

"Here," she said, handing Gabe a small drawstring pouch. "I made you these, when I was hanging with Hoot." Inside the bag were four awesome hand-sewn eye patches in different colors, navy, black, purple and dark green, with matching elastic and top-stitching around the edges, stars and little zigzags. The inside layers were soft cotton muslin.

"Those are fantabulous," I said. Gabe thanked her and put one on, and it fit perfectly. Like, it really looked sharp. She said they were fun to make, and she would teach me how to do it. I'm thinking this means she believes her house, Wynn's house, with all the sewing stuff in the spare bedroom, will still be here for a while.

"I brought some clothes from the garage, you can take what you want and leave the rest, but there's a catch," she said with a hopeful smile.

"Sure, whatever you want," Gabe said. She turned to

me.

"I want a ring. If you still have them. Claude said you might, he said you had found some beauties, and I thought you might let me take a look?" She clasped her hands in front of her chest.

I couldn't help it, I started laughing. "You can have all the rings you want, but not the black diamond. I want that one." Until I said it, I didn't know it was true, but it is. I got the jeweler's box and opened it close to the lantern, which made the diamonds sparkle but did not make enough light to look at the darker gems. I picked up the black diamond and slipped it on my finger.

"It could be a fake, but the rest are real. Take them all so you can look at them in good light," I said.

"I may not need to. That's why I brought this." She turned up her kerosene lantern until the room was bright as day. "Is that an emerald?"

"We think so," I said, and pried the ring from its crevice and handed it to her. It fit! I kind of begged her to take it, but she was easily convinced.

"Confession. After I heard about the unclaimed emerald ring I kept thinking about it. And about emeralds symbolizing hope and growth. Seriously, like wearing it is going to make me stronger or something," she said, stretching out her arm to admire the ring. "Do you think I'm becoming a witch?"

I reminded her that I was the one with the black diamond.

"Which one do you think Evelyn would like? If everyone else has new jewels, she should have one, too," Gabe said, mostly because he's thoughtful that way.

Sarah bent over to look at the rings again. "Diamonds,

yes, but diamonds and what? Fine jewelry is not my thing."

Of the rings Evelyn said were of great value, there was one left. The setting held a large feature diamond flanked by two sizable blue sapphires, with two more small diamonds after that. "She liked this one, and she said it was expensive because of the sizes of the stones," I said, handing it to Sarah, who looked at it and handed it to Gabe. He came close to the lantern and squinted with his good eye.

"Looks good to me," he said. I said I would take it to her in the morning.

As Sarah left to go home, we thought she had slipped or something because she screamed. We both ran to the door, but she was perfectly upright, smiling. "It's raining. Like, it's really raining," she said, tilting her head toward the sky.

It's true. There were actual drops falling, and standing on the porch you could hear water running into the rain barrels. Music to my ears, and to Wynn's, too. A few minutes later, we heard him playing Blue Eyes Crying in the Rain on his trumpet. I know the song because down at Wonderland they thought Willie Nelson was a god.

In the morning it was smokey and damp, but no longer raining. We packed our personal things into a grocery cart, and took a second cart loaded with propane, kerosene and other combustibles to Gabe's shop. Wynn had already dropped off two cases of bottled propane and aerosol cans of wasp spray and fancy hair spray. I squirted some into the air.

"It's Sarah's," Gabe said. "Sometimes she smells fruity like that."

I'd been thinking it was her shampoo.

Gabe brought the Samsung laptop to add to Treasure Mountain, though we have no plans to use it, at least not at this time. For whatever reasons, Evelyn's obsession with connecting with her son seems to have gone away. Like, poof! Instead she washes dishes and flirts with Rob. She compliments his kitchen management skills, telling him how much everyone depends on him. It's all true and I would stick three gold stars on Rob's forehead every day of the week, but it's getting kind of syrupy, like a Hallmark Movie.

I hoped giving her the ring would help. Like, make her feel wifey again, because it's probably what she wants. Past predicts future.

"I've never received a piece of jewelry that didn't have a man attached," she said when I placed it in her palm. I'm pretty sure she recognized the ring from when she saw my collection before. She knew it wasn't a cheapie. She slipped it on and spread her fingers to admire it.

"It's a classic beauty," Claude said, pausing as he kneaded a big lump of bread dough. "Should the Pirates come, they will see that our women wear beautiful jewels," he said. "That will make them think twice."

I hoped he was right.

Chapter 33 Mud

It has stopped raining, the skies are lightening up and the wind is puffing from the west, so the fire will soon find ways to feed itself. Wynn and Gabe think that two days of damp weather may have caused its own backburn, which could break the fire line heading in our direction. We have no way to know. The air is too bad to go jogging down to the overlook. We are preparing for the worst.

Our house might have a chance because of the big, open yard. We raked up all the leaves and sticks and threw them into a wet ditch. Until we ran out of water, we used a mop to slop water all over the deck, front porch and front walkway. Then we grabbed all of our empty water jugs and headed to the Manse by way of Wynn's to see if he needed any last-minute help. There was no Prince in the window, and all the water jugs were gone. They had already bugged out, leaving the deck soaking wet and the yard raked clean as a whistle. I was feeling like both houses just might make it.

But I was worried about the Manse, as in unreasonably worried.

What if we get trapped? Like, what if we're throwing water all over the house and it doesn't work and the Manse turns into an inferno?

Mud. We can roll up in blankets and roll in the icky black mud in our new swamp. Gabe can't remember where he heard of it, maybe in Scouts, but getting in a muddy ditch is one of the ways to wait out a fire.

"Huddling together in the mud is safer than jumping in the stream. Less risk of hypothermia," Rob said as we met in the kitchen to discuss the day's plan. I felt Gabe shiver behind me.

Buddy cleared his throat and spoke up. "Might be we can do better than that." He said there were some folding sawhorses and odd pieces of sheet metal in the barn we could use to set up a shelter in the mud.

I thought it was a great idea and signed up to be his helper, in part because everyone else was busy. Rob and Evelyn were cooking and making face masks from old tee shirts, Claude and Wynn were running a pulley system to lift jugs of water to a second story balcony, Gabe was installing our solar water pump at the spring to move the water closer to the house, and Sarah and Clare were building Treasure Mountain. Everyone was wearing masks and moving slow because of the smoke.

As we loaded the sawhorses and sheet metal onto a garden cart, I asked Buddy if he was scared. "Of course I am," he said, almost laughing. "But I got more than most, and I'm grateful for that. I ain't wishing for another thing in this life, until I see Candy and my family again." For Buddy, death meant reunion. He had just watched his cousin die, taken care of him, helped bear his misery. "On the other hand, I'm happy as a mule in green pasture here. It's a good life. I want to keep it going. Do my part."

Helping to balance the sheet metal in the cart made me a captive audience, and Buddy was on a roll. "Another thing, Little Girlie. If my house is left standing but yours ain't, I want you and Gabe to come on down there, snug in with me. We could get along good." I said sure thing, and that if things turn out different, he could stay with us.

Our assembled shelter looked safe from flying ash, but it was not exactly inviting. We were on our way to get some concrete blocks to hold down the sheet metal when Buddy stopped, muttered "Yup," then changed directions and pushed the cart toward a side door in the metal barn. At first it was stuck, but then he rammed it with his shoulder and it opened.

It was the tack room, full of all the things you need to ride horses, like bridles and saddles and little whips. Most of the leather had gone green with mold, but you could tell it had once been beautiful, especially the saddles. Buddy was after the wool saddle blankets, which were full of moth holes but still showed colorful weaving patterns. This is how the muddy floor of our emergency fire shelter became carpeted with wool, which naturally resists fire and stays warm even when it's wet.

We probably wouldn't die, but I was still not looking forward to rolling up on the ground like a muddy cigar.

I found Sarah and Clare taking a break in the gallery, where the air was slightly better. They were talking about Wynn and Claude, and the pulley they had rigged to lift jugs of water to the second floor. Sarah said Wynn thought of the idea in the middle of the night.

"He got up and sketched it out by candlelight," she said, laughing. "He knew there were some ropes and clips in the garage."

"Wynn is so amazing," Clare said. "The way he

organizes and keeps records, and his maps! If we were on a ship, he would be our navigator."

Sarah agreed. "He needs order. It's probably what saved me." I said I wouldn't even be here without Gabe, and Clare nodded and started laughing.

"Same here. At times the old Claude was insufferable, but would I have survived alone? I don't think so." She nudged my foot with hers. "And now I have you, and Sister Sarah, and a much-improved Claude. Life is good."

Except for a few things, like the wildfire. And Evelyn, who is as nervous as a long-tailed cat in a room full of rocking chairs. She copes with her anxiety by staying busy.

"Oh, there you are," she said, pushing through the door from the kitchen holding a large, open hat box. "Robert said you should have wool hats, no brims, so I looked through our landlady's closet."

It took me a minute to realize that Robert was Rob. Sarah sputtered slightly, trying not to laugh.

"Gina," Clare said, smiling a little too big. "I can absolutely picture her wearing hats."

"These have tags that say hundred percent wool. I cut off the pompoms, they seemed like little torches." Evelyn reached into the box and brought out a mauve pink beret, knit beanies in black and gray, a hand-embroidered black cloche, and a Virginia Tech beanie, brown with a flame stitch pattern in orange and white.

"Youngest firefighter picks first," Sarah said. I redid my ponytail into a high bun and pulled on the Hokie fire hat, and everyone clapped. Sarah went for the gray beanie and Clare went for the black one, which left the two prettiest hats for Evelyn. She tried them on and used us for mirrors. The beret was pretty fabulous, and earned oohs and aahs from all of us. She blushed, like her neck turned really red! It was cute. I am starting to kind of like the new Evelyn though I don't quite get her changing Rob's name to Robert. Must be a husband-catching move.

The smoke started to billow when the wind picked up in the afternoon, and you could hear pops off in the woods when it hit something combustible, a house or a car. We rotated watch, but basically hid from the smoke in the house, staying low and quiet and trying not to breathe. A downstairs bathroom was made into Prince's private apartment. It was late in the day when Wynn reported the hiss of live cinders hitting wet surfaces outside the house.

"Battle stations everyone!" he called, running up the stairs. "This is not a drill!"

Buddy and I looked like outlaws dressed in our hats and masks, but instead of guns we carried wet towels and plastic jugs of water. If little fires started close to the house, we killed them quick. There weren't many, and we were out back, watching the backyard and the barn, so I didn't see all the action on the firewall side of the Manse. But I did hear the men's voices as Rob spotted from the ground while Claude, Wynn and Gabe manned the three upstairs windows, slapping wet blankets or blasting water at cinders that attached to the side of the house. Clare moved from room to room with a fire extinguisher to catch live ashes that blew inside.

"Hit it with your blaster, Wynn!" Rob yelled at one point, when I was preoccupied with a small grassfire close to the barn. Buddy and I stomped it out with our muck boots, and then I caught a puff of smoke and was wiping my eyes and coughing into the cotton kerchief Evelyn gave me. That's the last thing I remember.

I woke up on the floor in the gallery, coughing. It was too dark to see, but a lantern light moved closer and I felt Sarah's soft hand on my shoulder. She kissed my head and handed me a moist washcloth. "Cough into it," she whispered. "Don't try to talk." She propped me up with some pillows, which made it easier to breathe. She was sniffing a lot, and when she leaned over me wet drops fell on my face.

"Where's Gabe?" I tried to ask, but it's like my vocal cords were out of commission. The body beside me rolled over, coughed, and reached out and squeezed my hand.

"We've been waiting for you," he said softly. "Glad to have you back, Des."

Then I heard Clare sniffing in the shadows. "Oh, sweetheart, you gave us a scare," she said, her voice weak and wobbly. Beside her, Claude tried to speak, but coughed instead. He sounded almost like Hoot.

It's when Sarah moved next to me and hugged me close that I lost it. I started crying, like sobbing, and my eyes and nose were running and she rubbed my back and told me everything was all right, everyone was okay, that it was over.

When I calmed down, she took me to the kitchen for medical care. "You have a few burns. Not bad, but that's what happened to your pants. We put aloe on your leg, but it needs more attention." I wanted to say that's what my mom would have done, but I couldn't. My throat was burning hot, and I was trying hard to stop crying.

In the kitchen, Wynn rested in a small recliner that had been moved close to the wood stove, with Prince on his lap. He jumped up when he saw us, attempting and failing to toot a vocal bugle call. He smiled and pointed to his throat, then came over and gave me a long, hard hug. Except for what looked like a big fever blister on his lip and a bandage over one brow, he looked pretty much okay.

"This is our ER," Sarah said, helping me into the recliner and covering me with a fleece blanket. "You're our last patient of the day." She felt my forehead and handed me a fresh washcloth. "I'm head nurse, and Evelyn is my assistant."

Evelyn appeared out of the shadows with a can of ginger ale. She popped the top and dropped in a bent straw. A straw! "See if you can swallow a few sips, or shake your head if you'd rather have water." I reached for the can and sucked down half of it, then burped. Nothing ever tasted so good.

The lantern moved around the room while Sarah gathered her supplies. I heard the heavy, uneven shuffle of feet, then saw Rob's red, swollen face in the lantern light, smiling and touching my cheek. There were whispered voices across the room, including Wynn's.

Sarah and Rob returned, holding the light close to my face. Sarah told me to look at Rob, so the light wouldn't hurt my eyes. I'm glad she did, because she held it so close I could feel its heat.

"Good, good," Rob said roughly. Evelyn stepped beside him and whispered something, to which he agreed.

"His voice, you know," she began. "He wants to say good, your pupils are responsive to light, which means you probably don't have a concussion. Do you have a headache?" I shook my head yes.

I heard the snapping of fingers, then the shuffling of paper. Evelyn read from a note. "Wynn wants to know if you have any problem with Tylenol or Mucinex?" I shook my head, then started coughing. When I caught my breath again, Evelyn was ready with a dose of each.

Sarah asked me to point to any places where I felt burning or pain, which would be my right thigh and a place on my right forearm. There was also a lump on my forehead. She checked my hands and feet to make sure I could feel my fingers and toes, then lifted the blanket to look at the burn on my thigh, a couple of inches above my knee. She asked if I was ready for some orange juice and smiled when I nodded yes.

It seemed like it took her a long time to get it, but she returned with a kid's drink box of OJ and Gabe. "I asked for a second opinion," she said.

"Hey Des," he croaked, holding the lantern close to the burn on my leg. It was maybe three inches long and an inch wide, and it was dark, like it had soot in it. "Do you remember what happened?"

I shook my head. "Buddy said you fell on a burning stick. It burned through your pants," Sarah explained. She turned to Gabe. "Should we cancel the plastic surgeon, forget about the skin graft?"

He smiled, nodded, and touched my forehead. Then he pulled up a kitchen chair, sat down on my left side, and opened the drink for me. When he started coughing, I saw that he had his own handkerchief, a red bandana.

He also had a green piece of aloe taped to the side of his neck.

Evelyn came around with baby wipes for me to clean up with, and I couldn't believe the black stuff that came off my hands, arms, and face. It tingled when I wiped the lump on my forehead, but there was no blood. The wipes smelled nice, like lemons, which was so much better than smelling smoke. Gabe gave his face and hands a good wipe down, too. When we were done, Evelyn brought us wrapped throat drops, gathered up our trash, and said she would have soup ready soon.

Sarah squirted something on my burn that stung at first, but only for a minute. "We just want to get it clean without mucking with it. It will probably blister, and then scab over," she said. "Maybe leave a nasty scar." She moved my leg to rinse the wound from a different angle, and started humming the chorus to Blank Space, a Taylor Swift song, my favorite one. When she stopped, I leaned forward to tell her to go on, and Gabe started tapping his foot in the steady rhythm of the song, at a slow tempo. Sarah moved my leg again, then started singing softly. It made me start crying again. "Sorry," she said. "But crying might help clear our sinuses." She covered the burn with a light gauze bandage.

The burn on my arm was a small one, which she treated by cutting a fresh piece of aloe from the big plant in the kitchen and taping it in place with white tape. She gave my legs and feet the lemon wipe treatment, and helped me into a pair of men's pajama pants with dogs printed on them and some thick black knee socks. Evelyn brought us mugs of chicken noodle soup.

I think all of this happened in the middle of the night,

because when I heard the roosters crowing I was still in the recliner, but it was Buddy instead of Gabe sitting in the chair next to me. It was barely light.

"How are you doing, Little Girlie?" he asked in a scratchy voice.

I managed to whisper "I'm okay" before I started coughing. I felt pretty good on my feet, but I was still glad to have his arm to hold onto as I made my way to the bathroom and back. My mind was still foggy. I had a headache.

So did everyone except for Sarah and Evelyn, who had spent most of the day inside. Buddy's right hand was wrapped with gauze, and there were scattered red spots on his face. A tired Evelyn with dark circles under her eyes appeared with Tylenol, cough drops, and lukewarm black tea.

"Thank you," I squeaked.

"You're welcome," she said, making a small curtsy.

In a hoarse, whispered voice, Buddy told me what happened. "You were stepping around a flare-up and started coughing, lost your balance and hit your head on the side of the barn, where there was a hard beam. I found you right away and carried you into the house, but both of us got burned by a patch on your pants. Could have been lots worse," he said, rubbing his chin.

I said I owed him, and the tears started coming again. He said please don't cry and handed me a clean washcloth.

As the morning grew brighter, you could see that the air was clearer, as in almost normal clearer. We really were on the other side of the dang fire.

Sarah breezed into the kitchen wearing a puffy pink

jacket over lots of black Lycra, carrying a bicycle helmet. "I'm off to check the houses," she said, grabbing a chunk of bread Evelyn was cutting on the counter. "Cross your fingers and toes!"

I looked outside and saw Wynn squeezing the tires on Sarah's favorite bike, saw him warn her to be careful. Then he held her tight, his treasure, and let her go. On this day, she was the only one with good enough lungs to make it up the hill.

I told Buddy I felt like moving around, and wanted to go check on Clare. I stood up, stretched my back, and bounced on my feet to get my balance. "Come on down to my house when you're ready," he said. "Gabe's already there, getting some sleep."

Evelyn offered me some bread to dip in Swiss Miss, which was wonderful. She asked if I would mind popping in to see Rob, who was in the bedroom off of the kitchen. Popping in, that's what she called it. She said he had a burn on his foot that made it hard to get around, but that he had been asking for me.

"There she is," he whispered when I entered the dim room. He was sitting up in the double bed, well-propped with pillows, with one foot sticking out from under the covers wrapped in gauze. His face looked crackly and weird, but then I saw green pieces and realized he was slathered with fresh aloe to cover what looked like a bad sunburn.

I sat down beside him on the bed. "Sorry you took a hit," I said, then pointed to my throat and shook my head.

"Me, too," he said, then started coughing. I picked up the small notepad and pen from his bedside table. "We can talk later. I love you," I wrote. He got tears in his eyes when he read it, but like Sarah says, crying might help clear our sooty sinus passages. I kissed him on the forehead and told him to rest.

I pulled my way up to the second floor, where Clare, Claude and Wynn were assessing damage to the bedrooms. Thumping noises led me to the large bedroom at the end, Claude and Clare's room. Clare was sitting cross-legged on the big bed. When she saw me, she smiled and motioned for me to join her.

"We survived," she whispered, squeezing my arm. "And the place is not totally trashed." Only partly trashed. Her voice was weak but workable. She said Wynn was closing off the small bedroom, Rob's old room, because it was covered with white dust from the fire extinguisher, which he said was caustic. "The bedspread was catching fire, but I got it pretty quick, and then we threw it out the window. Very scary."

Claude came in through the sliding glass door to the balcony, where he had been collecting wet towels, jugs and water blasters. He was moving slowly and seemed bent over, so he probably had about as much energy as I did. He flopped down on the bed in front of us, face down.

"End of Act One," he said, then coughed. Clare ran her fingers through his hair, which left a dark residue around her nails. I reached down and got the throat drops I had stuffed into my knee socks to share. The window was half open to air out the room, so it was cold, but it felt warm to sit with Clare and Claude, trying not to talk, just resting, enjoying our cherry cough drops.

Where did the cough drops and all the other Time

Before stuff come from? That was what I would have asked if I could. It was common knowledge that Wynn had basic drugs, and that Rob kept a stash of yummy things of which there were only small amounts, but ginger ale, orange juice and chicken noodle soup, just when you need it? They had to be in this together. I was thinking Sarah was also a prime suspect.

Her voice echoed up from the gallery. "Friends, Romans, countrymen, lend me your ears!" I jumped off the bed and stumbled to the stairs, but I could tell from her smile that the news was good. "Ring the bells and call the people, the town is saved!" she proclaimed. "Both houses!"

I thumped down the stairs to hug Sarah, then went down to Buddy's to tell Gabe, who was still sleeping but I decided to tell him anyway.

"Our house did not burn up. This is not a dream," I whispered in his ear. He twitched. "I repeat, this is not a dream." I was starting to laugh and cough at the same time.

"Oh, yes. It is." He cleared his throat. "It's a dream come true."

Chapter 34   No Bananas

January 20

Back when Hoot was around, he liked to give me advice about life. Like, that it's going to be hard so I should do it right, grab good chances when they come my way. He meant well, but my life so far has not been a fun park. In the time before, I worried about school shootings, selfies, needing a drivers license and a car, and if my kooky mom had paid the rent. It's different here in Hokie-ville, where I can be me and learn new things and it's that simple. I'm not being judged or rejected. There is no such thing as algebra.

I'm feeling okay, even if it's dreary and cold, because lately it's been snowing, but not too much. Only enough to make it pretty, and hide the blackness of the woods burned by the fire. Now we're back to surviving. Chop wood, carry water, and battle boredom.

We read books, work puzzles, study our instruments, and play games. The Hokies have been playing the Banana Game since before I got here, and it goes like this. It's a fact that there are no bananas, there will be no bananas coming from Honduras or anywhere else. Everything that falls into the banana category, a person, place or thing that will be no more, can be brought into the Banana Game.

"Banana Game!" Claude called from the corner of the kitchen where he read the old newspapers we use to light fires. Clare was working at the sink, crunching up dried veggies for soup, and I was kneading bread. Claude is teaching me to make sourdough. Clare laughed, and we sang the response in unison. *"Yes, we have no bananas, we have no bananas today."* That means you're in the mood to play the game.

"I have no bananas, I have no golf," he said, stretching his back and pretending to hold a club. "The neatness of the fairways, the deceiving tilts of the greens, the crack when you tee off just right." He faked a swing and said "Whoosh!"

"Good one," I said, punching at the dough. "I got nothing."

"I do." Clare wiped her hands on a dish towel and gracefully raised her arms as if they were wings, ending with a slight flutter. "The Washington Ballet. Tchaikovsky. Swan Lake. Such grace and beauty, such perfection of form." She twirled around the kitchen and landed in Claude's arms, then took a bow.

"Ding, ding, I say Clare gets a point," I said. I asked if she had been a ballet dancer and she said no, not since she was a kid. "But I do like to dance, for fun."

The burn on my leg is healing nicely, and it's now a fresh pink scar. The one on my arm has almost disappeared along with the lump on my head. Wynn had a hard time with the burn on his lip, which meant he couldn't play his trumpet, but at least it didn't get infected. I would hate it if I couldn't play my harmonica.

At Wynn's house there is a sewing room with all kinds of supplies, so that's where Sarah is teaching me to sew. So far, we've hemmed some cargo pants and made new eye patches for Gabe. Mine was pretty lame, but it's a start. I like working with needle and thread, the repetition and constant progress.

The bottom drawer of the sewing machine cabinet had a booklet that shows basic knots and stitches and a few easy projects. To practice my stitches, I used felt scraps to make a hand puppet that looks like a dog. It's really cute. Sarah got out her imaginary camera to take a picture.

"Destined to go viral," Wynn said, sitting down on the carpeted floor. He unfolded a paper restaurant menu. "I'm thinking of driving down to DJ's, pick up some burgers. Can I get you something?" he handed the menu to Sarah. "Maybe an Italian sub with a side of mozzarella sticks?" He raised his eyebrows enticingly.

"I love those things, I'll take a double order, and a bacon cheeseburger, all the way." She handed the menu to me, said it was her treat. No way I was getting chicken. I ordered a barbecue sandwich with extra sauce.

"Good enough then. As soon as I'm finished counting beans," he said, and disappeared into the den, where he really was counting beans. He's become an incredible farmer. Last summer he grew gobs of potatoes and sweet potatoes, and Buddy grew corn, but he says next year will be the year of the bean. When we find dry beans on a sugar run, he counts out two hundred of the most perfect ones and sets them aside for planting.

Not that we're dying of hunger, or that Gabe is going blind. His eye is much better, but it's sensitive to smoke or bright sun. He sees good enough to go hunting with Claude at the lake house, which did not burn up. The fire stopped on the far side of the ridge where it hit a road and a power cut, or at least that's how it looked when Gabe and I went down there to check on things. There was a lot of gray ash, but the house was intact along with Hoot's grave.

We rearranged the pine boughs on Hoot's grave and added a few stones from the edge of the lake. Gabe brought some green plastic chairs from the back deck of the house. Then we sat in the sun for a while, humming and whistling some old tunes Hoot liked, telling Hoot stories, it was nice. At the sunny end of the lake, wild ducks and Canada geese acted like we weren't there.

"Talk about sitting ducks," he said. "Ka-pow! Hoot would love it."

It's true they looked like easy shots, but I was always partly on the animals' sides, and some of those ducks were gorgeous. We make compromises. The ducks Claude and Gabe bagged a few days later didn't have much meat, but the rendered duck fat was so good! It's like butter, for real, butter being bananas at this point. According to Gabe, the overgrown pastures are producing more food than the wild birds can eat, which is why they are so fat. Last week we boiled some doves for stock and fat, mostly because there are a zillion doves. They taste like chicken.

Before Evelyn came, Rob didn't much play the Banana Game, probably because he had lost so much, his wife and two grown kids. He rarely said their names or told their stories, which was his way. The past was too painful, too many hard memories. I get that. Boy, do I get that.

But you need to give the good memories some air, too, and sometimes it's like that's what Evelyn is doing when she makes him talk about his wife, Natalie. What was her favorite food? Where did she like to shop?

Natalie loved a hot reuben sandwich and liked to shop at Target. She was allergic to shellfish. In summer, she liked taking the throw rugs outside to clean them with the power washer. Evelyn smiled and said she had always wanted to try one of those.

"Banana Game!" Rob said, getting to his feet. After the fire, Rob's face peeled pretty bad, but he is back to his normal color now.

"Yes, we have no bananas, we have no bananas today!" I sang, with Evelyn humming along.

"I have no bananas, I have no power washer," he said, pretending to hold a big spray wand with both hands. "It's dirty vinyl siding. You start at the top, get it good and wet with some dissolved OxiClean, keep the machine on low. After a couple of minutes, you crank it up to high and blast that baby, left to right, right to left, and green and brown dirt and mold goes running down, and you go back and hit the spots you missed, and it looks like new," he said.

I said he nailed it, and Evelyn said he should get an extra point for OxiClean.

Hanging out with them in the kitchen gave me the warm fuzzies, like I was visiting an imaginary aunt and uncle. It was also fun to see what Evelyn was wearing, which was always something nice from dead landlady Gina's closet. One day she might wear dark-washed jeans with a soft cashmere sweater, the next day a printed pullover and flowing lounge pants. She said it was mostly resort wear, so Gina must have traveled a lot, like rich people used to do. I'm thinking there are probably no more resorts, but I never went to one so I'm not missing them.

Gabe is keeping Dr. Kim's computer at our house, but it's not hooked up to a satellite dish and Claude turned off the Wifi, so they think it's safe to run. Only we don't, based on group discussions of what Karla wants, or anything good she might do for us. Which may not be much.

"We are not in desperate straits. We have no reason to risk anything," Claude said one day when he brought another laptop to check for movies and games. Sarah and Wynn were already here, playing darts on the board we found on a recent sugar run. As usual, the computer had a bunch of read-only documents and games and movies that won't open because they were accessed from the now defunct cloud.

"In video games, you would never call on Karla unless you needed a life-saving serum, or to slay the dragon who was eating the town's dogs and cats," Gabe said. "Neither seem to be happening here."

"Based on satellite imagery, it may look like we burned up," Wynn said. "Never to be heard from again."

Sarah said she liked the sound of that.

We still haven't heard shots from other hunters, so we think we are alone here and safe for now, maybe even forever. Why take chances? We are still laying low, only shooting to eat, and staying away from town in case there is trouble there.

We do worry about the Pirates. Those are the humans who live in western Pennsylvania and are known to outer space Karla, and who we assume were the source of the question about women. Do they have none of their own? Sad for sure, but don't come looking for me. I'm learning to shoot in the spring, and so are Clare and

Sarah. When they come for us, it will be the Virginia Hokies versus the Pennsylvania Pirates, and the Hokies will rule.

ACKNOWLEDGEMENTS

Special thanks to my brave first readers for being so generous with their time and guidance: Roger Kienzle, Anne Pendrak, Lorraine Skala, Angela Thompson, Chris Youngblood, Becky Pomponio, Kamala Bauers, Lori Graham, Tom Brody, and Jackie Crenshaw.

ABOUT THE AUTHOR

The author of many award-winning gardening books and former contributing editor to Mother Earth News, Barbara Pleasant has lived in Floyd for almost 20 years.

Made in the USA
Columbia, SC
28 May 2025